THE HAUNTING OF FRANK SCARPELLI

Marsh Rauser

Cover designed by: Anita Williams I DESIGN
ISBN: 1502345714
ISBN 13: 9781502345714

Also by, Marsh Rauser
Guardians Of The Innocent—YA
The Lions Revenge—Guardian/Sequel

Dedication

I would like to dedicate this novel to all the men and women in the United States Armed Forces.

My utmost respect, admiration and gratitude go to all who are serving—and to those who have fought in all prior wars. Your bravery and dedication, have kept America free from the tyranny of the regimes who seek to destroy our way of life. Thank you for your service. May God bless you all the days of your life.

In memorial—WW11 family veterans: George Rauser, William Rauser and George Rosner

Introduction

In the annals of world history, World War II will go down as the largest conflict the world had ever witnessed. Although there were many heroic campaigns the one that stands out is the Sicilian Invasion.

Dates: July 10, 1943 – August 17, 1943.

Mission: Occupy Palermo, Sicily to open the shipping lanes in the Mediterranean Sea by eliminating the island as an axis base for German occupation. The plan was devised in February 1943, by President Franklin D. Roosevelt and the Prime Minister of Great Britain, Sir Winston Churchill.

Execution: Jointly orchestrated between General Dwight D. Eisenhower and Sir Harold Alexander.

Strategy: To destroy all lines of communications between Africa and Italy, in an effort to secure the Mediterranean.

Purpose: To defeat Italy and bring down "IL Duce" or Benito Mussolini, the Italian Prime Minister.

Obstacle: A buildup of German forces (Italy's allies) had arrived prior to the invasion to support Italy's inadequate manpower and assault weapons. Sicily was considered a strategically located stronghold.

Prologue

July 10, 1943

Nineteen year-old Army Private, Thomas Callahan (aka--TC) boarded the 227-C47 aircraft from New York City. He and four other paratrooper-specialists were chosen for a military coup d'état called, HUSKY.

This time it was the real thing and not a practice jump and Sergeant, Thomas Callahan whom everyone called TC, started to consider the odds of anyone of them surviving such a dangerous mission. The reality was— the odds were against them. Still, it had been done before and TC has always been a fighter. He decided not to think about the mission so he focused on his past and what his life was like before the war, and before he received his draft notice. He smiled when he thought about his family and a life that was secure and predictable. That's how TC liked his life—planned, organized and predictable.

CHAPTER ONE

Who would have thought that Tom Callahan from Philly, PA, would be going to Italy? Most of my friends never got as far as New York City. They were happy just to hang-out in the neighborhood. I always had a hankering to see different places. In fact I always wanted to go to Italy. Who wouldn't? There are beautiful women good food and seeing old stuff but while on a vacation and not by putting my ass on the line. I'm as patriotic as the next guy but I'm young and I've got my whole life ahead of me. I wonder if the person who said, 'War was hell' had a concept of how scary hell was, when you don't know if today will be the day you'll come home in a body-bag or crippled.

Jesus, my mother will freak out if I don't come home. And then there's my wife, Anna Marie. I promised her I'd be back. But for some reason I have this gut feeling that this is it and I won't be on the return flight home. I wonder if the other guys feel the same.

I was born with the map of Ireland all over my face. Blue eyes, red hair and freckles you can't get more Irish than that. Dad was the one with the blue eyes and red hair. Mom calls it rust. I was brought up Catholic to an Irish clan in Philadelphia, and just one of, Thomas and Loretta Callahan's four kids. I have two brothers, Patrick is seventeen and Devin's fifteen. They have the dark hair and green eyes like mom. And then there's my little sister Blair, she's thirteen and looks like dad and me. My dad was glad when Blair was born he was afraid my mom would never stop wanting kids, until she got her daughter.

I'm the oldest and I was named after my old man, that's why everyone calls me TC. My old man is a second generation cop and I intend to follow in his footsteps. After all I'm his namesake. A lot of the cops in Philly are second generation and some are even third. I'm going to make the old man proud. Someday, I'm going to be the Chief of Police in our neighborhood precinct. I'm a shoe in, everyone knows me and I know them. And the one thing they know about me is I'm tough. I won't put up with any crap from hoodlums in my part of town.

My brother's, Patrick and Devin want to go to college. They don't want to be a cop and without an education their only option would be the mill or the mines. They have this high-fluting idea that they want to be a 'somebody.' Everyone knows you have to go to college to be rich. To me being the Chief of Police is a "somebody."

Anna Marie Cassandra, the love of my life. I've known Anna Marie since we were kids. Carmine is Annie's brother. He's a homeboy and my number one ace. We hung out together all through grammar school and high school. Annie was always following us around and we thought she was a pain in the ass. Carmine's old lady would always rag on him. 'Carmine, get in here and watch the baby.' Or, 'Carmine you take your sister with you." The only time we could get away from that brat was when we played at my house or, in the schoolyard.

This one day I was over Carmine's house. I was about sixteen. All of a sudden I noticed that Anna Marie looked different. For one thing she was dressed in a party dress. Carmine said she was going to some kid's birthday party. She had on this dress that kind of hugged her body. She didn't look like a kid anymore. For the first time I noticed that Anna Marie had big dark brown eyes and hair so black that it shined silver. I was also surprised that for fourteen her boobs were really starting to show. Man, was she stacked! She was no longer Carmine's kid sister, she was a beautiful babe.

Since that time Annie and I were like two peas in a pod. I really had the hot's for her and I think Carmine was a little jealous because, now we were a threesome and he still didn't like his kid sister following us around. After a while Annie and I started going steady. And before we knew it two years had gone by and we started talking about getting hitched after we both graduated from high school. I was graduating in June and in two years she would follow. Our plan was, I'd get a job, any job. And a couple of nights a week I would go to college and take a couple of courses in Police Science. When I turned 21 I would join the police force and live in the same neighborhood as our folks. We also planned we'd have two boys and a girl. Life would be good and predictable. So, when I got my draft notice two weeks before graduation I freaked out. Annie and my old lady cried and you know dads, 'I'm proud of you son you go over there and show those krauts what us Irish yanks are made of." I told him, "Yeah sure, I'll win this war all by myself. Are you nuts? I can be killed!"

"You won't get killed if you don't act like a jerk and take too many chances. For once in your life learn how to take orders." I got the impression that my old man thought that going to war was going to make a man out of me. On the other hand Annie decided that she wanted to get married before I left. She actually wanted to elope and not tell anyone. I nixed that idea, she's too young and she needed to finish high school. Besides, what if something happened to me? No, we'd have to wait however long it took for this war to be over. We're both young and we have the rest of our lives. I told her, "We'll get married as soon as the war is over." I usually caved in when Annie started to pout or cry. This time, I was sticking to my guns. The problem was Annie was one of those good Catholic girls which meant no sex before marriage and I was sick of waiting. The church and her mother told her it was a mortal sin to have sex before marriage. I tried convincing her it wasn't a sin if, we were in love but she wouldn't buy it. She actually thought that I was going to wait for her to be the first. She wasn't. I felt what she didn't know wouldn't hurt her. I wanted her body and soul and the other girls were just practice. Besides, practice makes perfect and I wanted to be perfect, for her.

The night before I left for Fort Dix my folks gave me a graduation and send-off party at the local Elks lodge. I think half the town showed up. After living in this neighborhood for all my life as did my parents before me you get to know everyone, especially the people on our block. My old man even invited the guys from his precinct.

I wasn't the only kid that got drafted a couple of guys from the neighborhood also got their notice. Carmine didn't and he was pissed. "How come you got drafted and I didn't?" That idiot actually thought this was some sort of honor the government was giving me because I was special. "Carmine, don't sweat the small stuff. My number came up and yours will too. Besides, why the hell do you want to risk your life fighting a war we're not sure we can win? You lucked out." As usual he didn't get it. He just looked at me with this wild stare and said, "Because you got asked first. You get everything first."

"Carmine, just for once get your head out of your ass. Being drafted is not an honor." He looked surprised and then, laughed. I also laughed. "You know, Carmine, I'm going to miss you, you grease ball."

"I'll be missing you too you dirty mick."

After the party I drove Annie home and begged her. "Let's do it before I go. I'm leaving tomorrow and who knows when you'll see me again? I might even get killed."

She looked at me and started to cry. "Holy shit Annie, I'm sorry I was just kidding. I won't get killed. You can't get rid of me. Besides, I have to come back to collect what you've holding out on me for two years."

She smiled. I felt her up as we kissed we did everything but go all the way and it was tearing up my insides. I finally got her give me a hand-job. It was a small sacrifice and not as fulfilling. She couldn't help it. It was like an old tune that kept playing in her head, 'God will punish you and only bad girls have sex before marriage.' And the dumbest of all, 'After you give into your boyfriend he will tell his buds and give you a bad reputation.' What a bunch of crap! But what the hell could I do? I loved the girl.

After I dropped Annie off at her house I started thinking— there is no way out of this draft situation so if I have to do this I'm going to do it right. I'm going to be a freaking hero. I will bring honor to my family and the whole damn town. But first I have to go home and pack.

CHAPTER TWO

Fort Dix, NJ: Six weeks -Basic Training

At six o'clock the following morning, me and the other local guys boarded the bus to Fort Dix, New Jersey. The bus ride was as hot as hell but we all knew we weren't going on a picnic. As soon as we arrived we went to a hospital for a physical-exam. They were pretty thorough and just a couple of guys didn't make the grade. It didn't mean they got to go home, they found them a desk job. Most of us had no problem passing we were all so damn young.

While in line at the hospital I met this straight shooter from, Baltimore, Maryland named, Jerry Stein. And it just so happened we wound up in the same barrack. We soon became buddies.

Basic training was everything I thought it would be and more. I wasn't sure I would survive the lousy discipline. But, I was determined to make it work. My self- imposed commitment was to get noticed and to at least make sergeant before getting out. At first they made it easy. They started us out with three weekly six-mile runs for fewer than fifty minutes. Then, there was the twenty-five mile march wearing all of our gear that weighed a hundred pounds. Then, it was a forty-eight mile march in eighteen hours besides, all the other crap we had to do, like marksmanship, mantling and dismantling artillery, climbing walls and doing calisthenics.

After I survived my six weeks of basic training, I signed up for Airborne School. So did Jerry. No way we wanted to be foot soldiers. This meant we had to go for another physical and instead of going to Signal Training we would be transferred to Airborne Training- Camp. It's said that paratroopers are the best-trained and physically fit troops in the army, because they could perform under any extreme condition.

I called my mother to tell her the good news. "Guess what mom, I decided to go airborne. I want to be a paratrooper." Obviously, she was not impressed.

"That's nice. When are they going to let you come home?"

"I'll be coming home in a few months. I'm being transferred to Fort Benning, Georgia."

"What do you mean? You have to go to Georgia before coming home? Why can't you come home first, and then go to Georgia?"

"If I do that, I'll get locked up for desertion. Your son is going to be a paratrooper! You should be proud— not everyone made the cut."

"Did I say I wasn't proud of you? I just want to know when you're going to be furloughed."

"That's what I'm trying to tell you if you would let me get a word in. I can't come home now. I have to go for paratrooper training. When I've completed my training I get to go home for a while. Then, I'll be sent overseas."

"Where are they sending you?"

"I don't know where. And even if I did, it's top secret."

"You can't tell your own mother? Remember, I'm the one that brought you into this world."

"Do we have to discuss this now? Mom, I've got to go I'll talk to you later. Other guys want to use the telephone. Bye. I can't hear you, bye. Mom, tell Annie I'll see her in a couple of month and, I'll write."

I finally hung up. Holy shit, she was making me nervous. I know how she feels. I'm her son but she didn't have to get so emotional. And to top it off my idiot brother Pat, enlisted in the Navy. Now mom is afraid she could lose two of her sons.

CHAPTER THREE

Ft. Benning, GA: Six weeks/Airborne Training

It wasn't long before we were on a train to Ft. Benning, Georgia. When we arrived we were assigned to the 505th division. Surprise! Surprise! Our first assignment was KP duty. I got to clean the latrines. Not the best job in the world, especially for a guy who didn't even know how to make his bed before he was drafted. Jerry's job was cooking and scrubbing the pots and pans. During the day we did push-ups, running and training.

After several weeks of KP, we started Airborne School. It was a six-week training program. I didn't think I would make it after the first week. It took a while to get the hang of it.

At first we jumped the thirty-four foot towers five days a week with one day off. Then, they put us through a couple of nights jumps, a week. It took a lot of practice to figure out how to maneuver the parachutes. Harder yet was learning how to hit your targeted area.

After three weeks we graduated to the Douglas-C-47 transport. My first night plane jump scared the hell out of me. Mostly, it was the flames shooting out of the engine. I was afraid my chute would catch on fire. It took several nights of jumping to get oriented and be able to distinguish and maneuver within a ground perimeter. My bud Jerry almost got himself killed. He pulled the ripcord and nothing happened. He must have panicked because he never thought to pull the reserve chute until it was almost, too late. We all watched in disbelief. Finally, it opened. What a relief! It sure scared the shit out of him. Literally! He stunk so bad that all the guys razzed him. He was embarrassed. I told him not to sweat the small stuff. He lived that was the main thing.

In order to graduate you have to advance from a single jumper in the door to jumping with five men. Then you have to jump with all the guys using both the doors. Some of the guys couldn't hack it and backed out. Jerry and I stuck it out we wanted our wings.

Annie wrote to me every day. Without those letters there would have been nothing to look forward to. She was eagerly awaiting me being furloughed. Although, I still couldn't give her a date. No, way we could leave before we completed our training and that took weeks or, even months.

Finally, Graduation Day! After six weeks of training I finally got my jump wings. General Marshall pinned them on me during a graduation ceremony. He stood back, saluted and said, "Welcome aboard, soldier, you're now airborne." Oh man what a day! This was great. I could now go home before going overseas. But knowing when I returned I would be going overseas. My anticipation was soon shot to hell when Sergeant Cox walked up to Jerry and me while we were in the mess hall and informed us that some of the men in our unit were being reassigned, in two days. All the other guys would be taking their furlough. Jerry and I were on the roster to be moved to Fort Bragg's 82nd Airborne Division for special training. That sucked.

CHAPTER FOUR

Ft. Bragg, NC: Six weeks-Special Training

The training at Fort Bragg was grueling. You need a lot of strength to carry one hundred pounds of equipment. We carried our parachute, reserve chute, two-day rations, a small shovel, four grenades, an M-1 rifle and several clips of ammo. Added was a change of underwear and a gas mask. For stamina we were made to march for 25 miles wearing all of our gear. Rumor had it we we're being trained for a secret mission therefore, preparedness was vital to our survival. We were also trained to expect conditions like hunger, fatigue, and severe weather. And have quick responses and to make fast decisions. Timing was also essential, especially when you're landing in, enemy territory. We practiced day and night. We also practiced jumps, night maneuvers, hand-to-hand fighting and foxhole digging. We learned how to use American weapons and the enemy's weapons. A few of us were trained in machine gun maintenance. It was six days a week which left little time to worry about our tour of duty or, what our next assignment might be. All we wanted was a couple of days off, but, there is no time-out in the military.

On March 10, they finally gave us a two-week furlough. We were also told that when we got back we would be going overseas. Where or when was top- secret. I didn't give a shit I just wanted to go home. I called the folks and told them I had my train tickets and that I would be pulling into the Pennsylvania station, at, five, pm. I asked mom to tell Carmine and Anna Marie that I was on my way home.

When I got off the train the whole family was waiting for me. That is everyone except my brother Pat. He was at, the naval station in Norfolk, Virginia. To tell the truth I got a little choked up. I didn't realize how much I'd missed them and obviously they missed me. Of course mom was crying, Dad was smiling and Anna Marie was a sight for sore eyes.

Just looking at her gave me a hard- on. Standing next to her was good old Carmine, a friend, till the end. Carmine didn't look too good he didn't look healthy. He looked kind of thin and scrawny. I thought, *TC, you are one lucky guy; you've got a good family, a great looking girlfriend and a best- friend.* It's funny how you don't realize what you have until you don't have it anymore. I was surprised to see how my kid sister had changed in the short amount of time I was gone. She went from a little girl to a beautiful teenager. I started thinking. *Those horny guys in school better keep their mitts off her. Or they'll have to answer to me.* What is it about being a big brother? You don't mind screwing someone else's sister you don't want anyone to screw yours.

We all hugged and we kissed. Then we took the party to my folk's house. Mom said she made a special dish for me, my favorite, corned- beef and cabbage. You would have thought that by now she would have known that I hated corned- beef and cabbage. It was Devin who liked it. I like steak. What the hell she meant well. I kissed her on the cheek and thanked her. "You know ma, I thought about your cooking the whole time I was gone."

She smiled and kissed me. "I know Tommy there's nothing like a Mothers home cooking."

We ate drank and laughed. They started catching me up on all the local gossip. Like who got married, who died and who got pregnant. I said, "As long as it wasn't Annie I couldn't care less." Both Annie and Mom darted me a look that could have killed. I guess I was out of line. I laughed anyway. My mother gave me another look and blasted me. "What's wrong with you? That remark was so disrespectful to Anna Marie."

"I was kidding. I was only kidding. I'm sorry. I guess I had too much beer?" It was getting late and everyone was getting drunk so we decided to call it a night. Carmine said his goodbyes and announced that he would take Annie home. I said, "No, you don't. Thanks just the same Carmine. I want to be alone with my girl." Dad threw me the keys to his 1940, black, Ford sedan.

Annie was silent the whole time I was driving her home. "What's up doll? You haven't said a word since we got in the car?"

"I can't believe you Tommy. How could you show such disrespect for me in front of your family?"

"I'm sorry. It just came out wrong. What I should have said was I didn't care about gossip. But you're right it was a stupid remark I'm sorry. Do you still love me? Or, have you already found someone else?"

"Of course not there's no one else Tommy, and there never will be anyone but you."

I didn't say another word until we got to her house. This was what I was waiting for, what I dreamed of, Annie and me alone in the car necking and making out and of course her hand pushing my hand away while I was trying to take off her panties. Same old stuff but it sure felt good. After fifteen minutes into all that good stuff Mrs. Cassandra appeared at the door and yelled for Annie to come into the house. She then yelled at me. "Hi, Tommy, welcome home! Why don't you come over tomorrow? Anna Marie has to come in now."

"Okay, Mrs. Cassandra. I'll stop over tomorrow."

Annie started laughing. "Good-bye, Tommy. See you tomorrow." I didn't think it was so damn funny. I gave her one final French kiss before opening the door for her. Annie's old lady was still watching and I wanted her to know how polite her future son-in-law was.

When I got home, everyone was in the living room listening to the radio. I excused myself and went into my room. I was tired with all that traveling and excitement. I'm sure the beer helped. I didn't realize how much I had missed my home, my room, and my own space until I walked into my room. Everything was exactly the way I'd left it, except for Pat. Pat and I shared this room. I used to hate sharing a room with him. I wanted my own space. But now, I would have given anything to see him again. I started thinking about us as kids fighting over the radio, fighting over who would turn out the lights and fighting over each other's toys. Although, when any kids picked on either one of us we joined forces. You couldn't take on just one of us you had to be ready to take on both. After all we were brothers. Many a time we beat the crap out of a kid and sometimes it was a couple of kids. And many a time they beat the crap out of us.

I must have been drunk. I started talking to him like he was in the room. "I miss you Pat. I wish you were here to see me before I go overseas. But we'll have a lot to talk about when I get home if, I get home. To tell you the truth kid I'm no hero I'm scared. I'm scared to death. But that's just our secret. Don't tell dad. I'm not as tough as everyone thinks I am. And when Annie and I get married you'll be my best man. Come home alive, brother."

It didn't take long to get back into the swing of things. I visited everyone I knew and then some. The hero had returned (some hero). I even went to visit my high school. I figured I had to wait for Annie to get out anyway, so I walked around and talked to all my old teachers. I couldn't believe how fast the time had passed since I had walked those halls. I felt like I had grown up and I didn't belong.

Just about every night I would meet up with Carmine, Carmine's girlfriend Louise, and my girl. We would hang at Tony's Pizza Parlor. We'd shoot pool and order a pizza. Carmine and I would drink beer and the girls had their cherry-cokes. Most of my buddies from school had been drafted but, the locals always stopped in to have a beer before going home. Dad's cronies also stopped in after their shift. I like neighborhood bars where everyone knows everyone. There was always someone to bullshit with.

On the Thursday of that first week we were at our usual table drinking, eating and clowning around. Carmine and Louise played the Jukebox and got up to dance. They played the new song, 'As Time Goes By' from the movie, Casablanca. Annie and I saw it three times. I told her, "If I could be like any movie star I would want to be Bogie."

I asked Annie if she wanted to dance, she said, no. "I want to talk to you alone."

"Alone? We're always alone."

She glared at me. "We're never alone. You always have a crowd around you. When are we ever alone?"

I flipped my mouth off. "That's because you never want to do what I want? You know what I mean." I relented. "Okay, what do you want to talk about?"

Her dark eyes shone as black as the night and out of that beautiful mouth came, "I want to get married."

"So do I. We'll get married as soon as the war is over."

Again, she looked me straight in the eye. "No, Tommy. I want to get married now. I want to get married before you go overseas."

"Are you are crazy? What if I don't come back? Besides you still have to finish school. Your parents will have a flipping fit. No, this discussion is over."

She started to cry. Christ, I can't stand to see a woman cry especially my woman. She then started in, "You don't love me."

"I don't love you? You're all I ever think about. It's because I love you that I want to wait."

"Then marry me. Let's elope. We can go to Elkton, Maryland. In Elkton you can get married at sixteen without your parent's consent."

"Sweetheart this doesn't make any sense. What about the church? We won't be legally married in the eyes of the church."

"I thought about that too. We can keep it a secret. When you get back we'll redo our vows and have a real, church wedding."

I tried to reason with her. "Annie, think about what you're saying. I say we wait."

"No. I love you and I want to marry you before you go overseas. I have it all planned. Tomorrow is Friday, you can pick me up after school and I'll tell my mother I'm sleeping-over Louise's house. Louise will cover for me. We'll be back on Saturday night and no one will know the difference. Think of it TC, you and me staying overnight at a hotel. Isn't that what you've been waiting for?"

I must admit 'the sleeping together' made perfect sense. "Okay! I'll tell Carmine."

"No. You can't tell Carmine he's got a big mouth and he'll tell my parents. I'll make Louise swear to God to keep her mouth shut. It also means she won't be able to see Carmine tomorrow night. I know she'll do it. She thinks eloping is so romantic."

"Okay Sweetheart. Here's looking at you." We both laughed. I made a lousy Bogey.

The following morning, Mom fixed me, ham, eggs, home-fries, with a lot of butter smeared all over my toast. She was spoiling me, and, she was also trying to fatten me up. Without realizing it I must have smiled I felt happy, and I guess it showed. Mom was also smiling when she asked, "What's up with you? Why are you so happy this morning?"

"Why not it's cold but it's sunny and I'm having breakfast with my beautiful mother, who is trying to get her son fat. Mom if you don't stop feeding me. I won't be able to get through the door of the plane." She laughed. "You got so skinny. You need some beef on those bones. People will think I don't feed you."

It's always been 'what people might think.' I wondered, *what they'll think when they find out that Annie and me got, hitched. At least they won't know for a while. I'll worry about the fall-out later-on.* "By the way mom I won't be home tonight I'm going to Pittsburgh to meet a buddy I met in Ft. Dix."

"What buddy?"

"Come on, mom you wouldn't know him if I told you."

"What's his name?"

"Jesus, do you also want his telephone number? I'm nineteen and I'm a soldier for Christ's sake."

"Okay, okay, but what did I tell you about swearing in this house and taking the Lord's name in vain?"

"I'm sorry but sometimes you treat me like I'm a little kid." I could always charm her.

She smiled and gave me a big hug. "I love you Tommy. This war scares me. Please take care of yourself."

"I love you too mom. Do me a favor and tell pop I'm taking the car for the weekend." She started to frown. "He's not going to like that." "I know but he'll get over it."

I had to pick up a few things from the store before meeting up with Annie. The first thing I did was go to a jewelry store outside of our neighborhood. I wanted to surprise Annie by getting her a wedding ring. I couldn't afford much so I got her a plain band that she could easily hide. At least it was real gold. I also needed to pick up some rubbers. There was no way I wanted her to get pregnant.

By three o'clock, I was waiting for her in front of the school. As soon as she saw me her face lit up. She and Louise ran to the car. That's when I noticed that Louise was crying, "Louise. What the hell happened? Did someone say something to hurt you? Point him out. I'll beat the crap out of him."

"No, TC. And stop acting so stupid. I'm crying because this is so romantic. You guys running away to get married. I wish it was me and Carmine."

I said, "Come on stop blubbering and remember, don't tell anyone about us getting hitched especially Carmine."

As we drove away I got a knot in the pit of my stomach. It wasn't that I didn't love Annie I just felt like I was taking advantage of her. You know, not doing right by her. You're supposed to protect women they're so fragile, so vulnerable and she was so young and beautiful. What if I didn't make it back? She'd be a young widow and she's much too young to be pining over me.

Annie must have guessed what I was thinking. She knew me like a book. If I was quiet, I was thinking. "Stop dwelling on this Tommy, I want this. Do you think you're the only married man going overseas? There are thousands, maybe even millions."

"I know, but they were already married when they were drafted."

Before I could finish she interrupted me. "Stop it. I don't want to hear this. It's my decision. I want to be Mrs. Thomas John Callahan. Besides, now you can't fool around on me. You wouldn't fool around on me would you, Tommy?"

"Are you kidding? You know me." I know. I'm a damn liar but those other girls meant nothing to me, so why hurt her on our wedding day? Besides, I wasn't married when I screwed around. "What about you Annie? Would you ever cheat on me?"

"Never—I'll wait just like any wife should. And when you get home we can retake our vows at St. Jude's. No one need ever know our secret except for Louise and of course God.

On the way to Elkton we listened to the radio and when the news of the war came on we changed the station. We sang all the way to Maryland to songs like, *I've Heard That Song Before*, *Don't Get Around, Much Any More* and *All or Nothing At All*—all the songs on the hit parade. When 'As Time Goes By' came on, Annie started to cry. "Hey, Baby what's the matter with you? You cry every time you hear that song. This is your wedding day. Don't forget it was just a movie." I did my Bogie routine. "Here's looking at you, kid." Annie started to laugh and her mood changed.

It took less than two hours to get to Elkton, Maryland, the eloping capitol of the East Coast. I checked around for a florist and found one on the corner of West Main Street. I ran in and bought Annie a white-rose corsage. I asked the girl at the counter if she knew where we could get married. She gave me directions to a little white house that was down the block. In front of the small white house was a sign that read: Justice of the Peace. And believe it or not, it had a white picket fence around it. We laughed. This was just like in the movies. Nervously, I rang the doorbell. A middle-aged man opened the door and asked, "Can I help you?"

I said, "Yeah, we want to get married."

"You look awfully young are you sure?"

"Yeah, we're sure. We're not as young as we look. I'm nineteen and Annie here is seventeen."

He smiled. "Oh, you're that old? I would never have guessed." He was a thin WASP looking guy, real tall at six foot two. He had light brown hair with a receding hairline. He called to his wife. "Margaret we have company." This older woman came running in with her apron on. His wife Margaret was the total opposite of him. She was short and pudgy. "Sorry, folks," she stated. "I was just cleaning up in the kitchen." She looked at us and asked the same thing as her husband. "Aren't you both too young to be getting married? I assume you're here to get married?"

"No Darling" he remarked. "He's nineteen and she's seventeen." They both laughed.

I was starting to get pissed. I felt like they were laughing at us. But Annie said I was too sensitive. I told them our story on how I was going overseas and how Annie and I had been sweethearts since we were kids. I explained that we were both Catholic and that we planned on getting re-married in Church, as soon as I came home. The guy smiled. He told me his name was, "Larry Jones."

We followed Larry and Margaret into a room they called the chapel but it looked more like their living-room. There were lace curtains on the windows. The only thing that set it apart was the podium. It had a fancy white lace cloth hanging halfway down and on top of it were silver candlesticks on each side of a large white Bible. Near a window in the corner of the room was an organ. On the wall behind the organ were photos of about a hundred couples.

The only other furniture in the room was a pink floral couch and a coffee table. It was easy to assume that the pictures were of all the couples that they had married. I stood there, looking at all the smiling faces. Larry came over and pointed to a picture on the wall that was way up the wall and to the far left corner "They were the first couple we married."

I looked at the picture and thought *they're probably old and have kids by now*. Also, neatly framed was his Justice of the Peace license. At least Larry was legitimate. He then handed Annie and me some papers to fill out. He said it was a Maryland state requirement. While filling out the papers Margaret lit the candles on the altar. As soon as we finished Annie went into the bathroom to comb her hair and change into the new dress she stashed into her overnight bag. When she came out she looked like a movie star. Her dress was pink with a full skirt that swayed when she walked. I handed her the box with the white-rose corsage. Rather than pin it on her dress she chose to hold it, as if it were a bouquet. By now Margaret was sitting at the organ. She asked if we had a request. I looked at Annie and then at Margaret. "Do you know As Time Goes By?"

"It just so happens, I do—except that's not the kind of song you play at a wedding."

"I know, but that's our song and in a couple of days I'll be going overseas. I want to remember this day as the day I think about when things get rough."

Gee-wiz, Annie started to cry and Margaret looked like she was going to blubber at any moment, women. Margaret never said another word she put her pudgy hands on the keyboard and started playing our song. *You must remember this-- a kiss is still a kiss.* I don't think the ceremony took more than five minutes. When I put the ring on Annie's finger Larry said, "Until death, do you part." I got a lump in my throat. I guess it was because I knew that the possibility of my death existed. Our kiss was long, passionate and embarrassing, until we finally let go of each other. It was done and it was legal. We were now man and wife.

We asked the Joneses if they knew of a hotel in the area where we could spend our Honeymoon. They recommended a boarding house that was called, The Elkton Love Nest. And if we hurried Mavis, the owner might still be serving dinner. That sounded good to me. I was starving, although, I wasn't keen on sleeping in a stranger's house. Annie deserved better. She deserved the bridal suite at the Ritz or at least a Howard Johnson, with a great restaurant. Dancing would be good, we both knew how to Jitterbug and do the two-step. Larry assured us that the only decent hotel was in Baltimore and we were too tired to make the trip. Larry gave us the directions on how to get to the Love Nest. He and Margaret wished us well and took our picture. This whole wedding thing seemed a little weird but I knew within the next hour or so, came the part I'd been waiting for. We would finally, make love.

The Love Nest was just a few blocks away. As soon as we pulled into the driveway the door of the house opened and there stood this woman who was almost as wide as she was tall. She had short blonde curls, rosy cheeks and the friendliest smile I had ever seen. "Come on Luvs, come on, I have dinner waiting for you."

So, taken by, surprise that for a few seconds we sat and stared at her.

As I walked through the door, I got this warm feeling. "This is a real nice place isn't it Annie?" She shook her head and smiled. She seemed more embarrassed then scared or, maybe just a little shy.

The woman introduced herself as Mavis Abbott. Mavis had an English accent. She explained that Larry called and told her we were coming and to take good care of us. "He also said you were hungry."

I thought, *Good old Larry.*

"You must be famished. I have chicken, mashed potatoes, gravy, string beans and apple pie for dessert. Is that alright?"

I said, "All right-that sounds swell."

"First off," she said. "Would either one of you like a nice hot cup of tea?"

21

Annie said, "Tea would be nice."

I don't drink tea so I asked Mavis if she had any coffee.

"No Deere. Sorry. I never keep the stuff in the house. Bad for the nerves— you see. But, I do have a bottle of brandy I keep for medicinal purposes or for special occasions. I would say this is a special occasion." Mavis ran into the kitchen to get the bottle of brandy and poured me a quarter of a jelly glass full. "Sorry about the jelly glass darling, but my crystal-stemware broke on the way over to the States."

"When did you come to the United States?" I asked. "And how long have you had the Elkton Love Nest?"

"Well Love I guess you could say I was a war bride. I met my Jimmy in London, in 1940, right before the war broke out. Jimmy was in London on some sort of banking business. I worked for the Bank of England and he handled his company's foreign accounts." He seemed like such a nice chap and good looking, too. So, when he asked me to have dinner with him that evening, I accepted. He waited for me in the lobby of the bank until I got off work. We walked to a Pub that was close by and we immediately hit it off. We saw each other every night while he was in England. And, like they say, 'all good things must come to an end.' He finished his business and went back to the States. We started corresponding and became such good friends. I was very fond of him. Then, one day Jimmy wrote and said he was going to enlist in the United States Navy. I thought I would never see him again. You know how that is, long distance romances, and all? We kept up the correspondence and before you know it we realized we had fallen in love. Then out of the blue I got a letter from my Jimmy, asking me to visit the colonies. He had a two-week holiday and he wanted me to meet his mum. I told him that was too short a time to make traveling preparations, and I couldn't afford to go. A week later he was knocking at the door of my flat. I nearly fell over. What a bloke! He picked me up in his arms, danced me around the room and told me I was a sight for sore eyes. And then he asked me to marry him. The rest is history. We got married in a small chapel in London. We had a wonderful two-week honeymoon, before he left for Hawaii.

Jimmy's mum called me and invited me to come to the States. She was a widower and said she would love the company. This way together we could wait for Jimmy to come home. I did and surprisingly there was little difficulty in getting a Visa, being, I was married to a Yank. His mum lived right here in this house and I've been here ever since."

Mavis looked rather sad as she told us her story. I asked where her husband was stationed and when she thought he would be coming home. "No, Love," she sadly replied, "My Jimmy's not coming home. My poor Jimmy is dead. He was stationed in Pearl Harbor. His mum died shortly after, from a broken heart. When she passed on she left me the house. I needed some income and I love company so I turned the house into a Bed and Breakfast. A 'Love Nest' for newly married couples like yourselves. You should see this place in the summer. Not a room to be had. That's enough of me. You must be exhausted. Let me show you to your room."

We followed Mavis to our room. The minute we hit the room Annie pushed me on the bed and said, "Just watch and don't say a word." There was no shyness, no fear or apprehension on her part. I was bowled over. This girl who held me at arms lengths for years, was doing a striptease. First, she took off her dress and danced around. Then she removed her slip and more dancing. Annie with her strict Catholic upbringing wasn't shy at all. She was dancing, bumping and grinding like she was Gypsy Rose Lee. I laughed until I thought I would piss my pants. This was definitely worth waiting for! What a babe. It wasn't until she took off her bra and panties that I realized Annie was no longer a girl she was a woman, and I never wanted her more than I did right now. I removed all my clothes and motioned for her to join me in bed. As she curled up into my arms I leaned over her and kissed her passionately. As our tongues met I could feel the pounding of my heart. I never had felt such love or happiness as I did at that moment. Her body was soft and her kisses moist. This was not the kid I fell in love with we had come full circle.

Being this was Annie's first time I tried being gentle. Although the passion was overwhelming I used restraint. This wasn't just about me I wanted her to enjoy making love to me. After some passionate kissing I fondled her breasts. When her nipples hardened I kissed and then suckled her breasts while I put my fingers inside her as she moaned. I pulled out and I gently put her hand on my erection. Annie sighed and arched her back. She put up her knees so I could go into her moist-opening. I moved up and down at a gentle pace until Annie started to moan and then yelled, "Oh, Tommy, oh my god." Talk about seeing stars! It was more than I had ever dreamed of. When it was over I told her I was glad we were married. Not so much for me, but for her. I knew there would never have been a honeymoon for Annie, without the wedding.

We fell asleep, hanging on to each other for dear life. I awoke in the middle of the night. The moon was full and it lit up our room. I looked over at Annie. She was sound asleep and she looked beautiful. Her skin was moist, her face flushed and her long black hair was tousled. I whispered, "I love you, Annie Callahan." She opened her eyes, looked up at me and whispered, "Mrs. Callahan." We kissed and then turned our bodies to spoon. I never wanted to let her go.

I awoke around seven o'clock in the morning and realized that I never used the rubbers I'd brought with me for protection. *My God, what if she got pregnant? How would she explain it to her folks? No, you can't get pregnant doing it just once, Isn't that what I always told Annie? We're goanna have to be careful from now on.* I finally fell back to sleep only to be startled by something crawling on my chest. I opened my eyes. It was Annie, (propped up in bed) and watching me sleep. Her fingers started at my chest then slowly she went to my stomach and on to Mr. Johnson. Obviously, Johnson reacted. "Annie," I laughed, "I created a monster. Hey, promise me that while I'm away you'll stay away from all those pimple-faced kids in your class."

"Not to worry. I'm yours, body and soul."

I laughed. "Hey, wasn't there a movie like that?"

We made love again, only this time I used a rubber. It wasn't as good but it was better than nothing. Again, she got so excited I could hardly stop her from yelling. "Honey, please Mavis will think I'm beating you." At first, she laughed, and then she got very serious. "Tommy, I'm scared."

"What are you afraid of? Do you think your folks will find out?"

"I'm worried about you going into combat. I'm afraid that something will go wrong and you won't be coming home."

"Come on Annie, you're scaring me. I'm coming home. Look, I'm not going to take any more chances than I have to. Don't worry Honey. I'm coming home."

"Then how come you can't tell me where you're going?"

"Because it's top secret—they didn't even tell me where I was going. Look Annie, on this day, at this time it is the best day of my life and I wish it would never end. I don't want to think about going back."

It wasn't until we went to shower that we realized what a cool room we were in. It was a little too fussy for my taste but I guess it fit the occasion. I figured it was called, The Bridal Suite.

Annie squealed, "How beautiful! Tommy, look how pretty this room is. I want us to have a bedroom as beautiful as this when we get married. I mean, when we get a house."

"Sure honey anything you want." I was starting to get scared. I was too happy everything I dreamed of was coming true. I had to be careful not to tempt fate.

When we came down the stairs, Mavis was smiling. "Good morning, my Darlings. how did you like your room?"

Annie gushed. "It is beautiful Mavis. Was that the bridal suite?"

"My dear, they are all bridal suites. But I gave you the best one. I thought I would make you a grand breakfast before you leave."

"Sounds great," I replied. "I'm really hungry."

Annie agreed. "Me too, that was some workout."

I couldn't believe she said that. Mavis remarked, "What did you say, love?"

"Oh, I meant that we like to exercise before breakfast. I read that exercise is really good for you."

Mavis laughed. "Well, you can call it whatever you like." We all burst out laughing.

Mavis gave us eggs, bacon and these things she called scones with marmalade. It was different, but tasty. She said she enjoyed having us stay with her. This was usually their off-season for weddings and she sometimes got lonely. Annie went over and hugged Mavis. She told her, "If it's alright with you Mavis I'd like to call you from time to time?"

"Oh, my dear, that would be ever so nice. You are such a charming young couple." Mavis insisted on only taking twenty dollars for the room and the meals. She said, "You should save your money for that grand wedding you will be having when you return from the war."

We hugged her and thanked her.

When we got in the car I asked Annie, "What do you say as soon as the war is over we come back and stay in our old room?"

"Oh, Tommy, that would be keen."

We were kind of quiet on our way home, neither one of us wanted to separate and go back to our parent's homes. I dropped Annie off at the corner of her street and kissed my wife good-bye. I reminded her to take off her wedding band. She took it off kissed it, looked at me with that silly little grin, and put it in her bra. Although the temptation to retrieve it was great, I forced myself to drive home. As usual, my mother was in the kitchen. I yelled, "I'm home!"

She yelled back. "Good. I'm making your favorite dinner. Corned-beef and cabbage."

"You've got to be kidding."

That night I couldn't fall asleep. My mind reenacted our first night together over- and-over again. And then it hit me. Carmine and me- we're not only good friends we were related. He's my brother-in-law—we're family. I started to think about Carmine. I felt kind of bad for him. He confided in me that he got his draft notice soon after I left for Ft. Dix, but he didn't pass the physical or was eligible for desk duty. Carmine has diabetes and he needs to take insulin shots on a daily basis. No wonder he looked so unhappy. I tried to cheer him up. I told him he was a lucky bastard, but he didn't buy it. All of our friends were either drafted or they enlisted. He felt alone. He was a guy who was stuck here with all the women.

Before I knew it my furlough was at an end, and it was time for me to go back to my base. Saying goodbye was the hardest thing I ever had to do. It was bad enough leaving my folks but leaving my wife was even harder. We had so little time together as a married couple. We had to have sex in the back seat of the car. It was just getting laid and not making love. There was no holding, no quiet conversation or spooning. At least I made sure I was careful about not getting her pregnant.

When it was time for me to say goodbye I felt like it was for the last time. I figured every soldier felt the risk and the odds were great. Deep down in the pit of my stomach I knew I wasn't coming back. Stupid- fears. I was a survivor and I knew how to take care of myself. I told no one about my feelings. It's not very manly to be afraid so I put on a very brave front. I was cocky as I hid behind my fears. This way no one would have to worry about me. I remembered that when I was a kid, if I cried that someone beat me up or whined, my old man would say, "Act like a man. Men don't cry." I wasn't a man. I was a kid. I made up my mind that I would never say those words to my sons. It made me feel weak— worse than that I thought my old man thought I was weak so I turned into a bully and kept everything inside. I pretended I was a big man. I now felt kind of bad for the kids I beat up and made fun of, for no reason at all.

I never saw my dad cry, not even at grandma's funeral. I thought he didn't care but mom said he did—he just had a hard time showing his feelings. I guess that's why he made a good cop; he never showed or acted like he gave a shit. I want to be a cop but I also want to give a shit.

Everyone that was there to greet me came to say goodbye, except that this time Annie's mom came to support her daughter. Annie made no bones about being upset, she was crying.

As the train started to move I put my head out the window and yelled. "See you next year. Pray for me." Why the hell did I say that? I sounded weak and scared. I hope my old man didn't think I was scared. Before leaving Pennsylvania I had received my orders. I was to meet my regiment for extensive training for a secret mission called *HUSKY*. On April 28, 1943, the 525th division would leave New York. Ten top jumpers would stay behind for more briefing. And then, five out of the ten would get to go on this mission. How they would be picked depended on their survival and jumping skills. They would then join the 505th on May 10th in Casablanca for their orders. The five chosen jumpers would go to New York, the point of embarkation for North Africa. That date had already been chosen. We would practice jumping the terrain at the DWP zones near Koradji, Morocco. If we survived, five of us would jump at an undisclosed designated area. The specifics wouldn't be given out until the last minute.

None of the jumpers would have a clue as to where this secret-mission was located. Briefing would come after the five men were chosen. I soon found out I was not only one of the men picked—but to my surprise I was promoted to Sergeant and second in command. Lieutenant, Harvey Bradshaw, would lead our unit. The other's chosen were, Leon, Jerry and Ralph. I was glad my buddy Jerry made the cut. Not sure if he was.

CHAPTER FIVE

Okay TC, that's enough daydreaming. You're aboard the 227-C-47 aircraft and you have to make the best of it. It had just dawned on me how quiet everyone was. Usually we're yakking up a storm. You could have heard a pin drop. I felt like I was going to puke. When I boarded the plane it took every bit of guts I had. We were told that the Paratroopers on this special mission were to be dropped south- west of Palermo. There, we were to rendezvous with Mario Moretti, the leader of the underground. With the exception of the pilot none of us knew where the drop would be. Lieutenant, Bradshaw was in command so we would follow his lead.

Mario and his band of Nazi and fascist haters would show us where the Nazi and Italian headquarters, and strongholds were. They also knew the terrain and the times the enemy was most vulnerable. Mario had informed the British Commander that said the Italian army would be easier to conquer because their weapons were old and they lacked training. The partisans also had maps and the locations of their headquarters, weapons and storage-facilities. Once we had the information we would radio our commanding officer with the intelligence information. He would then have knowledge of where to drop the rest of the paratroopers and the ground troops. It was risky but worth it. We would then meet with the rest of the 505th and liberate the Italian people whether they wanted it or not. We assumed they did, Mussolini was not a popular dictator.

Most important— knowing this information could save a lot of lives. Our mission was to defeat Italy and bring down Mussolini and the German forces. That would open the Mediterranean Sea route. If we had waited much longer the Germans would have beefed up their strength in that region. The way it was now, we out manned the German's stationed in Sicily. The plan was that all but the five paratroopers would be dropped at, Caltagirone. The infantry would invade the beaches at Gila, while the five of us would be dropped on the outskirts of Palermo. Once we radioed the information we gathered from Mario's partisans we would hook-up our ground forces. We had 48 hours to complete our mission.

The time finally came for us to jump. We were to get as close to southwest Palermo as possible. It was as dark as hell and we didn't know if we would be landing on the ground or in a tree. The saving grace was that we were expected so, the partisans guided us by flashlight. Once we were down and accounted for they took our parachutes and buried them in the woods.

This was a band of six men and two women. They put their hands over their mouths to show us not to speak until it was safe. This area was patrolled by the Germans using large spotlights. It wasn't until we reached a farmhouse that we actually saw who it was that was guiding us. It was dim with just a lit candle on an old wooden table, but at least we could see their faces.

Mario was the leader, all right. You could tell by his stance and the way he ordered everyone around. I thought this was probably how Bonaparte must have looked. You know small man with a large ego He was much younger than I had expected. He looked like he was in his early twenties. He had short black curly hair, bushy-eyebrows and a quick-smirk. His eyes pierced right through you. At least he knew how to speak and understand English. All this time I was worried about how we would communicate. I assumed that was why he was picked for this particular assignment.

Only three of the eight could speak or understand English, so there was a lot of interpreting. One of the women in the group was a beauty called Angelina. I thought the name suited her, she looked like an angel. She must have been about eighteen. She had blonde hair that she tied in a bun on the top of her head. She was tall for a woman, maybe 5'8", slim and in great shape. My thoughts were getting out of control and I had to remind myself that I was not only on an important mission I was married. *Jesus, forgive me my thoughts.*

I was glad that Harvey was in command. He was a good man—smart and not a glory boy. His motto was, "let's get this war over with and go the hell home." That was to my way of thinking. I didn't care about the medals.

As we sat around the table looking at the maps, one of the other women named Mary brought out some wine, cheese and bread, while apologizing that there wasn't more. It seemed when the Germans marched in they took most of the town's food. If it weren't for some of the farmers in the area helping them they would have no food at all. We assured them that we brought rations that we would be glad to share with them. They became indignant. No, we were their guests. Shit, this was no time for protocol. In their defense they really had a handle on this mission. They knew where and when to strike.

Mario said, "We should rest now. At dawn we go to the Cathedral of Monreale by foot—there we will meet up with ten more of my men and women. They will help by mapping out where the Germans hide their trucks, tanks, ammo and ships."

I reminded him that our mission was to also cut all lines of communication. Mario was quick to answer. "I know that soldier. The others will show you where the lines are and where the Italian military is located." They all laughed when he said, "Italian military."

Lieutenant Bradshaw asked, "What's so funny? Let us in on the joke."

The only ones who knew what Harvey asked, was Mario and Angelina. Angelina laughed as she explained in broken English, "Mario made a joke when he said Italian Army. All they have is light tanks, motorcycles, horses, bicycles and mules. If it weren't for the Germans they would have nothing to fight with."

We were all laughing. But inside I knew it was still a dangerous mission and it wasn't going to be a piece of cake. I was starting to get tired. I assumed the rest of the guys were too. We had been up for eighteen hours and the wine didn't help. Mario led us to cots and showed us where the outhouse was and it's pile of newspapers.

We all felt very uneasy about this band of partisans. Maybe it was because of the language barrier? The truth is we didn't trust them. Maybe war makes you paranoid?

I got up early the next morning. It's hard sleeping when you don't trust the people you're sharing your room with. Besides, I had to go to the can. When I went to the outhouse they call a bathroom I all but threw up. What a filthy rat hole. I decided to go into the wooded area that surrounded the farmhouse. I had just taken a piss when I heard someone coming toward me. It was kind of hazy and not quite light out. I drew my gun and said, "Hold it. I've got a gun."

A female voice said, "Cowboy, American Cowboy, don't you know when you hear the bushes rustle you're supposed to hide and surprise the enemy. You're going to get yourself killed if you stand there shouting. 'I've got a gun.' You would have made a good target and you would have been killed." She was right. I was trained to think like a soldier, but I acted like a green horn kid. Angelina was smiling when she came towards me. I asked, "What are you doing up so early in the morning?"

"It is not early Yank. You forget I'm part of this group and there is no time to sleep. We have too much to do. I, too cannot stand the smell of that filthy outhouse. I would rather go into the woods. Unlike you, I do not stink because I took a bath in the brook that's a few kilometers from here."

"Are you always this miserable in the morning? Or, don't like Americans?"

"I love Americans. I don't like arrogant men."

I couldn't help but laugh and when I did, she did. She was beautiful. In the light I noticed what I hadn't noticed last night. Her eyes were green. *I'll be damned, a blonde and green eyed Italian.* She must have read my mind by the way I was giving her the once over. "Northern Italy," she said. "My parents are from Northern Italy. Blonde hair and light eyes are not uncommon."

"How did you learn to speak English?"

"We learned from Mario. Mario was schooled in England."

She looked about fifteen but she told me she was eighteen. She also told me that a few months ago her best friend Rosemarie was raped and killed by 'fascist Italian pigs' and that she'll do whatever it takes to avenge her friend's death.

I reminded her that there was a chance that could also be her fate. "Why don't you go home and wait to be liberated? That's why we're here." That really pissed her off.

"Why don't you go back to where you came from Yank? This is my country and I want to be part of saving it."

"Boy, you've got some temper. You remind me of my wife Annie. She also has a hot Italian temper."

"At least you made a good choice in picking a wife. If you are married why aren't you home with her?"

"I guess you haven't heard about the draft." I quickly changed the subject. "Hey Angelina, where is that brook you were talking about? You're right I do stink."

She started down a path and I followed. "Come, I will show you. But be careful there might be snipers. So far we have been safe here, but you never know?"

I swear it was like a picture post card, the babbling brook, the morning mist, and the hillside was ablaze with the morning sunrise. I started taking off my gear and my clothes and Angelina's eyes never left my body. "Hey, Angelina, turn your head. You wouldn't want me staring at you would you?"

She laughed. "You have nothing I haven't seen before."

"Oh yeah, tell me more?"

She giggled. "No. What I mean is I have a husband and a brother. My husband is much bigger than you." Her remark caught me by surprise. I lost my footing and slipped on one of the slippery stones. "That's a low blow lady. And, I'm going to get you for that remark." The water felt good and clean. And for a brief moment, I felt like a kid again.

Angelina laughed as she watched me make a complete fool of myself. I poured water on my head while I pretended to be swimming in rough seas. After a while I got dressed. I ran up to her and said, "Now, you're going to get it." She made a mad dash for the woods but I caught up and tackled her to the ground. We were laughing and out of breath, then all of a sudden we were kissing. Strangers with different lives thrust into a war neither one of us wanted and all the while wondering if today would be our last day on earth. The sexual desire was overwhelming and we couldn't stop if, we wanted to. We were tearing off each other's clothes like we were on fire. After we came I started to shake. "Oh, my God what have I, done."

Angelina put her arms around me and whispered, "It is okay Cowboy. God will forgive us this sin and our few minutes of pleasure."

We got dressed, brushed the leaves from our clothes and went back to the house as if, nothing ever happened. As I walked in the door of the cabin Lieutenant Bradshaw asked me, "Where the hell were you? I thought you were my first causality. Don't you ever leave our unit without telling me where you're going? You could have gotten us all killed. Where the hell were you?" He stared at me, and then at Angelina. "Have you gone crazy?"

Leon and Jerry cut in. "Come on Lieutenant, he's here and he's okay. Nothing happened Let's get back to what we came here to do." Lieutenant Bradshaw reluctantly agreed and walked away.

I told the other guys, "The Lieutenant was right. I should have said something. But everyone was sleeping and I knew this was going to be a long day so I said nothing. I was wrong. I'm sorry."

Lieutenant, Bradshaw turned to look at me when he heard me talking to the guys and reprimanded us all. "Let me make this perfectly clear. Nobody takes a shit without telling me, understood?"

We answered in unison, "Yes, sir."

Mario broke the silence. "Let's go. We have to get out of here. We have a long walk to the church."

The Lieutenant asked Mario, "How many miles is it, to the church?"

"I don't know miles. It's about 24km." He asked, "Do you know Angelina?"

Angelina spoke for the first time since we got back. "I think it's about 15 miles."

Mario handed us some clothes. "Here, take off your uniforms and put these clothes on. We're going into town. You can't go to town in your American uniforms. You can pick them up when you rejoin your troop."

At the time it seemed to make sense. We took off our uniforms put on the street clothes worn by the locals, rolled up our gear and our weapons and started walking. I started to worry about the five of us being by ourselves and without any communication. We couldn't risk radio contact until this mission was in the bag. The scary part— no one from the 505th knew where we were and I was starting to feel spooked. What did we really know about these people? I asked Mario "What's the name of that church again?"

"It is the Cathedral of Monreale. Known to the locals as *'Our Lady'* King William the II, son of William the Conqueror built the Cathedral and dedicated it to the Virgin Mary, in-1172."

"Holy shit that's really old," Jerry said.

I said, "You know, Jerry you really have a way with words."

Mario decided to butt into the conversation. "That's the trouble with all you Americans you have no respect for anyone's culture or religion."

Mario's remark pissed off the Lieutenant. "Wait just a minute Mario. We're risking our ass to save yours." We all looked at each other. "You have some respect."

Mario apologized. "You are right of course forgive me." He then went back to telling us about the history of the Cathedral of Monreale. "Monreale is a small city in the province of Palermo. Palermo is old and like any old town the buildings and roads have shown wear and tear but is still very beautiful. You will see."

While tracking through the woods, we had to keep our voices down and our eyes and ears open. The German and Italian military patrolled the area. Luckily the partisans knew this terrain inside and out because we never saw a Kraut or an, Italian soldiers.

It was starting to get warm out so after walking for about ten miles we decided to rest and take a water break. Luckily we had filled our canteens with the water from a well before leaving the cabin. Mario was not one for lingering he never seemed to get tired. "Come on, come on we have to meet with the rest of my troop. You have only five minutes to rest." We were one tired ragbag of an army. Leon asked Mario, "How much longer before we get there?"

"Not long," he replied, "A couple of hours."

After an exhausting hour and a half we had finally arrived in Palermo. What we observed made us realize that without the guidance of the partisans, we could have easily wandered into a trap, Palermo was fortified. We saw many Germans and Italian soldiers patrolling the area. Mario was cautious. "We will wait for darkness and then make a run for the church. There, we will be safe." He was right. There was a lot of activity going on in town. It made good sense to be careful, and wait it out.

As far as I could see from the distance we were at I could understood what Mario was talking about. The town was old-world. In fact it looked pretty much like a picture postcard. *I started thinking of*

Annie. I bet she would like it here. Maybe we should go to Sicily, on our Honeymoon. I can't wait to tell the folks back home about this place. Too bad I can't pick up any postcards.

Angelina and I didn't look at or speak to each other during the entire trip. We both felt guilty. I know I did. Besides, no one did much talking there was no time to let our guard down Hanging around and waiting for it to get dark was difficult. So far we had lucked out but you never knew when lady luck will kick you in the ass.

Finally the streets started to empty out. The work day was over and the people were either going home or hitting the local bars. We noticed that the Italian army patrolled the area every 30 minutes. We also noted that the front steps in front of the cathedral would leave us exposed and vulnerable. Mario told Captain Bradshaw not to worry that we would be using a side-door that lead to a cellar that was only used by church staff. So, we waited until the Italian army's patrol passed. I thought it odd that not one person would be walking or wandering around town. But then this was war and there could have been a curfew. It was so eerie that the Lieutenant questioned the silence. "Where the hell did everyone go?" Ralph put in his two cents. "Probably home to have dinner and hanker in for the night—this is war where can they really go? Anyone who has a brain should stay indoors."

Mario remarked, "If you saw soldiers patrolling your town would you stay outside, yank?" Although the Lieutenant didn't like Mario's tone he let it go, for now.

With Mario and his band leading the way we split up in two's dashed to the door and went down several steps before coming to a room that had cobwebs hanging from the rafters, a damp dirt-floor and smelled of mold. The good thing was, we were in a wine cellar that was filled with wine barrels, several racks of wine bottles and a rack of wineglasses. Mario lit the oil lamps that were atop, some of the barrels. Then he picked out a glass wiped off the dust with his dirty, torn-jacket and opened the first bottle. "Come on everyone, drink up our food will be here soon."

I had thought about real food all day long. All we had to eat were a couple of cans of k-rations. After drinking our first glass of wine we heard the up-stairs door creak-open. We cocked our guns and pointed them at the stairwell. To our relief it was a Priest. He was introduced to us as Father, Michael Ferranti. As he entered our area I got up off the barrel I was sitting on. He said, "No, no, please sit." Father Ferranti looked to be in his mid-sixties. He was stocky, his hair was gray and his eyebrows were bushy. He stood about five foot nine. Most noticeable, was his kind eyes and smile. Although his English wasn't great he tried to communicate. What English he didn't understand Mario interrupted. He told us to rest as best we could with the less than elegant surroundings. The Lieutenant assured Father Ferranti that we were grateful for his hospitality. He smiled and stated, "I will have my housekeeper Louisa bring you food you must be hungry. We have pasta, wine, bread and cheese. Enjoy." As he turned to walk away I called out to him. "Father, would you have time for my confession before the rest of Mario's men get here?"

"Yes my son, I will be glad to hear your confession." I could see and feel Angelina's eyes burning a hole in me. I shook my head no. She understood and smiled. I knew I would have to leave that chapter out. Even though a confession is sacred the priest knows her. I don't care what he thinks of me I was just passing through. I felt I had to square things with God while I had the chance.

It wasn't long before Louisa came in from that same side door carrying a big bowl of pasta. It smelled terrific. She smiled and announced in Italian, "I will be back."

The two women in our group offered to help but Louisa shook her head and uttered one English word. "Dangerous." The rest was said in Italian and translated to us by Angelina.

"The soldiers were used to Louisa coming and going, she didn't want to raise any suspicion." Angelina followed Louisa anyway and came back with what looked like a feast. We ate like it was our last meal. I was stuffed. Between the food and the wine I was actually feeling good, I think we all were. After our meal the Lieutenant asked

Mario. "What time do you expect your men to be here with the intel-ligence we need? We only have 48 hours to complete this mission and we've already used up 24." Mario looked at his watch. "Let's see, it's 6:45. They should be here by, 7:30 sharp. You can be sure of that."

Again, Lieutenant Bradshaw asked, "I assume they will meet us down here?"

Father Ferranti interrupted, "No, no, we will meet them in the upstairs rectory. I locked the doors to the Cathedral, no one can enter. Don't worry you will be safe."

We started to let our guard down. We kept our voices low as we started making small talk. Actually, it was Angelina who started the conversation by asking us questions about the United States. She wanted to know about the Statue of Liberty and what New York City was like? We answered her questions until we heard a noise coming from inside the Cathedral. Mario told us to be quiet and to stay where we were. "I think it's my men getting here earlier than I expected, I'll go up and check it out."

Father Ferranti whispered, "I bolted the door. How did they get in?"

Mario went slowly up the stairs and opened just a crack in the door. He then came down and said, "It is okay to come up now it's one of my men." In groups of two we quietly climbed the stairs. When, we opened the door Mario was standing next to a man holding a machine gun and it was aimed, at us. Lieutenant Bradshaw asked, "What the fuck is this?" The five of us went for our weapons. Mario shouted, "I wouldn't do that if I were you. Everyone, drop your weapons." His fellow partisans stared in disbelief. He repeated in Italian, "All of you."

Angelina and the others yelled back at him in Italian. He just smirked.

"So what now" I asked. "We're prisoners of war?"

Mario's eyes met mine when he said, "No Yank we take no prisoners."

Father Ferranti, the last one up the stairs walked to the front of us as if to protect us. "What is the meaning of this? Have you gone crazy?" he asked in broken English and Italian. Mario turned his gun on him. Father Ferranti angrily yelled, "Get out of my church, you devil. This is a sanctuary. You cannot kill anyone in a church. It is a mortal sin." Mario and the other man looked at him and laughed. In a voice that sounded like the devil himself Mario said, "Get out of my way Father or you will be the first to go."

Man that Priest sure had guts. He turned his back on Mario and walked over to the altar, lit the prayer-candles and started praying. Mario became flustered as he shouted, "Everyone move closer to the front of the church. Move, hurry up!"

I walked over to where the Priest was standing. In English, he said, "May God, have mercy on your soul." Without warning the man Mario called Antonio opened fire on us American's first. I remember falling to the ground. Father, Ferranti tried to catch my fall but couldn't. I knew I'd been shot but I felt nothing. No pain, no fear, nothing. I just couldn't move I could only see and hear. I looked up at the ceiling and saw Jesus looking down at me. He looked sad and I could have sworn I saw tears in his eyes. I figured I must be dead. Then I remembered I was in a cathedral and had fallen to the floor beneath a large mosaic portrait of Jesus.

I watched Mario stand in front of Angelina and I heard her yell, "You traitor! You Nazi lover! I spit on you. And then I heard three shots and I saw Angelina fall to the floor. Then, there was nothing.

What's that smell? What the hell is that smell? My God it smells like corned beef and cabbage. As I stood in the kitchen of my home I saw my mother setting the table. She looked towards me, screamed and dropped the glass that was in her hand. "*Help me mom, I'm dying.*"

German and Italian forces surrendered in May 1943. Although the HUSKY campaign was successful, many lives were lost.

Dictator Benito Mussolini was arrested and imprisoned in July, 1943. In September, 1943, the German special-forces, rescued him... He was later-captured and executed along with fifteen leading Fascists, on April, 29, 1945. His body was then taken to Milan and hung upside down for public viewing. Those on the side of the Mussolini regime were shunned by their own people and considered traitors, while some left the country. Most Sicilians saw us as liberators who had saved them from German occupation and a tyrannical, injudicious dictator.

PART II

CHAPTER SIX

Cambridge, MA: Hotel Marlowe

Startled and with my heart pounding, I've awaken from a nightmare that has plagued me since childhood.

I see myself running through a forest and beside me is an American Soldier whose face is blurred. We stop running when we have reached a medieval Catholic, Church…We try entering, but, the doors are locked. The soldier pounds on the large-bronze doors and shouts "Open the door! Let us in! Open the door!"

A door opens, and a Priest says, "Come in and close the door." We hurry in, and close the door behind us… The soldier pulls out a Colt pistol and points it at the Priest—but, he doesn't shoot… The cleric ignores the soldier, and walks over to the pulpit and lights, eight prayer candles—he, then asks "Why are you here?"

The soldier shouts, "To seek vengeance." Suddenly, the crucifix that was affixed to the wall crashes to the floor…then the building starts to quake…The candles fall onto the alter-cloth-setting it, on fire…When the fire starts to spread the soldier and I run for the door—but, it's locked, and we can't get out…The smoke and heat, is so intense I feel like I'm suffocating… I can't get out—I'm going to burn to death…

That's when I wake up with my heart pounding, and my body drenched with sweat. I tend to play this scenario over and over in my mind and hoping I will find the connection that binds me to his hellish on-going nightmare.

According to the experts some people have the same or a similar dream over short periods of time or, it could last a lifetime. A recurring dream usually means that there is something in your life your consciousness refuses to acknowledge, and in all probability the dream will keep repeating until you have corrected the unresolved obstruction. Another theory is that people who experience difficulty in a recurring dream must have had past-trauma they have not dealt with. I have yet to find the reason or the connection between me and my nightmares.

My mother thought that I was re-creating a movie that I must have seen as a kid. I had seen some old movies on television, but if I was recreating a movie wouldn't the same actors be in the dream? Besides, I don't ever remember seeing a movie using that scenario. Still, questions remain, how would I know what a Colt pistol looked like?

I sat up in bed and tried to get my mind off the fire and the feeling of being suffocated. As before, my cognizant would not let it go. Lately the reoccurrences seems to be escalating. One of these days I'm going to see a shrink, but not until I have health-insurance and I'm collecting a paycheck. My education has put me in the hole for a hundred thousand dollars. It would have been a lot more if, my parents hadn't helped me out. The one thing I know for sure, I'm not going to let this nightmare ruin my day, because today, is my last day in Boston and one of the top ten days of my life. I'm a Harvard University graduate. And once I get my Law Degree, I can start the job that is waiting for me in Manhattan, New York. Graduating from one of the oldest and most prestigious law schools in the country has landed me a job with the law firm of, Mark Moran, Mark Moran Junior and Associates. Mark Moran, Sr., started the law firm several decades ago and is semiretired. I read he was a shrewd and calculating attorney who rarely ever, lost a case. Mr. Moran's sons have taken over the practice and they have decided to expand. To me it seemed like the perfect place to get the experience I'll need, as

I climb-up the ladder of success. As Jackie Gleason once said, "How sweet it is."

My family has always encouraged me, and they're proud of my accomplishment. I'm the first attorney in the family and the first college graduate. Hell, I'm proud of me. It was tough going for a while, but I finally did it. Now all I have to do is pass the bar exam

My dad's worked hard his whole life, and very secretive about his net-worth. Although, I'm sure he makes a decent living. I've never heard him complain about money, and he's been generous to all us, three kids. He never claimed that the money he gave me for college was a gift, so, as soon as I'm able, I'll start paying him back. God knows how long that will take

As much as I'm looking forward to graduation, I'm also looking forward to going to New York, and getting on with my life. Going against my requests to keep my graduation party, simple— my parents have planned to hold my graduation party at, the Marlboro Inn. It's a local high-end bed and breakfast mansion in New Jersey. History states that The Marlboro was built in 1840 for a Mr. Samuel Holmes and sits on three acres of prime real estate. It was then re-modeled and the name changed to, The Marlboro Inn Bed & Breakfast. Upper Montclair is known for its beautiful old mansions, most of them were built during the thirties and forties. Many years ago, Upper Montclair was the suburb for the wealthy.

I've been to the Marlboro on several occasions. That's where my uncle Frank had his daughter Robin's bat mitzvah reception. I guessed my parents-but mostly my mother, didn't want to be out-done by my father's brother. Personally, I don't know why they would want to go to all that expense, this place doesn't come cheap. A house party would have done just as well but they were adamant. Mom said that they were proud of me, and they wanted to share their moment with all the people who had endured her constant bragging, about her son, the lawyer. Dad, also added, "Your Uncle Frank, thought it would be fitting."

My mother always gets this look of disgust when anyone mentioned Uncle Frank. He's my father's brother, and his only sibling. She would like to disavow Frank Scarpelli. According to my mother, Uncle Frank has somewhat of a shady past. Rumor has it, he is, or was, in the Mafia. He not only denies it, he couldn't care less what people think of him. The buzz is, that he helped my dad out by loaning him the money to start his first- auto repair shop. Dad started with one, and now has five, Scarpelli, Auto Service Centers. Dad keeps reminding mom, that he paid his brother, every dime he ever borrowed from him. That loan caused a big argument between my parents. My mother said she didn't want a cent of 'mafia money.'

Dad and Uncle Frank are very close and it pisses him off when my mother makes snide, remarks about him. He keeps telling her, that she has no right to interfere with anything that goes on between them—that, his brother is a successful business man, and not, in the Mafia.

Mom still insists that Uncle Frank is a gangster and a bad influence on their children.

Mom no longer argues with my dad about his brother. The bond between them is unbreakable. The truth is, none of us really know what my uncle does. When confronted with accusations his wife, Aunt Dorothy remarks, "Rumors, just rumors. Would a Mafia guy marry a Jew? Some people are jealous so, they pass on stories." Anyhow, that's the story she tells her family and her daughter Robin, whose being raised in the Jewish faith. Except on, Christmas and Easter.

Most of the time my Dad is a kind, easygoing guy, but he also has an excitable nature, so he yells. When he does we know he's really pissed and we stay cool. We don't want his wrath coming down on us. He's a good father, he doesn't ask for much, and he gives a lot. Al, my brother, is four years older than me and he's a lot like my dad. They resemble each other and have the same temperament. Me, I'm not very emotional and I'm pretty easy going. It takes a lot to get me angry. When I do get mad I stay cool, but I tend get nasty and arrogant.

Uncle Frank was happy and proud when my dad named me after him, although, my mother was furious. Dad held his ground. Even if Uncle Frank had, had, a son, he couldn't have a namesake. In the Jewish religion, you name your children after deceased family members.

My Father's mother died of pneumonia when he was only twelve years old. And according to my dad, it was my uncle who took care of him. Although, my uncle Frank (his real name is Francis) is only three years older, he made sure his brother went to school, had clean clothes and money for lunch. Thanks to his brother, dad graduated from high school. Their father, (Pop) worked day and night in order to support his two boys. I suppose you could say they grew up without a mother or father. Pop never remarried.

Uncle Frank dropped out of school at sixteen and hustled the pool halls. Even as a kid, he spent some and saved some. He had a bank account when he was only sixteen years old. After taking a lesson from the local loan-sharks, he found there was more money in lending than in hustling. So he started a loan-shark business. Today it's a legitimate business and he's called a Venture Capitalist. He also branched out into real estate and the stock-market. In the beginning, it was on a small scale, after all he was still a kid. I don't have a figure on his net-worth; I just know he's very wealthy. Uncle Frank is a genius when it comes to investments; he's been taking care of my dad's finances since he set him up in business. He advised my dad, "Never buy what you can't afford to pay back. The interest rates will kill you. So, when Dad's business started to do well, Uncle Frank recommended that he should expand by purchasing a cost-effective structure- in a prime-location. "If the business goes bust, you lose everything. But if you own the building and the land, you still have an investment." I always thought that given the advantages that I had— my uncle would not only have gone to college, he would have graduated with high honors. As Aunt Dorothy has said, "Go figure, a high school dropout is a mathematical genius."

She's right, my uncle's analytical brain can figure immediately, while most of us would need a calculator.

I think Uncle Frank favors me a little more than my brother, Al, and my sister, Julia. He treats them great. And me, he's always busting my chops. I'm somewhat like him. I don't need coddling. I can take it because I can give it. I never start fights, but I also never walk away from one either. Many a time I came home beaten to a pulp, but I never cried. I figured it was as much my fault for not running away, as it was theirs, for starting the fight. Actually, I was more afraid of my mother's reaction than the kid who was beating the shit out of me.

It was my uncle who encouraged me to go to law school. I was just a kid when I knew I wanted to be an attorney. He said, "Go for it, go after your dream. Besides, we need an attorney in the family." I always enjoyed watching court trials on television, especially criminal cases. I was intrigued that in lieu of all the evidence stacked up against their client, they would figure out a way to seek doubt in prosecutorial evidence. Convincing a jury of someone's innocence takes a lot of skill. I even watched old, Perry Mason, reruns.

I also knew that in order to get into law-school, I would have to keep up my grade point average, so, I missed a lot of hanging out with the guys and other after-school activities. When I got a little older it meant missing out on dates, until high school. That's when I met Jessie.

Jessica, Smith, is a cute blonde with classic features and blue eyes. She was taller than most girls at, five-foot eight. She was also a popular cheerleader. She may have looked snobbish, but Jessie was down to earth and my steady girlfriend, all through Montclair High School. She was full of life and fun to be with and she liked sex. I guess you could call her my first crush.

A few days before graduation I received my acceptance to Harvard University. I ran over to Jessie's house to tell her the good news. Apparently, she didn't think the news was good. I guess she never thought I had a chance of being accepted. So, instead of congratulating me, she dumped me. She said it was because she did not want to wait the six years it would take, for me to finish my education. Jessie had her own agenda. She was going to Montclair State to become a physical education teacher. And after graduation, she would teach at a local school. She also informed me that, two-years later, she intended to get married and have two children, a boy and a girl. She wouldn't and couldn't wait for me because that didn't match her plan. She argued, "You're going to a prestigious school, and you will probably meet your own kind, and dump me anyway."

I said, "What the hell is my own kind supposed to mean? My kind is here in Montclair. So what if I'm going to a good school. I worked hard to get there. I know it's going to be tough, but we can work it out."

She said, "My point exactly, Frank. That's why you should go to a university within the metropolitan area. This way we won't be so far away from each other."

"Are you crazy, Jessie? I should give up going to Harvard because you're a spoiled brat, who's used to getting her own way? I'm so glad you have your life so neatly wrapped up with college, marriage, and babies. What you call picture perfect, is far from my expectations."

Jessie was right, right now, all I cared about was getting my law degree. I didn't know where I'd be, in six years. With my acceptance letter in hand, I walked out of her house and her life. I cared about Jessie, but nothing was going to deter me from getting my law degree, not even her.

My mother was heartbroken. She liked Jessie and the idea of my going to a college in New Jersey. Another thing about Italian mothers, they want you married and having babies as soon as possible, they live for grandchildren.

I have to admit Jessie was right. I would not have had the time that a relationship requires. I always knew that when I was ready for love and a commitment, it would happen. After all, I'm not hard, to look at. I'm six one with black hair, light hazel eyes, and a muscular build. And although I'm Italian, our family has been blessed with small, straight Roman noses from the Santos, my mother's side of the family. Thank you, God, and the Santos family.

My father's parents were from Naples and my mother's family is from Rome. In fact, my mother's parents live in Rome. Years ago they immigrated to the United States, and lived in Verona, New Jersey. They stayed for twenty-five years before deciding to return to Italy. Mom visits her parents every two years. I guess you could say, so far, I've had a pretty normal life. My only struggle has been dealing with my nighttime terrors. As they say, 'no one goes through life unscathed.' It might have been easier to handle if, I knew what created it, and how to get rid of it. Sometimes I'll go six months and not have one episode. I start thinking it went away and I'm finally free, only to have it return. I feel like it taunts me. My biggest fear is that I may have to live with it for the rest of my life.

When I was a kid, the dreams were not as intense as they are now. It seems to take on a life of its own and it's growing-up with me. It's almost like watching the same play over and over again then suddenly you notice that there are subtle changes. Another actor is added, or there's a change in the dialogue, and the setting is somewhat different. As soon as I find an apartment in New York and settled into my new job, I'll start looking for a psychiatrist. Hopefully, the dreams won't be as difficult to get rid of as I fear they'll be. My parents wanted to take me to a psychologist when I was nine. But I was afraid the kids in my school would find out, and call me crazy. So I lied—I told them the nightmares had stopped. They assumed I grew out of it.

My mother is unhappy about me moving into my own apartment. She actually wants me to live at home, save my money, and commute from Jersey to New York. She claims none of the children in the family moved out, until they got married. I reminded her that they all got married before they were twenty-four. I tried to explain, "Mom, a lot of my evenings will be spent in reading briefs and studying to pass the bar. Besides, if I work downtown, I should live down-town and not have to commute. I can afford to have my own place."

What I actually thought was—*it's time I started living the life that a young, twenty-four-year old should be living. It's time to have a normal sex-life.* With my heavy workload at college, my social life was kept to a minimum. I've been waiting for the day I'd have my own place, so I could come and go as I please. I dated some. There were a lot of smart, great-looking women to choose from— but you can't hang out at the bars, have a relationship and keep up your grades. Some did, and some flunked out. It's time I made up for lost time. In a couple of months I'll be twenty-five— other than some one-night stands, and a few friends with benefits, relationships, my sex-life was nothing to brag about. After haggling with my mother over my move, my father intervened. "Terry, please, it's enough already, you're giving me a headache. He's a grown man, leave him be. I want this conversation to end." *Thank you, Dad.*

CHAPTER SEVEN

Graduation went off without a hitch, except for a minor embarrassment brought on by my grandfather. As valedictorian I was asked to deliver the farewell address at the commencement ceremony. As I walked up to the podium Pop stood up and began clapping and shouting, "That's my grandson! That's my grandson!" Everyone in the audience laughed. I suppose at eighty-eight you can do any damn thing you want. Dad tried to calm him down, but he kept on shouting in his broken, Italian/New Jersey accent. I didn't care what anyone thought I was happy that he was well enough to attend. Six months ago, pop had a heart attack and we nearly lost him.

Besides my parents; my brother, Al, his wife, Barbara; my sister, Julia, and her daughter, Katie; and uncle Frank, aunt Dorothy, and their daughter, Robin. The smiles on my family's faces expressed how proud they were of my accomplishment. And, I was proud of them; they all looked great. One thing about the Scarpelli family, we know how to dress for an occasion.

Uncle Frank wore a very expensive, brown, tailored suit with a light yellow dress shirt. His tie was brown with gold diagonal stripes, and his shoes were brown, Italian -leather. He's five ten and in pretty good shape for a man of fifty-six. I imagine an older woman would think he was good looking with his dark hair graying, just enough, to make him look distinguished. To the world, he looked like the CEO of a large corporation. To my mother, he was a member of, the Cosa-Nostra. His wife, Dorothy is something else. She has long auburn, curly hair and in high heels she's about the same height as Uncle

Frank. She looks very young for forty. My mother said she's had cosmetic surgery. Maybe so, but she still looks hot. I'm sure she had on more diamonds than any other women there. A little tacky you might say but this woman is the salt of the earth and no one could be nicer. The most remarkable thing about this couple was their relationship. Every time she looks at my uncle, her eyes light up. She truly loves her man and he feels the same about her. I hope when I find my significant other we can maintain that same kind of loving connection.

Take my sister, Julia. She is twenty-seven and came without her husband, William McCray. Everyone calls him Willie. Willie is what Italians call a, *gavone,* (a real jerk) he's a drinker and a flirt. No one knows why Julia loves that idiot.

My dad gave him a job just so he could keep an eye on him. Willie was a wild, good-looking teenager. He stands slim and tall with blond hair and blue eyes. He had the kind of looks any young teenager would go crazy for. My parents went crazy when she brought him home to meet her parents. Julia was the only one of us who didn't go to public school. She went to parochial schools. My parents had big plans for Julia; they wanted her to become a nun. But Julia had her own plans and became pregnant when she was a senior, in high school. I thought my father would kill the bastard. Instead, he told Julia she would have to marry him. She said, "I knew you would feel that way dad, that's why I got pregnant!" And so they were married in the chapel at St. Josephs. She was seventeen and her daughter, Katie, was born six months later, premature, of course. Now mom is happy she didn't become a nun, she wouldn't have had Katie, who is her only grandchild. Katie is a great kid, in spite of her stupid father. We're all happy she's here. Although my brother, Al, has been married to Barbara for two years, they still don't have any children.

After the graduation ceremony, there was the usual picture taking and congratulatory hand shaking. I was surprised when, Dean, Robert Matthews came over to my family and shook everyone's hand, but held pop's hand just a little longer, and remarked, "It's OK to be proud, Mr. Scarpelli. You should be, your grandson is not only smart he's also a fine young man. Frank will make an excellent attorney." I was taken aback at his statement. I didn't know he knew anything about me. I don't think we have ever had more than a few words in the six years I was at the university.

With school behind me I was anxious to get on with the next phase of my life. I went through a mental too-do list, *graduation party is next. Monday, look for an apartment in Manhattan. Six weeks, I start my job.* As luck would have it, I didn't have to start until until August first. Mark Moran, Jr., the Senior, VP, told me I would need time to get situated. Besides, business slowed down some in the summer months. *I am one happy dude.*

At the end of the day I was to drive home with my parents. But first, we were all going to meet for a late lunch. Always one to go first class Uncle Frank made reservations at Anthony's Shack, a popular seafood restaurant. In fact it's one of Boston's landmarks. I don't know how he managed to get us a reservation on such short notice. I heard this place is booked several months in advance, especially this time of the year. And as usual he insisted on picking up the tab. We ate, drank, and Uncle Frank made a toast and not surprisingly there were tears in his eyes. When it came to family, he could get very emotional, but I know for a fact he's a shark when it comes to business. The waiter stayed by us like glue. I guess he knew a big tipper when he saw one. After lunch, we hugged, kissed, and went to our own cars for the long drive back to New Jersey.

It had been one hell of a day and I hadn't much sleep, so I decided to rest my eyes, but quickly fell asleep. That's when I saw my-self running through the woods alongside a soldier... We were running so fast my breathing became labored, the soldier looked at me and smiled. And although he had on a helmet, I could still see his freckled, face and blue eyes. This usual phantom of a man had a face, and seeing him for the first time startled me awake. I was in disbelief—but not frightened.

My mother asked, "Frankie, are you all right? Your breathing, it's so heavy."

"I'm good, just tired."

"Did you have one of those dreams again?"

"No, there's nothing for you to worry about."

My mother remarked in a joking tone. "Just because you're a lawyer, doesn't mean you tell me what to do. A mother's job is to worry—that's all I've got to do."

Dad and I laughed, but it was true. She drove us all nuts.

While on the trip home I finally had the time to evaluate my life and good fortune to be in such a loving family. Or maybe it was just the wine. I was actually getting emotional and allowing myself to feel something. For so much of my life, like any kid, I took things for granted. And like any kid, I didn't appreciate anything. Everything was about my fun, my friends, my career, and me. A new phase was about to begin, and I wanted to start by being a little grateful and, yeah, maybe a little humble. Of course, if I were really humble, I would have opted for a prosecutorial position in New Jersey. It was offered, but I turned it down. I preferred the established, accredited and money-making, law firm. Although, I would like to believe that I'll still be doing some good. I'll just get paid more.

I wondered why Uncle Frank never offered to throw me some of his business. He probably thought it would be small potatoes for me and the fees would be too high, although for him I'd work pro-bono. Actually it's best not to mix business with family. What if I screwed up?

For several miles we drove in silence, until my mother asked, "Why so quiet, Frankie?"

"I don't know mom. I'm just thinking. I was thinking about pop and how great he looks. I'm so glad he was well enough to see me graduate."

"Well, if you ask me, he was rude. Why did he have to be so loud? He should have kept his mouth shut and act a little more dignified."

My mother's remark infuriated my Father. In a quiet but deliberate voice he remarked, "Like you should, Terry. You should keep your mouth shut. That man raised two kids on his own, so show him some respect. He's an old man, and he's my old man."

"I'm sorry, Al. I know how sensitive you are about him." Dad gave her the eye look. I call it the evil eye. She got it and changed the subject. You know Frankie you never asked me who I invited to your graduation- party."

"I thought it would be family and some very close friends."

"If I did that," she replied, "I would have had it at home. We've invited a hundred guests."

"Mom, you have to be kidding. You invited a hundred people? Who did you invite?"

My dad finally joined in the conversation, "The whole, damn, town."

"Mom, who did you invite to the party?"

"Family, some of your friends, some of your father's friends, my friends, business associates, and of course, your Uncle Frank had to have some of his you know who, friends."

Dad looked at her. "Terry, what the hell is wrong with you tonight?"

"I don't know what's wrong. I don't know why I keep aggravating you. I guess; I'm just tired and excited about having my boy home."

Then she jokingly interjected, "At least we won't have to pay for his wedding."

Dad teased her. "How do you know he wants to get married?"

She started to laugh. "Al, you know how long I've waited for that day. By the way Frankie, I invited that nice girl from the neighborhood."

"What girl, mom?"

"You know, Jessica Smith, who is now Jessica Hart. It just so happens she is getting a divorce and she needed a pick-me-up. No one seems to know what caused the breakup. May-be we'll find out at the party."

"Why she's getting a divorce is her business, you and your friends shouldn't gossip." My remark meant nothing. She went on and on, so my dad and I kept still. We couldn't win. I guess in the six years I was away I had forgotten what a nag my mother was. The ride home reinforced my plan to leave the nest, as soon as possible. As soon as we arrived home, I went to my room. I was exhausted, but also, afraid to sleep. I didn't want to ruin my perfect day by having another nightmare. Not to worry, as soon as I hit the pillow I was out like a light.

The following morning brought mixed emotions about my graduation party. Although I looked forward to seeing my close family and friends, I thought a hundred people, was going overboard. It was actually embarrassing. What was my mother thinking? There was nothing I could do about it now— except skip town and that was out of the question.

I started thinking about Jessie. I wondered how she was holding up and why she didn't tell me she was getting divorced. The last time I saw her was at her wedding. Being there was rather awkward, although, I kind of liked the dude she was marrying. At least he seemed nice. Parker was a jock and the physical education teacher at the local middle school in Montclair, New Jersey. Not bad looking, if you like that type. Jessie looked beautiful in her wedding gown. As if possible, she was even more beautiful now, than when she was in high school. As she walked down the isle of the church she was smiling. Jessie was always smiling; it looked easy for her. She's a smart, great girl, every man's dream, then why didn't I fight to keep her? Was it ego? Maybe, after all she dumped me. How could she dump me and marry that jock? I was surprised that I felt some resentment towards him. It was as if he was stealing my girl, yet still knowing she wasn't my girl. She was once, my teen crush. We'd broken up years before he came into the picture and she had every right to fall in love. I suppose I was jealous that she found someone first.

The whole time I was at the university our correspondence amounted to short holiday messages. I received Christmas and Birthday cards, that, amounted to a few short sentences

Jessie got what she wanted: a husband, a teaching job, and the security of living in the same community she grew up in. And I had chosen my path: a career, leaving the town where I grew up, and putting some distance between my family and myself. Jessie was happy with the same old thing. I wanted to expand my horizons. I didn't want to be the local, family attorney.

The party was starting at 3:00 pm., so we arrived at 2:45 to greet our guests and make sure the bar was stocked the way my Dad and Uncle Frank liked it. Surprisingly, the guests started arriving on time. I guess they never heard of, fashionably late. But then we weren't those kinds of people, no pretense here. Everyone came up to me and congratulated me. Some were friends and relatives I hadn't seen in years, and it was good seeing them again. I wondered if Jessie would actually show-up. I watched the entrance until I grew busy greeting people and shaking hands. Suddenly I felt a tap on my shoulder. I turned and there she was. What a sight! I thought, *Holy shit, this girl is a knockout.* We laughed. We kissed. We hugged. Divorce seemed to agree with her. "Frankie, you look great. How the hell are you?"

I smiled when I said, "Jess, you can call me whatever but don't call me 'Frankie.' It sounds so juvenile." She started laughing. "Look at the 24 year-old, big man."

"I should have seen that coming." She laughed and I swear the room lit up, along with the lower extremities of my body. It had been a long time since I had had sex with someone I was really attracted to. And once again I didn't use my common sense and asked, "What's this I hear about you getting a divorce?" She stopped smiling and the expression on her face changed. I hit a nerve. Why did I have to bring up something that was obviously painful, at a party?

"You know Frank; everyone will be waiting to speak to you, why don't we discuss that, at, another time? I have the summer off, so give me a call. Maybe we can get together when things calm down. Give me you cell-number and I'll put it into my cellphone. I'm living in the same house Parker and I purchased after we got married. And yes, I'm still living in Montclair."

"I'm sorry Jessie, bringing up your divorce was inappropriate. But stay close bye. I want to be able to find you when the music starts."

She smiled. "You got it.

"My brother finally walked in after being a half hour late. I walked up to him. "Where the hell have you been?"

"What do you mean Frankie? This is your day."

"Thanks a lot bro, you know how uncomfortable I am with all this attention."

"Well, Frank, you better get used to it, with your high-powered New York job, the ladies will be flocking all over you. And it's about time you got laid."

"What the hell's wrong with you, you're acting weird? Where's Barbara? Are you drunk? Did something happen? You know, I didn't want this party."

His voice softened. "No, it's not the party. What are we 12? Yes, I'm drunk. I got drunk before I got here." Al put his arm around my neck and kissed me on the cheek.

I asked, "What the hell is going on? Why are you acting like a nut-job ?"

"Frankie, are you insinuating that I'm jealous of you?"

"Why the fuck is everyone calling me that, today?"

"That's your name, isn't that your name? It's like, we knew you when you were just, Frankie. As I was saying bro, I'm not jealous of you, I'm happy for you. In fact I'm proud of you. All that studying, all that missing out on parties, not to mention getting laid. You deserve this and more. Give me a hug, love you kid." He held out his arms and was coming at me I laughed and moved back. "Al, you stay the hell away from me."

"Don't you want to know why I'm drunk?"

"Sure, you probably became a lush while I was away at school. Okay, tell me why you're acting like such an asshole."

"I'm drunk because this morning Barbara gave me some great news and I didn't want to spring it on the family because, today is your day."

"Are you and Barbara having marital problems?"

"You dumb shit. I told you it was good news. We're going to have a baby, a bambino!" Tears were in his eyes. My big brother was moved to tears. I haven't seen him cry since he was nine years old and a twelve-year-old kid from down the street, beat the shit out of him.

"You see Frankie, I'm not jealous of you or anyone. I have everything I have ever wanted. I like working for Dad. I wanted to go into the family business. I have a beautiful wife who loves me and now I'll have a baby. I'm the happiest man alive.

First I hugged him, then I sat him down on a nearby chair and asked him to stay put until he sobered up. I found a waiter and asked him to get Al, a strong cup of black coffee. Barbara saw us from across the room and walked over. Barbara is as cute as they come. She's short, in good shape, with long dark hair and blue eyes, your typical Irish lass. She was beaming when she came over and kissed me. "Congratulations, Frankie. From the look on your face, Al must have told you the good news. He's been blubbering ever since I told him. Can you imagine this big hunk getting so sentimental?"

Here, I was worried that Al was feeling left out and maybe a little jealous of his younger brother, when the truth was, he had all he ever wanted. He wanted to be just like his father. He loved the business and he loved working in Montclair. He also knew that someday it would all be his and he deserved it. Having a family was the icing on the cake.

Al got me thinking about how two brothers from the same family can be so different. Al and I made our own choices, and for each of us it was the right one. I guess it's true that we all hear a different drummer. I kissed my sister-in-law and whispered in her ear, "Thank you for making my brother, happy."

She giggled. "That was the easy part. The hard part is telling your mother."

"You're right about that, that woman will drive you crazy."

My sister, Julia, noticed that we were together, and came over. "What's going on here? And what's wrong with Al? What happened?"

"Wouldn't you like to know," I remarked.

With that, she slapped me on the back of my head. I grabbed her hand to stop her from doing it again and we started laughing. It seemed like we had regressed into childhood. I whispered, "Al, will tell you later."

She whined, "No, now. I want to know now."

I remarked, "You know, Julia, you're still the same pain in the ass you always were." As usual, she gave it back.

"And you Frankie, Scarpelli, think you're the same boss you always thought you were."

Al decided to join in the conversation. "Come on kids, let's not fight." Then he looked at Julia and whispered, "I'm having a baby."

Julia had to have the last word. "You're having a baby? What about Barbara? Does she know?"

My brother slapped her on the back of the head. We started laughing so hard that my mother gave us a dirty look. Then my dad walked-over to reprimand us. "What the hell is wrong with you kids? You're all so loud, everyone is looking at you. What the hell is so damn funny? You kids never grow up!"

I put my arm around my sister and brother. "You know, it's like old times. It's really good to be home."

I walked over to my mother kissed her on the cheek. "Thanks, mom, this is a great party."

CHAPTER EIGHT

On Monday I left the house around 10:00 am, to avoid the rush-hour traffic into the city. I had to go apartment hunting. I stopped at a diner for coffee and once again, checked-out the rental newspaper clippings that were in, my pocket. Very few were in my price bracket. I had heard that apartments were not only expensive, they were difficult to come by.

I called the few apartments that were listed, and then some real estate agencies. Almost every answering machine had the same message: "The apartment that was advertised in the Sunday newspaper has been taken." With the exception of the one that sounded like a dump. It was an efficiency apartment with one large room, in a crappy neighborhood, and it was going for $3,500, a month, without a garage. I left the diner and figured I'd hit some realtors.

I walked around for blocks in all the trendy neighborhoods. I got the same old story; "Nothing on the market right now but if you leave your name and number, I'll call you."

The few subleases that were available were for the summer months, only. I parked my car at the Port Authority and took a cab to several less desirable neighborhoods and started walking. I went from apartment building to apartment building looking for something, anything, even if it was just for a year. I found nothing. The weather was hot and humid and I was sweating like a pig, so, I decided to grab a cold soda. As I sat on the bench in Central Park, I figured I'd call it a day and go home.

After spending three full day's in Manhattan, I was no closer, to finding a place to live. The afternoon temperatures were climbing, and I was getting tired and frustrated and the realization hit me. *I may have to live in New Jersey and commute.* I dismissed that thought. That was not what I wanted. I would have to keep trying. Besides there was always, Brooklyn.

I called several friends and some acquaintances, and asked if they knew of any apartments for rent or any lease that may become available? They all said the same thing, 'I'll check around and call you if, I hear of anything.' As a last resort, I decided to call my father. A lot of his customers lived in Montclair on weekends and holidays, but stayed in the city during the week, for convenience, and I'm sure in some cases, to screw around. His office was so noisy I had to shout, "Hi, dad. It's me, Frankie."

"I know who it is, why are you yelling? I'm not deaf."

"Sorry. It's so noisy; I didn't think you heard me."

"I hear you. How are you doing, kid?"

"I'm good. Dad, I was wondering if, you could ask your friends and customers if, they have an apartment in New York or, if, they know of someone who is looking for a renter. I knew I'm grasping at straws but, you know a lot of people."

"I'll ask around, kid, but I can't promise you anything. Are you having a hard time finding something?"

"It's impossible. I've been coming to Manhattan for three days and I only saw two dumps that were going for $3,000, bucks a month."

"Then why don't you live at home until something opens up?"

"I don't want too, it would be inconvenient. I want my own place and I thought you might know someone, who knows someone."

"You know, Frankie, you're so damn stubborn, I can't tell you nothing. You're just like your Uncle Frank."

"Thanks a lot dad. I'll see you later."

Suddenly, I heard, "Wait, kid." It was my uncle's voice. "Let me put you on speaker, I want to talk to you. What's the matter, kid? You can't find an apartment? I'll ask around but in the meantime, you can stay at my place."

"Thanks, Uncle Frank, but I don't want to live in New Jersey."

"Who said anything about living in New Jersey? I'm talking about my place in New York, I'll let you rent it, until you find your own place."

In unison, dad and I both asked, "You have an apartment in New York?"

"Jesus," he said, "I don't need you two broadcasting it all over town."

I heard my father say, "How come you never mentioned that you had an apartment in New York, before?"

All the while laughing I heard him say, "Because it's none of your damn business,"

My first thought was, that he was cheating on Aunt Dorothy. No way, they were so much in love he'd be the last person, besides my dad to cheat.

My father had no trouble questioning my uncle's loyalty. "What the fuck is wrong with you, Frank? Are you cheating on Dottie?"

And for what it was worth, I put in my two cents. "Are you?"

"You know, I should kick both your asses for thinking that I would cheat on Dottie. Besides, she'd kill me. You guys don't know what a temper my firecracker has when she gets mad. It's a business expense. I entertain my clients there and sometimes, I let them use the place when they're in town. It's actually a condo. I bought it a long time ago."

Again, we both said, "You own it."

"Of course, I own it. What did I tell you about paying rent? It's an investment. About ten years ago a guy owed me money and couldn't pay it back. He had secured his loan by using the condo as collateral so, I took possession and now it's tripled in value. Are you both happy now? Now, you know everything. Look kid, do you want it or not? Take it or leave it."

"Are you kidding? I'll take it. Where is it? What does it look like, and how much rent do you want?"

My uncle interrupted. "We'll get to all of that, later."

"Uncle Frank, does Aunt Dorothy know you have this condo?"

"Of course she knows. We go there from time to time to rekindle. You have to rekindle. Do you ever rekindle, Al?"

My dad remarked, "There's nothing to rekindle. It's already, burned out." My uncle said, "You are such a romantic son of a bitch, aren't you?"

I broke into the conversation. "Could we please get back to the condo?"

"I don't know how to describe it Frankie. It's got furniture, two bedrooms, and overlooks Central Park. It's on Park Avenue."

My dad and I both chimed in. "Park Avenue?"

"What is it with you two? Is this a comedy routine?"

My father sounded mad. "You never told me!"

"What do you want, Al? I should tell you everything? How about when I take a piss?" They both started laughing. That's how it was with them; they really only busted each other's chops. They never got mad and they always ended up laughing.

I started to raise my voice so I could be heard above the laughter. "Can we please get back to me, now?"

There was sudden silence. "OK," my uncle remarked. "Come home now. It's too hot to be in New York, today. I'll pick you up at your house on Monday and take you over to look at the place, then, we'll figure out how much it's going to cost you. There are no free lunches. I'll pick you up around nine o'clock. Be ready, you know how much I hate waiting." He then hung up.

As long as I could remember, Uncle Frank had stated, "There are no free lunches." As kids, whenever we needed money for something or other, we would go to Uncle Frank, not that dad wouldn't have given it to us; it's just that we would have had to listen to a lecture on how life was when he was a kid. Uncle Frank gave us the money and had us set a date, for the payback. He would ask, "When can you pay me back?" We'd stretch it out to several months, he would write it down and when the time came if we didn't pay up, he would ask us for it. After we paid he would say, 'Thanks for paying your debt.' You have to learn that in this world there are no free lunches," We always found a way to pay him back. If we didn't, we thought he would never loan us money again. We would do dishes, clean our rooms, mow the lawn, or, my sister would babysit. He taught us a good lesson. When birthdays came around, graduation or Christmas, he was very generous.

I went home, showered and had dinner. I looked forward to calling it a night, I was beat, and tomorrow was going to be a good day. I was taking Jessie out for lunch. We had a lot of catching up to do. I must have fallen asleep after the eleven o'clock news, because, around 2:00 am, it started. *I'm running as fast as I can through thickets of brush and I wasn't alone. Several American soldiers were running behind me—running alongside me was a red-haired, freckled face soldier, and we're all carrying our standard-issued weapons... One of the soldier's shouted, "Hurry up Tom!" The soldier next to me shouted back at him. "I am, what the fuck do you think, I'm doing?" We duck in the underbrush to make sure the coast is clear before crossing over to a medieval church, that by now, looks very familiar to me...We run to the door of the church, and it's locked...We've been spotted and we hear gunfire, behind us. Frantically, we pound on the door—a door opens and a Priest says, "Come in and close the door." We rush in and close the door behind us... The soldier alongside me pulls out a Colt pistol and points it at the priest— but he doesn't shoot... The priest ignores the soldier and walks over to the pulpit, lights eight prayer candles and asks "Why are you here?"*
The soldier yells, "Vengeance." All of a sudden the crucifix that was affixed to the wall—crashes to the floor. The building starts to shake— the candles fall and set fire to the alter-cloth. The fire starts to spread so we run for the door—it's locked and we can't get out...The heat is so intense I feel like I'm suffocating...I'm going to die.

As usual I woke up coughing and shaking. When I looked at the clock it was 2:05. Son of a bitch! Tom? I asked myself, who the hell is Tom? Maybe when I get to the end of this saga, the nightmares will go away. Still, questions, without answers, the end of what? This is so fucking bizarre, I think I am going out of my mind. That's it, maybe I'll go nuts before it stops.

CHAPTER NINE

This was the first time I had been invited to Jessie's and Parker's home. When she opened the door she had on her usual smile although, she could not hide the sadness in her eyes. She led me into the living room and said," Have a seat Frank, I'll be with you in a minute." As I looked around it seemed pretty much what I expected. The house was a nice, older mid-size home that was furnished in Early American furniture. Folk-art paintings and whimsical crafts were tactically placed around the room. It was homey, but it was certainly wasn't my taste.

Jessie soon appeared with a smile on her face and announced, "I'm ready to go."

"Nice house, Jessie."

"Thanks. It's a little big for just one person."

I put my arms around her and gave her a big hug. "I'm sorry, Jessie."

"Hey, it happens over fifty-two percent of the time. It just wasn't in my plan, but I'll live through it. Now tell me about you, Frank. What are your plans?"

"Well, unlike you, I kind of live from day to day. No long-term plan just a few career, wants. But you know that about me." We started walking to the car. "I wouldn't say that about you, Frank. You've been in school forever. You went to one of the best schools in the country that took some planning."

"In some respect, you're right. I wanted to be an attorney, and I followed it through. I didn't plan on going to Harvard, it became an opportunity and I had to work hard to meet the school's high standards. But now that part of my life is over and it's just day to day. I don't say I plan on being married in three years, or I will have two and a half kids in six years and then move to the burbs. You know what I mean? You never know what life has to offer."

"In a way you're right, Frank. I had my life all planned out and look what happened."

"I'm sure it wasn't your fault, Jessie."

"How do you know it wasn't my fault?"

"Because to me you're, perfect."

She leaned over and kissed me on the cheek and asked, "How is it you're not in a great relationship with some smart, great-looking woman from Harvard?"

"Maybe I'm not as smart as you think. And how do you know I'm not?" She looked me in the eye and asked, "Are you?"

I laughed. "No, I'm not. I dated some. I just haven't had the time it takes for a serious relationship or, I just wasn't in the right place at the right time."

"Tell me, Frank, how did you get the job you have and what's the name of the firm?"

"It's Mark Moran, Mark Moran Junior, and Associates and I was recruited. It's a midsize company, but they're an old and established firm. I felt it was a good place to start. It's not big, but it's not small either. Last March they showed up at the university to interview prospects looking for a job in New York. There were twenty applicants. We were all interviewed and later went through a process of elimination. My first interview was with Camille Powell, she's the head of human- resources. After she left several candidates were eliminated. Only five of us were picked to be interviewed by VP, Mark Moran, Junior."

Jessie added, "And you got the job?"

"I got the job."

"You know Frank you've lived a charmed life, everything comes to you. Look at you your handsome, smart and you're nice. And you're even modest about your accomplishments. And someday you're going to be rich. You're every woman's dream."

"All the things you said about me are flattering but that's your opinion. Let's face it. I never had a lot women knocking down my door in school or for that matter, in any of the schools I went to."

"Do you know why, Frank?"

"No, but I think you're going to tell me."

"You're aloof and you seem disinterested. It's like you're on a mission of some kind and that mission comes first. Women want to come first."

"What's that supposed to mean? What the hell are you talking about? What mission?"

"I don't know Frank only you know the answer. Maybe when you find Ms. Right, you'll snap out of it."

Jessie always knew how to push my buttons. "What about you, Jessie? Correct me if I'm wrong but you had a great home life and parents who paid for your education. You were popular in school and you lived the life you wanted. You're the teacher you've always wanted to be. You bought a home in Montclair, which is exactly where you wanted to live. You're close to your family and you got married. I'm sorry that it didn't work out for you, but you're young and beautiful. Maybe you think I'm spoiled, but you haven't done so badly yourself. So please stop with this 'pity me party' you're on. You got almost everything you've ever wanted. As far as I can see, you've lived a charmed life."

Tears rolled down her cheeks, and her nose started running. There she goes, making me feel guilty. Maybe I was too hard on her, but damn it, she didn't mind giving it to me.

"I'm sorry, Jessie. I don't mean to hurt your feelings, but if you're going to give it, you should also learn to take it." I reached in my pocket and gave her my hankie.

She wiped her eyes and blew her nose. "You're right, Frank. I'm as spoiled a brat as you are." We both laughed.

When we arrived at Bon Appetite, I decided to change the subject. "I hope you like the food here. It's always been one of my favorite restaurants."

"I know Frank. You brought me here, a couple of times."

"That's right. I did."

Before getting out of the car, we just sat there looking at each other. I started thinking that I wish I could tell Jessie I would like to resume our relationship, but I didn't know how I felt about her, and I wasn't sure if it was the right time. In fact, I wasn't even sure I loved her or, did I know how she felt about me.

"See what I mean, Frank? There goes that reserve."

"What the hell are you talking about? What do you want me to say? Come on, Jessie, give me a break. Are you insinuating that that's why you broke up with me?"

"I broke up with you because when you decided to become an attorney, you also decided not to go to a local college. You opted to go away for six years."

"That's right. I opted to go to a university instead. I don't see that, as being irresponsible. I saw that as a good career move. The plan for my future was not the same as yours. I didn't want to stay in Montclair, and I don't want to live next door to my parent's and I wanted a career that was challenging."

"I know that Frank, and I also know that you didn't love me enough. You never told me you loved me."

"Well, Jessie, you've heard the expression 'actions speak louder than words.'" That was my cue to get out of the car, open her door, and walk into the restaurant.

We got a table with a view of Manhattan and the Hudson Bay. I ordered wine and we toasted both our futures. I then asked her about the breakup of her marriage.

"Why are you getting a divorce? The last time I saw you, was at your wedding and you both seemed so much in love. What was that, two years ago?"

"I guess it was the same thing that happened to us. He fell out of love with me."

"You know, Jessie, I know you're hurting right now, and if it makes you feel better, just let it all out. Reality is we were just kids, childhood sweet-hearts, with deep feelings for each other. Or, maybe it was our hormones. Nevertheless, it was you who broke up with me. Looking back, I don't blame you. But, you and Parker were a different story. You were both out of college, more mature, and you loved each other."

Jessie's eyes welled up with tears, and I felt maybe I had been a little to blunt at a time when she needed sympathy.

She started to explain. "It started with one of his students."

I said, "What?"

"No, it's not like it sounds. There was this thirteen-year-old boy in his class whose father was a casualty of 9/11. He was killed in one of the towers. You can only imagine how this would affect any child, let alone a teenager. He not only lost his father, he had no male role models in his life. The family was from the Midwest, and they didn't have any close relatives in Jersey. His mother thought about moving back to Kansas, but decided to wait until; he graduated from middle-school. "His name is, James Masterson. Jimmy was a nervous, and shy, kid. His mother thought if she could get him interested in sports, his self-esteem would improve. So, she contacted, Coach-Parker and asked for help. After a couple of months and with a lot of coaching, James was starting to take an interest in football and soccer. Parker stepped in to help the boy by soliciting his help in setting- up the schedules for the coming season. He even brought him in on the strategy sessions with the players. It quickly developed into a big brother situation.

I said, "That sounds commendable, but how did that break up your marriage? Were you jealous?" She glared at me. "No. That's not it at all. At first, I was part of it. I wanted to help the kid as much as Parker did, so, I would invite Jimmy over for dinner and sometimes we would take him to the movies. Once we took him to Giant Stadium. Then Parker started tutoring Jimmy at his home. At first, it was one night a week then two, and then it seemed to me he was there, more than he was at home. I tried to be patient, but then I became suspicious and confronted him. I asked him if he was there for Jimmy, or for Jimmy's mother, Kim. I thought he would say, 'don't be ridiculous. I'm sorry I've been taking so much time away from home.'

"Instead he said, 'I'm sorry, Jessie, I don't know of an easy or kinder way to put this. I've been having an affair with Kim and I was going to ask you for a divorce. I was just waiting for a better time.' When would that have been? I told him to get the fuck out, that very night, and he was never step foot in my house again."

Jessie pulled away when I reached for her hand. Frank, I'm very angry right now and I don't want to talk about it anymore."

For a while, we ate in silence.

"When do you start work, Frank?"

"August, first,"

"Are you moving to New York?"

"Yes, I already have an apartment."

"When did that happen? I hear it's almost impossible to find an apartment in Manhattan."

I promised my uncle I would not to spill the beans on him being my landlord so I lied and said, "Could you believe the luck? A friend of mine is going to Europe for a year, so I'm subleasing his place."

"You see what I mean, Frank? You have a charmed life."

"Don't kid yourself Jessie. No one goes through life unscathed."

"Frank, do you still have those nightmares?"

"No, not since I was a kid."

"Come on Frank, save it for someone who doesn't know you."

"OK, yes and it's been happening a lot more often since, graduation. Before I could go months without having an episode, and now it's a couple of times a week."

"Why don't you go for help?"

"I've been wanting to, but it's only now that I'll be earning a salary and able to afford it. Even then, it will be a stretch on my finances. I won't be able use my companies insurance-plan. The claims are filed through the corporation, and I don't want anyone to know that I'm seeing a shrink."

"Why? Everyone I know has seen a shrink at one time or another."

"Would you go to an attorney who's seeing a shrink?"

"That's a stupid statement from such a smart guy. You don't have to tell your clients, it's none of their business. Why don't you try hypnosis?"

"I'm not sure that would be a solution. I don't think my nightmares are caused by an actual experience. They take place in what looks like World War II, which, in its-self is weird. My nightmares started when I was nine, what did I know about the second, world war?"

"You did go to movies. You read books or maybe a family member talked about their experience?"

"No, that's not it, Jessie. I've racked my brain to find the answer. To my knowledge; no one in my family was in WWII."

"Who knows, Frank? Maybe there's a good explanation."

"I don't want an explanation, I want it to stop."

Jessie held up her half-empty glass of wine and smiled. "I guess you're right Frank, we all have our problems. But you know what? We're going to be OK."

"You bet, sweetheart." We clinked, our glass to toast our endurance and left the restaurant.

On our way to the car, I had a thought. "Hey, Jessie, do you have to go right home?"

"No! Why? What did you have in mind?"

"Do you want to go to Verona Park? Remember when a bunch of us kids used to hang there?"

"Sure. Why not? After that big lunch, I could use a walk."

When we reached the parks parking lot we took off our shoes and walked around the lake and held hands, just like we had done in years past. We talked about old times. Kids were playing, Mothers were walking their babies and the lake was filled with paddleboats. We found this great old oak tree to sit under and we kissed. Jessie whispered, "I've missed you Frank, welcome home."

Uncle Frank pulled up to the house at, 9:00 am. I ran out to meet him to save him the embarrassment of my mother giving him that cordial but disapproving look. Instead of her being grateful that he was helping me out, mom felt Uncle Frank was interfering in her life, by helping her baby, move out.

"Nice car, Uncle Frank?" He buys a new Caddy every two years and it's always the color, black. "I picked it up last week. You know me kid I get the same car and same color every two years. It's my way. This way I know what to expect."

When I sat on the plush leather seats I realized it was not such a bad thing. It wasn't my taste. I would have preferred something sportier, or a muscle car. But for a man in his position, it was cool.

I reiterated my thanks to him for helping me out. "Uncle Frank, this is a godsend. I tried finding my own place but either the rents were prohibitive or the place was a dump. I couldn't find anything that was halfway decent in my price range. Actually, it was difficult finding anything, in any range."

"That's OK, kid. Glad to help out, but as you know there are no free lunches. You will have to pay rent."

"Sure, I expected to. What do you want for the place?"

"I don't know. Just pay the utilities and the homeowner dues. I'll figure it out. First, you have to see if you like it and, oh yeah, there's a garage below the building and you get two parking spaces. You know, all the buildings on Park Avenue are old, but the architecture is stately and timeless. That's what I love about New York; they don't tear down to put up new ugly buildings."

As we pulled into the garage and parked the car he announced, "This is it kid."

We took the elevator up to the eleventh floor and turned right to the door numbered, 1103. He opened the door, and I followed. "It probably stinks in here. The windows are closed and I shut the air conditioning off, when no one is here. Give me a hand, let's crack open the windows."

"This is so cool!" I couldn't believe that I was going to be living in an apartment that overlooked Central Park.

My uncle remarked, "It's Okay."

"Are you kidding me? It's more than okay."

The downstairs was decorated in black, white, red, and yellow. All the kitchen appliances were in stainless steel. The kitchen cabinets were black with stainless-steel knobs and the countertops were white marble. I think you might call this decorating style art deco, or modern. It looked like something out of Architectural Digest. I was certainly surprised. There's a staircase in the large black-and white marble entranceway. I ran up the stairs; there were two bedrooms. The master was huge, with a connecting bathroom, and walk-in closet. I shouted, "I can't believe this and I certainly can't afford it!" I ran down the stairs. If I were a kid, I would have slid down the white wood banister like I had done on many occasions at my uncle's house, in Short Hill, New Jersey.

"Frankie, will you please sit your ass down, we have to tie up loose ends and I don't have all day."

"I'll listen but I know I can't afford this place."

"Could you just keep your mouth shut and listen to what I have to say? I might stop in from time to time, but I'll always call first, in case you have company. If you know what I mean?"

"That's cool. Now let's talk money because I know my salary will not cover the cost of what this place is worth. What kind of money are we talking here?"

"I can live with you paying $2,000.00, a month."

"You know that's not nearly enough for a place like this."

"Look at it this way. If I make a profit, I'll have to declare it as income on my taxes. This way you can save some dough and get your own place." Uncle Frank smiled, "Once you become a hot shot lawyer. Let's go kid. I've got work to do."

I walked over to shake his hand, thought better of it and hugged him. "Thanks Uncle Frank, I really appreciate this."

"Hey, kid in a minute you're going to bring out my sensitive side and get me all choked up like a big galoot. Before we go, I want you to know how proud your aunt and I are of you. Six years of law-school is no piece of cake. You could have taken the easy road and gone into business with your dad or me, but you stuck it out and followed your own path."

I smiled. "I still have to pass the bar."

"Don't sweat it kid. You have the brains, you'll ace it. Here's the key, you can move in whenever you want."

On the way home we stopped at a diner in Jersey to have lunch. As soon as we walked in the door a man cleaning up the counter, came running over to my uncle and gave him, the bear-hug. "Welcome, Mr. Scarpelli, so happy to see you."

"Vito, I want you to meet my nephew and godson, Frankie.'

Vito shook my hand until I thought it would fall off. "Glad to meet you Frankie. For you I have a nice, clean, quiet booth. Your uncle and I go way back. He's not only my partner; he's also my best friend."

I looked towards my uncle. "You're Vito's partner?"

"I guess you could call it that."

"I didn't know you owned this place. We've been coming here for years and you never said anything about owning this diner."

"Half this place, Vito owns the other half."

"You know Uncle Frank there is a lot the family doesn't know about you."

"What's to know Frankie? Always remember, what you don't know, can't bite you in the ass."

"What the hell does that supposed to mean?"

He laughed. "It's a joke kid. Don't be so serious."

As soon as I got home I started packing. Not that I had a hell of a lot to pack. I had some clothes, trophies, picture and sports equipment. The six years I spent in college didn't give me the time or the money to accumulate things. I was sorry that my mother was taking my moving out, personally. She didn't seem to understand that I'm closing in on 25, and it was time to be on my own. I love my family and I like being around them, from time to time. But make no mistake I would do anything for them. Let's face it if, I lived at home I doubt I would grow into the independent man I wanted to become. I want to be like Uncle Frank, he's my mentor.

You would think having my mother clean my room, cook my meals and wash my clothes would be the way to go. I could sure save a lot of dough, but at what cost? She would drive me crazy. I've been away for six years; you might think she got used to me not hanging around, besides, I'm only moving to Manhattan, it's just a tunnel away. I have to admit my first year at school overwhelmed me with all the responsibilities of taking care of myself. Now I enjoy my independence and making my own decisions right, or wrong.

After I told my parents about my move to the city I called Jessie. "Hey Jessie I took the apartment and I'm moving in as early as tomorrow. If you help me move my stuff in, I'll buy lunch."

"I'm glad you called. I'd love to go into the city, tomorrow morning. What time are you going to pick me up?"

"There should be less traffic around 10:00. That's 10:00 sharp Jessie, I've got a lot to do."

"Okay, I hear you. I'll be ready."

On my way over to Staples to pick up some cartons and without realizing it I was smiling, after all how lucky can a guy get, an apartment literally fell into in my lap. I was on my way, baby.

CHAPTER TEN

J essie and I talked all the way to New York, mostly about her job. She loves teaching and talked a lot about the kids in her class. She really gets them. If anyone needed to have kids, it's she. And surprisingly I wasn't bored with the conversation. It was nice to hear about her experiences. Besides, most of her stories were so damn funny.

When we arrived, Jessie became very quiet. I parked the car in the garage and she helped me carry some of my stuff. We took the elevator to the eleventh floor in silence. When I opened the apartment door, she said, "OMG, this is awesome. Christ, are you lucky."

"I am, but please no lectures on how lucky I am. It sounds like what you really want to say is, what a spoiled brat."

"I thought that the minute you pulled into the garage, you bastard."

I smiled at the expression on her face. "Nice, Jess, real nice. Instead of being happy for me, you slam my good fortune."

"You're damn right you bastard. I'm fucking jealous.

We dropped the boxes on the floor as I looked for the air conditioning unit. The thought finally occurred to me that we had nothing there to drink, and it was as hot as hell. "You know, I should have stopped on the way over and picked up some beer or soda. I'll check the fridge. Hey girl we lucked out, we have Diet Pepsi and Perrier. What do you want?"

"I'll take the Diet Pepsi but first I'm going to look around. This is the most beautiful bachelor pad I've ever seen. So, tell me about this friend who is he and is he single?"

I tried to change the subject. "So, tell me, Jessie, how many bachelor pads have you been in?

She laughed as she ran up the stairs and yelled "Wouldn't you like to know? I don't kiss and tell. Good God Frank, did you notice the size of that bedroom and it's a loft? Wow, look at that bed!"

"What about the bed?" I shouted.

"It's a king," she yelled, "Its big enough for three people."

"Now there's an idea." She came down the stairs un-noticed, because before I knew it, she had thrown an ashtray at me, and it barely missed my head. "Hey you could have killed me with that thing. I thought you we're still upstairs?"

She started laughing, "Come on, Frank, stop being such a wimp, the ashtray is plastic. It would have only left a small dent. Damn, I thought I had a better aim. This carpet is so plush you didn't even hear me walk down the stairs."

Jessie was sitting on the couch in the living-room when I handed her a can of Pepsi and a glass. She wasn't paying attention when she stood- up to look out the window. Her hand hit the can and the soda spilled all over the couch, her legs and her shorts. "I'm so sorry Frank. I'll clean it up."

I got a dishtowel from the kitchen and started wiping the couch, her legs and her shorts.

"It's okay Frank. I'll do it. It's not a big deal. It'll dry." As I leaned over her she stood up and walked right into my arms. I became aroused and I kissed her passionately. She responded by arching her back and pressing her body against mine. I moved forward and guided her towards the couch. She never pulled away, so I started caressing and kissing her body, as I removed her clothes. Jessie unzipped my pants and moved my briefs to one side. The feel of her cool hands touching my warm body, aroused me to a fever pitch. While French-kissing our hands started exploring our hot-spots. I undressed then positioned myself on top of her and kissed her erected nipples. I was about to enter when she whispered. "Not here, Frank. Let's go upstairs."

As we ascended the stairs we held onto each other as we intermittently kissed and caressed, until we got to the bed. There we explored all the areas that excited our senses... As soon as I mounted, our rhythm became synchronized, and a few moments later, the frenzy accelerated and intertwined into a passion that had been suppressed and was finally released. We were exhausted and fulfilled. It had been seven years since

Jessie and I made love and it was obvious that we had both matured. After it was over, Jessie asked, "Did you plan this, too?"

"Hell no, but I'm sure you did."

We started laughing and hugging. Suddenly, we became very quiet, taking in the sudden intimacy while trying to figure out if it meant anything, or nothing.

I, for one wondered if the timing was wrong. I didn't want Jessie to think we were anything more than friends. I asked, "What are you thinking?"

"I was thinking how much better you are at 24 than when you were 17."

"I'll take that as a compliment. I guess practice does make perfect. So are you. It seems you've also had a lot of practice."

Jessie laughed. "I'll tell you when it's perfect."

We both got up. Jessie wrapped a sheet around her naked body. I couldn't help but laugh. "A little late don't you think?"

She laughed. "Shut the hell up Frankie."

Jessie washed her clothes in the bathroom sink then put them in the dryer. While we waited, we lay on the bed and talked about old times and the gang we hung with. We wondered where they were now. We even talked about putting up a website to see if we could find them and perhaps get together. We talked about high school and things I hadn't thought about in years. Finally, I asked, "Aren't you hungry?"

"Yes, I am. What do you say, after we put some of your stuff away, we look for a deli, get some take-out and walk around the park?"

"Good idea, Jessie. To hell with unpacking, I can do that later on. Let's go, girl."

While in the elevator she asked, "Do you want me to stay the night?"

"Only, if you want to." She thought for a while. "No, I guess not. You have a lot to do. You can take me home, but later this evening, I'm having too much fun to leave now."

We held hands as we checked out my neighborhood for a Deli. We didn't have to go far Nate's Deli was a block away from my apartment.

We sat on the grass and we people watched. Then we walked around Central Park, until dusk. I took her home around 9:00, pm. On the way home she was quiet and thoughtful. I figured she was just tired.

Before getting out of the car she looked at me and said, "Frank, on the way home I was wondering if our making out might have been a mistake? Maybe it shouldn't have happened? You're still not ready for a commitment."

"You're right, Jessie. I'm not, and neither are you. You're just getting out of a marriage and it's too soon for you to make any emotional decisions right now."

She looked at me like she hadn't expected me to agree with her. Although, her remark made me feel that maybe I had taken advantage of her, she was vulnerable. I didn't set out to hurt her. But, I also didn't want her to think it meant more than it did. I told her I didn't realize it was some kind of a commitment test.

"Don't be a dork, Frank. I'm not a kid. I could have said no. The truth is I wanted it as much as you did. Besides, what's better than having a friend with benefits?"

"I'm glad you understand where I'm coming from."

Before she got out of the car, I told her I would give her a call as soon as I settled in. She smiled and kissed me on my cheek.

Being I was already in Montclair, I figured I would stay at my folk's house for the last time. When I walked in they seemed surprised and happy to see me. Dad got me a beer and mom was smiling when she said, "I'm surprised you came back tonight. I thought you would be staying in New York?"

"I would have, if I didn't have to take Jessie home. She wanted to look over my digs. I was in the neighborhood so I thought I'd sleep in my room for the last time."

Dad remarked, "Smart thinking Frankie. No need to waste gas."

Mom got that faraway look in her eye and a smile on her face when she said, "I like Jessie. She would make a great daughter-in-law."

"Good night mom, dad, I'm going to bed.

CHAPTER ELEVEN

On the way to my apartment, I stocked up on groceries, toilet stuff and beer. I never did that kind of shopping before and I wasn't sure about the brands I liked so I picked out the stuff that was on sale and the few things I was familiar with. I also didn't realize how expensive everything was. It was a good thing I had enough cash on me because I forgot to bring my credit cards.

After I put all my clothes and groceries away, I started looking for a place to put my sports equipment. I had two baseball bats, a mitt, two-tennis racket, balls, golf clubs and my suitcases. Noticeable was a closet under the staircase. I checked it out to see if it was big enough to hold all the equipment, I would seldom use.

It was narrow, but deep, and luckily there was an overhead light fixture. I looked around for the switch and found a stack of opened cartons and a metal box covering the light-switch. I removed the boxes and turned on the light. There was room enough, but I would have to move all the boxes to the back of the cubbyhole if I wanted my gear to fit.

I pulled out all the boxes to re-organize, when I decided to check-out the opened cartons and the unlocked metal box.

The metal box was full with my uncle's cancelled checks, and some old photos. I assumed they were pictures of family members. I sat on the floor and looked through the photographs. They were yellowed with age and most of people I didn't recognize, they were obviously from a bygone era. There was a shot of ten kids who looked to be about 13 years old. They were standing pyramid style on the steps of a church. And somehow, I dismissed the fact that it looked vaguely familiar. On the top step was a Priest. I looked closely at the faces to see if, there was anyone I could recognize. It was impossible.

The pictures were too old to be of my Dad and Uncle Frank. The clothes worn were knickers and caps and soon realized they must be my grandfather's. snapshots.

Again, I stared at the photograph to see if I could recognize pop, but there was no recognition. Until I got this uneasy feeling when I noticed the likes of a second priest in another photo and, he looked familiar. But then, I get an uneasy feeling with every priest I see and the reason I don't go to church. Only after being threatened with bodily harm, did I accompany my family to Mass. I somehow associate all churches with my night terrors. I believe in God and I have asked him the same question over and over again, why, did this have to happen to me? What are these nightmares all about?

I looked at several more photographs while searching for a familiar face or landscape, but none of the terrain looked familiar to me. I soon realized that this must be where Pop grew up. There were a few pictures of a family. In it was a man, a woman and a boy and girl in their teens. I checked the back for a date and the names, but the script was in Italian, and the only thing I could understand was the date: 1941.

In another photo, there were five kids about eighteen. All boys with the exception of the same girl, that was in the other photographs. There was also an album that must have been Pop's and my Grandmother's pictures, some so old they must have been taken right after he had migrated to America. I recognized those pictures because my Dad had a couple of photographs of himself growing up that he kept in his sock drawer. And Uncle Frank also had a picture of his mother and father on the dresser in his bedroom. I did see the resemblance between my dad and his mother. Uncle Frank looked a lot like pop.

The next couple of pages were pictures of pop, Uncle Frank and dad that were taken in and around New Jersey. Considering their age now, these few photographs didn't seem like much in the way of a remembrance. My interest had peaked so I started digging in all the boxes. I soon found Pop's immigration papers— dated September 14th, 1945. The surprise came when I read he had emigrated from Sicily. *This can't be right Pop told us he was from Naples.* But there it was, Angelo Michael Scarpelli. *What's up with that?*

As I started to empty a small box of old clothes I found a rag that was wrapped around something fairly- heavy. I un-wrapped it slowly and was surprised to find a an old German Luger. Not knowing if it was loaded my first instinct was to drop it. What the hell is this doing here? I certainly can't ask Uncle Frank. I'm sure I wasn't supposed to be snooping around. And I wondered, *if Pop is from Sicily, why did he lie about where he came from?* I carefully put everything back as I found it. But now, I had some unanswered questions about my family and their heritage.

I wondered if my brother had any information about pop's immigration status. Now I was really curious. That thought reminded me; the family doesn't have my address. Tomorrow I'll give them a call.

After a while I walked to Nate's Deli to get some takeout. I ordered a corned beef sandwich, potato-salad, a dill pickle and a knish. I came home had my meal and washed it down with a beer while I watched the Yankees beat the Mariners. After the game I got ready for bed and watched the news, before calling it a night. I don't know what time the nightmare started. *"I'm running through the woods with a small group of soldiers. We're crouching down. We hear footsteps and artillery fire behind us—then silence. One of the soldiers whispers, "Quiet, Frank." I looked behind me— a soldier is smiling as he salutes me. It was the guy with the red hair. Still grinning he said, "You have to be quiet." His demeanor and intrusion into my dream annoyed me. "I am, can't you see I'm quiet? Who the fuck, are you?"*

"You know me, Frank. It's Tom."

"I don't know you, Tom."

"But you do, Frank."

I asked, "Why am I here?"

"You're here because I need your help."

"Help with what?" Tom reached in his holster and pulled out a gun. *"It's important you remember this gun."*

"I know that gun, it's a German Luger."

"That's right, Frank you saw this gun."

I opened my eyes. Oh, this is just great! I'm now carrying on a conversation.

This dream had to be related to me finding the gun in the closet. So that's what's going on here, I saw a gun and then dreamt about it. That's why I wasn't frightened. No rapid heartbeat and no sweating. I looked at the clock. It was 2:10. I got up, went to the fridge to get a beer, took a shower and went back to sleep.

I must admit, those couple of months with nothing to do was great. I got to hang with Jessie on several other occasions. We had fun times together. It took her mind off her ex-husband and I was finally free of the six years I spent in solitary confinement. It felt great to have some fun. But since that day in my apartment we hadn't had sex.

I even got to know some of the people in my building. Some were friendly and down to earth and some a little too high-class for me, although, polite. I also found where the best places to eat, drink and buy groceries were. And I got into the routine of jogging in Central Park, on early mornings, before the sun came out. Now there's the place to meet hot babes. I couldn't believe the amount of people that jogged before going to work. I took it a step further by weightlifting at the gym in my building, now all that hard work was starting to payoff.

I was feeling so good I invited the family over for lunch to see my new pad. It was great having them visit me, on my turf. Of course, my mother and sister brought all the food. I wouldn't know what to buy or, did I know how to cook. Besides, money was getting tight. It was also a great opportunity to speak to my brother about pop's pictures and his hometown.

"I don't know what to tell you Frankie, I also thought pop was born in Naples. Forget about it, what difference does it make?"

"I guess you're right Al. It's not a big deal. It's not like he hiding his past for a reason, or is there?"

"What the hell are you talking about? What would pop, have to hide? You're making something out of nothing. Forget about it!"

"You're right, there's no reason to stir up trouble."

CHAPTER TWELVE

The day had finally arrived. It was August first, and it was time to go to work. All the years I spent at the university, should start paying off. And right now I can really use a paycheck. Today is the first day in what should be the beginning of a successful career.

I never thought for one moment that I wouldn't be successful. If, it's one thing I have its confidence and faith in my ability to be able to transfer my will and education into reality, except when it comes to my fucking nightmares.

Lawyers may be called many things: counselor, attorney, solicitor, and even barrister. Then, there are some who call us: shyster, crook, leach and ambulance chaser until they get in a jam and need help in getting out of it. I also wondered what I would do if I knew my client was guilty. If it was a heinous crime would I want him or her, back on the streets? On the other hand, even the guilty deserve a good defense. Isn't that what our country was founded on? 'You are innocent until proven guilty.'

First impressions mean a lot so, for my first day at the office. I wore my navy suit, a light gray shirt, a gray tie with just a hint of red and my Italian black leather shoes and got a haircut. It was time to get a new conservative, I'm a professional who's working downtown' look.

I was instructed to report to Human Resources at 8:00 am, to fill out the new employee paperwork and to watch an introductory video on company policy. After the orientation I would be shown around the office and eventually wind up with Mark Moran, Junior, who would see me in my office.

I arrived at 7:45. After showing the guard my letter of employment I was allowed access into the building, and into my firm's administrative office. I, sat in HR and waited for the staff to appear. One-by-one they walked in and glanced in my direction, but made no attempt at communication. At 8:00 am, a woman walked in. sat next to me on the black leather couch and smiled. Being there were several un-occupied seats within the area, I was surprised she chose to sit, alongside me. I said, "Hello, my name is Frank Scarpelli is, this also your first day?"

"Yes, my name is Darlene Banks." We both smiled and shook hands. And in that moment in time I was fixated by her beauty, and I couldn't take my eyes off of her. I should have realized that staring at her was making her uncomfortable. I know I'd be if someone was gawking at me. I thought she was the most beautiful woman I had ever seen and believe me I've seen a lot. Darlene Banks was about 5'8," and her slender weight was distributed in all the right places. She had long curly, black hair. Good God, she was stunning and that smile. I was afraid if I said anything I would probably stammer like a sixteen year old so I said nothing.

Once again, Darlene started to converse. "I assume you're one of the newly-hired attorney's?"

"Yes, your assumption is correct. Today's my first day with the firm. I'm a recent graduate. Is this your first day?"

"Yes, it is, Frank."

I responded with, "I sure hope they hired you to be my secretary."

She quickly responded, "What makes you think I'm a secretary, Frank Scarpelli? Is it because I'm a woman or, is it because I'm African American?" Her voice was composed and articulate, and I could feel my face getting red with embarrassment. After giving it some thought I answered, "I'm sorry. I wasn't thinking. I didn't mean to offend you."

She good-naturedly laughed, "That's okay, Frank, I accept your apology. But you still didn't answer my question."

I looked towards her eyes. "I didn't take notice that you were African American, but I certainly noticed that you're a beautiful woman, so, I guess the only thing I can say in my defense is, it was wishful thinking that I would get to see you every day, all day."

"You know Frank you're digging yourself into a hole here. But you will be seeing me around. I'm also a newly hired attorney. You did a fair, but not a great job of getting out of your chauvinistic statement. You had better start practicing if you want to keep your female clients."

"You're right, Darlene I'm going to have to do a lot better if I want to compete with you. The first thing I have to learn is, to think before I speak."

I was saved when I was called in to the office to meet with, human resources manager, Maureen Sylvester. After I filled out the insurance forms and W-2 forms, I watched a video on safety and disaster protocol. Maureen also signed me up for a course in CPR. I was then escorted to the main lobby that would lead me into the firm's corporate offices.

I suppose I shouldn't have been surprised at the ambiance and the quality of the furnishings. Coming from a small town in New Jersey, I was used to a small–attorney office in Upper Montclair, where my dad did his business.

As I passed through the long wide entranceway noticeably was the shiny brass elevator-doors, the contrasting dark green walls and the ornate dark- oak woodwork, that blended with the dark oak parquet flooring that was underneath the largest Oriental runner, I had ever seen. On the paneled walls were four large portraits in wide-ornate gold frames. At the bottom of each frame was a brass placket with the names of the person in the portrait. Two were of Mark Moran, Senior, the founder. One was when he was about forty and in the most recent portrait he looked to be in his late-seventies. The portrait of his two sons, Mark Moran, Junior, and Timothy Moran, were of men in their early forties. I was surprised that there was little resemblance between farther and sons. Evident was senior's stern and disciplined expression.

I confided in Maureen that I thought Mark Senior appeared rather stern in his portrait and asked, "Senior, looks rather business like, what's he like to work for?"

"Well Frank, I've been at firm for ten years. I don't see or converse with Mr. Moran, that much, but, the times that I've been in his company he was soft-spoken and polite. Although his sons will tell you he's void of a sense of humor."

As we entered the large glass doors leading to the reception area, Maureen looked at me and smiled. "Don't worry Frank you will fit in just fine. They only hire the best and from what I hear, you will be one of the best,-just as soon as you get your sea-legs."

I needed her reassurance I was starting to feel uneasy. Maureen introduced me to each of the eight attorneys and soon after I was brought into what was to be my office. My office was a welcomed surprise. I really lucked out. I had a corner office with a large window overlooking the Manhattan ski-line. It wasn't long before Mark Moran, Jr. came into my office smiling and upbeat. He asked, "Well, how do you like your office?"

"Like it?" I replied, "I think it's great, Mr. Moran."

"Frank, call me Mark unless my Dad's around, and then you can call me Junior. But I warn you if you want to keep your job that's the only time you call me Junior."

I smiled when I responded. "You got it Mark."

"I assume you had the pleasure of meeting Darlene and the rest of the Attorneys? Darlene is a recent graduate of Yale with grades that were almost as impressive as yours."

"Now I want you to meet the heartbeat of the company, the workforce. Without them our job would be impossible. "First, I will introduce you to your secretary, Joan, and then to Bea, your right-hand paralegal. For now, you and Darlene will be sharing their expertise. We expect your workload to be light and with little overtime. We realize you both have to pass the bar and this will give you both ample-times to study."

I thanked him and told him I didn't expect this kind of consideration.

"Well, Frank, we've all been there and you're an investment. If you're treated well, you will make us all a lot of money."

I didn't know what to say to that. I knew they were taking a chance on a recent graduate and I didn't want to let them or me down, so I said nothing. But I admit I, was concerned about their expectations.

So, Darlene went to Yale? No wonder she was insulted when I inferred she was hired to be my secretary. Sometimes I'm such a dork.

Mark walked me over to my administrative assistant and introduced us. "Joan, I want you to meet, Frank Scarpelli. You know what to do. He's green and he'll need all the help he can get."

Joan appeared to be in her fifties. She had dark-brown hair and wore black rimmed glasses. Although somewhat overweight she was impeccably dressed. She held out her hand to shake mine and a feeling of relief came over me. *Thank God I won't have to try to impress her. She looks so nice. Better yet she probably knows more than I do.*

Mark told me that Joan Gold had been with the firm for fifteen years and that she trains all the new recruits. Joan beamed from ear to ear, "So nice to meet you, Frank. Let me know if there is anything I can do to make the transition easier for you? There is only one thing I won't do and that's get your coffee. I'm not your mother."

I smiled. "No problem, Joan. I know how to get my own coffee. Every morning I will stop at Starbucks on the way in to work." We all started laughing.

I then followed Mark to the break-room. "This is where you can get free coffee Frank. Do you know how to use a KEURIG?"

"No, Mark I don't."

Not to worry it's easy. If I can use it anyone can. That's pretty much it, Frank. The tour ends in the corporate offices. I left some briefs on your desk. I would like you to look them over and take notes because, every Wednesday we all meet in the conference room to discuss our most significant cases. We brainstorm each individual case. You'll be asked your opinion on what you think the options are for our client's best defense. We do this because nine brains are better than one. Don't you agree?"

"Absolutely, and it's seems like a great way to learn the ropes and reinforce my six years of training."

Mark concluded, "But whoever's case it is makes the final decision."

Mark seemed like an all right guy. I was starting to feel a lot more relaxed. My associates were friendly with no sign of attitude. But that was my first impression and it might be too soon to tell.

Mark walked me through the corporate offices. They were large and impressive, especially the office of the President &CEO, Mark Moran, Sr. Junior stated, "Now a days my dad rarely comes into the office and no more than once a week. He's 88, and although his mind is still sharp it's time he started to enjoy his life. We tried to get him to retire and lead the good life. Maybe travel abroad but he told me the good life was the firm, and he wanted to come in until he died."

"That's dedication," I affirmed.

"Not like today's young people. No offense. I'm talking about my kids. They're spoiled and soft. I was raised differently. My brother and I had to work hard. We helped my father build this business. In the beginning, we had some tough times, but it paid off."

"My Uncle Frank would agree with your philosophical views on the youth of today, only he expresses it differently. His family was poor so he never had the opportunity to go to college. But he was smart and now he's a very wealthy man."

"Your uncle sounds like a good man. That's what I mean about the older generation. My father was also poor, he came to the United States with little money and worked his way through college and then law school. This firm is like his child. I sometimes think he had us just to keep it alive."

I thought, *that's an odd remark.*

Mark quickly changed the subject. "You know Frank, your uncle may want to consider using our firm for taxes, investments or any other legal requirement. I'm sure there is something we could do for him?"

"That may be his one fault. He doesn't trust anyone, but himself. Although he knows a lot of people so I'm expecting to get referrals from him."

"Frank, is your uncle on your mother's side or your father's?

"My Fathers, in fact I was named after him."

Mark laughed. "I should have made the connection. I have heard of Francis Scarpelli. He's well-known in the corporate world. Any referrals from him will no doubt increase your commissions. Well Frank I have nothing more to say, unless you have any questions."

"I'm good."

As we shook hands Mark stated, "One more thing, although I have an open door policy, everyone has to go through my assistant."

"Good to know."

As I sat in my office I couldn't help but feel great. I enjoyed reviewing real cases, about real people. I started to take notes on what course of action I thought should be taken in the defense of the client. I wondered how different or how close I would come to my colleagues who were more experienced than I. Was I in the ballpark or far out in left field? Before I knew it, it was after five and I had skipped lunch. Joan peeked in my office and told me she was leaving and that I should do the same. "Go home, Frank. It's okay to leave your room." I looked up and saw her twinkling, eyes and a big smile on her face. "You're right. I'm leaving right now, I'm starved. Good night, Joan. Have a good evening." She waved her hand at me and left.

It was getting late and last night my uncle called and asked me to meet him at Nate's Deli. He needed to pick up some documents he left at the apartment and figured he should call me first, to see if the coast was clear. I laughed to myself. Where did he ever get the idea that I was this hot lady's man? I guess it was flattering. I suppose most guys my age are. Jessie could be right maybe I appear unapproachable, or maybe I just haven't met Ms. Right, yet.

Uncle Frank was at Nate's when I arrived. Although he was reading The New York Times he looked up and smiled. "Hey, kid look at you, you're as sharp as a tack haircut and all. I'm really impressed. You know you're really not that bad looking, in fact I think you look a lot like me."

I started to laugh. "What's so funny Frankie? You could look a lot worse than looking like me. You could look like your old man." He smiled. "Tell me, how did your first day go? And before I forget your father asked me to ask you how come they never see you? And, don't forget to call your mother.

"What's he talking about? They never see me? I'm there every Sunday for dinner."

He laughed. "I know kid but it's already Monday and they miss you."

"I was surprised you asked me to meet you here Uncle Frank. I didn't know you liked eating Deli."

"Are you kidding? That's why I married your aunt. That's the only thing she can cook. She microwaves the pastrami or corned beef, buy's a loaf of Jewish Rye and along with this gourmet meal is potato salad, or coleslaw. Sometimes she'll microwaves knishes-and calls it dinner.

But you know, Frankie, I relish whatever that women does for me. She excites me, but that's another story." He then acted like I was back in school after being off for the summer, and asked what I did on my first day.

I went into detail, but left out the Darlene disaster.

"Sounds good kid, you will do just fine. I have to go to your place to pick up a couple of ledgers I left in the closet under the staircase."

"Why didn't you just go in and get what you needed? You don't need an appointment. It's your place."

"Well, kid, I don't like barging in. You're young and single. Besides you're paying me rent. It's yours for now. The truth is, I wanted to see how your first day went."

"Speaking of the closet under the staircase—I hope you don't mind that I put some of my stuff in there."

"No, problem, there's nothing in there that's of great importance.. It's just some ledgers, and old IRS documents. If they were important, I would have kept them it in my safe. I don't like keeping the IRS documents in my office. I have people walking in and out, all day. Some of the stuff in that closet is, pop's."

"I know. I saw an album and some loose photographs in a carton, so I looked at them. I didn't recognize anyone. They were wearing old-fashioned clothes, so I figured they must have been Pop's and taken in Italy. I was surprised when I found pop's immigration papers. His last known address was from Sicily. Did you know he lived in Sicily? I thought pop was from Naples?" My uncle looked surprised.

"He told me, he was from Naples. You know how it was in those days, so many people coming in after the war? The authorities at Ellis Island could have made a mistake during his processing."

"Another thing I found, was a gun. It was in one of pops boxes."

"That's weird. I never remember pop having a gun, or for that matter any kind of a weapon."

"It's a German Luger and it is wrapped in a dirty rag."

"Okay, kid, let's go up to the apartment. I want to see what the hell you're taking about."

As soon as we got to the apartment, I went into the closet, unwrapped the rag and showed Uncle Frank the gun.

"Frankie, are you sure this was in that box?"

"Yes, I'm positive. It was under the photo album."

"It must be a souvenir or something. Why would pop have a gun? What's it wrapped in?"

"I don't know. It looks like a small shirt with a lot of dark stains on it. It looks like a kid's shirt."

"Why would he keep a gun in this rag? You know, he's getting old, he probably forgot he had it. He gave me these boxes when he moved into his new apartment. I thought it was just photos of our family. I never went through it."

"I guess I shouldn't have either. I'm sorry I didn't mean to snoop around."

"Hey, that's okay. I never told you to stay out of that closet. But, I'm telling you now. Just get what you need and stay out of the closet. Did you check to see if there were bullets in the clip?"

"Yes, there are two in the clip."

"Take them out Frankie. I don't trust a loaded gun in the house, especially with someone who can't shoot straight—then put it back in the box where you found it."

Soon after, Uncle Frank got what he needed and left.

I went into my office to open my mail and found a registration-form and an application to take my Bar Exam As I started filling it out my mind wondered and I began thinking about Darlene. After that I had a hard time concentrating. On the way to my bedroom my thoughts once again turned to my new crush. We hadn't seen each other since this morning and I wished I had, had, the guts to ask her out for dinner. Not that she would have accepted after acting like a mega ass-hole. I'll run into her tomorrow. And if I don't say anything stupid, I'll ask her out for a couple of drinks.

I have to admit, my first day on the job was exciting, but nerve wracking. I had no problem falling asleep, staying asleep was another matter.

"I was in the forest—we were hiding from the enemy. I was dressed in an American camouflage uniform. Someone tapped me on the shoulder and said, "Hello, Frank." I knew who it was before I turned to face him— it was Tom. I didn't say anything. I just stared at him. He spoke, "Frank, I need your help."

I asked, "Help with what?" I could feel myself getting pissed-off. "Why don't you leave me the hell alone?"

"That can't happen until you help me out." His remark agitated me even more.

"You dumb shit, you keep asking me to help you, but you don't tell me how."

"I'm telling you now. You have to find a mass-murderer and expose him to the world. You're the only one who can take him down."

"What the hell are you talking about? What murderer? He handed me a gun, it was a German Luger. You have to find the man that owned this gun."

I opened my eyes as the sweat poured down my face. It looked like pop's gun. This was getting out of hand. I knew I needed professional help. Then I remembered that Jessie said she knew of a good shrink. Without thinking about the time I called her.

"Hello?" she said. In a voice that was barely audible.

"I'm sorry Jessie. I obviously woke you up."

"Frank, are you alright?"

"Yeah, I guess I'm fine."

"You're fine? It's after 2:00 in the morning, who calls someone to chat after, two? What's wrong?"

"I said I'm fine. I'm sorry I woke you. I wasn't even thinking about the time. But I do need something. You said you knew of a good shrink in Montclair. Could you give me his name and number? I want to call him tomorrow."

"What's wrong, Frank? Is it the nightmares?"

"Yes, it's the nightmares. They're changing,"

"What do you mean they're changing?"

"Damn it Jessie, they're just changing, they're becoming personal." I was starting to get agitated and thought to myself, *Why all these fucking question's?* I must have sounded angry when I said, "All I'm asking for is a name and phone number why, the third degree?"

"Okay, calm down Frank. I'm just trying to put this all in perspective. No need to get pissed off. Hang on I'll get it for you." It took only a few seconds for Jessie to get back to me. "His name is Dr. James Bass. He's at 2113 Main Street, in Montclair, and his number is 222-222-222."

"And Jess, can you put it on my cell-phone?"

"Is there anything else I can do for you in the middle of the night? Maybe I should come over and hold your hand or whatever you want me to hold."

"I started to laugh. Thanks for the offer. I'm okay now."

"You know Frank, you may not need a shrink maybe you just need hypnosis. It is probably stems from a childhood trauma and manifests when you're uptight. And you sure are uptight."

"Thanks for the pop-psychology. I feel that what I'm going through is more complicated. Besides, what the hell could have happened to me that would to cause this?"

"That's exactly my point! You don't know. Hypnosis could bring it out in the open. It doesn't have to be something your parents did, it could be something you saw or read. I don't know."

"That's right you don't and neither do I. That's why I'm going to a professional to find out what the hell is wrong with me. And I hope the good doctor can rid me of whatever the hell it is, before I go postal."

"Goodnight Frank. I would love to chat but it's past my bedtime. Promise me you'll call and let me know if you get an appointment? I'll meet you afterwards. We could have lunch or dinner."

"I only hope he has Saturday or evening hours, I just started a new job. I can't take any time off."

"In that case why don't you go to a Doctor in New York, and save yourself a trip?"

"Because I don't want anyone to know I'm crazy."

"How would they find out if, you don't submit an insurance claim?"

"Think about it, Jessie. I work for a somewhat prestigious law firm. What if that particular shrink needed an attorney and came into my office? Worse yet, what if one of his patients sued him?"

"Good God you are such a worrywart. What are the chances of that happening? Besides, there is a law about patient doctor, confidentiality. You're an attorney you should know that?"

"Good night Jessie and thanks."

I tried to reconcile in my mind the actual events of the dream and wondered why after all these years it was changing from entering the church to hiding in the woods. And how come we're having dialogue, and who the hell is Tommy? It's not like a dream it's more like a happening and if I didn't wake up I would swear it was real. What does this all mean? Maybe it has no meaning? Maybe it's just what Jessie said, a memory of something I can't recall?

I'll call Doctor, Bass in the morning to see if I can setup an appointment. Let him try to figure out what's wrong with me if, he can.

CHAPTER THIRTEEN

I went to work feeling great. I was not only anxious to resume looking over the case files; I wanted to find Darlene's office, to see if I could get her to go out with me. Being we shared the same secretary her office couldn't be far from mine.

So I started looking for her office as soon as I arrived at the firm. I would have noticed if she was on the right-side of my office, that's on the way to the lounge and restrooms. I knew Norman Shire's office was next to mine therefore, I walked left which turned out to be, Bruce Thompson's office, but the office next to Bruce, was Darlene's office.

When I walked in, Darlene was at her desk reading a case-file and taking notes. When she looked up, she smiled. "Hi, Frank. Come in and sit down. What can I do for you?"

"Here you are? I was looking for you. Nice office."

"Do you really think so, Frank? It's not as nice as yours. You have the corner office with two large windows and the view of the city. I have one window and the view of a brick building."

"When did you see my office?"

"Well, it's no secret that from time-to-time I have to use the rest room and I have to pass your office."

"Why didn't you stop in to say hello?"

"I guess it's because you had your head buried in the case files we're supposed to review." Here was my opening. "That brings me to my next question why don't we have dinner this evening and discuss those cases? I'm talking, lighthearted friendly competition between

Yale and Harvard. It would be interesting to see if there were any variable differences, in the way we handle the individual cases."

"Come on Frank is this a real contest or do you want to pick my brain so you can come up with all the right answers when we're brain storming?"

I smiled. "Is that what you think? You got me all wrong. Maybe you're the one that's afraid that Harvard will show up Yale." We both started laughing. "To answer your request that we go out to dinner, I don't think it's a good idea to get involved with anyone I work with. Being we're colleagues. You know what they say about getting involved in office relationships."

"Trust me you've got me all wrong. Like you said we're colleagues and if you were a guy you wouldn't think twice about my offer. People working in the same office often go out for a drink or dinner. It seems to me you're gender-biased."

She smiled. "So, what you are saying is, this would be two colleagues going out for a drink?"

"You got it. We're two colleagues that are new to the firm, going out for a drink."

"Okay! Frank, meet me at, 5:15, in the downstairs lobby. Let's go someplace close by. How about the Marriott Hotel? It's right across the street."

"That works for me. Later." *I can't believe I pulled that off.*

I went to my office and waited for an appropriate time to call Dr. Bass's office to see if I could get a weekend appointment. I almost talked myself into waiting, but realized I had to resolve my situation if I wanted to lead a normal life. So, I called and lucked out, because of a last minute cancellation for this coming Saturday, at, 11:00 am.

The day just dragged. I couldn't wait to be with Darlene. Finally it was five. I ran out of my office so fast, that I noticed Joan's head spin around, as she watched me leave.

Darlene was also on time, but unfortunately it had started to rain. Luckily, we were just going across the street because everyone in Manhattan was looking for a cab. Neither one of us had an umbrella so by the time we got to the hotel we were drenched and tried shaking ourselves off, before entering the bar.

"You know Darlene if you like we can get a room and dry ourselves off and call for room service. Just a thought or, we can just go to the bar. You choose."

She looked at me with eyes wide open and a smirk on her face. "Now Frank, are you trying to tell me that if I was Bruce or Norman you would still make that same offer? After all, isn't this just one of the boy's night out?"

"If they looked and smelled like you, I probably would." We both started to laugh.

She affirmed, "You know, you're crazy, Frank. But you do have a certain charm about you."

"I'll take that as a compliment. I also noticed that about you, Darlene. I think we make the perfect couple."

Her eyes widened so I apologized. "I'm sorry, did I say couple? I mean, associate. What are you drinking? I'll buy this time. You can get me the next time we go out. I can see it now we're going to be good buddies." Again, we laughed. *Be still my heart and my dick, this lady turns me on.*

That evening, I couldn't get my mind off Darlene. I'm not sure if it's because I'm so damned attracted to her or, that I was afraid to fall asleep. I had such a good time being with her. She's smart and has a great sense of humor. And for some reason I'm wildly attracted to her. And I hope she feels the same about me. We just hit it off.

Unexpectedly my appointment with, Dr. Bass came to mind. I wondered what my sessions would be like. I had never been in analysis before. *What should I tell him and how can he treat something that is as evasive as a dream? I hope he doesn't prescribe drugs. I don't know how effective that would be. I have to sleep. I have to sleep. I have to.* And luckily I slept peacefully, the entire evening.

The rest of the week was significant, I practicing what I had been interested in my whole life, the law. And I was starting to get the hang of getting up early, going to the office and running into Darlene.

CHAPTER FOURTEEN

Saturday seemed to arrive in a flash and several times last week I thought of cancelling my appointment with Dr. Bass. But, I knew this week may have been a reprieve but in all probability, the nightmares would return. I arrived at the Doctor's office ten minutes early. It turned out I was the only patient in the waiting room. I figured he might schedule his appointments so his patients wouldn't run into each other. It was just as well. I knew a lot of people in Montclair. I just wanted to get this over with and I hoped he was on time. I was supposed to pick up Jessie for lunch, at 12:30.

Finally an office door opened and a man walked over to me to shake my hand and said, "I'm Dr. Bass I assume you're Frank Scarpelli." I thought I would burst out laughing I could hardly contain myself, he looked like all the pictures I had ever seen of Sigmund Freud. I stood up to shake his hand. "Hello, Dr. Bass. Yes, I am Frank Scarpelli."

"Please, call me James. From the look on your face you have noticed the resemblance between me and Sigmund. He's not an ancestor and the only connection we have is that we're both Jewish. Thank God my mother never named me Sigmund. Sometimes, I think I should shave the beard but it's kind of an icebreaker and my clients get a laugh out of it." I started laughing. It was a relief, and an icebreaker. At least the guy had a sense of humor. Still, my negative thoughts started to wonder, *What if this analysis proves nothing. What if I can't be cured and I have to go on like this for the rest of my life? I have to stop this negative thinking. At least I took the first step by, showing up.*

Dr. Bass's office was pretty much like you would expect from a psychiatrist. It was smartly furnished with a sofa on the far end of the wall and two comfortable chairs in front of his desk. On the wall behind his desk was a large bookcase filled with text-books.

As Dr. Bass walked behind his desk I sat on the chair adjacent to him and asked, "Can I sit here or do you want me to lie on the couch?"

"I prefer you stay seated Frank, unless you're tired and you need a nap. That's why I keep the couch in here it's for when I need a nap. Frank, relax I'm trying to alleviate some of the stress with my jokes, but I can see it's not working. Sorry about that."

"That's okay, Dr. Bass I'm glad you have a sense of humor. It's just that I come from an Italian family and my heritage dictates you're supposed to take care of your own problems and most of all you never let anyone know you have them. I don't feel hopeless or help-less I've come to realize that this is something I need professional help with."

Dr. Bass stopped smiling. "Frank, you did the right thing. Obviously, something is upsetting you or you wouldn't be here." He told me that he mainly used the couch for in-depth psychoanalysis or if hypnotherapy was required. He then asked me to tell him why I thought I needed his help.

I started at the beginning. "I have been having this one particu-lar nightmare since I was nine years old with the exception of slight variations. I can best describe it as watching the same play over and over again. As I aged there were minor changes to the dialogue and scenes but since then, excuse the expression, 'the shit hit the fan'."

Dr. Bass interrupted, "Describe the dream sequence you had as a child."

"I see myself running through a forest and running beside me is an American Soldier whose face is blurred. We stop running when we have reached a medieval Catholic, Church. We try entering, but the doors are locked. The soldier pounds on the large-bronze doors and shouts "Open the door! Let us in! Open the door!"

One door opens and a Priest says, "Come in and close the door." We hurry in and close the door behind us… The soldier pulls out a Colt pistol and points it at the Priest but, he doesn't shoot… The cleric ignores the soldier and walks over to the pulpit and lights eight prayer candles and asks "Why are you here?

The soldier shouts, "To take vengeance." Suddenly, the crucifix that was affixed to the wall crashes to the floor… At that moment the building starts to quake…The candles fall onto the alter-cloth-setting it on fire…When the fire starts to spread the soldier and I run for the door but it's locked and we can't get out…The smoke is so intense I feel like I'm suffocating…I soon realize if, I can't get out I will burn to death…That's when I wake up, shaking and sweating.

Dr. Bass asked, "Why are you frightened?"

"Good question Dr. Bass. I would think it's because at the time the dream seems real and I'm afraid I'll burn to death. I also think it's because I get a sense of impending doom."

Dr. Bass made another observation in clarifying the problem. "Why are you afraid to follow it through? You really don't know for sure what the next sequence would actually be. Once again, what are you really afraid of?"

Before thinking, I blurted out, "I'll die, in the fire."

"Why will you die?" he asked.

"I don't know why. I just feel like if I can't get out, I'll die"

"Are you in the dream?"

"Yes, and I'm with people I don't even know. I'm forced into a place I have no control over."

"I see," he said, "So, you're afraid you have lost control and you won't wake- up."

"I never thought of it that way, Dr. Bass. You could be right."

"Frank, think about this, do you will yourself to wake up? In other words, are you in control of waking yourself up or, are you so frightened that you wake up because it startles you?"

"I'm not sure. I really don't know. I think I wake-up because my heart is pounding and I'm sweating, profusely."

"This is what I suggest you do. I want you to put a notebook and a pen next to your bed. Every time you have this dream right down everything you remember, especially the changes. Try to focus on what causes you to wake up at that exact time.

Do you wake yourself up because you don't want to follow through and learn the outcome? If that's the case, you're in control of stopping the dream. Or, do the symptoms from the anxiety you're experiencing wake you up— such as the sweating and rapid heartbeat? Depending on your anxiety level you can either call me or email me with the information right after it happens. Or, if you prefer, bring it in on your next appointment and we can discuss it."

"Okay, Dr. Bass. I'll try to observe my reaction and write it down when I awake."

He went on. "You mentioned your dreams have changed. Do you remember when it started to change?"

"This past June, precisely, the day I graduated from the university. I fell asleep in the car on the way home from graduation I fell asleep. This time when the nightmare started there was a significant change in the sequence, but for some reason it didn't scare me. But lately there has been several changes. Now I'm conversing and interacting with the people in my dream, and their faces are no longer blurred."

"When did that start?" he asked.

"It started within the last couple of weeks"

"Think this over carefully before you answer, Frank. Did you ever notice whether there is a trigger that causes the dream perhaps a change in your personnel life, stress or an event?"

"No, I don't recall." I knew I should have been honest with Dr. Bass but I wasn't ready to tell him about pop and the gun. Besides, pop had nothing to do with my dreams. I've had them since I was a kid.

"I must say, Frank, this is very interesting but don't worry, we'll get to the bottom of it." I had just realized that Dr. Bass was taping my entire session.

"Okay, now tell me all about Frank Scarpelli. Who is he? What does he like? What was his childhood like? You know what I mean. You don't have to go into a lot of detail unless you think it has some bearing on your dreams."

On my way to pick up Jessie, I evaluated my state of mind and I felt hopeful. So before leaving Dr. Bass's office he suggested it would be best to go forward and not let too much time lapse between sessions. I agreed. It was time I faced my fear.

I was about to ring the bell when the door opened and she ran into my arms. She hugged me and asked, "Did you go? What happened? Are you alright?"

"Yes, to all your questions. I'm fine and I won't and can't tell you what happened. But, I will tell you that Dr. Bass said it was not contagious or terminal."

"That's real funny Frank. You scared the hell out of me the other night and now it's a joke. Please!"

I changed the subject. "We're not going to a fancy place for lunch I've just been taken to the cleaners?"

"No problem. This time I'll pay. You always pay."

"I was kidding Jessie, it was a joke. Get real, how do you think I'll feel when they bring the check and I hand it to you? I'll look like a cheapskate. No way, you're paying."

"You know Frank you are so behind the times. Where the hell have you been the last couple of years? Our age group does it all the time, it's called Dutch treat."

I smiled when I said, "I like taking care of the weaker sex." Jessie punched me in the arm and said, "you chauvinistic pig."

I couldn't help but laugh. "What? I thought I was being nice. Maybe you're right. It's the second time in the last week that someone insinuated that I was chauvinistic."

"Who accused you?"

I wasn't ready to tell her about Darlene so I told her it was one of the women I work with.

"You better watch that Frank. I'm sure you realize there are laws protecting women from harassment."

"No shit Jessie. You must be kidding? I just spent six years in law school and I didn't even know there were harassment laws? Stupid me! I thought the laws were for harassment, not being chauvinistic."

"There is a fine line, mister.

"Really, I better watch it the next time I offer to pay for someone's lunch."

"You're twisting my words. Screw you Frank Scarpelli, I'm ordering lobster."

CHAPTER FIFTEEN

It's Sunday, which means I'm expected to have dinner with the family in New Jersey. Even though it's passing up my mother's cooking, and its great having ties with the family there are times I would prefer not having to be there.

Italian families don't have the normal Sunday dinner, they feast. We start off with fruit cup or soup (depending on the weather), then pasta with meatballs, sausage, salad and Italian bread, and then, the meal. It could be roast-beef, pork or lamb, with potatoes and vegetables. Later, it's coffee, or espresso with Anisette. Last but not least, dessert. That could be, cannoli's, a rum *cake from Santo's Bakery* or a homemade chocolate mousse cake that happens to be my dad's favorite. My mother makes so much food that the rest of the week I have to run and cut down on my caloric intake.

Al, Barbara, Julia, Willie, Katie and me, (now that I'm back in the area) have our meals in the dining room and dinner can take anywhere from two hours to three hours or more because we're unable to leave the table. We can't move. It's also expected, that we repeat this ritual every Sunday. Pop comes every other week. He spends one Sunday with his son Al, and the other Sunday, he goes to Uncle Frank's house.

On holidays and special occasions we all get together at my uncle's place. His house is larger than my parent's home. Uncle Frank's house is six thousand square feet and has five bedrooms, five bathrooms, a large family room. And a game room that has a slate Brunswick table, a poker table, and a stocked- bar. As a kid I liked going to Uncle Frank's house, but after a while the talking and the noise was too much for me, so while the family was mingling I would go to one of the bedrooms and watch television. A couple of hours later someone would notice that I was missing and they'd comet looking for me. Eventually they'd find me, but in the meantime I had peace and quiet. I wonder if Dr. Bass would consider that, peculiar behavior? Here I go analyzing my strange, habits.

I'm not sure why I felt somewhat awkward when I walked into the living-room of my parent's house and saw pop sitting in the living-room. I repressed the emotion. I walked over to him and gave him a hug, "Hi grandpa how are you feeling?"

He smiled. "My boy, it's so good to see you. How is work? Do you like your job?"

I assured him I did and we made small talk. Pop started telling us how he and his neighbor, also a man in his late-eighties went to the Senior Center and met some fine ladies. My father went postal. "That's crazy. You don't need any women."

My mother heard his remark from the kitchen. "Al, you leave pop alone. What's wrong with him meeting a lady? He should be having a good time."

I started to wonder *how could I have mistrusted this man's integrity? I've known him all of my life. He has always treated his family with such kindness and respect.* I started to feel guilty about my unexplainable discomfort around him. *On the other hand why did pop lie about where he was from. And, why is he holding onto that old German Lugar and, that dirty rag? Do I really know him? Or, is this man a stranger? And why am I acting so paranoid? I'm sure there's a plausible explanation.*

A short time later the rest of the family arrived. Barbara was really starting to show and yet she looked beautiful. You know the other thing they say about pregnant women's emotional state is true.

Barbara started to cry when my brother said that my mother's meat-balls were the best. I can't say I'm sure if that's the reason, maybe she would have cried even if she wasn't pregnant?

As we gathered around the table it dawned on me that everyone was mated with the exception of pop and me. And they all seemed very happy, even Julia. No one knew how she could be happy with Willie, but she was. I wondered what would happen if I had brought Darlene to dinner? How would my family handle the interracial thing? I've never known my family to be particularly prejudice. I was never subjected to any slurs about other religions or for that matter, any racial remarks. The only person mom is prejudiced against is, Uncle Frank. It was almost like my mother was reading my mind. "Frankie, how come you never invite Jessie to Sunday dinner? You're still see-ing her aren't you?"

The question had all the earmarks of, what's going on with you two?

"Yes. We keep in touch by phone, text and sometimes we go out. If you want to know if we're more than friends mom, we're not."

Mom said, "You're so sensitive. Why don't I rephrase that? Why don't you invite your friend over for dinner? And why are you so secretive about your personnel life? We're family."

Willie my stupid brother in-law put in his two cents. "Yeah Frank why don't you tell us who you're banging these days?"

I thought my mother was going to faint. She went pale and speechless. My sister elbowed him in the ribs and my father got up and smacked him in the back of the head. "What is wrong with you? You have no respect for the women here, let alone your daughter?"

He put his hand to his head and started to rub it. "I was kidding. Can't you people take a joke?"

I started to laugh. That didn't sit well with my dad, he glared at me. Personally I thought it was about time someone let their hair-down. At the table we sat in the same order we did as kids. Only now a chair is added next to that persons partner.

I decided to change the subject and get some straight answers from my grandfather. "Pop, tell me what's it like in Italy? I was thinking of going there on my vacation. While I'm there I would like to meet some of your relatives."

"I was from Naples and we no longer have any relatives there."

My mother interjected, "You don't, but I still have family in Italy. You can visit my family in Rome. In fact I'll go with you."

My grandfather sadly stated, "I don't like talking about the past Frankie. It was a long time ago and my memory is not too good."

I pushed on. "Pop, did you come to the United States before or after the war?"

"Which war Frankie?"

"World War II."

He thought for a moment. "I don't remember. I think it was before World War II.

My father darted me 'the evil eye,' which meant shut up. So, I did.

After several hours, I said my goodbyes and went home to do my laundry. I only wash underwear and towels—I send everything else to the cleaners. I watched some TV and went to bed after the eleven o'clock news. It wasn't long before I could sense that I was going into a dream, state. *I'm in the forest with several American soldiers. We were crouching so low I could hear the sound of the brush rustling beneath my feet. Then, I woke up and I immediately jotted down the event and followed up with, I'll be damned, I can control it.*

CHAPTER SIXTEEN

Before going into my office, I checked to see if Darlene was in hers. She wasn't so I figured it was just as well. I needed to get to work and, to stop acting like a love-sick teenager. If only I could get her off my mind. I went to my office and re-read the notes I had made on several of the open cases and began, once more, to theorize my allegations. Trying to coming off as someone who knew what they were doing was, difficult. Knowing the fundamental law and applying it to a client's situation is difficult. Junior had asked us all to attend an impromptu meeting and I wanted to be in good form, just in case he happened to question me. I expect that I would have to describe in detail what legal method I might have used as a defense for a specific case. I felt my opinion at this point was moot, every-one of the litigator's were experienced.

While deep in thought Darlene came into my office with a beautiful smile on her face. "Good morning, Frank."

"Good morning, Darlene. How was your weekend? From the look on your face, I'd say it went pretty well?" She gushed. "It went real well." She then held out her left hand to show me a very large diamond, engagement ring. My enthusiasm waned. I tried not to act like a jerk and say something stupid. "Congratulations, I had no idea you were involved in a relationship?"

She looked surprised at my remark. "You never asked and we haven't known each other long enough to discuss our personal lives."

"You're right, of course. It's a beautiful ring and I hope you'll be happy. Who's the lucky guy?"

She smiled. "His name is Bruce Cortland. We met at Yale when he was a sophomore and I was a freshman. The rest is history we've been together ever since."

"What field is he in?"

"He's a physician. Right now he's living in Boston, but he will be doing his residency in New York. He's specializing in Pediatrics."

"Cool, which-hospital?"

"He's not sure. He's had several offers. He's not sure which one he'll choose."

"Bruce Cortland? Is he related to the mega bucks Cortland's from Boston?"

At first, she hesitated, "Yes, Bruce is the grandson of Thomas Cortland the founder of the Cortland Hotel, chain." She excused herself and muttered, "I have to go to work. See you later, Frank."

"Sure, see you at the meeting."

As she was leaving, she glanced back at me and smiled.

What is that ache doing in my stomach? And thank God the windows don't open. Holy shit, I feel like crap. Darlene is everything I have ever dreamed of in a woman. Beauty, brains and a good sense of self, and something more, she has charisma, and that perfume. I have to find out what the name of that perfume is, it, drives me crazy.

I have to get hold of myself. The pain will pass and I will move on. It's not like I'd been in a relationship with her or that she dumped me for someone else. It's not that I'm in love with Darlene. You can't love someone you just met, can you? I have to look at it for what it is, a strong attraction and most likely lust. Whatever!

Besides, now is definitely not the time to get involved with women and all the more reason to explore all my options. Right now I need to get rid of the only thing in my life that has caused me stress and uncertainty. Besides, I have to put a lot of time into my career. This firm has offered me a great opportunity and I have to show them I'm worth it. This is actually a good thing. I need to keep my mind clear.

Mark's meeting was in part to address the changes that would be soon be implemented. "I'm sure everyone here is wondering why I brought in two more trial lawyers. It was predicated on attracting more high-profile criminal cases. Although we've established our-selves as being credible and competent in wining most of our cases, we do not receive the media attention needed to attract high-profile clients. Frank and Darlene were hired to assist, until they are ready for first chair. I'm sure you're aware that Frank and Darlene have recently graduated from two of the best universities in our country. I might add they also ranked high in their academic achievements. So, let's move forward and put all our efforts into winning all of our cases. Right now we have a great team and that's exactly what it takes to succeed. Here is how it looks on paper but not in stone. Three of us trial lawyers will specialize in criminal defense cases. That person would need an associate sitting second chair. That position would be open to whoever is available, at that time. This way all five trial attorneys will get the experience needed for excelling in a special-ized field.

"In the past our firm's main focus has been in libel, white collar crime, real estate, accounting, corporate restructuring, bankruptcy, and so on. This firm had built its credibility in all of these areas. We now have the capitol and manpower to expand. I don't have to tell you that high profile cases, is where the big bucks are. Getting those cases will be difficult, but not impossible I have hired a public rela-tions firm to help out with re-marketing and establishing our firm as a brand.

"My brother Tim will remain in charge of taxes, finance and corpo-rate reorganization. Does anyone have any questions?" No one said a word, either for or against incorporating the company's new agenda. We then continued with our weekly staff meeting and reviewed the case-load. After the meeting, I felt inspired. Mark opened the door to a challenge: Win all my cases, bring in more business and last but not least, make more money. It sounded good to me.

I was surprised that soon after our meeting junior walked into my office. I was concerned because during the meeting I was asked to provide my opinion on an extortion case, and I did. I began to wonder if I was way off base on my assessment.

"Frank, I just wanted to tell you that I was impressed with your input during our session. As soon as a new case comes in, it's yours."

"Thanks Mark. I can't wait to get my foot in the door." I knew that until I passed the bar and have a lot more experience I could only be an assistant to the senior attorney. Hopefully, by this time next year I'll be ready to have my own caseload.

That day I ran into Darlene on several occasions and my state of mind hadn't changed and it got me down. I wondered if I should tell Dr. Bass about my feeling for her. I thought better of it. It didn't pertain to the reason I was seeing him.

CHAPTER SEVENTEEN

S aturday, I arrived at Dr. Bass's office at exactly, 9:45 am, and at exactly 10:00, Dr. Bass opened the door to his office and motioned for me to come in. I told him with the exception of last Sunday's nightmare, the week was uneventful.

He asked, "Tell me about the dream you had last Sunday and did you write it all down?"

I explained how it started. "I was in the woods crouched down and I stopped it. I actually stopped it."

"I suspected you had the control Frank. The only problem is you didn't complete the dream sequence so you still don't know why you were there. I also have a feeling there is more to this than you're willing to tell me. If you want help I need to know everything. Are you holding anything back? The smallest detail might help me understand if these are dreams or a suppressed memory. On the other hand you appear to have total recall of events and things that have happened in your lifetime. So, the likelihood that you're trying to suppress an event that happened in your childhood would have had to have been so traumatic that you repressed the experience by putting it into your subconscious. I feel we can count that out. Because your nightmares are of an era that took place before you were born. Another circumstance might be that an elderly family member recalled his experiences during WWII. Then again, you would have remembered enough of the details to notice a correlation between the story and the nightmares. A farfetched question is that this dream, trying to tell you something?"

"You mean a message? What kind of message?"

"At this point it's all conjecture on my part. We haven't really spent enough time together. But my experience tells me we would find out a lot sooner, if you would follow through with the dream. Would you object to hypnosis?"

"I don't know. What are the risks?"

"Minimal, compared to the insight and direction the dreams are taking. It should reveal if your subconscious is holding something back that could be useful to your situation." "Suppressing? You think I'm suppressing? I've been looking for the truth or the cause of these nightmares since I was a kid."

"That maybe what you feel, but in reality you have stopped short of letting the dream take you to its conclusion."

"That's right Dr. Bass. You know why? I'm afraid I'll die."

Frank, are you afraid you'll die or afraid you will have to face something you don't want to know about? Look at it this way did you ever dream you were falling?"

"Yes, doesn't everyone? I wake up before I hit the ground."

"My point exactly, you stop it, don't you?"

"Yes, but isn't that a knee jerk reaction?"

"Yes," he continued, "You wake up startled from falling. But you don't have the same fear or the symptoms that you experience from your nightmares. When in the midst of your dreams you don't know what to expect yet, you can still control the outcome by waking yourself up. It's obvious that your subconscious is trying to give you a message, and it won't let go until your conscious understands and deals with it. Does this make any sense?"

"Okay, doc I'm willing to try hypnosis if you feel it will help."

"I really feel it will. Frank, are you sure there is nothing you're holding back from me?"

"There is nothing of importance."

"Let me be the judge of that. What is it? Does it have anything to do with the changes in your dreams?"

"I think it might. Except I can't seem to, connect the dots."

"That's a curious remark. What is it Frank?"

"Dr. Bass, I found a German Lugar and pictures belonging to my grandfather. And what bothered me the most was the inaccuracies in my grandfather past. Like, how come no one knew about the gun? And why is he lying about what part of Italy he comes from? Most of all, why is that gun winding up in my dreams and what the hell does all this have to do with me?"

"Truthfully, I have no idea. All this stuff about your grandfather and his gun might have nothing to do with anything. You may have connected it to your dream because a German Lugar represents military combat. Hypnosis could produce a deeper contact with your emotional life. It could result in understanding why you are repressing your fear of finding out what your dreams really mean. Don't worry, I will stop the session if, at any-time your health is in danger. Deep hypnosis is actually a relaxed mental state and you should feel uninhibited and relaxed. This may be the only way I can access your subconscious mind. Did you want to schedule an appointment for next week or wait a few weeks to think it over? It's up to you. Personally, I think the sooner the better."

"To be honest with you, doc, this sounds a lot like weird shit and I have considered bailing."

"I know how it sounds to a layman Frank, but it's an option that should be considered. We have several other options, but in my opinion non are as fast as hypnosis. You certainly don't need in-depth analysis. You're very intelligent and if you're telling me the truth and I'm sure you are, you had a great childhood with loving and caring parents. You don't have a neurosis or psychosis. Everything about you is normal and just because you have nightmares doesn't mean you're not. If you can live with this I doubt it will kill you. But it will and has already upset the quality of your life. Wouldn't it be better if it just stopped? Something is causing these nightmares and we have to find a way to open that door."

"Okay, doc, let's make it happen. I can be here, next week."

"Frank, before you come in next week look through your grandfathers photographs. Also, check out the terrain of the photographs."

"I don't understand. What could be familiar?"

"That's what I think you're going to find out. And be sure to write everything down."

As I headed home, I decided to take a detour. Instead I walked around the city. I later went to Nate's for a corned beef sandwich and a knish. I then wound up at the Marriott for a nightcap, big mistake. The last time I was there was when I was with Darlene. It reminded me of her and it put me in a lousy mood. So, I had a few scotch and sodas and left.

As soon as I got home I had two more scotch and soda's and called Jessie. Tomorrow was Sunday and I would be heading back to New Jersey to have dinner with the family. I thought if I invited Jessie to have dinner with us my mother might get off my back. And just maybe, I could get Darlene off my mind. Without hesitation she accepted my invitation. After speaking to her, I started to get a twinge of guilt.

Then I dismissed it. I had enough to worry about without having to analyze every move I made. *She's my friend, I enjoy her company and she likes sex.*

I decided not to follow Dr. Bass's instructions, tonight. I avoided looking at the pictures. I told myself that tonight was not the night I needed to focus on the negative. I'll do it tomorrow. I was already feeling lonely and unhappy. It could have been all the booze. At least I slept peacefully.

On Sunday, everything went off without a hitch. Jessie was perfect, she fit right in. She was happy and my family was happy that Frank not only brought a date it was someone my mother approved of. And that was not an easy accomplishment. Yes, Jessie would be perfect, if only I was in love with her.

CHAPTER EIGHTEEN

I had to start focusing on my job and what was to be my first case in assisting a senior staff member. Right now I'm no more than a paralegal with six years of learning the principles of the law. Still, this will be an invaluable experience. Knowing the law is one thing applying it is another. In most cases people's lives, their livelihoods, reputation, their marriage or freedom could be at stake. And they are entitled to the best defense their money could buy. It takes years of experience in learning how to manipulate the interpretation of state and federal, law. Anyone who thinks otherwise is misinformed.

I was surprised when Junior walked into my office and handed me his case. I had no idea that I would be working for him. I never imagined that the senior partners would want my input. He put the file on my desk and said, "Read this over and get back to me on how you would handle, Dr. Fischer's situation."

I asked, "What situation?"

He laughed. "Read the report and take notes. When you're done buzz my assistant, Millie and tell her you want to see me. She knows when I'm available. That's it, Frank. I don't have time to explain. I'm a busy man. That's why I hired you."

I smiled. "You did, and you did the right thing." Mark smiled when he left.

I opened the Dr. Jerome Fischer file: Mr. Jerome Fischer, 80 year old retired physician is accused of killing his 82 year old wife by giving her a lethal morphine, injection as she slept. Mrs. Fischer had been ill with stomach cancer for over a year. Although she sought radical treatment it, could not contain the spread of her disease, which was now in its advanced stages. Her Oncologist's prognosis was that the disease was terminal and she would most likely die within the next couple of days or weeks. Dr. Fischer is being charged with fourth degree, voluntary manslaughter. If he's found guilty he could be facing up to ten years. Unfortunately, Dr. Fischer signed a confession shortly after his wife's demise. In his confession, Dr. Fischer stated that he killed his wife because he could no longer endure seeing his wife of fifty-one years wracked with the pain that would eventually lead to her death. The prosecutor's is seeking a criminal-judgment because it was premeditated. And being a Physician he had means and the intent to do bodily harm by waiting for Mrs. Fischer's caregiver to leave their home before administering the lethal dose of morphine. Due to the circumstances and his age the DA's office is willing to make a deal by offering him three-to-eight years for a voluntary manslaughter conviction.

Mark's note stated: Due to Mr. Fischer's age we're going to try and get him off. Get me enough evidence to prove it was a mercy killing. Hopefully, the jury will feel he did the right thing. If possible find a way to have his confession thrown out.

It seems Dr. Fischer's daughter, Annabelle King, called Mark as soon as her father was arrested. Dr. Fischer had been a client of Mark Moran, Senior, and had been doing business with the firm since its conception. At the arraignment, Junior convinced the judge to allow Dr. Fischer bail by claiming he was a prominent New York City heart surgeon with ties to the community. And, he was not a flight risk. The judge agreed, but asked that he surrender his passport. Although the prosecutor had asked that he be remanded, he didn't seem too upset that he was allowed bail.

My investigation would start at police headquarters. I decided to speak to the arresting officer's first. Then I will need to obtain a copy of Dr. Fisher's confession. The difficulty will be in trying to have it overturned. I will then speak to and take depositions from his daughter Annabelle, Mrs. Fischer's physician and her care-taker. I also needed to know Dr. Fischer's behavior before and during the time of the 'accidental' overdose. (I, assumed it was accidental). If needed, I will interview character witnesses, such as friends, colleagues and family members. But first, I had to go to the firm's library. That is where we keep the best law books that money can buy.

Soon after, Mark left my office— Darlene walked in and handed me a cup of coffee and asked, "You take it black, don't you?"

"You got it sweetheart." We both started laughing— I don't know why. I guess we were both a little nervous. I know I was. "You bringing me coffee is quite a surprise. What happened to wanting to be treated like one of the boys? My secretary won't even bring me coffee."

"You have me all wrong, Frank. I was going for coffee and I thought you might like some. It's just a common courtesy and it also gave me an excuse to come in and find out why Mark was in your office and, to tease you about being the teacher's pet."

"So, what you're really looking for is a little dirt? First of all I'm not the teacher's pet. Mark recognizes talent when he sees it."

Darlene got this 'Yeah sure' smile on her face. I told her why Mark was in my office, and explained the case. After her expression changed when she asked, "What's wrong, Frank?"

"I'm not sure what you mean, nothing's wrong. Why?"

"We used to speak to and kid around with each other a lot more than we do now. I guess what I'm trying to say is, you seem to be avoiding me."

"Well," I replied, "You're engaged."

Darlene looked confused. "What does my engagement have to do with our friendship?"

Of course she was right. I now realized how immature I had been acting. I was actually angry with her because she was in love with a guy she met before I came into the picture. Jessie was right I act like a spoiled kid when I don't get my way.

"You're right, Darlene. Your engagement has nothing to do with our friendship. I guess I thought if I had a girlfriend as beautiful as you, I probably wouldn't want her to be having drinks with a good-looking guy."

Darlene started to laugh. "Well look who is full of himself."

Actually, I've just been preoccupied. I've had a lot of personnel stuff on my mind lately. Let me make it up to you. If you're not busy tonight, I'll buy you a drink?"

"You're on. I'll meet you in the lobby at, five."

We meet up and we walked across the street to the Marriott. I held onto her arm as if, to protect her from the oncoming traffic. The truth is I wanted an excuse to touch her.

When we got to the lounge it was so crowded we couldn't even get a seat at the bar or, at any of the cocktail tables. While waiting for an available seat we stood at the corner of the bar. Finally, the bartender noticed us and took our order. I was about to speak when I felt a slap on my back. Thinking it was some kind of an impatient wise-ass. As I turned to face him I saw Darlene's eyes widen— as if to say 'don't start anything.' Nevertheless I was not about to let this go until I saw it was my Uncle Frank. He slapped me on the back again, and said, "Tell me the truth you were about to take a swing at me weren't you?"

"No, I'm with a lady. I was going to tell you to and back-off before I take I take a swing at you."

Wouldn't you know it he gave me a bear-hug in front of Darlene. "I love you, Frankie. You have such composure."

I turned to Darlene and introduced her to my uncle. "Darlene, this is my Uncle, Frank Scarpelli."

She held out her hand. "Hello Mr. Scarpelli, It's nice to meet you."

While shaking Darlene's hand he remarked. "It's a pleasure meeting you too, Darlene. And please call me Frank. Any friend of Frankie's is a friend of mine."

"Frankie," she repeated, "I'll have to remember that."

I gave her my disapproval look. She just smiled.

Uncle Frank asked, "What's the matter, kid, can't find a seat?"

"You got it. This place is so damn crowded. What about you, Uncle Frank? What are you doing here at this time of the night?"

"I'm meeting with some business associates. I usually conduct my business earlier but tonight was an exception. You know how your aunt hates it when I don't come home for dinner. Why don't you and Darlene join us? Our table is in the dining room." He pointed and waved at three men who looked and dressed as cool as he did.

I asked, "Who are they? They don't look familiar."

"That's because you wouldn't know them. Why can't you and your father understand that my business extends beyond Montclair, New Jersey? Why do you think I have an apartment in the city? You're just like your father, you don't listen."

"It's not because we don't listen. It's because when it comes to business you're not exactly straight-up."

"There's nothing to tell. I'm a venture capitalist and a real estate developer. Besides, this certainly isn't the time or the place to discuss family business."

He was right. I never should have put him on the spot like that in front of a stranger. Although, he didn't act like he was too upset.

"That reminds me, Frankie why haven't I seen you in such a long time? Dottie keeps asking, 'how come we never see Frankie?' I told her you're busy. She said no one should be too busy for family."

It had been quite a while since I went up to my uncle's place. I didn't know what to say. Lately, my Saturday's were spent with Dr. Bass and Jessie. And Sunday's, I had dinner at my parent's place. And I had no intention of telling anyone in my family that I'm seeing a shrink.

"If you're not busy this Saturday, I'll stop in." He slapped me on the back. "We're not busy this Saturday. I'll tell your aunt and Robin you're coming over. Come for lunch." Uncle Frank excused himself to get back to his clients.

I did notice that before leaving he said something to the wait-ress and handed her money. I figured he was buying us a drink. As it turned out she walked over to one of the tables and placed a reserved sign on it. After the couple left she tapped me on the shoul-der and pointed to the reserved table and whispered "Mr. Scarpelli said to put whatever you want on his tab."

Darlene looked at me and whispered, "I'm impressed. I'm really impressed."

I just grinned at her. I was more surprised than impressed. *How does he do it?*

Darlene declared, "I see good looks run in your family."

"You mean I'm not the only good looking one in the family?"

"That's right, you're not. Your uncle is a very handsome man."

"You really think so? I never thought about that."

"He's also very charming."

"So, you think he's handsome and charming? Well, don't get any ideas he's a happily married man."

She laughed when she said, "Bummer! Only kidding Frank, as you know I'm already taken."

We left the Marriott around eight. I called her a cab and gave her a friendly goodbye hug. I flagged down another cab and went home, alone. I had such a great evening that I hated to have it end. There lies the problem with just being friends. Darlene wants an associate-friendship and I want a relationship. My physical desire for Darlene boarders on lust—I'm at an impasse.

Before I knew it, it, was Saturday and I was on my way to my appointment with Dr. Bass to start my first session of hypnotherapy. Although I was reassured it was safe I was hesitant. I wasn't sure I believed in it, so, I did some research. Supposedly, the subconscious is the storehouse for all your memories. So while under hypnosis you're usually able to access events that had been stored in the subconscious.

That's the part that scares me. Apparently, I didn't want to remember. That's why I controlled the dreams and never followed it to the end. The question remained, to what end. I knew I would soon find out in this session or, in sessions to come if, I don't renege. I told myself to, *get that thought out of my head —that was not an option.*

As usual I arrived on time and as usual Dr. Bass came out of his office and greeted me in his usual manner. "How are you doing, Frank?"

I acted nonchalant "Great, I'm doing just great." If I was really great I wouldn't be there and he knows that, so why does he ask such a stupid question? I suppose it's an icebreaker and helps to alleviate the stress of sitting and waiting.

Once again, Dr. Bass recalled the method he would be using. "It's called Progressive Relaxation and Imagery. A method commonly used by psychiatrists. By speaking to you in a slow soothing voice you will gradually feel relaxed and focused. I will then ease you into a full hypnotic state. That usually takes anywhere from a few minutes to a half hour." He reiterated, "It doesn't always work on the first session if the subconscious resists in giving full disclosure. If that happens you could require one or two more sessions."

This time, Dr. Bass led me to the sofa, "Frank I think it best you lie down. It will help you relax and it's the position you're in when the nightmares occur. Before we begin I want you to know I'm going to tape all of our sessions. By the way, have you had any nightmares within the past week?"

"No I haven't." I smiled when I said, "Is it possible that I'm already cured?"

"That's wishful thinking Frank, and you know better."

Laughing at myself calmed me down. What the hell I had nothing to lose. If the dream continued after these sessions, I'd just have to learn to live with it. Still, while under hypnosis I wanted to take this dream sequence to the end. Whatever, the consequence.

Dr. Bass was competent and I trusted him. Not sure if it's because he's assured me that I wasn't crazy. After what seemed like a few seconds, it began. Dr. Bass asked, "What are you doing, Frank?"

"I'm running through some thick underbrush"

"Why are you running?"

"We're in a hurry to get to the church."

"Is someone chasing you?"

"No, but we have to be on the lookout for the Nazi's and their defense forces"

"Do you know where you are?"

"Yes I'm in Italy."

"How do you know that?"

"The local patriots are speaking in, Italian."

"Pause for a moment and look at yourself."

"I can't stop. I have to go to the church."

"Why is it so important that you go to the church?"

"We're on a secret mission. We have to rendezvous with another group of patriots. They have the crucial information we were sent here, to retrieve."

"I don't understand— what information?"

"Maps, key striking locations— German and Italian headquarters, and where they keep their arsenal. We also have to dismantle their communication system."

"Frank, are you in the service?"

"No, but these five Americans are."

"What branch of the service are they in?"

"They're in the Army. They're paratroopers."

"Frank, do you know what year it is?"

"It's 1943."

"Frank look at your clothes. What are you wearing?"

"I'm wearing my street clothes."

'What clothes are the Americans wearing?"

"They're wearing vintage farmhand clothes."

"Why aren't they in uniform?"

"Mario said they'd look less conspicuous, if they were spotted."

"The people you're with are they speaking?"

"Yes, but they're whispering."

"Frank, is someone coaching you on what to say?"

"Yes, TC is telling me what to say."

"Who is TC and what's he doing there?"

"He's Sergeant, Thomas Callahan—A United States Army, paratrooper."

"Continue on with your dream-state. Frank."

We reached the church and we're ushered into a dark, cold cellar... Everyone is eating and talking... Suddenly we hear footsteps above us. Mario checks to see who it is and then yells for us to join him in the church. As we enter, the building starts to shake and the candles fall off the pulp and a fire ensues, flames are everywhere. We start running for the doors. Their locked and we can't get out— we're going to die.

"Frank, do not wake up. The fire is a figment of your imagination. Get hold of yourself. Did the building stop shaking and the fire subside?"

"Yes, it did."

"Why does TC want revenge? What horrible thing happened at the church?"

"I don't want to talk about it! I don't want to talk about it!"

"Okay, Frank calm down. This is not real. This is only a dream and it can't hurt you. I won't let it. I'm going to ask you again, why does TC want revenge?"

"Mario betrayed them and he needs to be punished."

"Why? I thought he was helping you."

"He's a fucking murdering traitor."

"Frank, it is time to wake up now. When I count to five you will wake up and remember what has taken place. One, two, three, four, five— wake up."

When I came out of my altered state of consciousness, I was confused and shaken up. I looked at Dr. Bass and asked him, "What the hell just happened?"

He replied, "What happened is, we finally made a breakthrough."

I asked, "What kind of a breakthrough? I'm more confused now then I was before. Once again everything had changed. What does any of this crap have to do with me?"

"I don't know and we're going to find out. Being this was your first session believe me when I say, it went exceptionally well. Frank, think, before you answer my next question. Did you know anyone named, Thomas Callahan?"

"I have no recollection of anyone named Thomas Callahan, although, it's not an unusual name."

"I must admit your case is very puzzling. But I'm sure we will get to the bottom of this. It is imperative we continue with this kind of therapy. Will you be able to come in next week?"

"I don't know Dr. Bass, I'm very uncomfortable with this kind of treatment, and it's freaking me out."

"It may seem unorthodox or, that you're out of control. Believe me you're not. We've just started making headway. If you quit now you may never know why this has happened to you and worse— it may never stop. You came here to find out the truth, let me help you. I can assure you once you know what you're dealing with you will be able to get your life back. Do you need something for your nerves?"

"No, I'm okay, I think. You're right I need to get this over with before it drives me crazy. I'll see you next week."

I was sorry I told my uncle that I'd stop by for lunch. I was in no mood to see anyone or, did I feel like eating. I also knew if I cancelled my life wouldn't be worth a plug nickel. My uncle is a great guy, but you don't ever want to upset his wife.

When I pulled up to the driveway of Uncle Frank's house I noticed several changes and additions to the grounds. As you drove up the private road that lead to the driveway there was a large wrought iron gate that prevented you from entering the driveway or the front entrance of the home. And a wrought iron-spiked fence encompassed the entire perimeter of the estate. My first reaction was, "What the hell is this? Did I drive up to the wrong house?" I checked the structure, it was the right house.

On each side the gate, were two brick posts, the driver's side had an electronic intercom system. As I leaned out the car window to speak into the stupid box— a voice said, "Hello, Frank, we've been expecting you." The gate opened, I drove in and parked by an area of the circular driveway. As I walked toward the front door it opened. Aunt Dorothy was smiling and waving. When I approached, she hugged and kissed me. "Frankie, I'm so glad you're here. It's been such a long time." I asked, "What's going on here? The place is locked up like Fort Knox. When did you put up that fence and gate? And who was that person on the phone?"

"Oh please, I hate all this. It's your uncle's idea. He claims it's for my protection. Sweetheart, who knows what that man is thinking? He said we need protection from burglar's and terrorists. Believe me when I say, your uncle is getting paranoid. He even hired a bodyguard."

"He hired a bodyguard?"

Aunt Dorothy laughed, "Did you know your uncle was meshuganeh?"

I looked at her.

"Crazy! Sweetheart, it means crazy."

Pop heard me talking to my aunt and walked towards me as fast as he could with open arms. "Frankie; my boy, how are you?"

I walked into his arms and hugged him. He held me so tight I could hardly breathe.

"Hi, pop. How are you feeling?"

"You don't want to know. Besides you wouldn't understand how it feels to be old."

"You're not that old grandpa."

"Yes I am and it's time for me to go."

His remark hit home and it made me feel lousy. I couldn't imagine our family without him.

Aunt Dorothy chimed in. "Dad, please don't say that you know how it upsets everyone. We all love you."

He had this big grin on his face. "Now, you see why I love my daughter in-law. Isn't she sweet? Isn't she beautiful?"

"Yes, pop she is beautiful."

Aunt Dorothy was embarrassed. "If you guys only knew how much I had to pay for this beauty."

Pop interjected, "Don't listen to her Frankie. I knew her before Frank married her. She was always beautiful." For all that my aunt had in monetary value, there was never any pretentiousness or conceit. In fact, her affluence almost embarrassed her. I had the feeling, if tomorrow, it was all gone and all she had left was her husband, her child and her family, she would be as happy as she was right now.

"Aunt Dorothy is Uncle Frank here?"

"Of course sweetheart he's in his office. He's been waiting for you."

When I walked into my uncle's office he was at his desk reading a document and for a few seconds I just stood looking at him. *And Darlene thinks this middle aged older man is good looking. I guess from a female point of view he might be considered suave and debonair. But, if you ask me I think he's just average looking.* He felt my presence and looked up. He got up from his chair, smiled and gave me the bear hug my family was so famous for. "You look like hell Frankie, what's wrong?"

"Nothing is wrong."

"Come on, kid, what's wrong."

I had to make something up he's known me all of my life, and I guess my mood was on my face so, I lied. I was getting used to lying. "It's nothing. A couple of days ago I had this twenty-four hour virus thing. I'm better now."

He looked at me and grinned. I don't think he bought it, nonetheless he dropped the subject.

I asked him, "What the hell is going on here? Why the gate and the bodyguard? I didn't know you were on a terrorist hit-list."

He motioned to me to shut the door.

I repeated, "What's up with that?"

"It's a precaution. I loan out a lot of money and sometimes I have problems collecting. Sometimes I have to go to court, and sometimes, they can't take the heat and threaten my family. I don't want some nut finding out where I live and putting my family in danger."

I didn't buy his story. Since he went to all that trouble of making it up, I accepted it. "If you're in any legal trouble let me handle it. I'm the lawyer in the family and I might be able to help."

"No, it's nothing like that kid. It's just a precaution."

'Then, what's with the bodyguard?"

He laughed. "It's a favor. John's father is an old friend of mine. John was a guard at AT&T. They were downsizing and they let him go. John's a genius when it comes to technology. At first I was helping the kid out and now he's helping me out. And he keeps an eye on the house and works the new security system. John's a good kid, and I can trust him. "At that moment there was a gentle knock on the door. When I opened it, it was my aunt. She whispered, "Lunch is ready."

Uncle Frank said, "Come on in sweetheart we're through talking business."

When she entered they smiled at each other like they hadn't seen each other in days. *God, look at them they're still hot for each other after all these years. Why can't I find that kind of love? I guess there aren't too many people that feel the way they do.*

We followed my aunt into the kitchen, which suited me just fine. I hate formal dining room affairs. On the table was a large platter of cold cuts, shrimp cocktail, potato salad, tossed salad, lox, cream cheese, bagels, rye bread and apple pie. "How many more people are you expecting?" I asked.

"It's just, us."

"Aunt Dorothy, where's Robin? I wanted to see her. I got her a little something."

"Frankie you didn't have to do that," she said. "Robin wanted to see you but her best friend Sam was having a sleepover birthday party."

"What? You let her go to some guy's house to sleep over?"

They both laughed. My Uncle remarked, "Are you kidding me? Sam's not a guy. Samantha lives a couple of houses down the street."

I brought out the small box I had in my pocket and asked my aunt to give it to her.

"Frankie, would you mind if I opened it?"

"No. I'm kind of lame when it comes to picking out jewelry."

My aunt opened the box and picked up the gold heart locket with the small diamond embedded in the center. "This is so beautiful. You shouldn't have!"

My uncle agreed. "Dottie is right. You should be saving your money."

"Do you think she'll like it or, is it too old fashioned. I don't know what kids are wearing these days."

Aunt Dorothy said, "What's not to love, it's beautiful."

Pop, who had been very silent said, "That's very nice, Frankie."

My uncle announced, "Eat up, everyone. It's deli, the specialty of the house."

My aunt leaned over and slapped my uncle's arm.

He pretended it hurt. "Ouch, you hurt me. You better be careful I could sue you for abuse."

"Sue away. You deserved it. I'll get a good Jewish lawyer and take you for everything you've got. No offense Frankie."

I laughed. "No offense, taken Aunt Dorothy." We all laughed because no one at this table could imagine my aunt leaving the love of her life.

My uncle asked when I was taking the bar exam and if I'd been studying.

"I don't have to take it until February, and, I haven't had time to study."

"You haven't had time? You spent six years in school and now you're going to blow it?"

"No, I won't blow it. I have plenty of time to study. Besides it should be easier, I'm now practicing the law."

Uncle Frank changed the subject. "Hey, Frankie, tell us about your girlfriend?"

"I don't have a girlfriend."

"What about that beautiful girl you were with, at the Marriott Hotel?"

Oh boy that was all my aunt had to hear. She started in. "Who is this girl? What does she do? How old is she? What does she look like?"

I asked, "How come I cannot have a meal without any family member bringing up the fact that I'm not married or in a relationship?"

My aunt replied, "Because we want to see you happy."

"I am happy. I'd be a lot happier if, my family would stop playing, matchmaker."

My aunt ignored what I had stated. "Okay Frankie, you made your point. Now tell me about her."

"First of all she's not my girlfriend. Darlene is a recent Yale graduate who works in my office. She's around twenty-five, engaged and very beautiful."

"If she's only engaged you still have a chance."

I looked at her and shook my head. Everyone started to laugh, including pop.

"You got a girlfriend, Frankie? I thought Jessie was your girlfriend? That's what your mother said."

"No pop, I don't have a girlfriend. Jessie is just a friend. I promise to let everyone know the day it happens."

Everyone laughed, including me.

My aunt concluded, "I'm sure when you're ready, you won't have any trouble finding someone. You're very handsome."

"Thank you, Aunt Dorothy. In fact, Darlene thought Uncle Frank was very handsome."

She looked amused. "Well, it seems Darlene has very good taste in men."

My uncle put his hand on hers and they smiled at each other.

I asked them, "Do you want us to leave?"

My uncle laughed. "Watch your mouth big shot you're still not big enough to take me on."

I laughed. "That might have frightened me when I was ten, but look at this." I made a muscle.

My aunt asked my uncle, "Frank, look at that big muscle aren't you scared?"

My uncle made a fist. "You will never get big enough for this. I broke a man's jaw with this fist."

We started to laugh. I had forgotten how much fun it was to be with them. My parents are great but they don't kid around like Uncle Frank and Aunt Dorothy. I always' thought my parents took life too seriously.

My aunt reminded my uncle to tell me about their up and coming vacation to Las Vegas.

"Thanks for reminding me sweetheart. I had forgotten."

"Frankie, I was wondering if you would let pop stay at your place for a couple of days."

"I would, but I have to work."

"I know that. We can have him dropped off on Wednesday, and he can stay at your place until the weekend. On Saturday, you can take him to your father's place."

"Ordinarily that wouldn't be a problem, except that I have an appointment, next Saturday morning."

Uncle Frank asked, "Can't you cancel it?"

"I'm sorry I can't. Can't I take him to my parent's home before going to my appointment?"

"Yeah, sure, that's okay."

Pop said, "You know Frankie if you're busy, that's okay. I just wanted a change of scenery."

"Pop, it's not that I don't want you to stay with me, it would be great having you around. What, worries me is you wandering around the streets of Manhattan all by yourself. Uncle Frank do you think it's wise for pop to be walking around the city without an escort?"

"Are you crazy? Do you think I'd let my father wander the streets, by himself? I've got that covered. John will take care of pop until you get home."

"John? Who's John?"

"John is my bodyguard, security man and number one assistant. It's all settled. Dottie and I are going to Las Vegas. Robin will be going to Dottie's mother's house. And, you're taking care of pop."

After lunch I asked my uncle to show me his security system. He took me to the room that once was the recreation room. At one time my aunt and uncle used that large room for entertaining. It had a dance floor, a twenty-foot padded bar, refrigerator, you name it and it was larger than most apartments. Now it held all the surveillance cameras. I was a quite surprised when I met John. He looked like someone who could have been a contestant for a look-a-like Lou Ferrigno, contest if, he was more buff. He's a large and intimidating guy and looked to be in his early twenties. When he stood to shake my hand he looked to be around six foot five. John was clearly someone you wouldn't want to piss off.

My uncle said, "Remember this face, John. This is my nephew, Frankie. I wouldn't want you to shoot him by mistake."

"Does he carry a gun?" I asked.

They thought that was funny and started laughing. "You're a trip Frankie. Isn't that what bodyguards do?" my uncle replied.

John smiled when he said, "Don't worry, Frankie. It doesn't have a hair trigger. I'm in complete control."

"That's not much of a relief John, I hate guns. They have a way of going off when least expected. You do realize that you can't take a gun out of state, assuming it's registered."

Mockingly, he replied, "That's all been taken care of."

John sat behind this huge circular desk. In front of him were eight TV monitors that surveyed the front door, back door, the large entranceway, the bottom of the staircase and the top of the staircase. There were also another three camera's that scanned the property, including, the front gate. "Okay, now you're scarring me," I said.

"Come on now, this is not that elaborate. Remember, I go out of town from time to time. And the whole time I'm worried about Dottie and Robin. What's peace of mind worth?"

I agreed, "You're right Uncle Frank. This is your home and your business."

"So John, I assume you know you're to take care of pop while I'm at work?"

"He knows it now." My uncle replied.

He subsequently asked John. "Could you watch out for pop while Frankie's at work? Next Wednesday me, and Dottie are going to Vegas and pop will be staying at Frankie's place."

"Sure boss, whatever you want."

It's okay for pop to walk around New York; he needs the exercise—but don't tire him out. Just make sure you keep a close eye on him. No one is to lay a hand on him."

John smiled a toothy grin. He had large white teeth, with a small gap in his two front teeth. "Whatever you want, boss."

My uncle put his arm around his shoulders and in a calm voice reminded him that he was told not to call him, boss. "Call me Frank John, we're family, now."

John said, "I know but to me, boss is a sign of respect. My family and me owe you."

"Who said you owe me? You owe me nothing."

Before leaving I shook John's hand. Mine hand seemed small in comparison. I told him it was great meeting him and I meant it. He seemed like an okay guy. After we left I my uncle if John was from Montclair. "John lived in Newark. He was a tough street kid who needed a break."

I asked, "What did he mean when he said he owes you?"

He laughed and said, "You know kid, you're such a lawyer. You ask so many questions. There are things I don't like to talk about."

"I just think it's odd that all of a sudden you have all this security and now a bodyguard. You're not doing anything illegal, are you, Uncle Frank?"

He stopped walking. "No, kid, in spite of what your Mother thinks I'm a legitimate businessman who earns a lot of money. And like any other businessman, I have to be careful. Madone! You sound more like a prosecutor than a lawyer."

On the way home, I thought about Uncle Frank. I knew that besides his and Aunt Dorothy's family they have helped out a lot of people over the years. I heard stories about how he has given money to his friends, the Catholic Church and to many, many charities. Yet they never speaks about his good deeds. To my uncle, it was no big deal.

By the time I got home I was spent. What a day! I hit the bed around, twelve pm. At 2:05 I was in World War II and the year was, 1943. *I'm squatting behind under -brush as I look for German and Italian soldiers, when someone taps me on the shoulder. I turn. It's the red haired guy, called, TC.*

I asked, "What the fuck do you want from me?"

"What I want is what you're doing."

"What am I doing?"

"You're going to find Mario Moretti the mass murdering bastard, and you're going to make him pay with his life. When you have completed your assignment, I will be at peace and so will you."

"Why did you have to pick me?"

"Why I picked you doesn't matter."

"It matters to me."

"Right now there are reasons you could not comprehend. But in time, you will. I will continue to give you instructions and you will follow them to the letter. I've been waiting a long time for you to grow up—and we've come too far for you to back out— under any condition..."

TC whispered to the soldiers, "Come on guys, we have to go to the cathedral."

"Wait," I whispered, "Why do we always have to go to that church?"

"Actually, this is not just a church, this is the Cathedral of Monreale—I recreate the scene so you can be a witness. We were murdered in the Cathedral of Monreale... I have to go now Frank,

you're about to wake up. Find the owner of the gun and you'll find the murderer."

I started shouting, "That's bullshit. You're looking at the wrong person..." When I awoke I was still shouting "Don't leave you've got this all wrong." My heart was pounding and I was shaking all over. This can't be true. My grandfather could not have done such a unspeakable act. What the fuck am I supposed to do? If my grandfather was involved in this atrocity it would not only destroy him, it will impact the entire family. Does TC expect me to turn in my own grandfather for a crime that was committed, over 70 years ago?

I felt angry and cursed. Why is this happening to me? I got out of bed and went into the living room to clear my head. Then the thought occurred to me that maybe I should stop my sessions with Dr. Bass. I don't want him or anyone else knowing about the massacre or the gun. Maybe I should get rid of the gun it could be used as evidence. Then again, how do I know this is real? I could be making this up. Dr. Bass said that hypnotherapy is not an exact science. It just brings your subconscious to the surface. The answer to how and why I developed this scenario is still a mystery and I could be over-reacting.

On the other hand even if it's true a physician is bound by doctor patient confidentiality. The sessions with my psychiatrist was confidential, unless I give him written consent. Let's face it I need Dr. Bass's expertise in proving that this is a repetitious nightmare that has no validity. And once it's exposed as something I have concocted for some reason, the nightmares should leave my subconscious. Worse scenario: it's true and I was chosen, for God knows why to right this terrible wrong. If pop was involved and he knew that I had knowledge of this occurrence it could kill him. The question remains, do I want to protect a murderer who committed an unspeakable war crime even if, he's family?

I poured myself another glass of scotch and went back to bed. Being awake was turning into as much of a nightmare as being asleep. It was Sunday morning and I was in no condition to have dinner with my family. I figured I'd cancel, and I'd see if Jessie wanted to come to my place to hang. I was in no mood to be around my family but I also didn't want to be alone.

I waited until 10:00 am to call. My mother was disappointed and tried using guilt. When she realized it wasn't working, she put my dad on the phone. He on the other hand was okay with me not show-ing up. I then called Jessie. She agreed to come over. In fact she seemed happy that I had invited her. She expressed her need for some R&R. "I almost forgot Frank how did the hypnotherapy go?"

"I don't want to talk about it. And I especially don't want to go into any of the details." That didn't stop her. "Come on, Frank, tell me what happened?"

"Look, Jessie, I'm tired of thinking and talking about it. If you can't let it go don't come over. I'm looking for a fun day. If, you are too, let's do it."

"Okay, Frank, you're on. I'll see you around eleven."

I was glad she stopped questioning me. We've been friends for such a long time I tend to spill my guts and later regret it. I'm starting to sound like a wimp. I hate that in men. Women should do the whin-ing and the men the comforting. We're supposed to be the stronger sex. Wow where did that thought come from? Hard to believe that in this day and age I still think that way. Maybe it's the New Jersey, male, thing. You're supposed to take care of the little woman. She's not supposed to take care of you. As educated as I am I'm still a chauvinistic bastard. I'm going to have to work on that. Jessie would have my head if she knew how I really felt.

I made a pot of coffee and straightened up the place, took a shower, shaved and dressed. Before I knew it, there was a knock on the door. I unlocked the door. When Jessie walked in we hugged. She whispered in my ear "I've missed you. It's been a week since we've seen each other."

I went to pull away but she pulled me back and kissed me passionately. I said, "Jessie."

"Be quiet, Frank I know what I'm doing." We kissed again and this time our tongues met. The touching and caressing filled me with passion and a desire for more, much more. She wasn't wearing a bra and the touch of her erected nipples gave me a hard on. "Jessie, stop! I don't have any rubbers down here we'll have to go upstairs."

"You worry too much, Frank. I'm on the pill."

As my body pulsated, my mouth became so dry I could hardly speak. Our bodies became entwined. Not wanting to pull apart or break the bond that was holding us. I maneuvered us into the living room. We couldn't get our clothes off fast enough as we sank to the floor. Jessie moaned as I propelled. As the momentum grew I waited for her to succumb to her state of ecstasy. In unison we arrived at euphoria. Out of breath, content and quiet, we savored the experience for as long as we could. "You planned this, didn't you Jessie? You seduced me, didn't you?

She laughed. "Yes, I did. Now, try telling that to the judge."

"I will. I'm very persuasive. But in the meantime, are you hungry?"

"I wasn't hungry when I got here but after that workout I'm famished."

"What do you say we take a shower then go to brunch?" I French kissed her again. "You're, the type of woman who knows and goes after exactly what she wants, aren't you?"

She kissed me back. "True, but in the end I never seem to get what I want.

CHAPTER NINETEEN

On Monday morning I felt a lot better. I had a good night's sleep and I was ready to go over my one and only case with Junior. Although a pseudo case, I felt sure that I was the one in control. After all I was the one doing all of the footwork and research. Hopefully, Mark would go along with my strategic recommendations. To an outsider this may seem like a done-deal case but trying to get our client off without any time would render it, a considerable feat.

I no sooner arrived at my office, when Mark's secretary called and said that Mark wanted to see me, and I was to bring my notes on the Fischer case.

When I opened the door to his office, Mark was sitting at his desk. He looked up when he saw me standing in front of him. "Have a seat, Frank. I'll be with you in a minute. I just have to finish signing some contracts."

I sat down in the soft leather chair that was across from of his desk. His office was cool. All of the woodwork was done in a dark walnut finish. The ceilings were high. The top three quarters of the walls were painted dark gold. The other portion had dark walnut paneling.

His desk and all the furniture were ornate and blended with the wood tones in the paneling. In front of his desk were two tufted beige, leather arm-chairs. Wall to wall windows overlooked the Hudson River and lit up the entire room. Void of draperies the windows had wide wood blinds that must have been on a remote control device. In front of the middle window stood a large round table and four overstuffed gold and black striped chairs. A beige leather sectional sofa was on the wall to the left. The carpet was Oriental, with gold, beige, black and cream in an oriental style, all very plush and expensive. There were the usual paintings, licenses and copies of his diplomas. Junior had great credentials he graduated from Princeton University. While waiting I checked my notes. Within a few minutes Mark put down his pen and asked, "How was your weekend?"

Although it really sucked I said, "It was good, Mark. How was yours?"

"I had to work all weekend. I'm sure you've heard the expression. 'Having your own business is not what it's cracked up to be?' Have you given much thought to the strategy that would best serve Dr. Fischer?"

"Yes, I have."

"Good, let's hear it."

I handed Junior a copy of my notes. "I would rather hear your thoughts on the case before I go over your brief."

I started off with, "I'm confident that we could get Mr. Fischer indictment, dropped."

Mark asked, "Did you forget that he signed a confession,"

"After taking that into consideration, I still think we may be able to have it thrown out by going for the defense of, temporary insanity."

"That's a great defense Frank, but can we prove it? You do realize that very few cases have ever been won by using that tactic."

"I realize that Mark. There are a lot of extenuating circumstances in this case, and if we go with the defense of assisted suicide, Dr. Fischer will still serve time."

"Frank, in his confession, Fischer stated that his wife begged him to end her suffering. Even with a plea, it's still considered manslaughter. I doubt the Prosecutor will try to prove premeditated murder."

"Mark, if we don't take the manslaughter plea, it will go to trial. The DA will say he's a physician and, being a physician he would have known how much morphine was lethal. Then, they'll bring in the officer who arrested him as well as the two detectives that talked him into signing a confession, without representation."

"Frank, you made an excellent case, now tell me how we can prove he was insane at the time of the murder? How are we going to dispute the DA, s characterization?"

"Let me lay out some of my evidence and you tell me if we have a case. After all, you're the one with the experience. For one thing, there is motive. What was Dr. Fischer's motive for wanting to kill his wife? He's 80, he's a physician who knew she would have died within the next few days or weeks. Even if, he hated her he could have waited a few more weeks. And if he loved her, he couldn't bear to see her suffer. I have a copy of his written and taped confession. This written confession does not even resemble a man who knew what he was saying, let alone what he was signing."

Mark asked, "What do you mean?"

"His confession shows he must have been incoherent, check out the words and sentences for a man of his status and education."

I handed Mark a copy of the confession. "I see what you mean. Don't forget, he must have been terribly upset."

"It's not just that, he wrote it like he was out of touch with reality. According to the recorded confession, the detectives had to have helped him write his confession because it matches the recording, word for word. Note the grammar and sentence structure, it's incon-sistent and doesn't make any more sense than the recording."

"Spell it out, Frank. What have you got?"

"The taped confession confirms that his words were slurred and his voice, incoherent. He was more than upset, he was on drugs."

"How do you know this? Do you have proof? And why didn't they test him for drugs when he was at the precinct?"

"I don't know why he wasn't tested. But, nothing I have here indicates that he was, tested. That's something I'll have to follow up on. I assume that because he kept repeating that he killed his wife, they wanted to get his confession signed, as quickly as possible."

"What kind of drugs do you think he was on?" Mark asked.

"He was on amphetamines. Amphetamines are a stimulant drug that act on the nervous system, the brain, and the spinal cord. Large doses of amphetamines could cause psychosis and substance-related mental disorders. Add that to major depression and grief and you have a man who was insane when he killed his wife."

"Do you have proof-positive, that he was taking amphetamines?"

"Yes I do Mark. On Thursday I went to see Dr. Roberts. Mrs. Filchers, Oncologist. I received pertinent information that could help our case."

Junior smiled. "Go on Frank you're doing great."

I went on to say, "It seems their nurse came in during the day. She worked from eight in the morning until, six in the evening. She left right after she gave Mrs. Fischer her dinner and medication, although, most of her nutrients, were administered intravenously. A couple of weeks ago, Dr. Fischer asked him for a prescription for a stimulant, so, he could stay awake during the evening to attend to his wife's needs. Dr. Roberts said he didn't like the idea and suggested getting an evening nurse. Dr. Fischer said that wasn't necessary, that most of her care was administered during the day and she slept most of the night. Dr. Fischer just wanted to stay awake a few hours longer in case she needed him. Dr. Roberts gave him a prescription and told him he should take just one a day at, mid-afternoon. This should have kept Dr. Fischer alert for a few hours longer than usual. He gave him a two-month supply.

When Dr. Roberts was called in to sign Mrs. Fischer's death certificate, he saw an empty bottle of the prescription he had given Dr. Fischer, sitting on the night table. He will also sign an affidavit and will appear in court, if necessary. He will state under oath that if Dr. Fischer took that many tablets in that short amount of time, he could not have been in his right mind when he administered his wife's nightly dose of morphine. In the state he was in, there is no doubt, it was an accident."

"You sure have been busy Frank my hat goes off to you for being so diligent. Is there anything else?"

"I guess. Last Friday, I went to see Annabelle King, Dr. Fischer's daughter. And this is the statement she gave me." I opened the file on Mark's desk and handed him her testimonial."

Mother started to get sick about a year ago. My father took her to the best cancer specialist in New York, where she was diagnosed with stomach cancer. Unable to accept the prognosis my father took her to Johns Hopkins, for a second opinion. The results were the same— the cancer had spread and the only available treatment would make her uncomfortable and not prolong her life. They recommended he take her home and make her as comfortable as possible through a drug program.

My father heard of a clinic in Mexico that had great results in treating stage four cancer. Although it was in the experimental stages and illegal in this country, he was ready to try anything. After spending several weeks in Mexico he returned home. The medication didn't work.

When I picked them up at the airport, my father looked worse than my mother. He started grieving before her death. When we arrived home we put my mother to bed. My father refused to leave her bedside. He just sat and held her hand until she fell asleep, and then he started to cry. I told my father that my mother knew he did everything he could to help her. She was now in God's hands. He blamed himself. He stated that he killed her! I tried to reason with him. Everyone knew that he did everything humanly possible to save her life.

He became angry and somewhat hostile. He said he was a physician and he should have seen the signs. I reminded him that he was a cardiologist and that my mother had been seeing her own physician and no one saw it coming, until it was too late."

After a while I interjected, "Annabelle is willing to sign an affidavit, or go to court if it comes to that. She will state that he told her that he took full responsibility for killing his wife, before she passed away."

"This is good work, Frank. I'll bring in a psychiatrist to examine him. Also, speak to the nurse and some of his friends. I'm sure there are other people who must have seen a big change in his behavior leading up to the death of his wife. Let's see what the shrink has to say. If he agrees that Dr. Fischer is mentally incompetent. I would think the District Attorney would likely dismiss the case rather than lose, if, we go to trial. If, they do find him insane at the time of the murder, the DA will insist on him going to a treatment center until he's considered well, which is still better than jail. Now, I just hope we can get Dr. Fischer to go along with our defense."

I was feeling pretty good when I left Mark's office. He seemed to agree with the way I was handling things. But I still had to get an affidavit from Barbara Tate, Mrs. Fischer's nurse. If she did not concur with our other witnesses, or, saw any wrongdoing by Mr. Fischer she could blow our whole case, apart.

I worked all morning finalizing my strategy and contemplating my approach to when I was to see Ms. Tate. Instead of having my secretary set-up the appointment, I hoped that hearing my voice would be less intimidating, and hopefully, put her at ease.

"Mr. Scarpelli I don't think I could be of much help. I really don't have much to tell you"

"Please Ms. Tate, call me Frank. If you will allow me to see you, I promise I won't take up much of your time."

"Okay Frank. I'm in-between jobs right now so I have the time. Today would be a good day. Do you have my address?"

"Yes Ms. Tate I did get that information from Dr. Fischer's address book. But if it's all right with you I would like to meet you at a café. Maybe one that's close to your home, if, it's all right with you."

"That would be lovely. I frequent this café on Pike Street, called, Hoffman's Cafe' How about 2:00 pm?"

"Two it is. Thank you Ms. Tate, I look forward to meeting you."

Although, Ms. Tate thought she had nothing to offer, her statement was essential to our case. Even, if it obstructed our position. Because, if this case goes to court there is no doubt she would be called as a witness for the prosecution. At least we would know in advance, what her testimony would entail.

When I arrived at the Hoffman's Café I looked for a middle-aged woman who was sitting alone. When she saw me looking around and carrying a brief case she waved. After we shook hands I asked, "Would you mind if I recorded our conversation?"

"No Frank, I don't mind. Like I told you, I doubt if I will have much to offer on Dr. Fischer's behalf."

My first question was, "Had you noticed a difference in Dr. Fischer's behavior within the last couple of weeks?"

Now that you mention it, several weeks before Mrs. Fischer passed on. I noticed a big change in Dr. Fischer's demeanor. He lost a considerable amount of weight. I told him he needed to eat if he wanted to keep up his strength. He said he had trouble keeping food down and wasn't very hungry. He also appeared to be disheveled. He stopped shaving and combing his hair, and his clothes looked like he slept in them. When I was hired to take care of Mrs. Fischer, Dr. Fischer's appearance was that of a man who had a great deal of pride in his appearance, but for the past few weeks he didn't even look like the same person."

"Ms. Tate, I realize my next question is not in your field of expertise, but I'm sure with your experience you would have noticed if Mr. Fischer showed signs of severe emotional trauma?"

"He was depressed, just like anyone would be under those circumstances."

My next question was, "Did he act like any other husband, under these circumstances?"

"No, he was different."

"How did he seem different?"

"Well, like I said before, his appearance for one. And, he appeared to be exceptionally nervous. His hands would shake. He even had outbursts."

"What kind of outbursts?"

"Mumbling and crying."

"Did you ever hear Mrs. Fischer ask Dr. Fischer to help her die?"

She hesitated. "Yes, I did, once. It was two weeks before her death. I was just about to walk into the room when I heard her say in a very low voice 'if you love me, help me die. Don't look so upset my dearest, I will see you on the other side."

"What did he say?"

"Nothing, he said nothing. I pretended not to hear and went on with my duties."

"If you noticed these changes in Dr. Fischer why didn't you tell Dr. Roberts?"

"I was about to when Dr. Roberts called me to tell me that Mrs. Fischer had passed away."

Nurse Tate, in case we need your testimony for a hearing, would you be willing to sign a deposition as to your account of Mr. Fischer's state of mind before the death of his wife?"

"If you like. Mr. Fischer is a good man. He did everything humanly possible to help his wife through her terrible ordeal."

"I hope you don't mind me asking you a personal question. How do you personally feel about assisted suicide?"

"I'm a religious person Mr. Scarpelli I couldn't or wouldn't do it to myself, or to anyone else. But then, no one knows what they would do if they were in the amount of pain and suffering that Mrs. Fischer was in. We had to increase the dose of her morphine on a daily basis. It could have been an accident."

She said it without me prompting her. I shut off the tape recorder. Nurse Tate admitted that, it could have been an accident. We had a few more minutes of conversation, mostly small talk, I paid the tab and thanked her for seeing me. I offered to drive her home but she said she would like to sit for a few more minutes to finish her tea. She looked sad when I left, I'm sure she was feeling very sorry for a man who had been put in Dr. Fischer's position.

When I got home my thoughts turned to TC, and all the people he claimed were murdered. *If what he told me was true this action went beyond being a war-crime, this was premeditated murder. I had to talk to someone. I needed professional advice. I should call Dr. Bass and tell him about the latest encounter.* I was in such deep thought that when the phone rang it startled me. It was Jessie. She was her usual cheerful self. "Hi, Frank. I just called to see how your week was going, so far? I'm going on a field trip to The Museum of The City of New York and I wondered if you would meet me there and help me keep an eye on the kids?"

"Are you tripping?"

She laughed. "Gotcha, I knew that would piss you off."

"Well played Jessie. I'm going to hang up now. I'm really not in the mood for this."

"What's the matter Frank?"

"Nothing you can fix so let me hang up."

"Frank, I'm coming over. What happened? Is it your job?"

"No, it's not my job. In fact, right now that's the only normal thing in my life. Please Jessie, don't be offended, because I'm going to hang up now."

Her last words were, "I'm coming over."

Forty-five minutes later, Jessie was knocking at my door. With a beer in my hand, I opened the door. "Do you want a beer?"

"You scared the shit out of me and all you can say is, you want a beer?"

"I asked you not to come here."

"I know, but I'm here anyway. You would do the same for me—at least I hope you would." I looked at her and laughed. I couldn't help it. She was wearing a jogging outfit that was two sizes too big and she hadn't bothered to put makeup on. She looked funny, but cute.

She took the beer and walked over to the couch. I started telling her about my sessions with Dr. Bass and the dream I had the other evening. I also confided in her about the gun in the closet and my grandfather's repeated assertion that he was from Naples, and not Sicily.

After I finished, she reminded me that I was assuming that TC was a real person. "What proof do you have that this massacre actually happened? You said it was just a dream"

"I know what I said, but don't forget about the hypnosis."

"That's not proof, Frank. You're assuming your dreams are real."

I reminded her that Dr. Bass seemed to agree with that assumption.

"God, Frank, you're an attorney, you know you need concrete proof. You should know the difference."

"Thanks for reminding me of my shortcomings, Jessie. As if I don't feel crappy enough."

"Well," she stated, "If you really want to know the truth, find out. Either go online or hire a private investigator."

"That's great advice. Don't you understand the implication of this? You're obviously not getting the full picture. What if it's true and what if my grandfather actually did those horrible things? What do I do, turn him in to the authorities? I can't do that. Sure, I care about the families of the victims, but that was 70 years ago. If this information got out it will destroy my entire family. And if I do nothing, the nightmares will never stop. I pride myself on being smart but for the life of me I don't understand how this can happen. How am I reliving someone else's life when we've never met?"

Jessie leaned over and put her arms around me and held me close. "Frank, you are the most just and fair-minded person I know. I also know that when the time comes, you will do the right thing."

As gentlemanly as possible, I said "Are you trying to coerce me into having sex with you?"

"You conceited bastard!"

I laughed so hard at the expression on her face that I could hardly catch my breath.

Jessie handed me her empty beer bottle. "I'll have another. Thank you."

Jessie stayed a couple of hours and I was really glad she showed up. It was good to get it off my chest. Before leaving she offered to go on line and research all the information I had received from TC. She also promised to get back to me with whatever she found, even, if she thought it would upset me. We also discussed hiring a private investigator, but Jessie was sure she could get most of the information she needed online. On her way out the door she kissed me on the cheek, then, she put her tongue in my mouth. I resisted the turn-on and gently pushed her out of my apartment, before I weakened to the temptation. Jessie plays on being a seductive tease and she's hard to resist. But, I have to get my shit together. And I don't want her to think our sexual relationship is more than, friends with benefits.

CHAPTER TWENTY

My grandfather arrives today and we'll be hanging out for a couple of days. Yesterday I went grocery shopping and I tried to remember all of pop's favorite foods. The first thing I bought was three bottles of Chianti. Pop is from the old-school, he never got used to fine wine. I figured we would eat our main meals out or, I would pick-up, take-out. The only thing I know how to cook is eggs.

I tried to figure out what I was going to do about John. I had no idea if his plan was to stay at my place overnight. It's a two-bedroom condo where the hell would he sleep? The only bed big enough for him was mine, and I'll be damned if he's putting me out of my own bed.

When I arrived home, Pop and John were watching the news. John was drinking a beer and pop was drinking Chianti, in a drinking glass, which is also how he drinks his coffee and tea. I said, "Hi," to John and shook his hand. Pop stood so he could give me a hug. I felt guilty and sorry that I ever started this mess with TC. I had no idea what this was going to do to our relationship. "I asked Pop how his day went and where he had gone? He seemed happy and excited when he told me he had gone to the Metropolitan Museum. But, he also confessed he had difficulty in walking around. So, after an hour or so John took him back to the apartment for a nap.

He said he told John he could leave if he had other things to do. But John said he wouldn't leave him until he was back in New Jersey— safe and sound.

At some point, I realized that John had not said a word since I walked in the door.

"Well John, I'm here now. It's okay for you to leave. I want to thank you for taking such good care of my grandfather."

"I'm not leaving." John finally said, in that deep voice of his.

"It's okay John, I can take over now. Come back tomorrow morning around eight."

Again, John said, "I'm not leaving. The boss said I should stay with Mr. Scarpelli, so I'm staying until you take your grandfather to Albert's house, on Saturday."

I knew by the tone of his voice there was no getting rid of him.

"Okay! What do you both want for dinner?"

Pop said, "Pasta. I want pasta."

"Is that okay with you, John?" He nodded.

"I know of a great Italian restaurant we can walk to, but first, I want to get out of my business clothes and into casuals."

The elevator ride from my apartment to the lobby was embarrassing. It's quite obvious I look Italian. It's also quite obvious the three of us look Italian. You would think 'no big deal.' But, at this time of night everyone in the building was coming home from work, or going somewhere, so, the elevator was more crowded than usual. Here I was with this big galute, who not only looked like a bodyguard, he stood like a bodyguard. John eyeballed everyone who came in and out of the elevator, and to make matters worse he stood in front of me, and pop, as if to protect us from anyone getting too close. Talk about profiling; I got some very strange looks. I'm sure most of the people thought we were either gangsters, or, we were in the witness protection program.

As soon as we entered the restaurant we were immediately, seated. One look at John and they didn't want any trouble. This was real good for my image. *I'm going to kill my uncle. Tomorrow night, we'll order take-out.*

Of course John wound up in my room. Pop had the guest room and me, I had the couch. With John around I didn't have the time to talk to my grandfather about his immigration papers or the people in his album. Although, it was such a long time ago, I wasn't sure he could recall the time-frame. Maybe it was for the best. He was not well and there was no point in upsetting him. In spite of my reservations I enjoyed my grandfather and John's company. After pop went to bed, John and I watched football, hockey, movies and we played poker. He beat me out of, two-hundred bucks. And if he didn't leave soon, I would be speaking exactly like him. It took me six years to get rid of my 'Jersey' accent.

By Friday, I was able to complete my portion of the Fischer case. Before leaving work I left it on Junior's desk to be reviewed and critiqued. Tomorrow, pop and John would be leaving for New Jersey and I, would be going to my psychiatrist. And I was not looking forward to another hypnotherapy session.

On Saturday, as we were reading to leave I hugged pop and told him how much I enjoyed having him stay with me. He had tears in his eyes and thanked me for having him, and kissed me on both cheeks. I offered John three hundred dollars for taking such good care of pop but he refused to take it. He told me the boss had already taken care of him. And, he liked being with the old guy. John also offered to drive pop to my parent's place so I wouldn't be late for my appointment. I thanked him and went to shake his hand, which he dismissed and gave me the Scarpelli bear-hug. John's a good guy, and he's starting to feel like family. I just wish he would ditch the hug.

We arranged for Pop to drive with me until we got to a diner in Clifton, New Jersey, to have breakfast. While driving and conversing I couldn't help but look at this old man and feel anguish and regret for exposing the Palermo, massacre. He was in such a good mood, smiling and making conversation. It was then that I decided to tell Dr. Bass that I was going to renege on any further hypnotherapy sessions.

On my way to the Dr.'s office I got a call from Jessie. She wanted to know the time I would be leaving the doctor's office. "Why, what's up?"

"I'll tell you when you get here. When your session is over, come to my place, we have to talk."

"What? Tell me now."

She hung up after she said, "It's all true. Later."

I was ten minutes late for my appointment. This time Dr. Bass was sitting in the reception room awaiting my arrival "Hi, Frank. I was beginning to think you weren't going to show."

"Sorry I'm late doc. To tell you the truth I was hesitant about coming in. I had decided I no longer wanted to participate in hypnotherapy."

"Frank, come in my office so we can discuss the progress you've already made."

I sat across from his desk, leaned in and asked, "What progress?"

"Hypnotherapy has opened some doors and it's has moved us closer to what your sub-conscious is holding back. Whether fact or fiction, that door has to be opened to find out why these nightmares frighten you, and why, they keep reoccurring. In other words something in your life is unresolved."

My response to his analysis was, "All I know is, I still have the nightmares and of late, I'm experiencing daytime anxiety."

"Think about it Frank. Isn't that why you came here? Wasn't it to get to the truth? And now that we're getting close to making headway into your subconscious your fears are starting to surface. Let's talk about what you're afraid of. First off, you thought you would die if you let the dream take you to the end. But now you know it's not death you're afraid of, it's the truth."

I became defensive. "Forgive me Dr. Bass, but what the hell are you talking about?"

"You tell me Frank. You're the one that's holding back a kind of hypothesis that you're afraid to share or confront. Isn't that right?"

I started to deny his accusation then realized that there was no point in lying. Dr. Bass was trying to help me and he was correct in his analysis of the situation. I then divulged the extent of my conversation with TC. "I asked TC what, he wanted me to do? He said, 'I was doing exactly what he wanted— to find the murderer so justice could be served. Only then would we both be at peace. I asked him why he picked me. He said, 'You have the connection and I've been waiting for you to grow up.' I questioned him on why we have to repeat the same sequence's over and over again? He said, 'it was to recreate the incident. Dr. Bass do you realize that I'm having a conversations with a man in my dream— who's supposedly is, dead. Do you now understand why it's freaking me out? Now murder is on the table. TC said that eight people were massacred in the Cathedral of Monreale. And, his last words were; 'find the owner of the gun and you'll find the murderer.'

Dr. Bass looked stunned. "Did you check to see if there was a massacre in the Cathedral of Monreale, in 1943?"

"No, I haven't had time. I've confided in a friend and she's doing the research for me."

"To tell you the truth Frank your situation is uncanny. I now see why you're hesitant in going through with this. You're afraid for your grandfather and the fallout from your family."

"Right, on Doc., my grandfather is in his late-eighties and he's ill. What do I do? Turn him into the authorities?"

"So, you have already convicted him because he lied about where he was born, and he has a German Luger in his possession?"

"Yes, to me the evidence is overwhelming."

"Why? Has he ever shown any sign of violence? Does he fly off the handle easily? Did he beat his children?"

"No to all your questions. He was so distraught when his wife died that he never remarried, I assume it was because he loved her. He raised his two children by himself and without any family support."

"Frank, does he meet the profile of a mass murderer?"

"No, but lately I haven't been sure of anything. TC is messing with my head. I only know that the evidence is leading up to him and it's tearing me apart."

"Let's play the 'devil's advocate.' Even if it's true you need to know or, you will never be free of your nightmares. Can you live with that?"

"But, what if it's true? What do I do? Turn in my own grandfather?"

"That is a choice only you can make. Think about the victim's families. Don't their families need closure?"

"I know! But what does all this, have to do with me? Ever since I was a kid TC has been tormenting me and I want to know why."

Dr. Bass walked over to me and put his arm around my shoulder. "Frank, those are the questions you're unwilling to find the answers to. One thing I do know, if this is not resolved the guilt will destroy you. You may have to confront your grandfather."

"I can't do that. He's an old man with a bad heart. And I won't only be taking him down, my whole family will go with him, including, my own career. My father and uncle are respected businessmen. If this gets out it could destroy their businesses. Tell me, will I feel any better knowing the truth? Because just dealing with what I know now, is killing me."

`"Frank, you're upset and understandably so. I'm just trying to encourage you not to jump to conclusions until you know all the facts. Dealing with 'what ifs,' is, harder than dealing with reality. I don't think we should go on with the hypnotherapy today. I suggest you check into TC's account of what happened in Italy to see if holds any validity. And don't forget to inform me of any changes in the sequences of your nightmares. I shouldn't have to tell an attorney, 'you're innocent until proven guilty.' I'm here for you Frank we will see this through, together."

As I drove to Jessie's place I thought about what Dr. Bass had said. 'You're innocent until proven guilty.' I, of all people should adhere to that principle, yet I'm allowing my nightmares and irrelevant evidence to cloud my objectiveness because, it's personal and I'm afraid of the implications. As soon as I pulled up to Jessie's house, I experienced that feeling of 'fight or flight.' I wanted to flee, but I didn't. I walked up to the door but before I could knock it opened and a somber Jessie invited me in. I got this sinking feeling in the pit of my stomach and I knew what she was about to say as she handed me printouts and said, "You better sit down Frank. It's all here in black and white. TC was right. There was a massacre in 1943 in a church named, Cathedral Monreale-in. Sicily.

"It seems the United States and England launched a campaign called *HUSKY* to try and take control of the Mediterranean Passage Way. By the time they got to Sicily the Germans were already there. I have a lot of documentation to give you. While online I obtained a list of the men and women who died in combat during WWII. A, Thomas Callahan from Philadelphia was listed as being killed during that *HUSKY* campaign. Frank, I hate telling you this, but your dreams are true. This is all so freaky, weird. What are you going to do? It's as if this guy has been haunting you."

I tried composing myself. "I don't know what I'm going to do. All I know is I have to prove pop's innocence."

"How are you going to prove that? It happened over 70 years ago."

I don't know how, but I will. Pop is not the kind of man that would do such a horrific thing. TC said the murderer is the person who owned the gun; we don't know if pop owned the gun or somehow came across this gun. We don't even know if that's the same gun that killed those innocent people. The German Lugar will have to be examined by a forensic expert to see if there are any fingerprints on it. But without the bullet, I still won't know if the shots came from that gun."

"Well, Frank we're either jumping to conclusions or you're grasping at straws. There is only one way you're going to get straight answers you're going to have to speak to your grandfather."

"I don't have to get any answers. I can drop this whole damn thing."

"You can't do that."

"Yes, I can. Who's going to stop me?"

Jessie stared at me with disgust in her eyes. "You can't do that. It was a horrific massacre eight people were murdered in cold blood and two innocent people were wounded. If you do nothing you will probably live to regret it. for the rest of your life."

I was starting to get pissed and lashed out at her. "I will live to regret it if, I do. Can't you understand he's my grandfather? You know him can you see him murdering eight people in cold blood?"

"Truthfully I can't, but let's face it Frank no-one really knows what anyone is capable of."

"Jessie, give me one good reason why this can't wait until he dies? He's a sick man. He can go at any time."

"Listen to yourself. Did it ever cross your mind that your grandfather may want to repent? He is Catholic. Or, maybe he knows who did this?"

"I know who did it, Jessie."

"You do? Who is it?"

"Mario Moretti killed those people."

"Well then Frank what's the problem? Let's look for Mario Moretti."

"Mario Moretti had to have changed his identity or the Office of War Crimes would have found him by now. If, he's found he will most likely be sent back to Italy to face criminal charges."

"It's not that easy to hide. We now have computers and access to all kinds of information, and don't forget DNA and fingerprints."

"Come on Jessie, do you really think that they will find fingerprints after 70 years? Countless people might have been holding that gun, including me."

"Frank, if you knew the name of the person who did this why didn't you tell me?"

"TC revealed the name of the murderer while I was under hypnosis."

"Frank, why don't we see if we can find him?"

"I wouldn't know where to start. Although, I'd rather use that approach before going to my grandfather for answers."

"Why can't you get some answers from TC?"

"TC just orders me around. I don't know why he just doesn't come clean and tell me the truth. Is my grandfather, Mario Moretti? Jessie, do you realize how bizarre this all sounds?"

Jessie came over to the couch and put her head on my shoulder. She asked in a soft and gentle voice, "Do you still want to go to lunch or do you want me to make you a something to eat?"

"If you don't mind I just want to go home and figure out what my next move should be. I also have to read over the documents you gave me. Right now I'm working on a case, so, as soon as time allows I'll do some investigating on my own."

I hugged Jessie before leaving and thanked her for all her help.

When I got home I was emotionally exhausted which meant I had to run and clear my head. I put on my running gear and headed for the park. I ran like I had never run before. After, I stopped at Nate's and picked up a couple of hotdogs and went home. Instead of trying to sort things out I decided not to think about it for the rest of the evening. I watched TV and downed four scotch and sodas and tried studying for my exam, but I couldn't concentrate. So, I went to bed after the eleven o'clock news and hoped that I wouldn't have to deal with TC. Thank the Lord I slept peacefully the entire evening

CHAPTER TWENTY-ONE

On my way to the office I stopped at Starbucks and picked up black coffee for me and a latte, for Darlene. When I entered her office she was sitting at her desk reading the open, cases. Not wanting to startle her I cleared my throat. As she looked up at me I reached out and handed her the latte. "Being its Monday, I thought you might need this."

She seemed to force a smile when she thanked me. "I certainly do. How did you know?"

I smiled. "I'm intuitive. I guess you didn't know that about me."

Noticing her uncharacteristic behavior, I asked, "Are you okay? Do you want to talk?"

"Sure, what do you want to talk about?"

"We could start with, what's troubling you."

"It's nothing Frank. I'm just out of sorts today."

"Okay, but if you change your mind you know where to find me."

Darlene forced a smile. "Thanks, for the offer and the latte."

On my desk was a pile of folders with a post-it-note stating: Frank, you have to review these briefs by tomorrow. The meeting will start at 10:30. Mark, Jr. will be in attendance.

thank you, Joan, for giving me fair warning that Mark would be at that meeting. I had just started to read the first case when Darlene walked in my office and closed the door.

She sat across from my desk and said, "I think I owe you an explanation."

"Not unless you want to. I didn't mean to pry."

"I broke-off my engagement to Bruce."

I tried not to sound too ecstatic. "Why? What happened?"

"I'm not sure Frank. It was a few things, little things."

She broke off her engagement for '*little things*?' It didn't compute. "Okay, like what?"

"He decided he wanted to get married sooner than we planned. He said he decided to do his residency in California and not in New York, as we had planned. He also wanted me to put my career on hold, so we could start a family."

"What? And give up your career? Boy, that's a hell of a lot of nerve."

She smiled. "That's exactly what I told him when I handed him his engagement ring."

"Have you thought this through Darlene? Are you sure you won't regret this in a couple of weeks or months?"

She looked somber but not upset. "No, I don't think so. I was starting to have reservations."

"Can you be more specific?"

"I don't know Frank, I guess I was questioning as to whether I was really in love with Bruce or if, I just loved him."

"Is there a difference?"

Darlene smiled. "You know what Frank, you think about it. I have to go back to work." As she opened the door to leave I asked. "Did I say something wrong?" There was no answer. *Women!*

As soon as I got home I changed into my jeans, made a very large ham sandwich, got a beer and went to my office to do some research on WWII, and the campaign called, HUSKY. Now that I knew that my dreams had some validity and that my shrink's not even sure as to why I was having dream sequences of an event that happened in 1943— I was going to investigate this phenomena, by myself.

First, I checked the State Department website and The Office of War Crimes. I then checked out the website for The Coalition for International

Justice and The International Criminal Tribunal, who, was still looking for 21 fugitives, although none were from WWII. I checked the WWII site and found the *HUSKY* campaign, but still, no information that pertained to the massacre at the Cathedral in Monreale. I wondered if the Freedom of Information Act also applied to the Pentagon. I was about to start my search when my cell rang. To my surprise it was Darlene.

"Frank, I'll come to the point I've been walking around for an hour and I'm worn out. Can I come up to your place? I don't want to go home. I just want some company."

"Sure, Darlene, you could stay the night if you want?"

"For heaven sakes Frank, grow up. And if your think this is more than what it is forget it."

"I'm sorry Darlene. That was a very bad joke and an insensitive remark. Do you want me to pick you up?"

"No. I'll catch a cab."

I gave Darlene my address and called down to Harvey, the doorman, to let her in when she arrived. I was excited at the prospect of seeing her so, I had to control my emotions and not hit on her. She made it clear she just needed someone to talk to. I knew how she felt. I would rather confide in a friend than my family. They may act like their supportive— they don't just listen, instead, they offer advice and then they get upset when you don't take it.

I don't think it took me more than six seconds to answer the doorbell. When I opened the door she looked like she had been crying. "Hi, come in and have a seat. Would you like a glass of wine or some sherry?"

"Wine would be nice, Frank. Thanks." She walked into the living room. "This is some place you have here. I had no idea you were wealthy?"

"I'm not. I'm leasing it from a friend. Unfortunately, it's temporary."

"If you can rent this on your salary I'm not getting paid nearly as much as you are. I hope I'm not intruding. It was nice of you to see me."

I was starting to feel sorry for her and I didn't know what I could say that would make her feel better, because I get so excited when I'm around her that I put my big foot in my mouth. "You're not disturbing me, Darlene. I enjoy the company. Can I get you something to eat? Do you want a ham sandwich? Do you want to talk?"

She laughed. "Thanks for the offer of the ham sandwich but, I'll pass. I'll finish my drink and let you get on with whatever you've been doing."

"You don't have to leave. I was just searching the web."

"What were you looking for? Maybe I can help."

"I doubt it!"

"You never know Frank. I'm pretty smart."

"I'm not surprised. I knew that from the moment I met you."

"Right, that's why you asked me if I was hired to be your secretary?"

"See, you're not only smart you also have a great memory. I knew you weren't hired to be my secretary. I was trying to make conversation."

"You know what, Frank?"

I leaned in just a little closer. She leaned in even closer to me and whispered, "You are so full of shit!"

The remark came at the exact moment that I'd taken a mouthful of beer. It was so unexpected that I started choking. I stood up to catch my breath. At the same time Darlene started slapping my back, I took another swig of beer and it stopped. I turned to face her. I looked into those beautiful brown eyes and thought. *She is going to hate me for this.* I put my arms around her and kissed her beautiful lips. Surprisingly, she responded and then pulled back.

"I'm sorry, Darlene, I couldn't help it. I'm very attracted of you."

"It's okay Frank. I wanted you to kiss me."

I held her in my arms and kissed her again. This time she didn't pull away. She responded. Suddenly a thought popped into my head and once again I opened my big mouth. "Is this real, or am I playing second fiddle ?"

"What?"

"Are you on the rebound?"

She laughed so hard she was doubling over.

"Okay, let me in on the joke because right now I'm feeling like a schmuck."

"Frank, you jerk, you're the reason for my breakup with Bruce."

"What did I do to break you guys up?"

"I was having reservations about marrying Bruce because of the way I was feeling about you. And to tell the truth I'm not sure what this feeling is. I'm not even sure if you feel the same about me. That's the real reason I came over." And then she started to cry. First she was laughing and then she was crying. I didn't know what to do. "Darlene, please don't cry. I haven't had a lot of experience with women and you're freaking me out. I do feel the same about you and I'm just as confused as to why you're consuming my every thought."

She stopped crying, walked into my arms and kissed me passionately. My body responded. Then she uttered those terrible words. "Frank, we have to take this slowly. I have no idea where this is going."

"What's your definition of slow?"

"We have to get to know each other on a personal level."

"What's to know Darlene? I know you, you know me and we both have this strong connection."

"I don't know anything about you Frank. And you don't know anything about me or my family. We don't have to delve into this now, it can be a gradual thing."

I'd rather start now. I know! How about we sit on the couch and make out. This way, you will get to know the real me."

"I don't think so, that will definitely lead to something I am not ready for. Instead, let me help you find what your researching."

"Okay, but first I have to fill you in on the details. I have a friend who has a relative that was murdered in Palermo, Sicily. He knows the name of the person that killed his cousin, but he doesn't know where to find him. He asked me to help him out. He's a good friend so, this is pro-bono."

"Frank, this sounds like something the authorities should be investigating."

"Except that, this is a cold-case. It happened in 1943."

"That was during World War II."

"Do you see my dilemma?"

"Was he an Italian soldier?"

"No. He was an underground dissident, at least that's what every-one thought. In reality, he was a German spy. He was known to have killed five American soldiers, three resistance fighters, and wounded two other patriots. One, was a priest."

"Who's your friend?"

"He's a guy from the neighborhood."

"I may be able to help."

"I don't know Darlene. I've already checked the State Department website- the Office of War Crimes, the Coalition for International Justice and the International Criminal Tribunal. I was thinking of checking the Pentagon to see if I could find that person's name."

"Having his name is a plus. What's his name?"

"His name is, Mario Moretti."

Darlene repeated the name. "Mario Moretti."

"Do you have any ideas?"

"Yes, I'll just ask my father to investigate."

"Who's your daddy?"

She gave half of a smile. "Is that supposed to be funny?"

"From the look on your face, I would say, no."

She started laughing. "Frank, you're a nut-job. But to answer to your question is— my 'Daddy' is Matthew Walker Banks. I'm sure you've heard of him."

"You're four star General Bank's daughter?"

"Yes, I am the only child of, Matthew Banks. He might be able to find this under the Freedom of Information Act. Even though Mario Moretti was an Italian civilian, he would still be considered a Nazi war criminal. Frank, did you check to see if he moved to the United States? Look under Ellis Island to see if he's listed."

"Good idea, but I would think if he's a war-criminal he would have changed his name."

She smiled. "I'm glad I came here. My problem seems infinitesimal compared to the real problems in the world. You helped me put things in perspective. Thank you! You know, I'm starting to get hungry. I think I'll take that ham sandwich now. Hold the mayo, just mustard. And I take my coffee black."

"You see, Darlene. We do have something in common. That's exactly the way I take my ham and coffee."

I was in a great mood as I got ready for bed. Before Darlene left we checked the listing of immigrants coming into the country from 1943 to 1950, he wasn't listed. It's quite obvious that a criminal would have changed his name and used forged documents in order to get a passport. I didn't doubt that someone as devious as Mario Moretti would have had any problem in obtaining anything he needed, to enter the United States or, Canada. Darlene was going to see if she could find Canada's immigration laws during that timeframe.

I hated to see her leave. I suggested she stay the night, but she felt we didn't know each other well enough. I hope her wanting to get to know each other better, won't take too long. There is something about Darlene's scent. Not sure if it's her perfume or I'm experiencing the effect of pheromones. I wondered, if I should come clean as to why I was looking for Mario? On second thought, I'd have to know her a lot better before I could trust her like I did Jessie. Oh boy! Come to think about it what about Jessie? I can't get into all this now. I need to sleep. I have work, tomorrow.

When I entered my office noticeable on my desk was a Starbucks coffee with a post it note affixed to the cup. It read, *Thanks for last night*.

I called her office. "Thanks for the coffee and thank-you for helping me with my investigation. Although it was great seeing you, it was not as eventful as I would have liked."

She started laughing. "You do realize you will have to watch what you say in the office. It could be misconstrued as sexual harassment."

Before hanging up I laughed. "Come on now. Did I say anything about sex? You're the one with the dirty mind."

I still had a few hours before our staff meeting which gave me time to review the cases and my notes. I was so engrossed in my work that I hadn't noticed that Mark had entered my office. He said, "I thought I would find you hard at work and not at the water cooler. That is my feeble attempt at a joke. How are you, Frank?"

"I'm good, Mark. Did you get my notes and testimonials on the Fischer case?"

"Yes, that's why I'm here. I'm going to go with your recommendation for the insanity plea. Annabelle is coming to our office with her Father, and Dr. Morris Baker. He's the founder of the Baker Clinic, in Upstate New York. If they can get Dr. Fischer to go along with the plea, I'll setup an appointment to meet with the DA to see if we can do some plea-bargaining. I would like you to attend both meetings. How is your schedule?"

"I'm open and I'll be glad to attend. Thank you for the opportunity."

"You earned it Frank. That was good work. You convinced me that Mr. Fischer was out of his mind. Now, let's see if you can convince District Attorney, Michael Bonito. I'll have Millie give you a call when they arrive."

I didn't see that coming and I wasn't sure I was prepared for a face to face meeting with the DA. I heard he was a hard-ass.

When Mille summoned me to the Conference Room, Annabelle King, Dr. Fischer and Dr. Baker had arrived. Annabelle stated that she contacted Dr. Baker after hearing that he has had great-success in treating addictions, mental disorders, and, he was considered an expert in diagnosing and treating the mentally ill. Dr. Baker stated that although he read about the case in the newspaper, he had never met Dr. Fischer until last week. He then elaborated. "I agreed to see Dr. Fischer on the stipulation that Annabelle would allow me and my associate, Dr. Evan Smith, preform the diagnostic, mental and physical examination at the clinic and base our evaluation on the results."

Dr. Baker asserted that Dr. Fisher stayed at the clinic for three-full- days. Within that time, he and Dr. Evan Smith gave him a complete physical by using the usual standard testing to evaluate his competency, sanity and the degree to which he was cognizant at the time of the crime against him. Therefore, Dr. Smith and I both agree and could say for certainty that Dr. Fischer could not have been in his right mind when he gave his wife the lethal overdose of morphine or, when he was interrogated and confessed to killing her." He pulled a file out of his briefcase that were the test results and stated, "If it goes to trial Dr. Smith and I would be willing to testify on Dr. Fischer's behalf." Dr. Baker also presented Mark with a copy of his testimonial that alluded to his findings for the District Attorney.

Mark thanked Dr. Baker. "I will or my associate Frank Scarpelli will contact you should it go to trial. But because of your analysis we will try to get the DA's office to drop the charges of manslaughter. If he does I'm quite sure he would want some kind of assurance the Dr. Fischer was being treated for his illness and, that he would be confined to a clinic or institution until he was well. If Annabelle is in compliance I'm sure you would agree that Dr. Fischer would do well to enter you facility, for rehabilitation."

During this entire meeting Dr. Fischer sat quietly, never saying a word. It was obvious to everyone in that room that his world ceased to exist when his wife died— and he didn't really care what happened to him.

Annabelle stated. "I will certainly be in compliance if, the DA will go along with Dr. Baker's and Dr. Smith's analysis. I also feel my father would best be served at the Baker Clinic."

Before leaving for to the DA's office, Mark wanted to be reassured that Dr. Fischer would go along with the Insanity plea. Dr. Fischer did not consent nor did he reply. Realizing that her father was ignoring the proceedings she leaned in to face him and in a very soft voice she said, "Dad, you have to agree to the plea. Do you understand what's at stake here?" As a yes, he nodded.

"Okay, he agreed." Mark declared. Let's get going. We have to be in Michael's office in twenty minutes." Mark called Millie and asked her to have the chauffeur bring his car around to the front of the building. We had no time to lose.

When we arrived we were escorted into Michael Bonito's office. Introductions were in order. It was the first time I had met Michael Bonito and I was surprised by his appearance. He looked to be in his early forties balding, short, portly and casually dressed-actually a little sloppy. No tie, and he had a couple of stains on his shirt. We went over all the statements of the people we interviewed as well as the evaluation of Dr. Fischer's competency at the time of his wife's death and at the time he signed the confession. Michael was very thorough and looked over all the information we brought to the table. He said, "Okay, I'll plea it down to second or third degree manslaughter-three to seven years. With good behavior, he'll be out in a couple of years."

Mark stated, "That's unacceptable. For God-sakes Michael, Dr. Fischer is in his eighties he's ill and he could not function in that environment."

Then I decided to put in my two cents worth. "What have you got here Michael? If we take this to court you'll lose. The jury will see a distinguished, distraught physician and when we bring in the experts who will testify on his behalf, how do you think the jury will side? Is it worth the cost of a trial—plus, the publicity? The DA's office is going after an eighty year old respected cardiologist, without a blemish on his record, who was so distraught over his wife's suffering that he started taking amphetamines so he could stay awake all night, to care of her. Which in part brought on his psychosis. Here, read the nurse's statement again. 'She was in so much pain they had to increase the dose of morphine on a daily basis. It was an accident. What about Dr. Baker's evaluation? Do you really want to go to court with all we have?"

Mark asked Michael, "Why wasn't he tested for drugs when they picked him up? The detectives had to see he was incoherent. And why didn't they allow him to call his attorney before booking him?"

Michael stated, the officer in charge said, he was advised of his right he waived his right to an attorney."

Mark replied, "Come on Michael. In the condition he was in he would have admitted to anything. Look at the copy of his confession."

Michael looked at the confession and then at Dr. Fischer and his daughter. "Okay! But there will be conditions. And if they're not met there will be consequences and a trial date set. Mr. Fischer will be placed on two-year's probation—that will start on the day of his release from the clinic. But, before I release him into his daughter's custody I want a reassurance that he will leave here and go straight to the clinic where he will be treated for substance related mental illness. And that he will reside there until, he is considered cured by the attending physician. Upon his release you are to notify my office to start the probation. Is that clear to everyone here?"

We all shook our heads, except Dr. Fischer. Annabelle smiled at the DA and said, "Bless you!"

Not wanting to sound like a pushover the DA cleared his throat and said, "Thanks, but to tell you the truth I might have lost this one. This way I save the city of New York a lot of money on a trial."

After we left the DA's office Annabelle thanked us and told us how wonderful she thought we both were. And then she started to cry. Dr. Fisher finally broke his silence. "Don't cry my darling. Don't cry."

Back at the office, Mark admitted he was very pleased with the way things worked out. "Good work, Frank. You did a great job. I'm glad we went with your recommendations. You did all the footwork and you deserve the credit. I like your style. You keep quiet, you listen and then you spring into action. You're going to make a hell of a lawyer." I thanked him and told him I was just following his lead. And, I was impressed at how he allowed me to interject my views with the DA. Mark hit him from one end and me the other and this time it worked out.

During yesterday's meeting, Mark told everyone about the case we were working on. The minute I got back from the DA's office, Norman, Bruce, Darlene and Joan came into my office to ask how it went. I told them we won. They all shook my hand and congratulated me. My secretary leaned over and kissed me on the cheek and whispered, "I knew you could do it."

CHAPTER TWENTY-TWO

When I checked my cellphone there were several emails and a few voice messages. Dr. Bass called to say he opened a time-slot for me on Saturday, at 10:00, am, by rescheduling another patient. Jessie called to ask if I was up for doing something on Saturday night, she wanted to come into the city and perhaps stay overnight at my place. *Jessie-how am I going to tell her I'm dating Darlene?* I had already made plans with Darlene to go out to dinner on Saturday night. I was taking her to the, *Terrace in the Sky a restaurant that is said to be one of the most romantic restaurants in the city.*

Although I considered telling my family about my feelings for Darlene, I thought better of it. My family will go postal and ask me a million questions. Until I know if Darlene's feeling the love, I thought it best to wait. After all, she was in a long-time relationship and it is too soon for her to make any decisions about the future. Like she said, 'We have to take it slow.' As far as I was concerned I would just as soon take it to the max. I also have to stop thinking about Darlene and take care of business like remembering to call my Uncle Frank to see if he could meet me at my apartment on Sunday, morning. It's time I leveled with him. I may be taking a risk he's going to be pissed, but I need his input. And once again I'll have to call my parents and cancel Sunday. That should go over well.

First, I called Uncle Frank on his cell phone. He said he would come if it were important because he couldn't imagine what could be so damn important that he had to drive all the way into the city, on a Sunday. Still, he agreed. He also said that pop was happy to have spent time with me although, he didn't need John to baby sit him. He could take care of himself.

"How did you get him to go along with John watching over him in the first place?"

"I told him if John had nothing to do while I was in Las Vegas he wouldn't get paid. He bought it. He said he didn't want John to lose his wages. What time do you want me there on Sunday?"

"How about ten o'clock in the morning?"

"Good, that will give me time to have Sunday dinner with the family."

Coward that I am, called my father on his cell phone, "Hey dad, I won't be able to come for dinner on Sunday."

"Why tell me Frankie, call your mother. You know she's going to throw a fit."

"Yes I do, that's why I called you. You see I met this girl,"

"Say no more that ought to keep her happy. You finally have a date."

Sarcastically, I remarked, "Thanks a lot dad."

"I'm sorry Frankie, but your mother and I were wondering if you were queer."

"What?" I started to laugh.

"Why are you laughing? You're not, are you?"

"Dad, do you know how absurd that statement is?"

"It's only natural we think that, you're almost 25 and you're not even married?"

"I'm sorry dad but it's funny that you would presume I was gay because I'm still single at the ripe old age of 25. Besides the term is gay not queer and I'm not. Tell me dad, what if I was? Would you love me any less?" There was a pause. "Dad, did you hear me?"

"I heard you. No, Son, I wouldn't love you any less. I couldn't."

"I love you too, dad."

I called Jessie and told her I was busy on Saturday but I was free on Sunday.

"Sunday is good. How do you feel about helping me shop for some sexy clothes?"

"Not my usual thing to do but I could use some new stuff myself. We could have lunch at Noodles, but don't get here before, 1:00."

"Frank, if, it's okay with you, I'll park my car in your garage and meet you at the front desk."

"Cool. See you Sunday."

I had a full weekend coming up and no time to think. This was exactly what I needed.

Although, I was concerned, about my uncle's reaction to me meddling into, my grandfather's affairs and I would have to come clean about my reoccurring nightmares after lying, that I had outgrown them. I mentally rehearsed. *The nightmares were getting worse and they're causing me a great deal of stress and anxiety. My Psychiatrist, Dr. Bass, had determined that there was only one way it was going to stop— I had to face what was in my subconscious and deal with it.*

Let's face it I couldn't ask my father for help he gets too emotional, especially when it comes to pop. Uncle Frank is cool and introspective, he's more of a thinker than a hot head. The more I thought about it the more I realized I shouldn't have told Darlene about Mario Moretti. I appreciated her offer to help me find Mario but, she doesn't know the true story and I'm not sure I wanted her to.

I thought about pop's immigration papers and passport which appeared to be legitimate: Angelo Salvador Scarpelli, Palermo, Sicily. Date of birth: August 27, 1925. Height, five- foot nine, weight, l65 pounds. Then again, how would I know if he had changed his name for fear of criminal charges? How would anyone know? The uncertainty remains, is our last name Scarpelli or, is it, Moretti?

Luckily my professional life was on track and I knew I had made the right career decision. I find that working on a case or just discussing a case with my associate's energizes me. It's a lot like working on a puzzle. You know all the pieces have to fit, but finding them takes time and knowhow. I was looking forward to the weekend in more ways than one— it would no doubt prove to be full of apprehension and excitement. This was my first real date with Darlene and I hoped

I wouldn't blow it. I think I finally got what Darlene was trying to say about her relationship with Bruce. She loved him but, she was not in love with him. I love Jessie but I'm not in love with her. I don't feel the same intensity and excitement that I feel when I'm with Darlene. I hope Jessie make too much of our reconnecting and realizes that we're just friends. Nowadays, it's not considered unethical to have sex with a friend as long as you have an understanding.

Colleagues, Bruce and Norman invited me to go with them for a couple of drinks I took a rain-check and decided to go home. I decided to veg-out and have a couple of scotch and sodas and maybe watch a basketball game or, a couple of movies. I also decided not to go to the closet to re-examine pop's stuff. I didn't want to take the chance of triggering a TC episode. And I certainly wasn't looking forward to tomorrow's hypnotherapy session. Although, Dr. Bass assured me he would stop it if, I went ballistic.

I awoke the next morning to a windy, cold, rainy morning. It surprised me that I felt calm and in control. I wasn't the least bit nervous or apprehensive about my hypnotherapy session.

I was also aware that what TC might tell me, could be the worst thing that has ever happened to our family. But if pop did this we should all have a say on how to handle the situation. Like it or not, the fallout will affect the whole family. I also had to remember to downplay this whole thing about my grandfather, with Jessie. I never should have confided in her.

There was little traffic on the way to the doctor's office so I had time to stop at the diner to have breakfast. I decided to go to Uncle Frank's place. Vito noticed me and came over. "Yo Frankie, what's up? What are doing here so early on a Saturday morning?"

"Hi Vito, I stopped in for breakfast I have an appointment in Montclair."

"You're a lawyer, aren't you kid?"

"Yes, but un-officially. It won't be official until I pass the Bar Exam"

"Your Uncle Frank talks about you all the time."

"He does?"

"Yeah, he's a great family man. Do you have any idea how many people that man has helped from the neighborhood?"

"No, he doesn't talk to me about his work or his relationships."

"That's smart thinking because sometimes, it's better not to know."

I asked why? "Why shouldn't I know?"

Vito smiled when he said, "Frank always kids around and says, "What you don't know, you can't testify too."

"Why does he say that? Is he doing anything illegal?"

"Calm down, kid, I've got a big mouth. I just hear rumors I don't pay attention and you shouldn't either."

"Only after you tell me what you meant, by that remark?"

"It's like this: your Uncle is a very successful business man and highly respected, especially in New York and Jersey. When you're in business and you're rich you can make enemies. That's all I'm saying. Some people start rumors about successful people, and sometimes they have to go to court to clear their name. That's all I'm saying. I need to get back to work, let me know what you want for breakfast and I'll get it for you."

"I already know what I want Vito. I'd like a Taylor ham and cheese sandwich on a hard roll, tomato juice and black coffee."

"You got it, kid. And Frankie, don't tell your uncle we had this conversation."

"Not to worry Vito."

I was just starting to learn that some of my family members are not as kosher as I thought they were. Maybe, Uncle Frank is right? Maybe, it was better not to know. I imagine every family has some skeletons in their closet.

I walked into Dr. Bass's office hoping that this would be my last visit. I also knew it would depend on how well today's session went. After waiting for only five minutes Dr. Bass came out to greet me. We shook hands and he asked, "What's up Frank? You sounded like this visit was urgent."

"It is to me Doc. I appreciate you seeing me on such short notice."

As he opened the door to his office I went straight for the couch.

"I assume you're ready to resume the hypnotherapy."

"Yes, I'm ready. I want to get this over with. Is it possible for you to direct me to the church at the time of the shooting?"

"I can, but only if you're receptive. Remember what I told you about free will? You have been avoiding this scene for most of your life."

"True, but you said I would know when I was ready. I'm ready."

I lay there listening to Dr. Bass's voice and then I heard the command. "Frank, go straight to the Cathedral of Morale. Are you in the church, Frank?"

"Yes, I'm in a church that looks exactly like the one in my dream, it has same stained glass windows and a large mosaic icon, of Jesus Christ on the ceiling."

"Is TC with you?"

"Yes. That jerk is smiling at me."

"Is there anyone else in the church besides you and TC?"

"There are several people here. To the side of me is a Priest. He's lighting the candles that are on the altar. And, he's speaking in Italian."

"What is TC doing?"

"He's standing next to a woman and several men."

"Are the Americans wearing their uniforms?"

"No. They're dressed in dated, civilian clothes."

"What are they doing?"

"They're staring at the front doors of the church."

"Do they have their guns with them?"

"Yes, everyone is carrying a firearm."

"Frank, are you carrying a gun?"

"No, I'm not carrying a gun."

Are they all Americans?"

"No. TC and four other men are speaking English, and they're weapons are in a side-holster. The other people here are speaking in Italian. TC is yelling at a guy named Mario."

"Mario, where the fuck are your men with the information you guaranteed us? You know damn well that we're running out of time. I knew you couldn't be trusted."

Mario said, "Don't worry they'll be here."

Mario is walking over to the front doors of the church. Mario is now opening the door to the sanctuary and a man is entering. In his hand is a machinegun. The patriots know him and they're shouting and waving their fists at him, and Mario. Oh my God, that guy is raising his machinegun and he's pointing it at the group of patriots, who are standing next to the Priest."

"Frank, how do you know what Mario is saying?"

"Mario speaks English."

"What's going on now, Frank?"

"TC is talking to his superior, 'I don't like this Captain, let's get the fuck out of here. Stand away from the doors Mario.'"

Mario is now pointing his gun at TC. Jesus, it's a German Lugar. Mario is smiling, the bastard is smiling. Jesus, he shot TC and the woman standing next to him."

"What's happening now?"

"Mario gave the order to the guy with the machinegun to shoot everyone in the room. Everyone is panicking as they're running towards a side door. Oh, my God, bullets are flying everywhere. Everyone is down, and there is blood everywhere. This is horrifying, that fucking bastard. This is a massacre and there is nothing I can do to stop it."

"Frank, are you alright?"

"I can't breathe."

"Frank, I'm going to wake you up."

"No. I'm trying to compose myself. I have to see Mario's face. Wait, there is someone banging on the front doors and they're shouting in Italian, 'Let me in, open the door.' Mario looks scared. I can't believe it— he just shot the man holding the machine gun. He's now running towards the side door. No, he's coming back into the church. He looks trapped. I hear gunfire. Someone is coming from that side door. It must be a stairwell. It's a young-man and his shoulder is bleeding. He starts yelling and waving his gun at Mario. Mario is now running to the front door of the church and he's unlocking it. As he opens the door the priest yells, "You are the devil himself." Mario stares at the priest and shoots him. That bastard is getting away and there is nothing I can do."

"Tell me what you're seeing right now, Frank?"

"Right now it's quiet. I'm the only one standing in the middle of the church. As I look around there is blood and bodies everywhere. I can't breathe. I'm dying."

"Frank, when I count to five, you will wake up: One, two, three, four and five."

"I can't breathe, Dr. Bass. I'm going to die."

Dr. Bass ran over to his desk drawer and handed me a paper bag and a pill. "You're just hyperventilating, breathe into this bag and take the sedative."

"No thanks, Doc. I have to drive home"

"It's just a mild sedative, it won't impair you driving." I took the sedative hoping it would help me get the vision of that massacre off my mind.

"I suggest you lie down and wait until the medication takes effect. You've had a very bad experience. Did you see Mario's face?"

"Yes, but I didn't recognize him. With the exception of the priest, they were young adults. Without seeing a photograph from that era I'd never be able to recognize them. By now, they're old men."

"Frank, do you understand Italian?" "Somewhat. I picked it up from my grandparents."

Dr. Bass suggested I go home and look at my grandfather's old pictures to see if I could recognize anyone from my hypnotic state. "I could, Dr. Bass, but I don't know who the people in the pictures are?"

"Ask him Frank. Ask your grandfather."

"Dr. Bass I want you to tell me the truth, what's wrong with me?"

He hesitated at first and then tried to explain. "I have to be honest with you. I've never had a patient who has had this kind of experience before. But, I have heard of it and our profession hates to admit it exists. You're experiencing what is called a Psychic Phenomenon. It's something that can't be explained."

"Does this mean I'm psychic?"

"No, more likely you've experienced a phenomenon. I can't say for certain. In fact I can't really believe it myself."

"Dr. Bass, please spit it out. I have to know what I'm dealing with."

"It appears that you're being haunted by a WWII, American, soldier. Another explanation would be you've been communicating with the dead. For some reason you were chosen to know about a terrible event that took place 71 years ago. Why? I don't know. It may be to expose the murderer. What did TC tell you? 'You were handed the gauntlet'? Do you believe in God, Frank?"

"Yes, I do. What I don't know is why I'm being punished for something I didn't do."

"There is one thing that puzzles me your experience in the church is somewhat different than your dreams."

"It was, there was no fire and I can't explain why I feel trapped in a church that's in flames during my nightmares. When I was hypnotized there was a massacre but no inferno."

"This is just speculation on my part. The crime took place in a house of worship, could TC have conjured up the fire as a symbolism for hell, or, to frighten you into investigating the event. For some reason he chose you as a vehicle to expose the person who massacred how many people?"

"Ten people were shot, two survived."

Dr. Bass went on. 'Vengeance is mine saith the Lord.' That's a quote taken from the Christian Bible."

I'm still not sure I buy it and the question still remains, why did TC pick me?"

"I don't have an answer to that question. But I think you will know why, once you know the truth about what really happened in the Cathedral of Monreale, in, 1943."

Dr. Bass asked if I would give him permission to document my case if, he promised not to use my real name. "I'm sorry, Doc. I can't let you release my records until I know to what degree my grandfather is implicated."

"You're right, of course. What if he is Mario? What are you going to do?"

"I don't know. If this gets out it could not only destroy the integrity of my family in the community, but our careers as well. This decision will have to be decided by the whole family. What happened in that church was horrific and believe me, I should know. It's what nightmares are made of. I only hope you're right, that if Mario is exposed my torment will also be over. Do you know how successful 'being regressed' while under hypnosis is? Like, before they were born?"

"Yes, I have read text on that subject. You're referring to reincarnation. It's not a science and highly suspect. Why Frank? Do you think you were reincarnated?"

"Lately, it has occurred to me."

"Are you thinking you're TC?"

"I'm not sure, but I was wondering about that possibility."

"No, that doesn't seem to be the case and frankly I don't believe in reincarnation. While under hypnosis you confronted him. He said you were an observer. In all of your meetings with TC you responded as if you were a witness. You use words like, 'they,' or 'TC said.' You never said 'I'. Plus, you don't know locations or the names of the people involved. If you were TC, you would know the names of the people and the places. In other words you would be TC, telling your story and not observing it. Can you imagine how bizarre, this is to me. Psychiatry is a science and I believe in science, not voodoo. And, I can't for the life of me give you a scientific explanation. But if you ask me for my analysis it would be that this has something to do with your grandfather. Your grandfather is very close to you. I think that after you were born and during your childhood you intuitively picked up on his fears or maybe, his regrets. That's conjecture on my part and not a scientific, explanation."

"You could be right. When I think about it some, but not all of my nightmares had occurred after, I had been in the presence my grandfather. Before seeking your help I never made that connection."

"Well, Frank it certainly seems we're on the right track. I'm just sorry I couldn't have been of more help."

"Are you kidding? You gave me the courage to follow through. I thought I was going meshuga."

Dr. Bass laughed. "Tell me Frank how does a nice Italian boy like you know the word meshuga?"

"It helps if you have a Jewish Aunt."

We shook hands before I left his office and with the knowledge that he was as bewildered as I was. I went home feeling like I had been in a war and in essence I was. Thankfully, I was going home to some peace and quiet, until it was time to pick Darlene up. I couldn't wait to see her. I needed a diversion.

Darlene smiled when she greeted me at the door. I got that stupid schoolboy feeling like some Goddess just recognized my existence. She looked that great. I wasn't surprised when I entered her apartment. The furniture was comprised of period pieces, maybe antiques, with a big striped gold and white overstuffed couch and loveseat. If I were a connoisseur of fine quality furniture I, would say her place was what you would call, elegant. "I like what you did with the place. Did you do the decorating or, did you hire someone?"

She laughed. "On, my salary, I think not. A lot of these pieces are family hand-me-downs."

On the way to the restaurant Darlene did most of the talking which was okay with me. With all the crap on my mind I wasn't in the mood for small talk. Besides, I enjoyed listening to her. We talked about the interesting cases our firm was involved in. And, what most people are talking about these days, the scope of the violence in our country. When, we arrived at the Terrace in the Sky it was packed. I made reservations for the Terrace Room. It was smaller than the other rooms and I thought it would be more romantic. While drinking our wine Darlene remarked, "I forgot to tell you, my dad did some checking for you. He found some information on Mario Moretti."

"He did what?"

She repeated, "You know, the information on Mario Moretti? I have the report in my purse."

When Darlene handed me the printout of the report I tried acting nonchalant. "That's great. Thank your father for me."

I thought to myself, *I spent the good part of my morning with Mario Moretti. Just enough time to hate his guts.* I took the folded piece of paper and put it inside my jacket pocket, acted cool and smiled. Although, I was anxious to see what was in the report I wasn't going to let Mario or TC ruin my evening. They had already ruined my day.

After dinner, we went to the Marriott to listen to some music. We had a couple of drinks and danced. I warned Darlene that I wasn't Fred Astaire. Darlene was such a lady she never said a word when the music was rock-n-roll and I looked like a nerd while try-ing to find a beat. We danced until two, pm. The last song of the evening was an oldie called, At Last. I felt like they were playing it for me. I was having a great time. Darlene and I have the same caustic sense of humor and we laughed a lot. This lady was far from boring.

When I brought her home I kissed her goodnight outside her door. I asked her if I could come in, she said no. "Why, not Darlene? Unless you're going to tell me your husband is due home at any moment."

Darlene laughed. "I told you, I want to take it slow and why put temptation in the way of our good sense?"

"Well, at least it's nice to know you find the possibility of us making love tempting. Okay, you're running the show, for now" She arched her eyebrow with that remark, as I knew she would. I kissed her and she kissed me back. I whispered in her ear, "Do you want me to walk out of here looking like this?" I looked down so she would notice the bulge in my pants. At first she didn't get it, and looked down. She laughed and slapped me on my arm. "Yes, Frank, as tempting as that is, the answer is still no." "You're a heartless woman, Darlene Banks."

She kissed me again and this time she French kissed me and whispered, "I know darling, but I'm worth waiting for."

Leaving her was difficult. It wasn't just the sex. I wanted to spend the night holding her.

The moment I got home I opened the report.
The Office of War Crimes
Washington, DC,
At large is Mario Moretti— Publicly indicted for WWII War Crimes in Sicily Italy on, July 09, 1943 Mario Moretti, was working as a spy for the German Army and betrayed his partisan comrades and the American Military, by murdering five American soldiers, three, resistance fighters and wounded two Italian patriots in, the Cathedral of Monreale. Sicily.

The United States and the Italian Governments have issued an indictment for this individual for Crimes against Humanity. These murders were committed without provocation. The United States government calls on all citizens to help apprehend Mario Moretti and bring him to justice for the murder of: Captain Harvey Conroy, Sergeant Thomas Callahan, Private Jerry Stein, Private Ralph Watson and Private Leon Jones. If you have any information that would lead to the capture of Mario Moretti, call, The U.S. Department of State: 111-111-1111, or your local Law Enforcement office. The Italian Government is expected to seek extradition.

Exceed with caution. Mario Moretti was born in 1924, in Palermo, Italy and he is believed to be living in the United States, or Canada. There is a two- hundred- thousand dollar reward for information leading to his arrest.

There was a lot of military and tribunal documentation. Noted were pictures of the American Soldiers that were familiar to me. Unfortunately, there were no photographs of the resistance fighters.

The photographs of Mario, was that of a young adult. How would anyone, be able to recognize him as he looks today? Then again, his picture could be age-enhanced by photo enhanced software. How strange is the fact that I witnessed the massacre from my hypnotherapy session? I saw it as if, it was happening now. If anyone told me they had dreams or visions of a murder that took place over, 70 years ago I would have thought they were twisted. I have no connection to TC. We're not even related. He's Irish. I'm Italian. He's from Philly. I'm from New Jersey. So, why has TC dominated my life? Before going to bed I downed a couple of Scotch and soda's.

CHAPTER TWENTY-THREE

My uncle was due to come over at any moment and I was wasted from last night's binge. When I heard the rapping at my front door I knew it had to be him, not because he was on time, it was because he always used a signal; rap, rap, rap pause rap, rap. He'd been doing that for as long as I can remember. When I opened the door he stretched out his arms and gave me the ole bear hug.

When he entered the apartment he said, "It's good the way you keep this place. It's clean. I like that."

"I made coffee, Uncle Frank, and I picked up some Danish."

"Just coffee I'm trying to cut down on the sugar." He patted his stomach. "It's all going here."

"Are you kidding? You look hot for a man of your age."

"A man of my age?" I'm not sure if it's a compliment or an insult."

"I can assure you it's a compliment."

"What's up, Frankie? You look like shit this morning. Are you in any trouble? You've got me worried."

"I'm not in trouble, but I have a problem that I need to talk to you about."

"What can I do for you kid?"

"This is hard to say because you're going to be pissed at me. But regardless of the consequence, I have to do this."

"Do what?" I started to hem and haw. To tell the truth, I was a little afraid of his reaction, the Scarpelli boys are very protective of their father.

"Get to it, kid. I don't have all day."

I started with, "Do you remember that when I was a kid I had repeated nightmares?"

"Sure, I remember but you said they went away."

"They didn't go away Uncle Frank. I told everyone they did because I didn't want to see a psychiatrist. Since graduation the nightmares are appearing more often and more difficult to deal with. Obviously, it's starting to affect my life and my job. I can't be up all night fearing that if I sleep the night-terrors will come. So, I went to see a psychiatrist in, New Jersey."

"What's the shrink's name?"

"His name is Dr. James Bass. He was a referral from a friend. I didn't want to see anyone from New York. Although, it's a big city, it's too close to where I work."

"What did the doctor say?"

"He said there was something in my subconscious that I couldn't deal with."

"What things, Frankie? That's a load of crap. You have a good family and great parents."

"It's not like that Uncle Frank. It has nothing to do with my parents or my childhood."

"Then what the hell is the problem?"

"I know this is going to sound weird. I keep dreaming about a place in Sicily. The year, is, 1943. And I'm in the middle of, WWII and I witness a massacre being committed in a Cathedral called, Santa Maria, La Nuova, in Monreale, also called, Cathedral Monreale."

"I don't understand. What does any of this have to do with you? You could be dreaming this whole thing up."

"That's exactly what I thought until I went through hypnotherapy. It seemed so real that I checked it out. It seems the United States and Great Britain went there to invade Sicily in 1943. A joint campaign that was to block the Mediterranean-Sea before the Nazi's built a stronghold. They called it, *HUSKY*. The American's sent in five paratroopers to meet with a group of Italian freedom fighters who were supposed to help them. One was a traitor and a murderer.

He killed eight people and wounded two in the Montréal Cathedral. Five were American soldiers and the others were civilians who were his comrades and friends. And while under hypnosis I witnessed the massacre."

"Frankie, this can't be real. You have some imagination."

"I know how this sounds but it's true. I checked out the story, after, I saw it happen. That's not all it gets weirder. I was told by one of the soldiers, that if I found a German Lugar, I would find the murderer."

"What are you saying? It's pop's gun, the one that was in the closet?"

"I'm afraid so. Look at the evidence. Pop said he was from Naples, but his immigration papers said he was from Palermo, Sicily. The same town as the Cathedral of Monreale, and it's the same year and place of the HUSKY invasion. I have to know why pop won't come clean about his heritage."

"Listen to yourself, you know this man, I know this man. He could never do anything like this. He goes to church every Sunday. It would be impossible for him to commit such a sin. Who did you talk to about this?"

"My doctor knows."

"Drop this Frankie or you will destroy my father and our whole family. I mean it. Drop it."

"I can't do that Uncle Frank. Until the truth is known I will be plagued with these nightmares for the rest of my life. I can't go through this horror night-after-night. Do you have any idea what it's like to witness a deranged man use an automatic weapon to kill innocent people? And do you have any idea how much blood there is in the human body?"

After seeing how upset I was Uncle Frank moved closer to me and put his arm around my shoulder. "Okay, kid, now what do you want me to do?"

"I just want you to ask pop about the gun. I swear Uncle Frank, I won't go to the authorities and my doctor cannot divulge anything I tell him, its privileged information."

He said in a very low voice, "Do you realize how much this could upset him? Are you willing to live with the consequences?"

"Why are you putting this on me? I'm just as much a victim as the people who were killed. I love my grandfather and I wouldn't do anything to hurt him or the family. You want me to drop it? Okay, I will."

"You know kid this is the kind of weird shit that I don't have a handle on. I deal in facts and figures but, I believe in you and I trust your judgment. I'll talk to pop. But before I do, I'm going to do some investigating on my own. I'll get back to you. Don't sweat this and don't get upset, I'm going try and help you. But this is just between you and me."

"I hear you Uncle Frank. Thanks."

He slapped me lightly on the face looked in my eyes and smiled. "You know you're a good-looking kid. Did anyone ever tell you that you look a lot like me?"

I laughed. "Yes Uncle Frank, Aunt Dorothy and pop told me I looked like you."

Before leaving Uncle Frank went to the closet and took out the gun and the rag it was wrapped in, as, well as pops photographs and documents. "You know I don't need to take this carton with me you got a bag to put this stuff in?"

"Sure, do you want paper or plastic?"

"Are you working part time in a grocery store? What the hell do I care if its paper or plastic? Madone, just give me a damn bag." He started to laugh. "You know kid sometimes I worry about you." He put everything in the bag including the information Darlene's father had given me and left.

No sooner did my uncle leave when I got a call from my brother, wanting to know why he never sees me anymore? I reminded him that I missed two Sundays out of how many? He reminded me I had missed a lot of Sundays in the six years I was away at school. He also heard that I had a girlfriend and he wanted to know what she was like and when the family could meet her?

"Al, I've been real busy at work. I'll make it sometime soon."

"Frankie, you do know that the baby is due at any time and that everyone is expected to show up at St. Barnabas Hospital for the birth."

"Hey bro, there's no way I would miss the birth of your first child. You can count on me being there."

"Good. Later."

Earlier, my sister had called. "Frankie, mom is really upset"

"Why?"

"You know why. The only time she gets to see you is on Sunday and this is the second week that you're not showing up."

"I'm sorry, Julia, it can't be helped. I'll be there next Sunday."

She went on and on about when was she going to meet my girlfriend "What's her name?"

"Her name is Darlene. She's one of the attorneys in my office."

"What about Jessie, Frank? Have you thought about her feelings?"

"Jessie and I are just friends. And I don't really have time to talk about this right now."

"Really, Frankie, is that all she is to you? Are you sure? Don't you hurt her she doesn't deserve it. First, her husband walks out on her and now you?"

I started to feel the pangs of guilt so I went on the defensive. "Why don't you mind your own damn business? You have an enough to worry about with that idiot husband of yours."

"That's a cheap shot, even from you."

I was too pissed to apologize. "I'll see you next Sunday Julia, I'm hanging up now."

Before hanging up, she said, "I love you little brother."

She was right. I was going to have to tell Jessie about Darlene. But right now, I didn't need this shit.

When Harvey, the concierge called me to tell me Jessie was in the lobby, I asked him to tell her I'd be right-down. I didn't want her to come up to my apartment, not that I didn't trust myself.

Who was I kidding? Now that I had a chance with Darlene, I didn't want to screw it up by jeopardizing a new relationship with lies. I just hoped that Jessie realizes that there was nothing more than friendship between us.

When I got down the lobby Jessie was sitting on a big over-stuffed chair wearing a suede jacket, with a heavy sheared lining.

I asked, "Are you going to the North Pole?"

"It's cold out there and you're not dressed warm enough. You better go up and change."

I had on a heavy wool sweater and jeans. "Thanks for the advice mom, but I'm fine. Let's go."

"You must be desperate for company Frank. I never thought I could get you to go shopping for clothes."

"Under normal circumstances you would be right, but I also need some stuff. I was in school a long time and I had no idea what the best dressed attorney is wearing these days."

"Oh please. I think I'm going to puke."

We both laughed. She hated when I acted full of myself and she always put me in my place. I only talk like that to piss her off.

We went to Bloomingdales, that's where we found a few outfits we both agreed on.

Jessie would hold up an item and I would shake my head yah or nay. And we did the same in the men's department. I should have known better than to ask for her opinion. If she didn't like what I chose her remarks were loud and far from flattering. With our packages in hand we headed to Fifth Avenue to a restaurant called, Noodles. The weather was starting to get even colder but unless I was frozen stiff I wouldn't have complained because of, 'I told you so." We both warmed up by having a brandy. Jessie asked, "By the way did you do anymore research on that Mario guy?"

I lied and said, "No. I've been too busy at work to do anymore research. I'm going to drop it for a while."

"Drop it? Are you kidding me?"

"I'll get back to it when I can. I'm busy and work comes first. Jessie. I have something to tell you."

"You look serious what's up?"

"It's nothing bad and I'm sure you'll be happy for me."

She got serious. "What is it Frank? Did you meet someone?"

"Well, I didn't just meet her, she works in my office and we started dating."

"Just like I had predicted, someday you will find and fall in love with your own kind."

"Don't do this, Jessie. It's not that she's my kind, there is no kind. You were my kind. It has everything to do with how I feel when I'm with her. Just like you must have felt when you met and married Parker." Her eyes welled up like she was going to cry. I was starting to feel like shit. "Jessie, this isn't payback for dumping me when we were kids. We have never really been in love, we're just good friends. That's why you were able to fall in love with someone other than me. As for me, it's taken me a long time to find someone I care about. Besides, it's too soon to know where this is going. I just wanted to be on the level with you."

Her demeanor changed to anger and resentment. "You fucking-bastard. Did you tell her that you've been screwing me?"

"Wait a minute and please keep your voice down before every-one in this place hears your filthy mouth. You were the one who made most of the advances."

"You're some gentleman Frank Scarpelli. I didn't hear you say, no."

"Who the hell in their right mind would? You're a beautiful and desirable woman. I would have to be nuts not to want to make love to you."

Tears started streaming down her face and I felt like the biggest asshole on earth.

"Do you have a hanky?" I pulled one out of my back pocket and gave it to her. She blew her nose and wiped her tears. "Does this mean we can't see each other anymore?"

I reached over and held both her hands. "No, you're still and always will be my best friend. And, I love you very much."

"What's her name and what does she look like?"

"Darlene Banks."

"Is she any relation to General Matthew Banks?"

I quietly responded, "Yes, she's his daughter."

Her eyes opened wide and she had that shit-eating grin on her face.

"Jessie, I'm buying what do you want for lunch?"

When I got home I called Darlene. I wanted to tell her what a great time I had last night. She seemed happy to hear from me but her voice was a little down. "Are you alright, is anything wrong?"

"No, nothing is wrong. "I also had a wonderful time last night."

I started to feel uneasy. "You sound a little down. Are you missing Bruce?"

She laughed. "No, Frank I'm not missing Bruce. I'm missing you."

I felt relieved. "Well, that can be rectified. I can be over in ten minutes or you could come here."

She laughed. "Thanks, but no thanks. I'll see you at work, tomorrow."

"I suppose if I can't convince you to see me tonight I have no choice but to wait. And don't forget it's your turn to pick up the coffee. I don't want to spoil you. You know how I like it, black and hot."

She laughed. "You know, sometimes you're just like a little boy?"

"You're probably right, and you know, that men never really grow up."

CHAPTER TWENTY-FOUR

When I arrived at work I was surprised to find a cup of coffee on my desk. I was kidding around when I had suggested that it was her turn to bring the coffee. As I walked into her office to thank her I noticed that her perfume had permeated the room. I walked up to her and said, "Thank you for the coffee. Tomorrow, it'll be my turn."

She smiled and looked towards the door to see if anyone was coming, kissed me on my cheek and said, "You're welcome."

"Is that it, a cold cheek kiss?"

She said in a low teasing voice. "While at work we have to conduct ourselves accordingly."

"You're right Ms. Banks. I'll just mosey to my office and get to work."

As I picked up the pile of briefs on my desk, notably was a note that read: Priority. See me ASAP. Mark. I started to read the contents of the folder and thought it quite interesting. It seems our client killed her abusive husband with a frying pan while he was in the midst of choking her to death. Unfortunately, her husband was Herbert Smith, a prominent New York, judge. I was surprised Mark asked me of all people to help him with such a high-profile case. Other than Darlene, the firm's attorney's had way more experience than I. Came to mind was the fact that I didn't have any trial history with the honorable Herbert Smith— therefore, I could not be prejudice, for or against him.

I was just getting into Mrs. Smith's statement when I heard a commotion in the reception area. Someone was obviously upset and excited but I was un- interested in finding out who they were, or why they were here. Until, Joan came running into my office and announced, "Someone is here to see you Frank. He doesn't have an appointment and he refuses to leave the premises. He said he's your grandfather and he's with this big guy who looks kind of scary."

Are you kidding me, my grandfather is here?" As I walked towards the reception area I noticed that all eyes were on me. I felt uneasy and concerned when I saw pop and John standing in front of the receptionist. I asked John, "What's wrong? What is pop doing here?"

He responded in his usual calm manner. "Pop asked to see you so, here he is."

"Why did you bring him here? Why didn't you go to the apartment? I could have met you there. You should have known better than to bring him to my office. Grandpa, what's wrong? Why are you so upset? If you wanted to speak to me why didn't you call? Please calm down and catch your breath."

He looked as if he had seen a ghost and I thought about calling, 911. People stared at us as they walked in and out of the office and I was starting to feel uncomfortable.

"Pop, are you all right?"

"No, I'm not all right, Frankie. I have to speak to you alone. I can't talk with everyone looking at us."

"Sure, come into my office we'll be alone in there."

"John, you stay here!"

"I can't do that Frankie. Your uncle told me to watch him and I can't watch him from here."

"For Christ-sake John, it's okay when he's with me. You don't have to take my uncle so literally."

"Sorry Frankie, I have to go with Mr. Scarpelli."

"Okay then the both of you come into my office we're creating a scene." Just then Mark came out of his office and asked if everything was alright? I apologized for the commotion and introduced Mark to my Grandfather and John. Mark shook their hand. "It's a pleasure meeting you Mr. Scarpelli. John."

"Frank, why don't you take your grandfather into one of the conference rooms? He obviously needs to speak to you." After hearing Mark's comment Sandra, the receptionist added that conference room two was free. I led my grandfather and John into the room closed the door and calmly asked "What is this about, pop? Why was it so important for you, to see me?" He looked awful and I was getting worried. "Pop, I think we should take you to the hospital. You're not looking well."

"I'm okay, Frankie. I just need a glass of water."

After John left to get him a glass of water, pop scolded me. "I am surprised at you! How could you? How could you think I could do such a horrible thing?"

"I asked, "What horrible thing?" I played dumb in case he wasn't talking about the massacre."

You know Frankie, the slaughter at Santa Maria la Nuova. How could you ever think that I was a murderer, a criminal and a traitor?" He started to cry.

I started to explain, "I am so sorry. I found the gun in the closet."

At that moment John came back into the room with the cup of water and handed it to my grandfather. "John, I think we should take my grandfather to the hospital."

"Ya think?"

"Yes, John, I think."

My grandfather was adamant. "I'm not going to a hospital right now."

I started to speak but pop cut me off. "Tell me, Frankie how long have you been looking for Mario?"

"Actually, it's only been a couple of weeks. Why?"

"You have been looking for Mario for a few weeks while I have been looking for Mario, for 68 years. And here he is, right in your office."

"What are you talking about grandpa? Do you know what you're saying?"

John furrowed his brow and gave me a dirty look. I lowered my tone. "Pop, please explain what you're talking about?"

"I'm talking about the pictures outside the elevator doors." He put his head on the table and his voice became labored. I uttered, "John, call, 911."

John not only called 911 on his cell phone he called my uncle and told him what had happened, and that he would let him know where the paramedics would be taking him.

Pop's breathing was getting worse but he continued to speak. "The picture in your office is off Mario Moretti. Thank you, dear Lord. I finally found the bastard." He then passed out.

It wasn't long before the paramedics came. They said he was alive but it didn't look good. Pop was the midst of a heart attack. They gave him oxygen and a shot before taking him to the hospital.

Most of the office staff was in the reception area, including Darlene and Mark. Mark told me to go with my grandfather and to stay with him for as long as he needed me.

When John and I went to the lobby to catch the elevator I checked out Senior's portrait. Is that what got my grandfather all riled up? How could that be? No way, Mr. Moran is from Great-Britain, he couldn't be Mario Moretti. Right now I felt as guilty as hell and I didn't give a shit about Mario, TC or myself. I prayed to God not to let him die. This was all, my fault.

John and I followed the ambulance to Bellevue Hospital and watched as they wheeled him into the Intensive Care unit. They hooked him up to every monitor known to medical science. Because they refused to let me in his room, John and I waited in the nearby waiting room. My uncle and father showed up forty minutes later and they were visibly shaken and upset. I suspected that when they calmed down their anger would be directed at me. I asked, "Where Al?"

My father replied, "I told him to stay in Montclair. Barbara is due to have the baby at any time and he shouldn't leave town."

My father asked, "Did, you talk to the doctor?"

"No. Since we got here no one's come out of his room."

He glared at me, "What the hell happened, Frankie?"

"Pop showed up at my office to see me. He said he got upset after seeing the portrait in the hallway. Pop allotted to the fact that he recognized the person in one of the portraits and it was Mario Moretti. That's all I know."

Uncle Frank stated, "You've got to be kidding. Pop has been looking for Mario for 68 years."

My father started to get excited and upset. "What the hell did you do, Frankie? What is all this crap you made up? Frank told me all about it on the way over here. Why did you have to get your grandfather involved?"

My uncle came to my defense. "Stop it, Al. He had no choice and in a way it was my fault. I shouldn't have had John drive pop to his office. He said if John didn't take him, he would take the bus. Other than locking him in his room I had no other choice. Who knew it would cause him to have a heart attack."

My father looked at me with disgust when he said, "Stay out of this, Frank, this is between my son and me."

"I'm sorry dad. I had no choice."

"What do you mean you had no choice? I could kick your ass for what you've done to my Father and this family."

Now I was starting to get hot. "Watch it dad. I'm not a kid any-more and I won't let you intimidate me."

"Tell me Frankie what are you going to do if I walk over there and beat the crap out of you?"

"You'll force me to defend myself. Keep in mind I'm younger and in much better shape then, you are." As he took a step toward me Uncle Frank positioned himself between us.

"You know Al you're acting like a jerk. I know you're upset but you don't have to take it out on the kid. I was just as much to blame as he was. I was also concerned that somehow pop had been involved. So, last night I confronted him about the gun and where it came from. I also showed him the printout that documented the massacre that took place at the Cathedral of Monreale. And then I asked him if, he knew anything about it? He finally told me the whole story about what happened that July, in 1943. After confiding in me he said he wanted to see Frankie to explain what really happened. He didn't want his grandson to think he was that murdering bastard, Mario." Uncle Frank turned to me. "Frankie, you said pop saw a picture and said, he was Mario?"

"That's exactly what he said. It blew me away. He hadn't seen Mario since he was a kid and the portrait of Mr. Moran is of a man in his forties and another of a man in his sixties. I met Mark Moran Senior, and he doesn't have an Italian accent."

My father was starting to get impatient. He not only hated our conversation he was also getting mad at the doctor who was treating his father. "Where's that freaking doctor? I don't trust him. I want them to bring in a specialist."

John, who had been silent the entire time, finally spoke. "Who wants coffee? I'm going to get some." In unison, we all said, "Me."

Uncle Frank said, "Let me tell you what really happened at the church, in Monreale.

Pop had a twin sister named Angelina. Pop, Angelina and Angelina's husband, Peter Sorrento belonged to a group of resistance-fighters. It seems Mario, was the self-appointed leader because he had been schooled in London and he spoke English, fluently."

I asked, "How come he was schooled in England?"

"Pop said it was because he was always getting into trouble. He was stealing, fighting and just a big pain in the ass. Fearing he would wind up in jail his uncle, Salvatore Moretti who lived in England offered to take Mario to live with him in London. Once there he sent him to a boarding school. Anyway, Mario lived in London for about five years. When the war broke out his uncle thought he would be safer in Italy so he sent him back to Palermo. Pop said they had started the resistance before Mario returned, but once they realized how well he spoke English they let him take charge.

His uncle stayed in London and became friends with a British diplomat. When they started discussing Italy's alliance with Germany Mr. Moretti informed him of the Palermo resistance and that his nephew could be of help to the British, armed forces. So when Great Britain and the Americans planned the HUSKY invasion they realized the dissidents were strategically located in an area that could benefit their cause. The diplomat contacted Mario to feel him out. Mario came across as a patriot who wanted to help free his people from Mousseline's tyrannical government.

On the evening of the HUSKY invasion to free Sicily, pop, Angelina, Peter and a few others were with Mario the night the American paratroopers landed. When the American's told them what they needed to complete their mission, Mario instructed pop and Peter to follow through with some of the best men in their group. Knowing they had just 48 hours to complete their mission they sprang into action, and collected all the information the Americans had requested. They knew where the Germans and Italian's hid their arsenal, their headquarters, outposts and communication systems. The also procured a detailed map of the area.

After completing their mission they went to the Cathedral to handover the information the invaders desperately needed. As they approached the front doors of the church they heard yelling and screaming. For a few seconds they banged on the door. When they heard gunfire they went to the cellar's side-entrance and ran up the stairs. Peter was the first to enter the sanctuary and was shot when he opened the door. He started to fall back but soon regained his balance and kept on going. The rest of the band followed him into the church. Pop said they expected to see German Soldiers instead they saw Mario holding a German Lugar. When he saw them all pile in with their weapons drawn he dropped his gun and ran out the front door. Pop said he couldn't believe his eyes. Everyone in the church had been slaughtered. He walked over to Angelina. She was lying next to a young dead American soldier and she was still breathing. Pop took off his shirt and tried to stop the blood. Angelina whispered, "Make Mario pay." And then she was gone."

"That's how pop got her blood all over his shirt. They checked to see if anyone was alive. Father Ferranti and Antonio Pasco were alive, but badly wounded. Pop picked up Mario's gun and swore in God's house that he would seek a vendetta. Pop has been searching for Mario for 68 years."

Uncle Frank shook his head. "What your dad and I didn't know was that on the nights he came home late, he was searching for Mario. Sometimes, he got a lead. An informant from his home town said they saw a man that looked like Mario in Princeton, New Jersey. He went there and walked all over town. The problem was that he had no idea what alias he was using. None of the leads ever amounted to anything, until now."

"But you knew all about this didn't you, kid?"

My father asked, "What is all this bullshit about? And how come you never told your mother and me about this nonsense?"

"Why do you think, dad? It's because of the reaction I'm getting now. I knew you wouldn't believe me."

"All I'm saying is you should have just kept your trap shut."

I was about to respond to my father when I heard loud talking and high-heels clicking down the hallway. There was no doubt that the Scarpelli ladies had arrived. My mother, sister and aunt walked into the waiting room. My mother and sister were somber and obviously upset whereas, Aunt Dorothy was sobbing. My uncle stood up to comfort her. "Don't cry sweetheart. Pop's will to live is strong. He's waited a long time for Mario Moretti to get what's coming to him. That alone will keep him alive."

My mother asked, "Did pop have another heart-attack?"

We all nodded.

My dad finally noticed that my mother was in the room. "Terry, how did you get here so fast?"

"John picked us up."

We looked up to see John holding a carton of hot coffee with all the makings.

My uncle remarked. "Good kid that John,"

"You got that right, Uncle Frank."

We sat in silence for what seemed like eternity. Finally, the doctor walked over and approached us. "Are all you people here for our evaluation on Mr. Scarpelli?" My uncle and dad got up to face him. "Well," the doctor said, "Thanks to the paramedics he survived a heart attack. But, he's going to have to take it easy and avoid as much stress as possible. And, his caretaker will have to make sure he's taking his medication. Mr. Scarpelli confided that today, he forgot to take it. That and stress most likely prompted this attack."

My uncle stated, "Don't worry Doc pretty soon all of his worries will be over. When can I take him home?"

"If Mr. Scarpelli's condition remains stable, he can go home in a couple of days."

My father asked, "Is it okay if I go in and see my old-man?"

"Yes you can all go in and see him but, keep in mind he's weak and he's been sedated. You can stay for a few minutes to pay your respects and then leave. But first, he asked to see his grandson Frankie, alone."

I was surprised, but glad. I needed to apologize and set things straight. When I walked into the room and saw how frail and vulnerable he looked I could hardly contain my emotions, but I did. I smiled and went as close to him as I could and asked, "How are you feeling grandpa? You gave us a scare."

His voice was low and hoarse. "Don't worry, I'm okay. I want you to know that my heart attack was not your fault. It had nothing to do with you. I forgot to take my pills, this morning. And, I know I shouldn't let myself get so upset, but when I saw Mario's picture in your office I got upset and happy at the same time. Thank you, God!"

"I don't want you to think about that now. The doctor said you shouldn't get upset."

"I'm not upset now. I want to live so I can see that devil get punished and knowing that it was me that found him made all those years of searching, worthwhile. Frankie, you have to promise me he will pay. Ruin his life the way he ruined my family's lives. You're a lawyer you know what to do."

"I do and I will."

He smiled at me. "Good boy! I can now die a happy man."

"Sorry pop the family is not ready to let you go."

He smiled again. "It's nice you all love me. I love my whole family, especially you Frankie. Did you know you were always my favorite?"

"No, I didn't. You were kind and loving to all of us kids."

"Don't tell the others, Frankie. That's our secret."

I could hear my voice quiver as I assured him that I wouldn't tell anyone our secret.

"It's up to God. He will take me when it's time. I'm grateful he let me live long enough to find, Mario."

He looked exhausted so I kissed him on his cheek and opened the door for everyone to come in to see him. My father came over to me and hugged me. "I'm sorry Son. I don't know what got into me?"

I reassured him that I understood and I did. But I also realized that this was a wakeup call for my father. His children we're grown and we would no longer allow him to bully us.

Together, they walked into pop's room and stood with the rest of the family. Pop said, "I'm okay everyone. Not to worry."

My Aunt Dorothy started to cry and my uncle put his arm around her.

Pop said, "Don't cry. No one cry. I'm a happy man thanks to my grandson."

My dad looked at him, then back at me and asked, "How could he be happy when he's just had a heart attack?"

At that moment pop closed his eyes, panic set in. My uncle dashed out of the room to find a nurse. She checked the monitor and assured us that he was sleeping soundly, and advised us to leave. On the way to the parking lot I asked my uncle if

``I should I quit my job. "Where is your head Frankie? We need someone on the inside. Besides, pop is old. He could have been mistaken. The last time he saw Mario was when he was 18 or 19 years old. I have friends who can help. I'm going to have Mark Moran, Senior, investigated."

"I did notice that Mark Senior looks nothing like his sons."

Uncle Frank slapped me on the back of the head. "You're an attorney and you call that evidence? It's probably the dumbest thing I've ever heard you say. So what if he doesn't look like his kids."

I laughed. "Trust me! That's not the dumbest thing I've ever said."

When I got back to the office I asked Millie to let me know when Mark would be able to see me. I wanted to speak to him about the

Maude Smith case. She agreed to set-it-up and inquired about my Grandfather. I felt no embarrassment for this morning's disruption. I vowed never to be embarrassed by pop or for that matter any member of my family again. One-by-one, my associates came into my office to inquire about pop's health. After they left Darlene asked me to call her. I told her I would but it would be after I got back from the hospital.

There is no doubt the firm's connection to a mass murder would ruin the firm's reputation and credibility. Should forensic evidence prove that Mark Moran, Senior is, Mario Moretti, I doubt it could survive that sort of bad publicity. Junior and Tim are decent hard-working guys and I felt bad for them. They had no idea the kind of man their Father was. I know how I felt when I thought pop was Mario. The repercussions will also fall on the employees. No doubt everyone would have to look for another job. Nonetheless, I promised my grandfather I would ruin Mario's life and I will do everything in my power to make it happen. If Mark is Mario he will finally get what's coming to him. This is what we Italians call, a 'vendetta.' Of course I had no intention of having him killed. My family and I will see to it that he's punished by the full extent of the law. In this country premeditated murder brings the death penalty and murder carries no statue, of limitations. And if Sicily tries to get him extradited, we'll fight it. He murdered five American soldiers and there is still a warrant out for his arrest.

We will have to be very careful. If Mario has a clue that we're on to him, he'll leave the country and go somewhere where he could possibly have immunity from extradition. But so far this case is hearsay and considered circumstantial evidence. Mark Senior may not even be Mario, but my bet was on pop.

After work I went to the hospital to visit pop. Although he continued to profess he feels fine and wants to go home he appears weak and frail. Aunt Dorothy and John got there a few minutes after I did. I kissed my Aunt, and asked, "Where is Uncle Frank?"

"He's on his way. He's bringing Robin with him." It occurred to me that for all the squawking I did about John I now realized what an asset he was to our family. I had such peace of mind knowing a member of my family was in his hands. It's funny how you tend to misjudge people, by their image.

Aunt Dorothy started fussing over Pop by fixing his pillow, straightening out his bed-sheets and, his blanket. You would have thought he would hate being fussed over, I would have. But then, I'm a pain in the ass. He just let her do her thing without so much as a grimace on his face. Rather, he looked like he enjoyed the attention. "Now pop, isn't that better?" she asked.

He smiled and nodded.

A few minutes later my uncle walked in the room with Robin who immediately ran up to pop and kissed his cheek. "I love you, Grandpa." She then placed this huge bouquet of flowers on his nightstand. His face lit up at the sight of her. She was an unspoiled and loving child who had to baby sit for extra spending money. I was sure it was because her father told her, 'there are no free lunches.'

Uncle Frank walked over to me and whispered, "Let's go outside I want to talk to you."

We walked into the waiting room. "I just wanted you to know that I hired a private investigator to do a background check on Mark Moran. I expect it will take several days for all the information to be accumulated. And, if there's no paper trail we'll have to find another way to prove his identity."

"There has to be something Uncle Frank. He went to a university. He got his license to practice law from Princeton."

"That's true, but if he entered this country as Mark Moran and his English was impeccable there would be no reason to question him."

"Uncle Frank, what if his papers were from England? What if he went to England first and then came to the United States?"

"You may have something there. Why don't we check immigration? Only this time see if he's listed under the name of Mark Moran. And for his country of origin, he would have to have used England or Canada. Don't forget he had to have a passport to get into the United States."

"What about the gun Uncle Frank, It could still have Mario's prints on it. I know my prints are on it and whoever else handled it. There is a chance it could still have Mario's prints on it. If it does we could match the gun prints to Mark's prints to confirm his identity."

My uncle asked, "How can we get his prints? You said he rarely comes into the office." "That's true but his office is full of his prints. I can try to lift them off his telephone or his desk. I have a key to the office."

He was emphatic when he said. "No, it's too risky. If you got caught you could kiss your career goodbye. No, I won't let you do this. I'll take care of it."

I asked him, "How?"

"How many times do I have to say this?" You don't need to know."

"Right, then I can't testify."

"You got it. The genius finally got it."

Pop was very quiet during our visit and I was starting to worry that even if we did find Mario he might not live long enough to see him punished.

Before leaving the hospital, I text Darlene to let her know I was on my way home.

Her message was, call me.

I called Darlene and told her the details of my grandfather's illness and his prognosis. We also made a date for Friday night, on the stipulation that pop's condition did not worsen.

I then called Jessie and told her about pop's heart attack. She felt terrible, but kept questioning me as to why he was at my office. I told her he was in New York and decided to pay me a visit. Her constant questioning every detail pisses me off big time. Although she's great about wanting to help me the problem is she gets too involved and doesn't know when to back-off. It's imperative that we keep our next move secret. At this stage in the game I regretted confiding in her. "Calm down, Jessie. I don't want to discuss this right now. I'll call you later."

"Fine, Frank, you do that."

It was, 1:30 in the morning when the phone rang. I was scared to death— I thought it might be a family member calling about my Grandfather. It was my Uncle.

"What's up? You scared the hell out of me."

"It's done. Frankie."

"What are you talking about?"

"We got the fingerprints."

"You burglarized my office?"

"Of course not, they only lifted Moran's fingerprints. No one will ever know."

"How did you know what to do?"

"I didn't,. his guy I know went in. He took a friend who's a forensic expert."

"Uncle Frank, is there anyone you don't know?"

He laughed. "This is not the time for this conversation. I just wanted you to know that we will know in 24 hours if, Moran is Moretti."

"And what if the prints match Uncle Frank? We can't go to the DA's office. They'll ask how we got Moran's prints."

"Let me worry about that kid. Before we go through all the trouble of looking for further evidence we have to know who and what we're dealing with."

"Uncle Frank did you tell my dad what we're up to"

Are you nuts? I can't tell your father because he'll tell your mother and she would have had my guy arrested for burglary— and me, arrested for hiring him. The only reason I called you, was because I was afraid you would do something stupid, like snooping around and being obvious."

"Funny you should think that. I was actually working on a plan, of sorts."

"Well forget-about-it. I'll take all the risks. You have a career to think about."

CHAPTER TWENTY-FIVE

I was sort of apprehensive about going into work the following morning. Although I'm sure my uncle's friend did a good job of covering their tracks because he hires professionals. He said the only thing taken would be seniors fingerprints. The question remains, is there honor among thieves? This time my uncle was right, no need to know.

When I arrived at work it seemed the same as usual. I said my usual good mornings and went into my office. Although I started to feel somewhat apprehensive when Millie came into my office and told me that Mark wanted to see me, a.s.a.p.

As usual I knocked before entering. "Come in Frank."

He expressed concern for my grandfather and asked if I knew what got him so upset?

"My grandfather has a heart condition and he had forgotten to take his meds. What got him so upset was that he thought Sandra didn't understand who he was looking for— because of his thick Italian, Jersey accent."

"Who's the big guy?"

"That's John. He is a very close family friend. He offered to drive my grandfather into to New York. My grandfather came in to have lunch with an old friend. After lunch he intended on going to my apartment to wait for me to come home. Later on, I was supposed to drive him back to Jersey. He came to the office, because he needed the key to my apartment."

"You're lucky Frank. I never knew my grandparents on my father's side. They both passed away before I was born."

"I'm sorry to hear that Mark. Was your father born in the United States?"

"No, he was born in England. I think it was London. He came to the United States in 1946 after World War II. My mother is an American citizen. They met in the U.S.

Like they say the rest is history. I really admire and respect my father he had nothing when he came to this country. He worked his way through law school and look at all he's accomplished." "I'm impressed, Mark. That's a real Horatio Alger story. No wonder you're proud." I thought I was going to choke on my words.

"Well," Mark said, "let's get down to business. I asked to see you because I need your help in the Maude Smith case. But, I now wonder if you think your grandfather's illness will interfere with the time needed to work-up a defense strategy? If so, I could have someone else assist me."

"My grandfather's illness has no bearing on this case, my job, or the time it will take to prepare an outline for a believable, self-defense strategy. I assume you're going for self-defense?"

"Yes I am Frank. Unless your investigation un-covers underlying problems— we should go with an affirmative defense strategy or justifiable homicide. The problem will be in proving either. That's where you come in. So, I suggest you get started?"

That was my cue to leave. The meeting was over.

I went to lunch at a nearby coffee house and called my uncle to give him the information I had just received from junior, about his father's past. As soon as he answered I told him, "I have some information that could be of interest to your investigation."

"I have some information for you, too. The prints match. Mark Moran is Mario Moretti."

I can't say I was surprised. I was surprised that they were able to get the prints off the gun after such a long period of time.

"Okay, I told you mine now you tell me yours."

I told him what junior had told me about his father being born in England, and that he came to this country in 1946."

He said, "That doesn't make any sense. We know he's Italian and that he was born in Sicily. But then, it's doubtful that he told his kids the truth and kept to a script. He's been covering his tracks since he high-tailed it out of Sicily. It's still a place to start. Good work Frankie. Now keep your ears open and your mouth shut. I don't want you to do anything that would tip our hand."

I assured him that I was smarter than what he gave me credit for. He laughed so hard, I hung up on him. When will my family stop acting like I'm a wet nose kid? I no sooner hung up from talking to Uncle Frank when Al called. "I'm on my way to the hospital, it's time."

"Okay. Now take it easy and calm down. Maybe you should ask dad to drive Barbara to the hospital?"

"No, I'm fine. I'll see you later. Come as soon as you can."

I assured him I would. Who had time to work?

At three pm, I called my father. "Dad, is there was any news about the baby?"

"No. The first one usually takes a long time."

"Do you know when pop will be getting out of the hospital?"

"The doctor said he can check-out tomorrow, providing his vital signs stay consistent for the entire day."

"That sounds rather soon to me."

"I thought the same thing but what do I know? I'm not a doctor. He's going to be living with Frank and Dottie. Frank doesn't want pop living alone, anymore."

"I Have to go now, I'll see you at St. Barnabas in a couple of hours."

I returned to reading Maude Smith's statement and started taking notes. I got so involved that I never noticed the time, it was getting late and I had to drive to Livingston, New Jersey through a shit load of traffic. But I knew if I didn't show-up my life wouldn't be worth a plug nickel.

Julia and Katie had arrived minutes before me. Al was a wreck. He would walk into Barbara's room and stay for a few minutes then he'd walk into the waiting room, to tell us 'the baby's not ready'. My mother said, "He's going nuts. He's been doing that same routine for five hours."

I picked up a magazine and started flipping through the pages as if I was actually reading it. I thought if it looked like I was engrossed in reading the family would leave me alone, and I wouldn't have to converse with anyone, or answer any questions. I was 15 minutes into my magazine when I heard laughter. I glanced upward to get in on the joke until I noticed they were all laughing at me. I checked my socks, they matched. No stains on my suit and tie. I asked them, "WHAT?" They just kept on laughing. My dad finally said, "We didn't know you liked reading The Ladies Home Journal?"

I looked at the cover and shook my head in disbelief. *I am really losing it.* I didn't want them to know that I didn't know what I was doing, so. "Hey, it's a damn good magazine. It's time I got in touch with my feminine side. Right, Dad?"

My wise-ass sister smiled. "I'm glad you like it. Maybe now we'll finally have something to talk about." Again, everyone started laughing.

This time Al was upset when he came out of Barbara's room. "Can you people quiet down, you're disturbing Barbara." My mother shrugged her shoulders like, 'what's up with him?' I guess we were all tired because the look on my mother's face was priceless, which got us laughing all over again. Al shook his head and went back into Barbara's room.

This had been one hell of a week for our family. First, there was the anguish about pop's heart-attack and now a new baby was on the way. Although no one said anything, there was always the concern that the baby and Barbara get through this without complications.

I was starting to get hungry. "I don't know about you guys but I'm hungry. I'm going to the cafeteria to get something to eat. Call me when the baby arrives." Everyone got up and followed me to the elevator. The only people that didn't leave, were Barbara's, parents.

A half hour later, Al showed up. "Where did everyone go? What's with you people? Doesn't anyone in this family care about my baby?" His behavior was so out of character for him. My father said, "We're hungry, Al."

My mother chimed in, "Eat, Al. You should eat."

"I don't have time to eat we had the baby. We had a baby boy and no one was there."

We got up, hugged him, left the rest of our food on our plates and ran to the elevator. Al was so excited when he described what the baby looked like. "He's beautiful. He's eight pounds and six ounces. And he's twenty-two inches long."

Single file and with my mother leading the way we walked into Barbara's room and took turns kissing and congratulating her for a job well done. The poor girl looked exhausted. Al was beaming when he said, "His name is Michael. Michael William Scarpelli."

I thought, *Thank God. I can now go home*.

On the way home I started thinking about how much had happened since graduation. Prior to that time my six years at school were routine. I would go to school, go home for the summer, and just the major holidays. Come September, I'd go back to school and start the same routine all over again. That went on for six years. But since this past June it was like all hell broke loose. It was not bad just different. I guess that happens when you move on, and grow up.

CHAPTER TWENTY SIX

I tried falling asleep but my mind wouldn't let go of pop's hellish involvement in a confrontation that has plagued him since 1943. How could anyone forget the experience of seeing your sister and your friends butchered by a, psychopath. Reaching out for help with my night-terrors was the smartest thing I could have done. Luckily I haven't heard from TC since my last hypnotherapy session. I assume TC knew he was getting what he wanted, the justice he had been haunting me for. I wondered if I would ever see him again. I hoped I never would.

And now that that our investigation had proof that Mark Moran was Mario Moretti, I had to consider our next move. Establishing a pre-mediated murder prosecution was going to be difficult. Hearsay and proof are two different things. Having a witness would help. The question remains, will pop be able to withstand his convictions under cross examination? And being Mark Moran is an attorney who had lived what seems like an exemplary life, and well known in the annals of the New York justice-system. His high-priced attorney might have a few angles going for him. He might even flee the country.

Wait a minute! Pop said his brother-in-law Peter Sorrento, survived. I wondered if he's still alive. He would be around the same age as pop and Mario. I'm going to check that out. If he is, we could bring him here to collaborate, pop's testimony. With two witnesses, photographs and fingerprints for identification, the government would have a foolproof case. And if we have too, we could hire a forensic artist-to use one of pops photographs of

Mario and have it age- progressed. Pop said he recognized Mario the moment he saw his portrait, because, Mario looked exactly like his father.

I was in a sound sleep when the phone rang. Uncle Frank asked, "Is it a boy, or a girl?

"Are you out of your mind? It's 3:00am, in the morning and you need to know that now?"

He started laughing. "You know Frankie, this is funny. Rarely have I ever seen you lose your temper. Good to know you have some Scarpelli in you."

"Your damn right I do."

He kept laughing. "What a tough guy. You really scare me."

I was ready to hang up when I thought about Peter Sorrento. "Uncle Frank, we need someone, to collaborate pop's account of the murders. I was wondering if Peter Sorrento was still alive."

"I'm way ahead of you kid. Peter is alive and he's willing to testify. And look at that- I never even finished high school. Actually, that's the real reason I called."

I said, "Swell. As usual you're one step ahead of me. And, it's a boy. Bye."

On the way to work I stopped at Starbuck for my morning coffee, and I picked up Darlene's favorite latte. When I handed her a latte, she remarked, "Well look whose here. I haven't seen or heard from you in quite a while. I was wondering if we were still on for Friday night."

"I'm sorry Darlene. I've been busy with family matters. I didn't even have time to call you. As you know my grandfather was hospitalized and I've been spending evenings visiting him. Then, last night, I had to rush over to St. Barnabas Hospital in New Jersey, because my brother's wife was having a baby. By the way, it was a boy and they named him Michael."

Darlene smiled, "You have been busy."

"I should have called or at least text you. I'm afraid I'm not making a very good impression on you. But finally everything is starting to fall into place. My grandfather will be moving in with my aunt and uncle. I miss you Darlene, so why do we have to wait until Friday to see each other, why can't we go out to dinner tonight?"

Darlene's eyes lit up. "You're on Frank, our usual place?"

"I'm cool with that. Later."

On the way to my office my cell-phone rang. It was my uncle. "I just got the report back from the investigator. It seems Mario changed his name to Mark Moran when he sailed to London, in 1943. Probably close to the same time he left Sicily. He enrolled at City University, in London, that's where he met Alice Crenshaw, an American who was married to an English soldier. Their relationship started as a friendship until, Alice received word that her husband had been killed in action. Alice was due to graduate in a year, so she decided to stay in London to complete her education. Shortly after graduation, Mrs. Alice Crenshaw and Mark Hudson Moran got married on July 25 1945, at the All Saints Church, on Margaret Street, London. November, 25 1945, Mr. and Mrs. Moran came to the United States. Being the husband of an American citizen Mr. Moran applied for and received a Visa through the American Consulate. When they arrived they moved to the town of Princeton, New Jersey where Mr. Moran was accepted on a scholarship at, Princeton University—where he received his law degree.

They moved to New York City in 1954. He got a job at the law-firm of Johnson, Johnson and Mayhew. Mark worked at, JJM for five years. After being successful in generating a backlog of cliental he started his own business. The Moran's adopted two male children who were named, Mark Hudson Moran, Junior and Jeffery Crenshaw Moran. The Moran's ordered that the adoption papers be sealed. Apparently, Mark and Jeffery where never told they had been adopted.

Mark Moran Senior is known as a proficient and ruthless attorney who specialized in winning fraud, embezzlement, divorce and what is known as white color crime cases for his wealthy clients. The only thing we don't know, is, how he got out of war- torn Sicily.

"This is a good thing Frankie. At least we have a paper trail, besides fingerprints and witnesses. There is no doubt that Mario Moretti is, Mark Moran. I'm giving you a heads up, John and I are coming over tonight to discuss how this is going to go down."

"I can't do it tonight Uncle Frank. I have a dinner date with Darlene."

"Then break it this is too important."

"I can't. It's just for a couple of hours. Can't we do this later in the evening?"

"How about I buy you both dinner, at the Marriott?"

"Thanks, but no thanks. I want to be alone with her."

He laughed. "You're right kid. Sorry. I forgot, at your age the hormones are really kicking in."

"Me? What about you and Aunt Dorothy? You're married fifteen years and you both still give each other that secret eye thing. Then there are those sly innuendos you think no one notices. I didn't know that people your age still had Testosterone."

"Let me tell you something smart-ass. I may be in my fifties but I've still have more Testosterone then you will ever have. You're right about one thing Frankie my woman is the light of my life. Without her I'm nothing. Changing the subject, John and I will wait for you at the apartment. What time will you be finished?"

"I'll call you before I leave the restaurant."

This time it was different, when Darlene and I walked over to the Marriott the anxiety was gone. Instead of heading for the bar we decided to have dinner in the dining room. There we could have a private conversation. After we sat down Darlene started to look around."

"Are you meeting someone else, here?"

"No, I'm looking around for your Uncle Frank."

I asked, "Why, do you have a thing for him? If so, you better get over it he's a happily married man."

"No, I don't have a thing for him. I enjoy his company. He's different. In a way he has that Frank Sinatra, Humphrey Bogart thing going. You know, tough with the guys but a gentleman around ladies. He also gives the impression that he's strong and in control. Women like to feel protected and safe. I actually have a thing for his namesake who is very much like the man I just described."

"Wow you got all that from one meeting with my Uncle. I guess I should sharpen my impression skills. Although, I'm glad you clarified your observation, because his namesake has a thing for you." It took all I had not to lean over and kiss her, passionately. Instead, I controlled my emotions. Every time I look into those beautiful light-brown eyes with the dark flecks I wished we were naked and in my bedroom. And then reality set in. *Darlene, could be in danger, if it got out that we were tight. Mario Moretti is a ruthless killer no telling what he would do to stop my grandfather and Peter from testifying. I have to level with her. And after tonight, other than at work. I won't be able to see her until Mario is taken into custody.*

"Darlene, I have to confide in you about something that might sound twisted, but I assure you every word is true and I will need you to keep what I have to say in strict confidence, or the consequences could be disastrous to me and my family."

The look on her face was somber. "What is it, Frank? It sounds ominous."

"There's going to be a big shakeup at the firm and it might be in your best interest if you started looking for another job. In fact you should leave the firm as soon as possible."

"What are you talking about? Why would I do that? What kind of a shakeup? I'm sorry Frank you're going to have to be more specific."

"I can't go into all the details. All I can say is the firm as we know it will no longer exist."

"Are you trying to tell me that the firm is having financial difficulties?"

"No, it's not that simple. My family is in the process of providing evidence that will show that Mark Moran, Senior, is a mass-murderer."

"Are you kidding me? What kind of proof?"

"You know the information you gave me on a war-criminal named Mario Moretti. Well, we have evidence that proves Mark Moran is, Mario Moretti. I know it sounds crazy but we have forensic evidence and two credible witnesses who are prepared to sign a deposition, and swear in court that Mark Moran is Mario Moretti."

"Frank, shouldn't you be talking to my father about this?"

"No. I don't want anyone to know until my uncle and I decide how we're going to initiate his arrest. There are many factors to consider. After I leave here I'm going back to my place to meet with my uncle and John. We're going to discuss how we're going to have Mark apprehended and, by whose authority. This is not just a war crime. Mario was not in the Italian or German, military."

"Maybe so Frank but he killed five American servicemen and three Italian civilians."

"I know that Darlene. This is also a family matter. I recently found out that my Aunt Angelina, my grandfather's twin sister, was one of the freedom fighters killed in the massacre. It turns out, that she was married to Peter Sorrento, who was also a partisan. Uncle Frank is flying Uncle Peter into New York to collaborate my grandfather's testimony."

"Frank, what are the legal ramifications? That crime was committed in Italy."

"I know that but pop and his brother-in-law actually witnessed the murders."

"Oh my God Frank that's horrible."

"Once we coordinate all the evidence we're going to see, DA, Michael Bonito, to see if the State of New York can press charges against Mario for killing those five Americans before Italy puts in a request to the State Department for extradition. Then again, we might be able to turn him over to the United States military and try him for the murder of the five American soldiers."

"You know Frank you had better be careful and watch your back. I think it would be safer if you stayed at my place."

"You would do that for me?"

She leaned in real close and said, "Yes, I would do that for you."

"Thanks Darlene. There is no way I would put you in that kind of jeopardy. In fact, after we decide what action we're going to take we will have to cut off all our communication, until Mario is indicted."

"Don't be so sure, Mr. Scarpelli." I didn't like the way she said that and I certainly didn't need to be worrying about her. Right now I had enough on my plate.

After dinner, I drove Darlene home and walked her to her door. We kissed and once again the excitement was overwhelming and I wished I were inside her door instead of outside. But before we could begin, I had to settle an old score.

When I arrived home my uncle and John were watching football and drinking beer. Uncle Frank looked up when I entered the room. "Hi, kid, you're just in time to watch the end of this game. The Giants are winning."

"Come on, guys I cut my date short just so I could meet up with you. Why don't we get started? I'll get a beer and we'll hash out a plan." Unexpectedly, there was a knock on my door. My uncle and John looked towards me. "Don't look at me. I didn't invite anyone over. Uncle Frank did you ask my dad to join us?"

"Are you kidding?" John stood up and took his gun from Its holster."

I asked, "Are you out of your mind? Put that damn thing away. Holy shit when did you get so paranoid?"

My uncle agreed and told John to put the gun away.

I opened the door, it was Darlene. "Didn't I just drive you home?"

"Yes. I figured two good attorneys were better than one."

"How did you get past the doorman?"

"I told Willie that I was your surprise birthday present and it would be a shame to spoil the surprise."

My uncle shouted, "Let her in Frankie. She's one smart lady."

John and Uncle Frank stood up to greet her. Darlene smiled and sat down. "Hi guy's, don't worry about me. I'm bound by client confidentiality not to repeat anything I hear. Little Frank is now my client."

"Hey, I don't like that little Frank crap."

"Well, how am I going to distinguish to whom I'm speaking? You're both named Frank."

"I see your point. Okay, you can call me young, Frank."

"My uncle groaned, "I don't think so. Young Frank as opposed to old Frank. I'm not ready to be called, old Frank. Why can't Darlene call you what the family calls you when we get together? Frankie."

They all looked in my direction.

"Okay. Frankie. But only when my uncle's around."

Darlene stated, "As I see it gentlemen this is a very complicated case and I wish you would let my father help."

"I wanted you to stay out of this. What kind of respect will your father have for me if I drag his daughter into a dangerous situation?"

"He's been a military man for most of his life. He could advise you on how to conduct this investigation and what the government options are. This is not a domestic case it happened during a conflict so technically it's a war-crime. The Department of State should probably be the branch that would handle this case."

I interjected, "I know the United Nations Security Council established the International Criminal Tribunal for Yugoslavia, but I don't think it applies to this circumstance."

My uncle intervened, "I don't understand a word you two are talking about. As far as I'm concerned Mario Moretti killed eight innocent people. And one was my Aunt. Now, I realize we can't prosecute him for the crimes he committed in Italy. The thing is, he was a civilian and he murdered five American's in cold blood."

Darlene reiterated, "That's my point Frank. They were not American civilians. They were American soldiers that invaded Sicily during wartime. Please, let me ask my father for his help?"

I insisted, "No, Darlene."

"You are so stubborn Frankie. I had no idea you were so pig-headed." She looked so cute when she got mad. I started to laugh.

Then she started to laugh. I realized in a lot of ways she was a lot like me, quiet, a quick sense of humor, not very emotional, in control and stubborn as hell.

"I've made a decision," my uncle announced. "What we'll do is make an appointment to see the DA and put our cards on the table. Let Michael tell us who has jurisdiction. In the meantime he can have him arrested on murder charges and hold him without bail. This way he can't flee the country." We all agreed.

Darlene asked, "Does anyone want coffee?

We all said, "Yes."

Even though we had reached a tentative agreement we were up half the night hashing it all out.

After everyone left Darlene helped me clean the coffee table and put the cups in the dishwasher. I followed her into the kitchen and stood behind her while she was loading it. I put my arms around her waist. "You were wonderful and you don't let me get away with a thing. I like gutsy women. Or, did you just come here to see my uncle?"

She turned around to face me and put her arms around my neck and her fingers through the back of my hair. She said, "All kidding aside Frank. I want to help."

"That's out of the question. I'm adamant about this one thing and I don't want to discuss it. You could be in danger and I won't allow that."

"I know and I'll be careful. If you're not going to ask my father for his advice at least keep me in the loop."

"Okay! That's a promise. This could go down in a couple of days, or in a week. We have to wait for Peter to get here before we can make an appointment to see the DA. Now didn't' you say you had a birthday present for me?"

"Come on now you know that was just a way to get past the doorman."

"So, you're the kind of person that offers a gift and then takes it back?"

"Not usually but in this instance."

I unbuttoned Darlene's blouse, than I unhooked her bra. As our tongues met I caressed her body. I then kissed her breasts and her nipples as I unzipped her jeans and slid my hand into to her panties and whispered, "Please, stay the night?"

She pulled away and walked towards the hallway. I thought, *Shit, I blew it and now she's out-of-here.*

When I followed I was glad to see that she was walking up the stairs. She shouted, "Come on, slowpoke." I ran to catch up to her. We laughed all the way up the stairs then stopped when we stood alongside the bed. Darlene unbuttoned my shirt and unzipped my pants. I took off her blouse, her bra and helped her step out of her jeans and panties. I couldn't help but remark, "Oh My God, you are so beautiful." We excitedly kissed but we wanted more. Our hands explored the most sensuous and sexually receptive parts of our bodies. My adrenalin peaked as my desire for her became intense. I picked her up, placed her on the bed and penetrated the opening that was waiting for my erection. At first I took it slow and then to a fever pitch until she moaned, "Don't stop." At first I was a little nervous. I wanted to please her more than any other woman I had ever been intimate with. I not only wanted her approval, I wanted her to want me.

Afterwards, I told her I loved her and she professed her love for me. With our naked bodies still embraced we made love again. After it was over I reached for the Goose down comforter to warm our now cooled down bodies. We lay there in silence until Darlene looked up at me with a serious look on her face. I asked, "What?"

"Frank, I'm worried about how this relationship is going to work."

"What do you mean? So far it's working out just great? I have no complaints."

"That's not what I mean. Your family is Italian and they're from New Jersey. They have roots in the community. You grew up in an all, white neighborhood. How are they going to take the fact that their son is in love with a woman of color?"

"I never gave that a thought so I guess it doesn't matter what they think."

"It does Frank, it matters. Your family is close and I don't want to come between you, and them. That's not the way to start a relationship."

I asked, "What relationship? You gave me a present and I took it."

She started laughing. "When is your birthday, anyway?"

"Early December, I'll tell you when it gets close I'd like the same gift that you gave me tonight." She kicked me.

"What about your family Darlene? How will they feel about you seeing an Italian, white guy whose uncle is rumored to have ties to the Mafia?"

"I doubt that race would be an issue. Both my parents had careers and we moved around a lot. We were used to being in a multi-racial and ethnic diverse environment. My parents had friends from all over the word. My father's concern will probably be your character, your behavior, and possibly your capacity for earning a living. You've heard the expression 'Army Brat?' Well, that was me for the first ten years of my life. My father graduated from West Point and my mother from Yale. They met right after my mother completed her doctorial in biochemistry through mutual friends. My dad was ten years older than my mother and he was already established in his military career.

We moved so frequently that we never maintained a relation-ship with our biological families. It was not the life my mother had envisioned and the higher he went up in rank the less time he spent at home. She had her education but not the career she longed for. Finally, after twelve years of marriage my mother told him she had applied for a professorship at Yale University and she had been accepted. She informed my dad that she and I would be moving within the next couple of weeks and had hoped that he would join us. She wanted a home, a real home and roots for her daughter."

"What did your father say?"

"He was stunned and in his stern voice he said, 'What can I say or do to change your mind Veronica?' She said, 'Nothing. My mind is made up. Please say you'll come with us.'

He said, 'You're willing to break up our marriage for a career?'

She said, 'Why couldn't I have both? You do.'

He walked out the door and he didn't return. We moved to New Haven in August of 1988. My mother bought a lovely home that was not far from both our schools. My dad called me from time-to-time, but he never asked to speak to my mother. One Christmas Eve there was a knock on the door, when my mother opened it she was surprised to see my dad with so many gifts in his arms you could barely see his face. He struggled to take off his hat and threw it in the hallway. He asked if he was still welcomed. My mother pushed the door all the way open and told him, 'Always, my love, always.' So, my mother went back to teaching and my dad would come home whenever possible. It was an arrangement they were both happy with because, they had compromised."

"When can I meet your parents, Darlene?"

"My mother died five years ago."

"I am so sorry. You must have been devastated."

"My mother was killed by a motorist. She had parked her car and was walking from the parking lot to the mall when a speeding car went out of control and killed her. That was the darkest day of my life." This was the first time I had ever seen Darlene vulnerable. We fell asleep, with my arm around her.

The following morning I dropped Darlene off at her apartment and rushed back to my place to change for work. I got to the office on time and went to work on the Maude Smith case and carefully re-read her deposition. On paper her story was plausible for self-defense or, by using the 'Battered Woman Syndrome'. But was her statement true or was she trying to get away with murder. We needed people who could give evidential testimony to Mrs. Smith's allegations and credibility. Mrs. Smith will have to give us a list of the people who could benefit her case. Later on, I'd speak to the people who would most likely give damaging evidence to the prosecutor.

First off I had to see Mrs. Smith and go over her statement. It is imperative her statement be consistent no matter how many times she has to repeat it. Especially under cross examination or, the prosecutor will tear her testimony apart. I also needed the name of her doctor, her family, housekeeper, nanny, neighbors and friends. People she might have confided in. And, I had to check the hospital to see if she had ever gone there for prior treatment. My first stop meant a trip to the penitentiary where Mrs. Smith was being imprisoned until her trial. Mark tried to get her out on bail at the arraignment, but Judge Markham said he would not give her bail because she was a flight risk. Mark and I thought it had more to do with the killing of one of their own.

Finding an unbiased judge was going to be difficult. I called the correctional facility to make an appointment for, 11:00 am.

This was the first time I had actually walked into a jailhouse. When they brought Mrs. Smith in to speak to me she looked surprised, and asked for Mark.

"Hello Mrs. Smith. My name is Frank Scarpelli. I'm Mark's assistant. My job will be to gather all the pertinent evidence that pertains to your case. Mark will be in to see you within a few days." She smiled and shook my hand. "Nice meeting you, Frank. Please call me Maude." Behind the smile you could see the eyes of a terrified women who was probably wondering how she got into this mess. Maude looked younger in person than in her photographs. She was tall, slim and had long red hair. Even without make-up, she was beautiful. And in a way that was detrimental to her case. She was beautiful and rich— no one will feel sorry for her unless we could prove self-defense. In other words, we had to prove our case.

"Tell me the truth, Frank. What are my chances?"

"That's something you should discuss with Mark. But, between you and me if everything in your statement is true and we receive collaboration and, if we can get you a mostly female jury I think you have a very good chance of being acquitted."

There was an actual sigh of relief on Maude's part. I also stated, "I want to give you hope but don't forget your husband's position in this community could make it difficult. On the other hand Mark is an excellent Attorney and not without influence."

We started going over her deposition. Several times during my questioning her eyes welled up and tears rolled down her face. I found her statement plausible.

They started fighting and she ran into the kitchen to get away. He was in rage. He followed, grabbed her and was strangling her. Her hand reached for something on the counter to stop him. The nearest thing she could reach was the frying pan. She hit him and he fell to the floor. She thought he was just unconscious when she called 911. She did have to go to the hospital with defensive wounds. Still, we would have to let the evidence tell the tale. Her story never changed nor did she contradict any of her past-statements. I even tried tripping her up. When it was over I got the names of the people she thought could testify in her behalf. She said, "I gave Mark my telephone book with all the numbers and addresses of the people I know."

As I was getting ready to leave Maude asked, "Do you know how my son is doing?"

"No, I don't, but I'll have someone check in on him and get back to you.

When I returned to the office Millie told me that Mark wanted to see me. She called him and told him I had returned and he told her to send me in. I was taken aback when I walked in and standing in front of me was Mario Moretti.

"Frank, come on in. I want you to meet my father, Mark Moran, Senior." I think I must have stammered when Junior introduced us. "How do you do Sir? I have heard a great deal about you."

He replied, "I have also heard good things about you Frank." His handshake was firm for a man in his late-eighties. If my grandfather had not recognized him, I would find it hard to believe that at one time he was an Italian immigrant. The only distinguishable thing was his eyes. They looked cold. Just as they looked in that torn old photograph my grandfather had of him.

"My son told me he is expecting great things from you." He then looked at Junior and asked, "What's the name of the new woman you hired?"

"Darlene. Darlene Banks."

"He said that he thinks you will both make a distinguishable contribution to this firm and that we're fortunate in having you."

"Thank you Sir. I appreciate Mark's confidence."

"I was told your grandfather came in to see you and was taken ill. Has he recovered?"

It just now occurred to me, had Senior been in the office on that day he might have recognized my grandfather.

"He's getting better Sir. Thank you for asking."

"Your grandfather, he's from Italy, isn't he?"

"Yes, he is."

He asked, "What part of Italy is he from?"

"Naples. In fact, my grandfather still has family back there."

"That's a beautiful city. Have you ever been there?"

"No, I haven't, but someday." He just wouldn't let the interrogation go.

"Scarpelli, I would imagine that's a common name in Italy?"

"I would assume so. I know our family goes way back."

"What's your grandfather's first name?"

"Francis. His name is Francis."

"I see. You were named after him. That is a very nice tradition." It finally dawned on me as to why pop lied about his origin. He wanted to find Mario before Mario found him.

Junior finally interrupted. I'm sure he didn't quite understand why his father was going on and on about my grandfather. He asked, "How are you coming along with the Smith case?"

"Fine, Mark. In fact I just got back from seeing Mrs. Smith. My next step will be to check her credibility and court records. But I was impressed with the fact that throughout our meeting she stuck very close to her statement."

There was a pause in the conversation. It was time to leave. I told Mark Senior I had enjoyed meeting him and I left the office. Under my breath, I vowed to see him rot in hell.

When I got to my office I made notes pertaining to my visit with Mrs. Smith, I was so engrossed that I had no idea how late it was until Joan came into my office and asked if there was anything she could do for me before she left for the evening. "No Joan, you have a nice evening. I'll be leaving, shortly."

Darlene stopped in my office to say goodnight and asked if we were still on for Friday. I suggested we do something different. "Do you like old movies?"

"I'd like that Frank. I love old movies!"

"Then, what do you say we break open a bottle of wine and I'll pick up some Chinese food, or Deli? You get to pick."

"I want Chinese food. I would like Shrimp in lobster sauce and don't forget the egg rolls."

"Chinese, it is. Bring your jeans or sweats, or whatever is comfortable. We'll put on the fireplace and gorge ourselves while we watch a movie. Sounds like a perfect evening."

She smiled her broad smile. "I agree. A relaxing night at home sounds wonderful."

CHAPTER TWENTY-SEVEN

On Friday I spent most the day trying to set up appointments with some of the people on Maude Smith's list. I desperately needed some collaboration for a case of abuse. Between that case and reading the briefs for the following week's meeting the day went fast.

I was to meet Darlene in the lobby after I picked up the Chinese food. When we met up I was carrying bags of take-out and she was carrying a small duffel bag. We took the elevator to the garage and as we were about to get into my car, Junior drove by and saw us together. He waived and so did we. Darlene said, "Uh, oh the cat's out of the bag."

"It's no big deal. For all he knows we could be going out for a drink."

She held up her duffel bag. We started to laugh. We were in such a good mood we didn't even think about being careful or considering the circumstances.

After I parked my car in the garage I took my seatbelt off and leaned over to kiss Darlene. She pulled away. "I've noticed that you don't like public displays of affection."

"It's not that I don't like it Frank. I'm not used to it. I feel a little embarrassed by it. I guess it stems from my childhood. Don't forget my father was in the limelight throughout his career. He showed little emotion or affection."

"Well, I come from a family where even the men hug and kiss each other. We kiss when we come in and we kiss when we leave.

It's probably a bit much. But I can understand how you feel. I'll try to watch it."

"No! Don't stop Frank. I don't want you to be like my father. That's one of the things I love about you, you're so romantic. I like that. I'm just going to have to get used to it."

"That's probably why they call me the Italian Stallion."

"That still has to be proven."

"Seriously, what about the other night?"

Darlene smiled, "Like I said, that still has to be determined."

"Well, I never had any complaints before."

Darlene's eyes got real big when she smiled and said, "Well played."

"You know sweetheart it's a good thing I'm secure in my masculinity you could sure deflate a guy's ego with that remark. But not me, because I know I'm good. And not that I hold any grudges. No Chinese food for you."

Once we got into the apartment we dashed to the bedroom and changed our clothes. Darlene put on her jeans and a tight blue tee shirt. "You know you really didn't need all those clothes."

She smiled. "Now, stop that Frank."

"You're right our food is getting cold.

I put the gas fireplace on and opened a bottle of wine. I put all our food on the coffee table and put the disc in the DVD player. "What movie did you get?"

I smiled. "Wait for it." Soon her idol came on. It was Bogie in, Casablanca.

Her eyes lit up and she smiled. We ate, drank and made remarks about today's terrible movies in comparison to the oldies. As soon as the movie ended Darlene fell asleep on the couch. I didn't want to wake her, so I decided to nod off myself. I don't know what time it started. *"I was crouching in the bushes while hiding from the German forces that were on patrol... I turned around to look for TC. He was standing behind me and smiling.* "Hi Frank. I brought you here to warn you."

"Warn me about what? I'm doing everything you've asked me to do."

"That's my point, kid."

"Who you calling, kid? You're younger than me."

TC laughed. "Had I lived I would be 88." His face got serious. "Listen to me Frank. Once Mario gets wind of what's going on he will most likely set out to destroy you and your family. This man is a ruthless sociopath. Be careful. And there is something else."

Suddenly, I heard a voice that seemed to be coming from a distance. "Frank, please wake up."

When I opened my eyes Darlene was staring at me with a concerned look on her face. She asked, "Are you, alright? You must have been having a nightmare."

I composed myself. "I did, but I'm okay now."

"What was it about? Do you want to talk about it?"

"Darlene, I have to be honest with you there is something you don't know about me and I guess now would be the best time to come clean. However, I must warn you, you're going to find the story I'm about to tell you freaking weird." I proceeded to tell her when the dreams had started and how Dr. Bass was in the process of helping me face my night terrors through th hypnotherapy.

"While under hypnosis Dr. Bass directed me to follow the dream to its conclusion. That's when I witnessed the horror of the massacre in the Cathedral of Monreale." Darlene looked stunned. "I didn't tell you about this because I was afraid of what your reaction would be."

"Frank, you do realize how this sounds?"

"You think I don't know that? I've had to live with this my whole life. Now that we've hit on the cause of the problem it should finally come to an end."

"How could you know that?"

Supposedly, the purpose of the nightmares was for me to find Mario Moretti and make him pay for his crime. Dr. Bass feels that once he's found and punished there will no longer be a need to haunt me. I know what you're thinking and I wouldn't blame you if you walked out of my life. This sounds like I'm some weird, nut job."

"Does your uncle know?"

"Yes, I told him a couple of weeks ago."

"Did he believe you?"

"Only, after he spoke to my grandfather. Pop confirmed everything I told my uncle."

"I don't understand this. You believe a dead man whom you've never met has not only appeared in your dreams, he's controlled them? This is too strange for anyone to make up. What did your psychiatrist say about this?"

"He was as skeptical as you probably are— until he put me through a few sessions of hypnotherapy. He said there is no scientific explanation as to why I not only know about TC, I know what he looks like. And I can describe in detail the Cathedral of Monreale without ever being there. I witnessed a massacre that happened in 1943. Why me? I have no idea."

"Oh my God does he materialize. Can he see us making love?"

"No. He just likes haunting my dreams and putting me through what he went through."

Darlene leaned in and kissed me passionately and I responded. This time she was the aggressor. We undressed and lied down in front of the fireplace. She went on top of me and took control. She kissed my mouth, then my chest and all the way to the groin area where she fondled my erection. Although she wasn't gentle, it was a real turn on and I had difficulty in containing my excitement. Finally, she allowed me access and it was pure pleasure. When it was over, I asked, "Where did you learn that move?"

"You see, Frank, I had this dream" She made me laugh. "That's real funny Darlene, but I don't buy it"

We then went to the bedroom and crashed. I was hoping to go back and visit with TC. He said he had something to tell me. This was the first time I had looked forward to my encounter with him. The following morning I drive Darlene home. She had a luncheon date with a few girlfriends. I suggested she leave some clothes at my place.

However, she thought it was too soon. I wondered if my nightmares had any bearing on her decision.

When I returned home I called my uncle to tell him about my encounter with Mark Moran Senior. I also told him how he had questioned me about pop's region of birth and his first name. "What did you tell him?"

"I told him Pop was from Naples and his first name was Frank."

"That's good. But watch it Frankie this man is cunning, we have to work fast. That reminds me the good news is, Peter got his passport and plane tickets. He will arrive this coming Wednesday. John will pick him up at the Newark Airport."

"That's great. They work fast in Italy."

"Not really. I had to pull a few strings."

"Like what?"

"Madone, what difference does it make?" He then disconnected.

I decided to stay home and do all the stuff I hate doing but has to be done. Like cleaning, grocery shopping, washing clothes, dusting and vacuuming. First I would go for a run. I also decided to leave my phone at home. I needed peace and quiet.

When I returned home there was a message from Darlene. "Hi, Frank. I was thinking things over." My heart sank and I thought here it comes. "Very few things are out of the realm of possibility. So, what I'm trying to say is- I believe in you and I love you weird crap and all. Later" Needless to say, she made my day.

Once again I decided to let the chores go for a while and studying for the Bar Exam. It was already November and I hadn't even opened a book. Besides, I would rather study then do laundry. I started taking notes but I couldn't keep my mind on what I was reading. I kept thinking about TC. I was wondering what he was about to tell me before Darlene had awakened me. I decided to try and contact him without being hypnotized.

I went to my bedroom, lied down on the bed and made myself comfortable. I started to repeat, "TC, TC, TC." Nothing happened. I started to count 1, 2, 3, 4, 5, still nothing. I got up and lit the candle on my night table. I stared at the flame and cleared my mind of any thoughts. Before I knew it *I was "crouching down in the woods, but it was different. No one was there. It was quiet and I was alone. I stood up and looked around. That's when I saw TC, walking toward me and smiling. He said, "This is a surprise you actually came looking for me?"*

"You started to tell me something before I woke up. What was it?"

"I wanted to tell you there is another way to identify Mario Moretti. Mario has a tattoo. There are two crossed saber swords about three inches in length on his chest. I noticed it when he changed his shirt."

As soon as I awakened I decided to visit my grandfather. I wanted to question him about Mario's tattoo. On the way over I called my uncle's place to make sure they were home. My aunt answered the phone. "Frankie, darling, how are you?"

"I'm good Aunt Dorothy. I was wondering if was alright to come over and speak to pop"

"Darling of course you can come over. I'll make you something to eat."

"Aunt Dorothy, don't go to any trouble."

"No trouble. I have corned beef, pastrami, Cole slaw and knishes. I'll make you a great sandwich.

"Thanks. I can hardly wait."

"Oy-vey, between my mother and my aunt it's a wonder I don't weigh 300 pounds."

When I arrived at the gate, my aunt let me in. This time around I was glad they had security. Even though I doubt Mario would have the guts to try something in the United States. On the other hand a man who can murder as many people as he did wouldn't think twice about hiring someone else to do it.

My aunt was as hospitable as ever. Pop must have heard my voice because he came into the hallway to greet me. He hugged me and asked, "Do you have any news Frankie?"

Although pop looked frail his voice was stronger than it was in the hospital. I hoped that this ordeal didn't kill him. Not knowing what my Uncle saw fit to tell him I was reluctant to go into too much detail. I walked into the kitchen where there was coffee and Cannoli's waiting for me. "Oh, boy, Aunt Dorothy, Cannoli's my favorite. Thank you!"

"I know that sweetheart, and you are welcome."

We sat down and started to talk about Al's new baby and that Barbara and Al brought the baby over to see them. Pop said, "It's a beautiful baby. The new come in and the old go out."

I said, "You're not going anywhere."

"I am, my boy, but not for a while. First, I have to see Mario rot in jail for the rest of his life." He was starting to get excited so I changed the subject.

"So, Pop, I hear your friend Peter will be here next week? I bet you're anxious to see him?"

"Yes," he replied, "I want to see Peter— it's been a long time. And this sweet woman is letting him stay here, with me."

My aunt smiled at Pop and said "Why not? We have plenty of room."

I was about to ask pop about Mario's tattoo when my uncle walked in. "Well, look whose here. Hi, kid."

My aunt immediately got up to get her husband a cup of coffee. Their eyes met and he smiled. "Thank you, sweetheart."

I started wondering if it was just me who noticed they had a relationship that transcended them from being your average couple.

I casually asked Pop, "Did you know that Mario Moretti has a tattoo on his chest?"

"I don't remember, Frankie."

My uncle said, "If you can't remember the tattoo, how did you remember his face?"

"His face is burned into my brain and I told you, he looks just like his papa. Don't bother me right now, I have to think."

We smiled as he sat there staring at the wall until he said, "Yes, yes, he did. He got the tattoo in London. When he got back to Palermo he bragged about what a big man he was."

I asked him, "What did it look like?"

"I think it was two crisscrossed knives."

I said, "Close enough! They're crossed swords."

My uncle stated, "You should have told us, dad. That would have been helpful in identifying him. Unless, he had it removed."

"He could have, Uncle Frank, but laser removal has only been perfected within the last couple of decades. I doubt if he thought to have it removed."

Pop said, "So what Frank? So, I forget sometimes. How much will you remember when you're my age?"

We all laughed. I put my arm around my grandfather and told him that he was doing great. Pop asked, "How did you know that Frankie? How did you know Mario had a tattoo?"

"The same way I knew everything else about Mario Moretti. TC told me."

My uncle remarked, "Don't start that crap, again."

Pop asked me, "Who's this TC person?"

"He doesn't matter. I just wanted to know if Mario he had any distinguishing marks on his body, and you said yes."

"Good, Frankie. Let's nail the bastard."

Pop said he was tired and he was going to take a nap. My aunt asked him if he took his medication he nodded. My uncle confided, "I'm really worried about him he's not doing well. I think the only thing keeping him alive is revenge."

I agreed and stated, "I would have reservations about their testimony should it go to court. Peter is Pop's age and I'm afraid Mario's defense attorney would tear their testimonial-recollections, apart."

My uncle said, "I'm pretty sure it won't come to that. Mario is a fugitive with a price on his head and he's wanted in two countries. All we have to do is prove that Mark Moran is Mario Moretti. What surprised me was that the egotistical bastard kept the same initials. He must have thought he was so clever and no one would ever find him. Do you realize that if you didn't find the gun and if pop didn't go to your office, in all probability, Mario would have gotten away with murder?"

"It's even stranger than you can imagine Uncle Frank."

He said, "I don't want to hear any more about that stuff."

My Aunt chimed in. "What are you guys talking about?"

My uncle answered. "Nothing much sweetheart, we're just having a discussion on coincidences."

"I don't believe that for a minute Frank, there are no coincidences."

He laughed, "Don't you start." We all started to laugh. My Uncle changed the subject. "I really like your girlfriend Frankie. She's smart and gutsy. I like that in a woman."

"Good because she's a keeper if she'll have me."

He asked, "What do you think your mother will say?"

"You mean about her being African American?"

"That's exactly what I mean."

My Aunt asked, "Do you love her, Frankie?"

"Yes, Aunt Dorothy, I do. I love her very much. But we're just starting to get to know each other. For years Darlene had dated and was engaged to that guy she met at Yale. Although we haven't been dating long, I think she's the most fascinating woman I've ever met."

"Frankie who cares what anyone thinks? If you love her go for it. When I started going out with your uncle it was the same thing. I'm Jewish and his whole family is Italian. My family wanted me to marry a Jewish doctor. No surprise there. And your family wanted him to marry a Catholic, Italian woman who could cook and have lots of babies. When both families realized that nothing they said would change our minds—rather than lose us both they accepted our decision. Your parents love you and they won't risk losing you. They will accept your choice, believe me."

I hugged her. "You're a wise woman Aunt Dorothy. And you're right. If they don't accept Darlene they will lose me because I won't risk losing her." I asked my aunt, "How does your family feel about Uncle Frank now?" She smiled at him. "They love him because he makes me and Robin very happy. And, if I'm happy, they're happy. It will be the same for you and Darlene."

When I got home I called Darlene and it went to voicemail, I left her a message. "I received your message and I'm happy with your decision. Call me when you get in. I love you!"

No sooner had I left the message than the phone rang. I answered it up without looking to check out the caller. "That was fast!"

Jessie said, "Really?"

"Hi, Jessie, how's it going?"

"Everything is good. I wanted to know how things were going with you and the good doctor."

"Great, it's going great. Thanks for recommending him. I think we've made great strides and the end is finally near. I actually feel some kind of relief."

"That's great Frank. I'm happy for you. You hadn't called in quite a while?"

"I know, sorry. I've been working on this case for my boss and it occupies most of my time."

She paused and asked, "When am I going to meet your girlfriend?"

"Just as soon, as things calm down around here."

"You're a lucky guy. I hope it works out for you better than it did for me."

"Come on now Jessie, life is a risk. Just because it didn't work out with him, doesn't mean it won't work for you with someone else. There are a lot of men out there who would give anything to be with someone like you."

"Really, Frank, do you know of any?"

She put me on the spot. I thought of Norman Shires. "Yes, there is this guy in my office. I'll talk to him. Maybe we could all go out for a couple of drinks?"

Jessie perked up. "What's he like?"

"I don't know. He's just a guy. He's an attorney."

"Is he cute?"

"I don't know what a woman thinks is cute. He's thirty-two, kind of tall. I don't know."

"He sounds okay Frank. Let me know if he's up for it."

I assured her I would and hung up.

On Sunday, Darlene and I connected for breakfast and later on I went to my family's house for dinner. I knew if I didn't show up my life would be hell. I invited Darlene, but she said she wasn't ready to meet my family.

When I arrived, I got the third degree. Everyone wanted to know what my girlfriend was like. I told them she was beautiful, intelligent and the nicest person I had ever met. My mother asked if she was Italian. I told her, "No. She's African American." Suddenly, it grew so quiet-- you could have heard a pin drop. Finally I said, "Could someone please pass the meatballs?"

My mother stated, "You know I'm not a prejudice person Frankie, but if you get married do you realize the problems you and your children will face?"

"Mom, this is the 21st. Century. If we get married and have children I don't foresee any problems. If we do, we'll deal with it."

My father asked, "What about Darlene's family Frankie? How will they feel about you?"

"Her mother passed away several years ago. And to tell the truth I 'm not sure her father will approve of me."

My mother got huffy, "How could he not?" Spoken like a mother who loved her son.

We all laughed. "Well, Mom he might just want her to stay within her own class."

My mother nearly dropped her fork. "And what class is that?"

"Politically, and militarily connected. They are well known in Washington's social circle. I'm sure you have all heard of, General, Matthew, Banks. Darlene's his daughter."

Everyone nodded. Not another word was spoken, except from Al. He asked me to pass him the meatballs.

CHAPTER TWENTY-EIGHT

That evening Uncle Frank called to tell me that we had an appointment with, DA, Michael Bonito. And we were to be in his office on Thursday at, 9:30, am.

I went to work as usual on Monday, but never told Darlene about my appointment with the DA. Darlene was brought up privileged and she knows little about the underworld. From now on and for her own safety I had to keep her out of this. She already knew too much. Junior, seeing us together in the parking garage, concerned me. I would never forgive myself if any harm came to her because of me.

I found that the prospect of finally having closure on my cold-case was no longer fearful but exhilarating, as my adrenaline started pumping. For a moment, I evaluated my choice of being a Trial Attorney. Maybe I'm on the wrong side? Making someone pay for their crime excites me. Maybe I should become a prosecutor? What am I thinking! This is not the time to make any major decisions. I still have to pass the Bar. In fact, Darlene and I should be taking it at the same time. How embarrassing, if she passed and I failed? Now I was being ridiculous.

I went back to work and made several appointments to visit some of the people who might be able to collaborate, Maude Smith's statement. Judge Smith may not have been the nice guy he pretended to be but a wife-beater and a tormentor, was still, questionable. This was not going to be an easy case. Her statement also indicated that his aggressive behavior was never in the presence of family, friends or associates. She stated, 'It wasn't until we were alone did he berate and beat me' In other words there were no witnesses. It occurred to me that I needed professional help on the symptoms and consequences of spousal abuse. I approached Millie and asked if we had a psychiatrist on retainer for such evaluations? "Yes we do Frank. His name is, Dr. Willard Converse. And his office is in our building."

I was glad that I didn't' have to trek all over traffic-congested New York. I called Dr. Converse's office and made an appointment. A thought came to me. *If, the judge was that cautious in front of family and friends, he might not consider the public a threat, because they wouldn't know who he was. I'm going to contact his first wife and children. They could be of some help. Then, I'll call Maude Smith and asked her for the names of the local restaurants, pubs and other places they frequented.*

Maude quickly answered my request for her and her husband's usual routine. My first stop was a restaurant called, The Downtown Bistro. Upon entering I asked to speak to the manager. He came over and asked if he could be of some help. His name was Ryan Clark. I gave him my card and introduced myself as one of the defense attorney's for Mrs. Maude Smith and stated, "Mrs. Smith said that she and the judge frequented this establishment quite often."

"Yes, the Smith's came here a lot."

"Then maybe you happened to have noticed Judge Smith's behavior while they were dining?"

"I'm not sure what you're looking for."

"Mr. Clark, Maude could use your help in establishing a motive. Do you know anything that might help her case? It could help influence the outcome of the trial." "I don't know much. All I can tell you is that Mrs. Smith was nice and polite to all my employees. On the times that I had to pass their table during an evening the judge always had his teeth clenched and he always seemed angry. She's a beautiful woman and men being men, stared, although she never seemed to notice. She mostly looked down— kind of like a child who was being reprimanded. I suppose she was afraid that he would create a scene."

"Why? Did he ever create a scene?"

"A couple of months ago they came in and I gave them their usual table. She got up to go to the ladies room and he followed her. I had to pass them on my way to the kitchen so I noticed that he grabbed her arm and twisted it behind her back. She pleaded for him to stop, he was hurting her. When he saw me looking at him, he let go and went back to their table like nothing had happened."

"Was this the first time you saw Mr. Smith abuse is wife?"

"Yes, mostly I heard a lot of emotional abuse. There was a lot of swearing and name calling that was directed at her throughout the evening. It seems the more he drank the more abusive he got. I don't know why she stayed with that looser. You might want to speak to the evening servers. I'm sure they can collaborate, my statement."

I thanked him and left.

My conversation with Dr. Converse was quite shocking. I soon realized I had lived a sheltered life. I'd been punished from time-to-time with a swat on my butt but only when I deserved it. I never saw my parents hit or hurt each other in any way. They bickered back and forth until one of them stopped. It was usually my father that walked away. So, I was surprised when Dr. Converse said that statistics show that fifty percent of all women have experienced some form of domestic violence and emotional abuse from a spouse, partner, or a family member. I asked, "Dr. Converse if he would you be willing to see and asses Mrs. Smith allegation of spousal abuse."

"Yes, I read about her case and it sounds very interesting. With all of my years of experience I'm quite sure that I would be able to tell if she is lying in order to cover-up the murder of her husband. There are indicators that a trained physician looks for. Including the symptoms, of, Post-Traumatic- Stress- Syndrome."

I decided to end our conversation until Dr. Converse visited Mrs. Smith at the correctional facility and could give us his diagnosis and deposition. All the while hoping it would be in our best interest. I went back to my office to compile my notes on this case and download them into my computer. I would also talk to Junior about Mrs. Smith taking a polygraph-test.

Darlene stopped at my office on the way to the lounge to get a cup of coffee and announced, "I'm working on a case with Norman."

"Great what's it about?"

"One of our clients was picked up for indecent exposure in a parking garage. It's only a misdemeanor, but this is the third time he's been charged."

"You had better be careful, honey. If he takes a look at you he might do it again."

She had a paper cup in her hand and she threw it at me. I ducked. "You could have killed me with that. Why do women throw thing?"

She smiled. "If I wanted to kill you, I would have. And who knows? I still might."

I laughed. "I didn't know you had such a temper?"

"I usually don't. I'm still not used to that Jersey caustic wit of yours."

"Now that I know it pisses you off, I'll try to remember to keep it real."

She smiled that sensuous smirk of hers. "Don't stop now. I'm starting to get used to it. And soon Frank Scarpelli, I'll be able to give it back." She walked out of my office and did a wiggly Marilyn Monroe exit.

It was funny and I started laughing. Darlene was usually sophisticated and understated It was a playful side of her I hadn't seen before. She was full of surprises. I suddenly realized how much I liked my job and the people I worked with. *Hopefully it will work out for them? Or maybe they will be able to wait out the bad publicity. It could work, if they changed the name of the firm. I sometimes feel like a traitor. What choice did I have?*

CHAPTER TWENTY-NINE

I t was Thursday, and today Mario will get the shit kicked out of him. And I was glad to be part of seeing him go down. My instructions were to meet up with my family in the DA's waiting room. The weather was cold but clear and with Christmas just six weeks away how fitting it would be to have Mario behind bars on a religious holiday. I called Joan and told her I wouldn't be coming into the office. She assumed I was sick and told me if I ate some chicken soup I would feel better in the morning.

According to my uncle Peter was in culture shock. He had never been out of Sicily before, now. The energy and population of our area overwhelm him. Although he spoke little English, pop was able to translate. It must have taken a lot of hate or righteous indignation to get an 89 year old man out of his comfort zone and on a plane to New York.

When I got to DA's office, they were all sitting in the waiting room, including, John. I greeted everyone and introduced myself as best I could to Peter. My Italian was very rusty to say the least. He stood up, hugged and kissed me on both cheeks. *Oh yeah, he's part of the clan.*

Pop said Peter was thrilled when Francis bought him a cappuccino from Starbucks. He wanted to know if they were from Italy, even though he had never met anyone with the last name of Starbuck. We all laughed, including him. Although I doubt he knew what we were laughing at. Finally we were told that Michael would see us. We filed into his office. He got up and shook our hands then walked over to Uncle Frank and hugged him. "Where the hell were you last week? You never showed up for our poker game. How are you're two beautiful girls doing?"

I was stunned Uncle Frank said, "Dottie and Robin are good, thank God."

Referring to my uncle Michael asked, "What can I do for you, Frank? You sounded kind of secretive when you called. What's up?"

"Mike, isn't your family from Sicily?"

"Yeah, my mother's people are Sicilians, but my father's family is from Florence."

"We came here to get your advice on how or who should handle a warrant for the arrest of Mark Moran, alias Mario Moretti. The warrant stems from a massacre that took place in the church of Our Lady in Palermo, Sicily in 1943, during WW II. Five American soldiers were murdered, along with three partisans by a German spy, called Mario Moretti. The priest and Peter Sorrento were wounded. The Priest is now deceased but Peter Sorrento is here to give testimony. What we need to know is who has jurisdiction of New York resident, Mark Moran? Or, do we turn him over to The Department of State, because he killed five soldiers during the time of war? Also, Italy has a warrant out for his arrest and they will probably ask for extradition."

Michael sat dumbfounded. "I assume you have proof of these allegations?"

Uncle Frank, answered, "Yes, we have the murder weapon with his fingerprints on it and Two witnesses. Mark Moran can also be identified by the two crossed swords that Mario Mario had tattoo on his chest while living in London. Uncle Frank handed him a large envelope with all the evidence we had gathered, including a report from a forensic specialist and the wanted print out showing Mario Moretti as a fugitive. Michael looked it over, than called his secretary. "Marge, get Alvin Feldman in here. We need to take a few statements."

Michael stated, "I know Mark Moran, Senior. I never came up against him but I've heard he's a formidable opponent. On the other hand Junior is smart, but not nearly as ruthless as his father. How come Frankie is working for the firm?"

I replied. "That's the strange thing about this case. I knew nothing about this until a few weeks ago."

Michael asked, "How the hell did you find out about this? What made you investigate a cold case?" My uncle was obviously afraid I would tell him about my nightmares because he ever so slightly shook his head. I felt like saying I'm not that stupid. Instead, I told Michael, "My grandfather mentioned it when he was in the hospital. I then went home and did some online research. I soon found that everything pertaining to the incident was correct."

Pop said, "That's right, I told Frankie."

Michael stated, "The feds will want him. But I want New York to get the collar and the publicity. So, we're going to get out a warrant for his arrest and a search warrant for his office and home. But first I have to make sure the evidence fit's the warrant. If it does we can take him into custody and hold him as a flight risk. He may have been able to have this overturned due to the fact he doesn't look anything like his picture. And I'm sure he will use mistaken identity as a defense. But seeing you have two witnesses, evidence, and professional-photo enhancements, it looks like an open and shut case." Michael smiled when he said, "Tell me Frank how did you get Mark Moran's fingerprints?"

"It was still on the gun he used to commit the murders."

"No Frank. I mean Mark's fingerprints. How did you get a match?"

"No problem there Michael I got it from the doorknob of his home, right out in the open."

Michael looked at him and laughed, "Yeah sure. Everyone should stay at Frank's house in Jersey. No telling what a man like that would do to try and stop his witnesses from testifying."

I angrily said. "There's no way I'm going to let that psychopath force me to run with my tail between my legs. I'm staying in Manhattan. If need be I'll go to a hotel."

Michael was insistent. "Don't be stupid. I don't have the man-power to protect you."

"I don't need protection. I met him, he's an old man. What can he do in jail?"

The DA and my uncle looked at each other. My uncle said, "Frankie, you're being stupid and naïve and if you were smart you would stay at my place until this blows over."

"No, Uncle Frank. I think you're being overly cautious. There's no way he'll be allowed to make bail once it hits the media. The feds will be jumping all over him. They might want to try him in a military tribunal. Mario Moretti is going nowhere."

Michael asked Alvin, the Assistant, District Attorney if he knew who had jurisdiction, the U.S. Government or the Italian Government?

"The U.S. Government did. "But the Italian Government might want him extradited for the murders of the civilians. Who the hell knows? Whoever gets here first can have him"

Michael said, "Mr. Scarpelli and Mr. Sorrento please bear with us, we will have to take your statements and, go over all the evidence in minute detail. I will also need Frankie's cell- number."

I glared at him. He started laughing. "Busting, your chops kid, with some DA humor."

"I didn't know district attorney's had a sense of humor?"

Everyone started laughing except Peter. He didn't understand a word of what anyone was saying.

The meeting was finally over and now all we had to do was to wait for Mario to be indicted and to see who would claim jurisdiction over the case against him. On the way to my car I received a call from Darlene. She asked, if, I was really sick. "No. Actually, I'm on my way to get a strong, hot cup, of coffee."

"Frank, talk to me what's going on?"

"No, I want you to stay out of this."

"It's too late, Frank. Please don't shut me out. As soon as I leave work I'm coming over."

"No, Darlene, I have to be firm about this."

When she started to laugh I didn't know what to say. That line always worked when my father used it on my mother."

All right, if you don't want me to come over to your place then I want you to stay at mine."

"I'll be fine Frank. I think everyone is blowing this danger thing out of proportion."

"And you're not taking this serious enough! What's the harm in being cautious?"

"Darlene, I don't want to talk about this anymore. I'll catch up to you as soon as Mario is behind bars and taken into custody. When the coast is clear and only when it is, I'll call you."

Darlene hung up on me after stating, "And you said I was stubborn."

After I had coffee and read the Wall Street Journal I found myself aimlessly walking around the city until I realized I really needed to go grocery shopping. The only thing in my refrigerator was cold water and beer.

I arrived home a couple of hours later and put the television on to catch the news while I put my foodstuff away. During a political discussion there was an announcement: 'Breaking News': "Mark Moran, Senior, a prominent New York Attorney and founder of Mark Moran, Mark Moran, Junior and Associates— has been accused of living a double life. With a clientele that spans over three decades. Mr. Moran, Senior, has been arrested for the brutal murders of eight people in Palermo, Sicily in, 1943. While posing as a freedom fighter during WWII, he was actually spying for the Nazi régime. Five, of the murders were United States military personnel. Mario Moretti, alias Mark Moran has eluded the Italian authorities and the United States government for 70 years. Mark Moran claims, 'it's a case of mistaken identity.' The names of the military personal have just been released: Captain Harvey Conroy, Sergeant Thomas Callahan, Leon Jones, Jerry Stein and Ralph Watson. The Italian civilian partisans were, Angelina

Sorrento, Mary Sorrento and Anthony Pasco. Wounded during the massacre were Father, Michael Farrenti and Peter Sorrento. Our cameras are at the court house. We will bring you an update after, Mark Moran's arraignment."

The camera caught Mark Senior being brought in for custody. He made a statement to the press: "I'm innocent. This is just a case of mistaken identity. I will be out of here, shortly. And I would expect nothing less than a formal apology from District Attorney Michael Bonito. Or, I will sue him and the State of New York for a false arrest."

I poured myself a double scotch and soda. *That lying bastard! Bullshit—mistaken identity.* Soon the camera's turned to Michael Bonito as he walked up the steps to the courthouse. And stopped to address the press: "This is an especially heinous crime. A warrant for Mario, Moretti has been in effect for over 62 years." He held-up the Wanted Poster of a young Mario Moretti and photos of the murdered soldiers. "I'm sure the family of these victims will finally be assured that justice has been served. And that our country did not let them down. We have an open and shut case against Mr. Moran."

My cell phone started ringing. It was Darlene. "Frank, the office is in chaos. Junior, went to the courthouse to help with his father's defense. They're going to try and make bail. Do you think he will get out on bail?"

"I can't see how? He would be a flight risk and the offense is premeditated murder. No way will a judge let him make bail."

"I have to go now. Please, keep me posted."

Then my dad called. "Do you really think this was the right thing to do right now?"

"If not now dad when? There is no right or wrong time. That bastard killed eight people in a church, for God sake. Dad, he killed your aunt. You think he should get away with this? Pop has been waiting for this day for most of his life."

"I know Frankie. You're right, it's your mother. She's worried about you."

Every time my father worried about any of his children, he blamed my mother. "Frankie, do me a favor and come over and stay with us. She'll feel better."

"Thanks for the offer Dad. I'm fine and I want to stay here tonight. I'll stop by tomorrow."

He said, "You're going to have to look for another job."

"I know. I'll wait until the media blitz dies down."

"Do you need any money?"

"Not for a while. I've been putting some money away. I have enough for a while."

After we hung up I got a call from my uncle. "Get your bony ass down here, right now!"

"Why? What's wrong? Is pop sick?"

"What's wrong is your father. He's out of his mind with fear for your safety. Get down here now. John's on his way to pick you up— and I told him to use force, if necessary."

I started to laugh. "Frankie, this is not funny. Mark Moran made bail."

A shiver went down my spine. "What? Are you kidding? What idiot judge did that? He's a flight risk."

"Apparently, he had some kind of connection with the judge. I haven't heard the whole story. John will be there soon."

"Okay, I'll get some things together. You people are so paranoid."

"And you're young, foolish and naïve."

"I said okay. I'll leave as soon as John gets here."

That when I heard a knock at the door. "I have to go Uncle Frank. Someone is at the door. It's probably John."

He started yelling, "Don't answer it until I call John on his cell phone."

I heard another knock and Darlene's voice.

"It's okay Uncle Frank. It's Darlene."

"Don't hang up on me. Frankie."

I saw no reason to leave Darlene waiting at the door. I yelled "Just a minute Darlene." I opened the door to find a strange man standing behind her. He proceeded to push her into my apartment and locked the door. I dropped the phone and asked him, "What the hell is going on here? And who the hell are you?"

"I'm going to kill you and your girlfriend if you don't tell me where you're grandfather and his friend is."

"I don't know where they are. They're in protective custody. Go ask the DA."

"Listen to me, you wiseass kid don't hand me any bullshit. I know your uncle lives in New Jersey and I also know he has a security system. If you don't tell me the code, I swear, I'll kill your girlfriend in front of your eyes and then I'll kill you."

"How the hell would I know the security code? Now take your fucking hands off Darlene and see if we could make some sort of a deal. I can offer you more money than you're getting now."

He laughed. "As tempting as that is the answer is no. I'm going to ask you one more time, what is the security code to your uncle's place?" I said nothing. He then reached over and grabbed Darlene's hair in an attempt to move her closer to where he was standing. He was hurting her and I feared for her life. I had to stop him. I caught him off guard when I lunged at him and grabbed and Darlene from his grip. I yelled "0Run Darlene, run." As we struggled for the gun, it went off. I don't remember feeling any pain, as I fell to the floor. I just couldn't move. I heard Darlene scream and then I heard another gun go off. I counted, one shot— two shots. I tried to get up but I couldn't. Darlene was silent. I feared that she was hit by the stray bullet.

I also remember feeling the wetness of my own blood. I then saw a blurred face leaning over me. It was John's face. He whispered, "Stay with me Frankie, stay with me. The paramedics are on their way."

I whispered, "Is she dead?"

"No, she just fainted. Lie still. It's over."

I don't remember the paramedics putting me on a stretcher or putting me in the ambulance.

My next recollection was me standing in front of the church of, 'Our Lady.' TC was standing in front of those large bronze doors. He saw me, smiled, and walked towards me.

I said, "It's finally over, isn't it?

"Yes, thanks to you."

"No one is around it's so quiet."

"I wanted to say good-bye Frank, and to thank you for all your help."

"I'm dead, aren't I?"

"No you're not. You'll wake up when you're ready."

"No offense TC, but I hope I never see you again."

TC laughed, "No offense taken, Frank Scarpelli."

When I awoke my thoughts were of Darlene. Was she really alright? When I opened my eyes I saw her sitting with my family. *My God, the whole family is here, including Jessie and John.* I was about to say 'what's up' when I felt this excruciating pain in my chest. So what I actually said was, "Ouch."

Everyone looked up and came over to my bedside. My mother started to cry. My father and uncle looked like someone had kicked them in the gut.

"Mom, please stop crying."

"I can't help it. How are you?"

I muttered, "Sore, very sore. Darlene?"

They all made way for Darlene to get close. I asked her, "Are you okay?"

"I'm fine! You're the one I'm worried about." Tears rolled down her cheeks. "You saved my life."

"No, I didn't. John did."

Her eyes welled up and she was sniffling. "If you didn't act like the fool you are and pull me aside, he would have killed me."

"I was terrified, of losing you."

She reached for my hand and started to cry."

"Darlene, please don't cry."

"Did John get into any trouble for shooting the perp?"

My uncle assured me, "No. John has a permit to carry a gun and used it to save a life. He's not in any trouble."

I reminded him that he had a permit in New Jersey, but not in New York.

"You know, kid I could smack the shit out of you. You're near death and you're concerned about the damn law? Just to relieve your sense of justice, John has a permit to carry a gun in New York. He's a bodyguard. Madone!"

I tried to laugh but it hurt too much. "Thanks John, I'm very grateful."

My dad said, "All this happened because you're so damn stubborn and won't listen to reason."

My uncle glared at his brother. My father shut up.

I could hear Pop in the background asking if I was all right. "Yes dad. Thank God, he's going to be fine."

I asked my uncle how long I'd been unconscious. "It's Sunday. You've been out for three days. You had a guardian angel looking over you kid. That bullet grazed your heart. You're lucky to be alive."

"I take it, this was Mario's doing?"

"Right after he was released from bail he put out a contract to get pop and Peter. But, they didn't know how to penetrate my security system. So they went looking for you.

"Uncle Frank, can they connect Mark to me being shot and Darlene abducted?"

"Not sure, they're tracing the money. I heard about the contract through a friend. You don't have to worry about Mark Moran anymore. He's dead—he had an unfortunate accident."

I was about to ask about the circumstance of his death when the doctor came in and yelled at everyone for not telling the nurse that I had awakened. He asked everyone to immediately leave the room, and not to come back until he had completed his examination. Speechless for once, they all left.

The doctor asked me how I felt. "I'm in a lot of pain."

"I'm glad you're awake, Frank. You're lucky to be alive. If it wasn't for your age and the best cardiologist in this city I doubt you would have made it. Right now, you need to rest."

That was the last thing I heard before falling asleep. I don't know how long I had been asleep. It could have been fifteen minutes or a full day. I only know that when I awoke it was dark and quiet. I asked the nurse who was taking my blood pressure, "Where is everyone?"

"The doctor advised them to go home, to get some rest. You're a brave young man Frank Scarpelli."

"Why? What did I do?"

She smiled. "Did you also lose your memory?"

"I don't think so. Could you please turn on the TV? I'd like to see the news."

"I don't think so. The doctor doesn't want you to get upset."

"Please, I won't tell him. And, please call me Frank, nurse?"

"Nurse Baxter. Okay, Frank, if you promise to try and eat something solid."

"What did you have in mind?"

"You can have Chicken-soup and Jell-O."

"You only eat Chicken soup when you have a cold. Fine, I'll eat the chicken soup but lose the Jell-O."

After watching a few boring commercials the news finally came on. On screen was a film-clip of Mark Moran, Senior leaving the courtroom after posting bail. The commentator announced: "The funeral services for Mark Moran, Senior, will be held tomorrow at a small Catholic church on, Long Island. Due to the nature of this case the name of the church is being withheld. According to court documents, Three days ago Mark Moran was arrested for premeditated murder. Mark Moran, alias Mario Moretti was accused of killing eight people and wounding two in the Cathedral Monreale, during World War II, in 1943. Five of the murders were United States military personnel. Captain Harvey Conroy, Sergeant Thomas Callahan, Leon Jones, Jerry Stein and Ralph Watson. The Italian civilians were

Angelina Sorrento, Mary Sorrento and Anthony Pasco. Wounded during the massacre was, Father, Michael Farrenti and Peter Sorrento. Witnesses claim that Mario Moretti posed as an Italian resistance-fighter while spying for the Nazi regime.

It was a strange turn of events when Mark Moran was killed by a hit and run driver minutes after his son, Mark Moran, Junior dropped him off in the secured garage, of his New York apartment building. So far there are no witnesses or clues to the car involved in the hit and run death of, Mr. Moran. The police are asking for witnesses to come forward or, if you have any information leading to the driver and make of the car—to please notify the DA's office."

The United States Department of State claims he never should have been released on bail and they are investigating Judge White's misuse of power. A full investigation is ongoing.

The latest report shows that Frank, Scarpelli's condition has been upgraded from serious, to guarded. Frank Scarpelli was shot by Carmine Dietz in a home envision at the Westward Building, on Fifth Avenue. Carmine Dietz held Frank and his girl-friend, Darlene Banks, (General Banks' daughter) at gunpoint as he interrogated Frank on the whereabouts of the two witnesses in the Moran case. After threatening to kill Ms. Banks, Frank pushed his girlfriend aside and reached for the gun. A struggle ensued and the gun went off. Frank Scarpelli was severely injured during the encounter. Carmine Dietz is a known felon with numerous convictions. Carmine Dietz was shot and killed by a family friend who happened to stop by Frank Scarpelli's apartment. The police are looking into the connection between the assailant and, Mark Moran, Senior. Buzz has had two prior convictions of attempted murder and is suspected to be a hit-man for hire. In a prior interview District Attorney Michael Bonito stated, 'This was a bizarre twist of fate. And in all his years as District Attorney he had never had a case where two suspects were killed prior to their trial.

I commented, "The DA sure has his work cut out for him."

Nurse Baxter claimed, "While you were unconscious the media had full coverage of you and Darlene on the night they brought you into the emergency room, half-dead."

"Well I'm glad I was unconscious and didn't get to see it. Please, shut that off."

When the nurse left I had time to collect my thoughts. *So, Mark is dead, talk about coincidences. Thank God, pop and Peter are safe. That's twice Mario missed killing them. I don't know if pop could have survived the trial. He is weak and the stress might have killed him. It's finally over. Uncle Frank said he was going to see that Peter gets the reward money. He deserved it.*

I fell back to sleep after my watered down chicken soup. When I woke up I was in a lot of pain, so I hit the buzzer for the nurse. There was no response. I tried again and I looked through the window to see if I could see her coming. All I could see was the shadow of a large person. I then tried yelling for the nurse, but I didn't have the strength. I could see the shadow moving closer and closer and he seemed to be heading straight for my room. In my semi-conscious state, the thought occurred to me that maybe there were two hit-men and he was coming to finish the job. I felt helpless. So, it was a surprise and a relief when John said, "What's the matter, Frankie?"

"John, thank God it's you. Please, get me the nurse the pain is unbearable."

He walked into my room and put the light on. "Hang on. I'll be right back."

A few minutes later, John was literally dragging the nurse into my room. He walked so fast, she was out of breath. "What happened here? I thought you died. This big galute dragged me all the way down the hall." I tried to laugh, but couldn't. "I'm sorry John was trying to help me out, the pain is really bad. Can you give me something, anything?"

She looked at my chart and said, "You're due for a shot of morphine." When she was done giving me the shot she stopped, looked at John gave and gave him a dirty look then walked out of the room. He just shrugged his shoulders and laughed. "I didn't even hurt her. She wouldn't come. She said she was busy."

If I hadn't been in so much pain, I would have laughed. What a sight! "John, what are you doing here so late at night?"

"I came to visit you but you were asleep. I wanted to see if you were alright."

"It's a good thing you did. Man, the pain gets pretty bad."

John sat beside my bed. "You scared the hell out of me, Frankie."

"Thanks to you Darlene and I are still alive. I owe you man." I held out my hand. He pushed it away and hugged me lightly, knowing that a good squeeze would probably send me into cardiac arrest.

"John, would you mind keeping me company for a while?" He nodded. I thought this would be the perfect opportunity to ask him about himself and his family.

"You know John I know so little about you. What's your story?"

"I don't have a story," he replied.

"Everyone has a story. What's your family like? Do you have any brothers or sisters?"

"No. I'm an only child. I live with my mom, she needs the income. My, dad, comes and goes."

I started to pry a little more. "What made you work for my uncle? How did you get to know him?"

"I've known Mr. Scarpelli all my life. He and my old man were friends from the old neighborhood. You don't know much about your uncle, do you Frankie?"

"Sure I do. I've known him ever since I was born. What makes you think I don't know him?"

"You know of him and respect him but no one in his family really knows him—except, Mrs. Scarpelli."

The pain was finally subsiding and I was starting to get a buzz on. "I don't know John I think I know my uncle better than you do. I know that no one dare double cross him."

"No offense Frankie, but I don't think you do."

"Okay, John you tell me what I don't know about Uncle Frank."

"Do you or your family know how much he gives back to the community?"

"Yes, I know he's altruistic."

"I'm not just talking money."

"Okay, give me an example."

"Take my Dad he was a heavy duty gambler. We lost our house and we were always on the move. Just one step ahead of paying our monthly rent because he used every dime he had, gambling. He was always waiting for that one big score. Then he got into the mob for one hundred grand and he didn't have a dime let alone a hundred grand. So, he got scared and took off. He just left us. My mother got a job in a grocery store but she barely made enough to pay the rent. The mob kept watching the house to see if he'd come home. Then one day they came knocking on the door. They took one look at me and said, 'Come on, kid, you're coming with us.' My mother freaked and said, 'You can't take my boy. What do you want with him?' They said, 'we'll hold him until your husband comes back and pays us the money he owes us.' I was scared to death."

"How old were you, John?"

"I was a little over ten. My mother threatened to call the police. They told her if she did, she would never see me again. They thought she knew where my old man was, she didn't. No one in our family would help her. They never forgave her for marrying my dad. She must have called your uncle. Because he not only found my father hiding in some dump; he gave him the hundred grand, so I could go home. In a way it was a good that it happened. Your uncle told him, if, he didn't go to Gambler's Anonymous, the next time he'd let the boys kill him for being such a coward and putting his family in jeopardy. My old man went for help and your old-man gave him a job. Your uncle never spoke of it again or, did he ask for the money back. He's helped so many people I couldn't name them all."

"What about school? Didn't you go to school?"

"Sure, and I got teased a lot. People thought because I was big I was dumb. I was just a kid and the teasing hurt my feelings. So my mother who's really smart, home- schooled me until, high school. I still had to pass a test, to qualify. I did, and passed at the same grade level as all the other kids my age. On my first day at school the football coach passed me in the hallway. He took one look at me and told me to meet him in the gym at three. I did. He looked me up and down and said, 'I finally got his quarterback.' I joined the football team and I was good at it. I had finally gained respect from my classmates. Those were the best four years of my life. After high school, I went to the Chubb Institute, in Jersey City to learn computer programming. It's supposed to be a hard course. I aced it."

"John, didn't you ever want to have a career besides being my uncle's bodyguard?"

"I'm not just his bodyguard. I'm his chauffer, I work on his computers, and I customize programs for his businesses. I'm also with him on his business trips, and I'm learning all about finance from the master himself. Your uncle is a financial genius. He should have articles written in magazines about him. Frankie, do you have a clue smart to how wealthy he is and how many influential people he knows? People like politicians, judges, builders, architects, bankers and even move-stars. I could go on and on. He loans a lot of important people money and they also invest in his multinational partnerships. I have a great job and he pays me well."

It was now time to ask the ultimate question about my uncle. The question I should have asked him, but never had the nerve. "John, is my uncle in Organized Crime?"

I don't see that Frankie. He doesn't hang with them or go to any meetings. He knows a lot of people in the mob. They're his friends from the old neighborhood and some are business acquaintances. Most of them go to him to invest in legitimate businesses. They trust him. He also knows how to keep quiet about their business dealings."

I asked, "What if the businesses fail? Won't they come after him?"

"No, they're not stupid. No business venture is one hundred percent guaranteed. Besides, it's a tax-write off. They win either way. Your uncle is too smart to get mixed up in anything that could land him in jail. He doesn't have too he's got all the money and power he wants. He's more like the legitimate, Chairman of The Board."

Take your school for instance."

"What school? Do you mean Harvard?"

"Yes. Look it how he helped you get into that university."

"What the hell are you talking about?"

"Oh, you didn't know about the donation?"

"What donation?"

"Forget it. I spoke out of turn."

"Oh, no you don't. What the hell are you talking about? I got excellent grades on my own. No one bought my grades. I worked my ass off in school."

"Don't get excited Frankie, I shouldn't have said anything."

"Well you did now tell me what the hell you're talking about?"

"Your uncle was really proud of you when you were accepted in Harvard. So, he gave a large donation to the school in good faith. That's what he does when he's grateful. He gives."

"He didn't pay for my grades, did he?"

"Of course not— you can't bribe a university like Harvard. And he wouldn't do that anyway. He just wanted the Scarpelli name to be remembered, as, an alumni."

"Holy shit," I said, "I had no idea." Then, I remembered the Dean coming over and congratulated me after graduation. *That's how he knew me.*

I started to getting tired but I wanted to hear more about John. "Do you have a girlfriend John?"

"No, I get all stupid around girls. Don't get me wrong I'm not gay or anything. I'm such a big guy I'm afraid I'll hurt them."

"Don't put yourself down you're a great guy. I can't imagine a woman not wanting to date you."

"Come on Frankie, look at me. You're a good-looking guy. You don't know what it's like to be afraid to go up to a woman and ask her out."

"Are you kidding me? No one wants to date a geek who has his nose in a book all the time. That's all I did for six years. When I met Darlene I went spastic. I could hardly speak to her."

John noticed I was starting to fade out. "I'm going now Frankie, I'm glad you're going to be okay. I've already talked way too much."

"Thanks for coming John. And you were right. You do know my uncle better than I do. But thanks to you I now know him a lot better." He smiled and left.

The following morning my physician checked my surgical procedure and read my chart. "If you keep on improving at the rate you are, you will be able to go back to your life with some restrictions. But work is out of the questions for at least three weeks."

"That's okay, Doc. I don't have a job to go back too. In time, will I be able to resume my usual routine?"

I expect in six months you would have made a full recovery if you follow my instructions to the letter. No jogging, no exercise and no sex.

"What! No sex?"

"Especially no, sex. Today you sit up and tomorrow you get on your feet for a few minutes and increases on a daily basis, until you get some of your strength back. Right now you're on a restricted diet. In a couple of days you can go back to a normal, healthy diet." As he was starting to leave he said, "Believe me Frank. I'd like to get you out of here. Then I wouldn't have to deal with your pain in the ass family."

I laughed. "I know what you mean. But, I also know I'm a lucky bastard to have them?" The doc agreed. "You are lucky to have such close family ties, in this day and age."

One-by-one they all came in smiling, because I was sitting up. My aunt came in with a box of candy and my mother brought flowers. It wasn't until she looked around for a place to display them did I notice that my room was filled with flowers. I asked, "Where did all these flowers come from?" My mother started reading me some of the cards. "This is from your several people that worked in your office. This one is from Nate's Deli. This one is from a Dr. Bass. And this one is from a Theresa Callahan, Sullivan. Who's she, Frankie?"

"I don't know a Theresa Callahan Sullivan. And then it hit me. TC. Thomas Callahan. *It must be a relative?*

"Mom, can you read me the note."

"May God bless and heal you Frank Scarpelli. I want to thank you and your courageous family for finding my father's murderer. I can now have closure in knowing that justice has been served. Thanks to you, my mother's soul can now rest in peace. My heart felt prayers, for a speedy recovery. Theresa Callahan. 333-333-3333." I asked my dad to dial the number for me. It rang for quite a while. I was about to hang up when a woman answered. "Hello?"

"Hello, this is Frank Scarpelli. I would like to speak to Theresa, if I may."

"I'm Theresa. Frank, are you alright?"

"I will be. Thank you for your prayers."

"I just got back from church Frank. The whole congregation was praying for your recovery."

"I appreciate their concern. Thank everyone for their prayers and thank you, for the flowers."

"It's me who should be thanking you for finding the man who killed my father and his friends. It's like a miracle. How did you ever find him?"

I wanted to tell Theresa that it was her father who found me. I also wanted to tell her that he was finally at peace. But how could I? Besides, she probably wouldn't have believed me.

She said, "If my mother were alive she would have been so pleased that the murderer of her husband paid for his heinous crime. For many years she wondered who could have done such a horrible thing especially, in the house of God. And wondered why they weren't taken as prisoners."

"I'm sorry to hear about your mother's death. When did she pass away?"

"Mom passed on, ten years ago. She and my grandparents raised me after my father was killed. My mom went to school in the evenings, got her Bachelor's Degree and became a teacher. This way she could have the summers off. She taught school for over 35 years."

"It sounds like your mother never remarried."

"No, she never did. She never got over my father's death. My Dad was her one and only love."

"What about you?"

"I married Robert Sullivan a fine Irish lad, and we have two children; Thomas and Anna. And, I have three grandchildren. I, better go now Frank I don't want to tire you. Thank you for calling me. And may God bless you."

I got all chocked up. I guess it was the drugs. Everyone asked who it was I was speaking to. I told them it was a friend's daughter. My mother then stated, "I almost forgot to tell you Frankie, Darlene said she will be here around ten."

"Well?" I asked, "What does everyone think of my lady?"

Everyone gave a nod and a smile of approval. To my surprise, my mother disclosed her feelings. "I do like her Frankie. And for what it's worth you have my blessing. While you were in the operating room, Darlene in her blood stained clothes sat with us until the surgeon came out of surgery to tell us that you were still alive. John took her home to change her clothes and she returned soon after. She never left your side. I'm sure she loves you very much."

"Thanks, Mom. That means a lot to me. How do I look? Do you think I should shave?"

My father spoke up. "Frankie, you almost died. Darlene's happy you're alive. I'm sure she doesn't give a damn if you need a shave."

I heard the clicking heels of a woman walking down the hall and I hoped it would be Darlene. It was Jessie. She came over and kissed me on the cheek. "I'm so glad you're okay. When are you going to introduce me to your girlfriend?"

"You know you're nuts, don't you? Can't it wait until I'm just a little better?"

She laughed. "I'm just busting your chops, Frank."

"I know that Jessie. When aren't you?"

"Come on, Frank. Don't tell me Darlene doesn't tease you. What fun is that?"

I looked at her and gave her the Scarpelli evil eye. I didn't like where this was going, especially in front of my family. I'll be damned, the evil-eye worked. She actually shut up. I should have done that a long time ago.

Dad informed me that John was driving Peter to Kennedy Airport. His mission was over and he wanted to go home. In fact, half the town of Palermo was going to greet him at the airport and, the bells of 'Our Lady' would be ringing in his honor. I was glad that pop had a chance to see his old friend before his time ran out.

As I looked through the window of my room I could see Darlene walking with a very tall distinguished looking man who looked some-what familiar. As they got closer I could see it was her father, General Matthew Walker, Banks. I got nervous, I wasn't sure if I was up for this. Darlene walked in and greeted everyone in the room. She came over to me and kissed me on the cheek. I pointed to my mouth. She shook her head and whispered, "Behave, yourself." She smiled when she said, "I'm so happy to see you sitting up." She then approached my family and Jessie and said, "I would like everyone to meet my father." The General went around to everyone and shook their hand. He then came close to my bed. As not to disturb the IV and all the other tubes in my arm he gently, held my hand and said, "I wish that we were meeting under better circumstances. However, I felt it was important for me to thank you for saving my daughter's life, in person."

"Thank you, for coming Sir. But I feel guilty for putting her into that situation."

"She told me the whole story Frank. How you insisted on her staying out of this until it was safe. I know my daughter and I think you should know that my daughter is stubborn and bull-headed."

"Dad, I think Frank already knows that."

He went on. "But, I must confess, Darlene inherited that trait from me. Thank God she has her mother's looks."

We all laughed. I was speechless. He was as he looked in all his photos. Pleasant, distinguished, controlled and he had a presence. All eyes were on him. General Banks stayed for twenty minutes and then excused himself. He had a plane waiting to take him back to Washington, DC. Before leaving he said, "Please, take care of my pigheaded daughter. She can get herself in all kinds of trouble in a city like New York."

"It would be my pleasure, Sir."

I assume that everyone in the room realized that Darlene and I would like some alone time because everyone started to leave, including Jessie. However, before leaving she kissed me on the mouth. Darlene arched her eyebrows and whispered, "When everyone leaves, we have to talk about Jessie."

"Sure, Honey I'll tell you almost anything you want to know."

Darlene pulled her chair closer to my bedside and reached for my hand. "I really appreciate your family leaving so we can be alone." I looked at her and confessed, "Do you have any idea how scared I was at the thought of you getting killed? You know what else scares me, is, how much I love you."

Darlene's eyes started to tear-up "When you were shot I thought you were dead. If you hadn't pulled me out of his way, that Dietz character, might have killed us both."

"I didn't do anything Bogie wouldn't have done."

She smiled, kissed me on the lips and started to cry.

"Honey, please don't cry. The doctor said I'm going to be fine. Is John going to be alright for killing Dietz?"

"Yes, after they took you to the hospital and revived me, because I fainted. I can't believe I did that."

"There is no shame in fainting."

"Don't you patronize me Frank, Scarpelli. Seeing you lying on the floor bleeding to death scared the shit out of me. As I was saying, after I was revived with the smelling salts the paramedic's had given me I went with John as his unofficial attorney, to interpret the statements he would have to sign. It was all good. John won't face any criminal charges.

You know after the operation the surgeon said that you were still alive but, it was touch and go— and we wouldn't know if you were to survive until you woke up from the induced coma. The doctor told us to go home, that you would be unconscious for at least 48 hours. John took me home to change my clothes and when I returned to the hospital, your mother said they were all leaving and I should too. So, I left to try and get some rest. But John was so worried that someone else might try to kill you, that he stood guard outside your door until the following morning. He left when we all started to return. John is a good and loyal friend. Once we heard Mark was dead, the only thing we had to worry about was you surviving."

"I feel somewhat relieved that John was at the hospital at the time Mark was killed and I assumed murdered."

"John couldn't have done that. Besides what makes you think Mark was murdered? They said it was an accident, maybe a drunk?"

"I can't say for sure but it sounds too much like a coincidence to me."

"Okay, now that we're alone tell me about Jessie."

"Jessie and I go way back to high school. She's a very good friend and I hope she will be yours, too."

"She doesn't act like just a friend, Frank."

"You're right she was more than a friend. But that was all over when we started dating. Now we're just friends."

"Are you sure it's over between you two? After the way she kissed you it didn't seem that way."

I laughed. "That was more for your benefit then mine."

"Oh, I see. She wanted to make me jealous."

"I can assure you that our physical relationship is over. Jessie was my first crush in high school. She broke up with me when she realized we had different agendas. Besides, we were just kids."

Darlene leaned over and kissed me lightly on my lips. "I can live with that. Do you realize we no longer have a job?"

"I know and I feel bad about the firm and the employees taking such a hit."

"Chances are we will no longer be working together."

"I hope you're not planning on moving out of New York?"

"Hell no, if, I left New York, I wouldn't be able to keep an eye on you, and that bleach-blond, cheerleader."

"I'm glad. I'd hate having to commute."

"All kidding aside Frank, I've been thinking about changing my vocation. I'm pretty sure I want to get out of the private sector and apply my legal expertise as an assistant to the District Attorney."

"Why would you want to do that? The money's lousy compared to private practice."

"I'm thinking I would prefer helping the victims and the public by putting these criminals away and getting them off the streets?"

"Does this decision have anything to do with what happened to us?"

"It probably does. We were victims and I felt vulnerable and scared. Take a man like Dietz he has a record a mile long yet, they keep letting him out."

True, but now with the three strikes law it should help, somewhat."

"Don't forget there has to be three trials before they're sent away for good. That's if you catch them. In the meantime there could be many, more victims we don't know about."

"I understand what you're saying Darlene but not everyone who needs a defense attorney is guilty. There are a lot of innocent people who are accused of a crime. And there are also circumstances when a crime is committed in, self-defense. Take the case I'm working on right now. I should have said, was working on. Mrs. Smith said she killed her husband in self- defense. I didn't have time to collaborate her story of abuse, but if she had been beaten and abused by her husband and she found the opportunity to save her own life the prosecutor will try her for premeditated murder. My gut feeling is, she's innocent."

"That's true Frank, but what about the case when you know your client is guilty? Do you want to be responsible for putting them back on the streets?"

"I'm sure all attorneys have to struggle with that scenario. In the United States, everyone is entitled to a defense and I don't have to tell you, 'they are innocent until proven guilty.' If the prosecutor does his homework and has enough evidence the jury will find him guilty. I guess as an attorney we have to choose sides. If you do decide to work in the prosecutor's office there's a good possibility we will be adversaries, in court."

She smiled. "I realize that. May the best person, win!" She finally brought up the subject of the nightmares. "Frank, do you think you have seen the last of your nightmares?"

"Yes, I do."

"Why do you think you had those terrible dreams for such a long time?"

"I'm not sure. My gut feeling is that Dr. Bass was right. It could have been Devine Intervention or however you want to define it. Maybe Mario had to pay for his sin against humanity?"

"That is a very spiritual analysis. I didn't know that about you."

"I know. The truth is I don't know what to think. Look at me, I'm alive. The doctor said he couldn't understand how I survived. Some things like my dreams are just as unexplainable."

I was taken off guard when Mark and Tim Moran walked into my room. They seemed somber, but who wouldn't be. They have gone through the same hell. my family went through. They not only lost a father, they had their lives and their careers turned upside down. Mark asked, "How are you feeling, Frank?"

"I've felt better. How are you guys holding up?"

They replied almost in unison. "We could be better." Then Mark spoke, "We came here to tell you how sorry we are for all that's happened to you, Darlene and your family."

I asked, "How is your mother holding up? I'm so sorry she had to go through this."

Mark said, "My mother is taking it badly. Never in her wildest dreams did she think her husband was capable of committing such an atrocity. Apparently he had a dual personality. He was a respectable attorney living a proper conservative lifestyle, and underneath, a psychopathic criminal. My father was not an easy man to live with.

He had fits of temper but he never physically hurt us. He did set our standards so high, that, it was impossible to attain his expectations. My mother finally told us that we were adopted. It seems mother wasn't able to have children so my father went to a friend that ran an adoption agency. His friend told him of a woman in New York State who became a diabetic after the birth of her second child. She was poor, and too ill to care for us. We were very young when we were adopted. Tim was only a couple of weeks old and I was two. Right now our only concerns are for our families. Our mother needs medical care and the notoriety has made her a social outcast. Her husband and our father disgraced the name of Moran. There is no doubt it will affect the firm. We're also sure that in time, people will forget and life will go on."

I was starting to feel bad for these guys. "I'm sorry that you and your family became the innocent victims. Mark, Tim, there is no way you're to blame for your father's actions. The One thing I couldn't understand was why you told him that I was involved with Darlene? That knowledge gave him the leverage he needed to have her abducted."

Mark said, "I didn't tell him. My father was in the backseat of my car when he saw Darlene get into your car. He surmised you were having an affair. I have never discussed office politics with him or with any of our employees. That was conjecture on his part when he saw Darlene holding an overnight bag."

Tim spoke for the first time. "Frank, we want you and Darlene to come back to the firm, when you're well."

"Are you kidding? After all that's gone down you still want me to work for you?"

"Yes," Tim stated. "It makes good sense. The vendetta between our families is over and none of it had anything to do with us. People will eventually forget, but in the meantime the bad publicity will kill us and we can't survive the fallout. There is no doubt that most of our clients will leave and we will have to close down. Everyone in our office will lose their jobs. They are good competent people, Frank and they don't deserve to get caught up in our family's problems. My father may have started the business, but Mark and I have doubled its revenue since he retired. If you come back our clients will stay. Without you, we cannot continue to exist. What do you say?"

"I have no quarrel with you guys. Won't I be a reminder of this whole mess?"

Mark answered, "What my father did was horrific and we're mortified, but it was his doing not ours and certainly not yours. Business is business. You need to learn the business and we're willing to give you that opportunity. We know with your credentials you could get a job with any upscale firm. But, we're expanding and promotions will be made, along with pay raises. Keep in mind you will receive no special favors, you will have to earn it. By the way, we have already taken legal steps to change the name of the firm. It's now M. Moran, T. Moran and Associates. What do you say, Frank? Is it possible to put the past behind us and start the New Year, in a new firm?"

I looked over at Darlene. She smiled and put her thumb up. She liked the idea. I was going to ask for time to think about their proposal but the truth was, I liked the location and the staff. I also thought Mark and Tim were good guys. "Okay, I'll come back." As best I could, we shook hands to seal the deal.

After everyone left and I was alone I thought about all I'd been through in the last five months. What a hell of a roller coaster ride. Most of all, my nightmares are gone and I had fallen in love for the first time in my life. I feel I've grown and matured from this experience and right now life is good. *Oh shit, here comes the pain again. Crap, it really hurts.* I hit the buzzer to call the nurse. As usual, there was no response. I started yelling, "Nurse Baxter, if you don't get your ass in here I'm going to call John, then you'll be sorry.

CHAPTER THIRTY

Before leaving the hospital I had to listen to my Doctor lecture on my post-operative do's and don'ts. "And most important, no strenuous exercise and no sex until after you're next examination. Is that clear young man?"

"Are you kidding me doc?"

"If you want to fully recuperate, you will abide by instructions. See you in two weeks."

My mother graciously offered to have me stay at her home so she could take care of me. That was definitely out of the question. I told her I had to stay at my place to study for the Bar Exam. And that's exactly what I did. What else could I do?

On the ride over to take our Bar Exam Darlene and I were unusually quiet. Each of us hoping the other would pass but secretly, we wanted to outsmart the other. I sure in hell didn't want Darlene getting a higher grade than me. As it turned out we were as close in our test scores as we were academically. And I would never admit it to her, but I was damn glad I scored several points higher. I know it sounds petty. She's just as smart as I am, but she's also condescending. I didn't want her lauding it over me for the rest of my life and I knew she would. On the other hand, I'm a lot more humble.

Although our relationship had been going great she refused to move in with me. It seems she preferred her independence. If I didn't know her like I do, I would say she wasn't sure she loved me. I know she does. And she's smart enough to want to make sure that we can stand the test of time. Forever is a long time.

As soon as Darlene got her license she called District Attorney, Michael Bonito. She informed him that she had passed the bar and she was interested in working for him. And should there be an opening she would like to be considered. Michael told her she was in luck. Jennifer O'Keefe, his top assistant was leaving to go into private practice and he needed a replacement. He also reminded her that she would have to take a cut in salary if she wanted to work for the state.

A month later, Darlene was working for the DA and enjoying every minute of it. I would have preferred her working for M. Moran, T. Moran and Associates. I used to like running into her at the office. I was also not looking forward to us being adversaries. I wasn't sure any relationship could take that kind of punishment. But, we would deal with that when and if, the time came. Personally, I think her decision was commendable. There is nothing like a tragedy to put things into prospective. After my mother got to know Darlene she really liked her. She began to admire Darlene for her activist modern approach to self-awareness and what her role was, as a woman and not just a wife.

A funny thing happened at one of our Sunday dinners. My father kept asking my mother to get him this and that. Usually mom would jump up and get it for him. After we were finished eating and still talking at the table, he asked my mother to get him another cup of coffee. She looked at him and said, "Al, get up and get it yourself. I spent hours cooking this dinner, the least you can do is get your own coffee." Not knowing what to expect we all looked at each other,. My father looked at my mother and started to laugh. I mean really laugh. My brother Al asked him if he was alright. "She's right, Al. I can get up and get it myself."

We all started to laugh. My mother looked at Darlene and winked.

I leaned over and whispered to Darlene, "See what you started, troublemaker."

She smiled, "I don't know what you mean. I never said a word." And then she started to snicker at her own private joke.

Pop decided to face his fears and go back to Sicily to visit Peter and the Scarpelli gravesite. We all tried talking him out of it. He said, "I'm going. It's time to put the past behind me, by facing it." He planned on staying a month and he should be back after New Year's.

They never caught the hit and run driver who killed Mark Moran. No one was surprised, including, the DA. Because of the efficiency in how it took place we all knew it was a Mafia hit.

I kept my promise to Jessie and fixed her up with Norman. So far so good. They're really hitting it off. Darlene is not thrilled about that situation. Although she tolerates Jessie, they are as different as night and day. Occasionally we double-date and its obvious Darlene and Norman are not comfortable with the bantering that goes on between Jessie and me. It's that sister and brother thing we have going.

It was great going back to work. Everyone greeted me when I walked in and Joan had a Starbucks coffee siting on my desk. "You're going to spoil me, Joan."

"No, I won't because as soon as you're back to normal you can get your own damn coffee."

I wasn't in the office ten minutes when Mark came in. He shook my hand and told me it was great seeing me looking so fit. He also congratulated me on passing the Bar Exam with such a high score. I said, "That was a nice surprise."

"Not to me," he remarked.

I asked Mark about the outcome of the Maude Smith case. It seems Maude lied to us in her deposition. She was having an affair and she had intended to leave Judge Smith as soon as the separation papers were filed. Maude swears that the judge was in a rage and attacked her. She feared her life was in danger when she grabbed the only thing close to her, to save her life. Mark had Judge Smith's ex-wife's statement that accused her ex-husband of being a brutal and sadistic man. She also stated that the day he left her for Maude, was the happiest day of her life. She also confided that she was too afraid to leave him.

After hearing the numerous statements confirming the abuse, Michael Bonita relented and offered her a one-time deal rather than taking it to court and having all these witnesses come forth and discredit a New York State, Judge. Mark also reminded Michael of how this would play in the media. Maude walked away with Justifiable Homicide. After, Maude walked a free woman, Michael leveled with Mark. "None of us know and can't know what really happened in that house. If the guy was the bastard people said he was he deserved it. But, if you ever tell anyone I said that. I'll deny it."

After Mark told me the story he headed for the door. I called his name and he turned to face me. "You're good, Mark you're damn good. There's a lot I can learn from you."

"Thanks, Frank. I appreciate that."

As soon as he left I got out the hammer and picture-hook. I took my newly framed license from my briefcase stared at it and smiled, as I affixed it to the wall of my office.

Phenomena: Reference Webster's Dictionary

a. A fact or occurrence that can be perceived or observed.
b. A rare fact or occurrence that occurs.
c. An extremely outstanding or unusual person or thing.

Ghostly occurrences have been documented since time began—but there are sceptics. Although statistics show that two-thirds of the American population believes in ghosts. Do you?

Made in the USA
Middletown, DE
21 February 2019